THE DARWIN AFFAIR

The Darwin Affair

a novel

TIM MASON

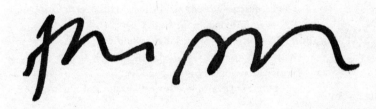

ALGONQUIN BOOKS
OF CHAPEL HILL
2019

Published by
Algonquin Books of Chapel Hill
Post Office Box 2225
Chapel Hill, North Carolina 27515-2225

a division of
Workman Publishing
225 Varick Street
New York, New York 10014

Printed in the United States of America.
Published simultaneously in Canada by Thomas Allen & Son Limited.
Design by Steve Godwin.

LIBRARY OF CONGRESS CATALOGING-IN-PUBLICATION DATA
Names: Mason, Timothy, [date]– author.
Title: The Darwin affair / by Tim Mason.
Description: First edition. | Chapel Hill, North Carolina :
Algonquin Books of Chapel Hill, 2019.
Identifiers: LCCN 2018037996 | ISBN 9781616206345 (hardcover : alk. paper)
Subjects: | GSAFD: Mystery fiction.
Classification: LCC PS3563.A799 D37 2019 | DDC 812/.54—dc23
LC record available at https://lccn.loc.gov/2018037996

10 9 8 7 6 5 4 3 2 1

First Edition

For Leo

We are living at a period of the most wonderful transition, which tends rapidly to accomplish that great end to which indeed all history points—the realization of the unity of mankind.

—Prince Albert of Saxe-Coburg and Gotha,
Prince Consort of the United Kingdom

On the view of descent with modification, we may conclude that the existence of organs in a rudimentary, imperfect, and useless condition, or quite aborted, far from presenting a strange difficulty, as they assuredly do on the ordinary doctrine of creation, might even have been anticipated, and can be accounted for by the laws of inheritance. —Charles Darwin, *On the Origin of Species*

God prosper long our noble Queen,
    And long may she reign!
Maclean he tried to shoot her,
    But it was all in vain.

For God he turned the ball aside
    Maclean aimed at her head;
And he felt very angry
    Because he didn't shoot her dead.

—William McGonagall

THE DARWIN AFFAIR

LONDON
December 1859

Her Majesty disliked what she considered to be over-heated homes. As a consequence, the many other occupants of the palace this chill December morning shivered as they moved from room to room going about their business. The Prince Consort himself suffered acutely from the cold; on the subject of maintaining proper fires in the scores of palace hearths, Albert's appeals to Victoria were unavailing. He rubbed his hands together, opening and clenching the fingers, trying to restore feeling as he read over the list on the desk before him yet again. The prime minister's aged first lieutenant stood waiting, suppressing a rising urge to sneeze.

"Yes," said Albert, turning the page around and sliding it across the desk toward the man from Downing Street. "This should do. Have the goodness to deliver it to the minister."

The old civil servant opened the battered attaché case used to convey messages of state to and from Downing Street. He drew the Queen's

Honors List toward him, his watery eyes flicking over the names of those to be knighted in the New Year, stopping abruptly a quarter of the way down at a name that had not appeared in the prime minister's draft.

Charles Robert Darwin.

Only three weeks earlier *On the Origin of Species* had been published to enormous uproar. The first edition had sold out in a day; the papers were full of it. The name of Darwin was praised, ridiculed, and thunderously reviled. The man from the ministry glanced up at the Prince who stared back steadily.

"Cold, is it not?" said Albert in his clipped German accent.

"Yes indeed, sir. Quite."

Albert pushed back his chair and stood, signaling the dismissal of the man from the ministry.

A thin rain fell all the afternoon, beginning to freeze as dusk approached.

Around that hour a messenger emerged from a great house in Whitehall, adjusting his cloak and scarf against the weather as he crossed the forecourt. He mounted the waiting curricle, its horses held by a groom. The messenger settled onto his seat and pulled on his riding gloves. He flicked a whip over the horses' heads and clattered off onto the slick streets for the road to Oxford, bearing an urgent communication for the bishop.

There is scant historical record of the actions taken by a small body of like-minded men in response to the message in the courier's valise. Rumors circulated here and there for a time among members of the court of Victoria, at Oxford, and within the Metropolitan Police, whispers of a bizarre series of murders and one man's dogged pursuit of a killer. Perhaps the stories merely faded with time; perhaps they were suppressed. But history is crystal clear on one point at least: Charles Darwin never received his knighthood.

PART I

1

June 1860

The heat moved like a feral thing through the streets, fetid and inescapable. Chief Detective Inspector Charles Field, sweating in his shiny black greatcoat, ducked into the shadowed portico of a house near St. Albans Street, just bordering the Mall. Because of the view it offered, as well as the protection from the elements, it was the spot he invariably used to monitor royal processions along this stretch. The horses pulling the royal carriage plodded solemnly, resignedly, their tails flicking at the flies. Victoria and Albert, their faces glimpsed within the open coach, had a wilted look, but they seemed to be conversing nevertheless. Today, given the heat and the mundane nature of Her Majesty's errand (she and the Prince Consort were to open a public bath in the West End), the crowd was understandably thin. But because the Queen already had survived several attempts on her life, the royal coach was accompanied by a couple of the Horse Guard. A few police constables, Field's men, walked here and there along the route, watching the spectators and licking perspiration from beneath their mustaches.

Inspector Field, his face glistening, clutched his stiff top hat behind his back. Tall, dark, and burly, he was clean-shaven, unlike most of his contemporaries, and gave the impression of not having been properly introduced to the clothing he wore. His shifting gaze touched each onlooker, one by one, and then came to rest on a skinny, threadbare figure on the curb directly before him.

I know you.

Little Stevie Patchen was an eighteen-year-old pickpocket and occasional purveyor of stolen goods. Field and his men had hauled him before the magistrates more than once. "Hatchet-Face," as Stevie was known to his intimates, was a very small fish in London's large pond of criminality, but what was he doing here among these mostly provincial sightseers? And what was he holding in a bundle of rags wrapped round his right hand?

As the royal carriage drew abreast of him, Stevie's arm rose. "Oi!" shouted Field, starting to move. "Stevie!"

The youth glanced nervously over his shoulder, saw the policeman bearing down on him, and flung away the bundle of rags. He hadn't run more than a couple of yards before Field tackled him, tumbling him and then immediately hauling him to his feet again, and frog-marching him back toward St. Albans Street. The royal carriage continued slowly on.

"Leave off!" cried Stevie. Field spun the lad around and shoved him against the railings of a grand house at No. 44 St. Albans, introducing the back of his head to the iron rods. A fine spray spurted from Stevie's nose. "Now look, I'm bleedin'!"

"It was a gun you just pitched away, was it not? Assassination? You're out of your depth, Stevie!"

"This all you got to do now you're famous, Mr. Bucket? Persecute the lowly?"

"My name is Field, not Bucket. He's a fiction, and I am a real, daylight fact, right here before you. Whatever do you have against the Queen?"

"I don't know what you're on about." Stevie wiped his bloody nose with a sleeve.

"I'll tell you what *you're* about, young man, you're about the hangman's rope that is someday a-waiting you, that's all. You know it, and I know it, and I'd wager your mother knew it, too, to her sorrow, as you partook the maternal refreshment."

"Sod off."

"I beg your pardon?" said Field, danger in his voice.

Stevie's eyes darted furtively. "Think you're so bleedin' smart."

A fearful thought occurred to the inspector: *I'm looking at a decoy.*

"Damn," he muttered, shoving the little man from him and then abruptly running, pelting along the broad Mall, scattering pigeons as he ran. The sudden crack of a pistol shot smote him like a blow.

Oh, dear God.

Field sprinted down the dusty road, trying to make out what was happening.

Another shot.

He saw a confusion of blue and red and black surrounding the carriage and heard the cries of men and frightened horses. A couple of onlookers had got someone on the ground, thrashing and cursing. The horses of the Guard were rearing, and the coachman was trying to calm the steeds harnessed to the royal carriage. As Field came abreast of the entourage, he saw the Queen, flushed and wide-eyed, talking rapidly to her husband, gesturing and scanning the horror-struck crowd. And then Prince Albert's furious gaze came to rest directly on him, Inspector Field of the Detective.

Her Majesty's alive, anyway, although my own prospects are dim.

The figure on the ground was no longer struggling; a policeman sat on the man's chest while others pinioned his arms and legs.

"Kilvert!" cried Field, and one of the constables, a rail-thin, dour Welshman, appeared at his side. "You and Llewellyn see to it no other blighter in the crowd's got a bloody gun—I've got Hatchet-Face back at St. Albans with a gun or something like it."

"Yes, sir!"

There was a cry and the crack of a whip, and the black-and-gold carriage lurched into motion once again, making a wide arc and turning back toward the palace, its royal passengers seemingly safe after yet another assassination attempt. Field was running in roughly the same direction, back toward St. Albans, determined to find Little Stevie and wrest from him a name, a face, a description.

Stevie, however, as Charles Field, deep in his dark policeman's heart already feared, was no longer available for questioning. What Field hadn't anticipated, however, was to find him just round the corner from where he'd left him. The young man sat beneath the wrought-iron railings behind No. 44, his back against the rods and his head resting on his left shoulder. His narrow face was tilted sideways to the pitiless sky, his waistcoat scarlet and glistening, his throat sliced to the bone.

Inspector Field quickly looked up and down St. Albans Street and then knelt in the widening pool of Stevie's blood. The young man's right hand was thrust into the pocket of his trousers. Field gently pulled Stevie's arm, and the hand emerged, fist still clenched. When he prized it open, a bloodied sovereign dropped from the fingers. Field got to his feet, picking up the coin and grimacing at the sticky feel of wet at his knees and hands.

"You there!"

Two young constables Field didn't recognize ran toward him. One thrust the inspector against the railings and pinned him there with his truncheon.

"Whoa, now!" shouted Field. "Get your hands off!"

A liveried servant, wigless and unbuttoned, approached, carrying a toasting-fork, looking both fierce and frightened. "That's 'im!" he cried. "'E did it, I saw it all!"

"Constable," said Field, "you must be new to the Metropolitan. *I am chief of detectives, do you understand me?*"

The other policeman, crouching beside Stevie, looked up and said, "'He's dead all right."

"Murderer!" cried a woman from the corner. She and several others were approaching.

"I saw it all!" repeated the servant from No. 44, shrilly.

"You will release me this instant!" shouted Field. "I've work to do!"

"I believe you already done your work here, sir. You're half-covered in blood, in case you hadn't noticed."

"I was inspecting the body, idiot!" Field glanced down, following the constable's pointed gaze, and saw that not only were his knees and hands wet with gore, but his shirt front and waistcoat were speckled with a fine red spray.

"He had nosebleed, for God's sake!"

The other constable rose to his feet, and as he did so, Stevie's head fell like a lid to the right, exposing vertebrae, oozing clusters of tubes, and a gaping hole where the left ear should have been.

"Good God," murmured Field.

"Nosebleed, right, then." In less than a moment Inspector Field was roughly handcuffed to the iron fence, with the body at his feet.

Meanwhile the alarm surrounding the assassination attempt had risen, with bells sounding in the distance, horses' hooves pounding up and down the Mall, and police whistles blowing. The crowd in St. Albans, watching Field's arrest and morbidly eyeing the nearly head-less figure of young Hatchet-Face, had grown. Police Constable Kilvert pushed his way through the throng.

"Josiah!" cried the inspector. "Get me clear of these fools!"

"Officers," said Kilvert, "you've made a grave mistake here. Just up from the provinces, aren't you, and soon to return at this rate."

The constables looked abashed, but the man in footman's livery was sputtering. "It weren't no mistake! I was watchin' from the winder all mornin', an' there wasn't nobody but 'im in the road—'im and the bloke 'e done for!"

"That's enough out of you, Brass Buttons, this man here is Detective

Field!" Kilvert grew indignant. "Mr. Charles Dickens called him Bucket!"

"Shut up, Kilvert!" said Field.

"Inspector Bucket of the Detective!"

"Kilvert, you ass," said Field, "just get me out of this!"

As the inspector was released, there was renewed scrutiny from the crowd. It was clear that many of them had heard of Dickens' fictional detective. For a person who did not in fact exist, Mr. Bucket was quite the celebrity, and so was his model.

"I don't care who he is," cried the woman from the corner, "he's been a-murderin' the populace!"

"You there!" said Field, thrusting a large forefinger at the liveried servant. "You're going to tell me what you saw from the window, lad— that's what you're going to do."

The young man with the brass buttons, somewhat abashed by the turn of events, muttered, "You know wot I saw."

"I do *not*, in point of fact. I know what *I* saw, but I've a keen interest in *your* observations. Go on. You were watching, you say. You saw no one but me and the, uh—this fellow?"

"That's right. Just you and 'im, and you weren't poundin' 'im, oh no, *you* weren't!"

The onlookers murmured ominously.

Field put a fatherly arm round the servant's narrow shoulders, caus-ing the young man to shudder.

"What's your name, son?"

Looking as though he wasn't eager to expand the acquaintance, he replied, "Willis."

"Right, then, Willis. You saw no one but me and . . ." He tilted his head in the direction of the corpse. "No passersby? No tradesmen? Not so much as a nurse pushin' a pram?"

"Not to mention, no. I mean, there was an old lady just now."

"How old was she, Willis?"

Willis glanced over his shoulder at the crowd and felt their support. "A hundred and twenty-six, sir."

The laughter was universal and no one seemed more pleased than Inspector Field.

"Delightful lad," he said, beaming. "So we got one crone, we got me and the dead bloke, and that's all, that's it, there ain't no more, we can all go home now, is that right, young Willis?"

Willis was beginning to enjoy the show. "That's about it, sir. Oh, there was a dog, I was forgettin' the dog."

Gusts of laughter from the crowd.

"The dog could be important, Willis, you never know," said Field, still smiling and nodding. "What was the dog doing?"

Groans now from the crowd, whose impression of the police as a bunch of sorry buffoons was being confirmed.

"Doin'?" said Willis. "Dog was doin' 'is bizness, wasn't 'e?" Laughter, tinged with scorn. "'Doin' 'is bizness an' sniffin' up the butcher's man, just like always."

"Which butcher's man was this, now, Willis?"

"Comes every second day, don't 'e? Brings a joint to No. 42." Field flicked the merest glance at Kilvert, who nodded and moved quietly through the crowd toward No. 42 St. Albans.

"I see," said Field. "Comes every other day, wheeling a barrow with a joint or a haunch, and the dogs all love him 'cause his apron's covered in blood, is that about right, Willis, my boy?"

"That's about it, sir!" cried Willis triumphantly, looking around and grinning as though he were about to take a bow. The crowd, however—or at least a number of them—had assumed more thoughtful expressions and did not look as likely to applaud as they had a moment ago.

Police Constable Sam Llewellyn, a black-haired, pink-cheeked lad from Abergavenny, arrived breathlessly. "Sir, you're wanted." Llewellyn's gaze fell on the body of Stevie Patchen. "Good Lord. Where in God's name is the blighter's left ear?"

"Well, *I* haven't got it, Mr. Llewellyn. Get the crowd back and have a look round. Also, Stevie threw a bundle into the bushes back there—find it."

"Yes, sir. I was sent to fetch you, sir. You're wanted at the palace." His voice dropped to an undertone. "It seems the royal family is not best pleased."

"I imagine not," muttered Field. "Thank you, Willis, you've been most entertaining." To the policemen who had arrested him, he said, "Cover the corpse decent, you lot, and wait with him till the coroner arrives. My men, Llewellyn and Kilvert, are in charge here, you answer to them."

"Where is Mr. Kilvert, sir?" said Llewellyn.

"He stepped round to No. 42. What did you make of the fellow who took the shots at Her Majesty?"

"Lunatic."

"Like the others, you mean?" said Field, and Llewellyn nodded. "But, Sam, the assassin wasn't acting alone, was he. I'm guessing Little Stevie here was set on deliberate to get me out of the way, and the gun I thought he was raising against the Queen will turn out to be a lump of coal or something like that. Come to that, if *any* of us had seen Hatchet-Face pointing a bundle of rags in Her Majesty's direction, he would have had our full attention, I think you'll agree. Whoever engaged Stevie promised him a sovereign if he was successful in distracting the police." Field held up the bloody coin he'd found in the corpse's pocket. "*This* one. Whoever did *that* was dressed in a butcher's bloodstained clothes and pushing a butcher's barrow. 'Meet me here, Stevie,' says the bloke, 'after you've foxed Mr. Bucket. I'll give you this shiny coin.' Which he does, and whilst Stevie stuffs it in his pocket, the butcher slices his throat. The body was supposed to go in the barrow, covered with a butcher's cloth and wheeled far away, only something interrupts the killer and he's got to make off quick, leaving Stevie where he lay."

"What about the ear?"

"Haven't a clue, have I. But I reckon Kilvert will find the kitchen at No. 42 in a state, 'cause of the usual butcher never arriving this morning. Don't you see? For the first time in all these attempts on Her Majesty's life, we've got a real live conspiracy, but instead of hunting it down, I've got to go and squander precious breath on a gaggle of court folk."

With that, Inspector Charles Field turned and strode through the staring crowd.

"Whatever has become of my hat?" he muttered under his breath. "Never mind. Too bloody hot, in any case."

CONSTABLE KILVERT FOUND distress in the kitchen at No. 42 St. Albans, just as Inspector Field had predicted. Cook indeed had been expecting a leg of lamb and a half-dozen hens for her mistress's supper party. They were never delivered.

"Just put yourself in my place, Officer, if you will. Wot am I to do now, wiv guests expected and Mistress such a sharp 'un?"

Kilvert had a suspicion that Cook, an ample woman in her forties, was rather a "sharp 'un" herself, as her little kitchen maid's red eyes and soggy handkerchief testified.

"There, there, Cook," said Kilvert, in low, comforting tones. "Perhaps the butcher was delayed by the commotion in the Mall. He'll come by-and-by."

"I have me doubts, Officer," shrilled the woman. "The man drinks!"

"Shocking." (Kilvert was, in fact, a teetotaler; strong drink made him bilious.)

Moments later he rejoined Llewellyn at the crime scene. A wagon had drawn up to receive the corpse of Stevie Patchen, and the coroner's men were supervising the operation.

"Look at this, Josiah," said Llewellyn, showing him a crude toy gun made from two wooden blocks, nestled in a bundle of rags. "Found it in the bushes, just like Mr. Field said I would."

"He's a wonder, is Mr. Field. Any sign of the missing ear?"

Llewellyn shook his head.

"Sam," said Kilvert, "where would you go to find a drunken butcher?"

"Let me think for a moment," said his partner, as though people were forever asking him just this.

IN THE SHIMMERING midday heat, the butchers' stalls of Smithfield Market reeked of flesh and blood and dung. On the street, sewage moved sluggishly through narrow channels toward open drains. Smoke rose from a dozen firepots, blurring vision, tickling the throat, and muffling the cries of those who still labored here. Recently much of the market had been shut down, following years of protest at the stench and the cruel treatment of the beasts (protest led in part by Charles Dickens). There were now more humane slaughterhouses in the northern borough of Islington. To the public, though, Smithfield remained synonymous with meat, and a contingent of the Worshipful Company of Butchers' Guild continued there, even as railway tracks were being laid near the site and construction begun on a new market. The area had resounded with the cries of men and dying cattle for nearly a thousand years; now there was the additional din of construction.

Tom Ginty, aged fourteen, butcher's apprentice, ginger-haired and freckled, blinked sweat from his eyes as he collected offal from the hog that his master, Jake Figgis, was jointing. The other butcher attached to his stall had gone off early that morning and not returned (*Drunk again*, said Jake), so Tom's workload was heavier than normal. But he knew how lucky he was. To have a chance of someday becoming an initiate of the Butchers' Guild was more than enviable. It was only because of his dead father having been mates with a few of the Worshipful Company that he'd been accepted as 'prentice—that, and a payment of one pound six that his mother had conjured from God knows where. Tom knew that if he were to put one foot wrong, there would be a score of lads waiting to take his place.

Which was one of the reasons he was reluctant to say anything to anyone about the man who struck him as odd.

Tom took him at first for another butcher because of the bloody apron he wore, but he didn't move right for a workingman. He seemed to glide, as though he were on skates, crossing a frozen pond. His smile seemed frozen as well, Tom thought, as he glanced up from his work and shoved his sweat-matted red hair back from his eyes.

Like he's livin' in a cool day somewheres else, but he ain't enjoyin' it, smile or no. Like he's this toff who just stepped in shit.

Tom's eyes dropped down to the man's feet.

Red shoes?

But they weren't shoes; they were made of cloth, like a baby's bootie, only red. Or mostly red. And now the man (*it's a gentleman, no mistake, the way he moves*), weaving his way through the crowd, paused, stooped, and undid the strings at his ankles. When he stood and moved on, he'd left the red things behind and was wearing gleaming black leather shoes. The scraps of red cloth were quickly trod over by the shifting throng and were lost to Tom's view. The gliding man's smile remained unchanged.

He's coming this way.

Tom felt a tingle of fear. Maybe it was the fixed smile. Tom looked up at Jake, who, drenched in sweat, was still fully engaged with the hog. When Tom looked back, the gentleman was gone, vanished, lost to the ever-moving crowd of buyers and sellers.

Tom felt a huge wave of relief and wondered why.

It's the heat, i'n'it.

Something white fluttered past his line of sight. It was reflex: offal bucket in one hand, Tom put out his other and caught the flying cloth before it hit the pile of bloody rags that accumulated each day behind the butchers' stall. It was wet and red and sticky. Tom looked up in time to see the gliding man, now apronless, as he glanced back over his shoulder; in time to see the man with coal-black eyes return his stare; in time to see a frown suddenly cross the smiling face.

The gentleman, never releasing the boy from his intense gaze, smiled again, put a finger to his lips, and shook his head. Then he turned and glided on into the crowd.

2

Inspector Field sat gingerly on the flimsy ornate chair on which he'd been placed, hoping it wouldn't shatter beneath him. He'd been led to this gilt room in the palace by Commissioner Mayne and Sir Horace Dugdale, a member of the royal household. Sir Horace was watchful and almost entirely mute; Mayne was angry.

"A *conspiracy*?" said Mayne, incredulously.

"At least three in it, sir," said Field. "The shooter, the decoy, and whoever set it up and topped the decoy."

"I have talked to *the shooter*, or tried. He's raving, the man could not conspire to do up his boots!"

"Even if he *is* insane, that don't mean he acted alone!" Field, easily angered, checked his rising heat and lowered his voice. "He might have been recruited *because* he was off."

That Detective Inspector Charles Frederick Field should find himself in Buckingham Palace, even to receive a dressing down, was something of a miracle. The son of a sometime publican in Chelsea, Field had nourished high ambitions as a boy—but they did not lie in this direction. There were few people on earth apart from his wife who knew that, as a young man, Charles Field had wanted more than anything to be an actor. A life on the stage would be his escape from the sour brutality of his parental home.

In pursuit of his passion, Field had committed to memory long stretches of Shakespeare. He created disguises for himself and went out in public as a whole gallery of characters. He adopted alien accents and strange walks. A beloved sister, long since dead of typhoid fever, used to fashion his costumes late at night when her own work was done. Young Charles Field went out as rich man, poor man, beggar-man, thief.

One day his father, drunk since the night before, caught him at it yet again (posing as a young gentleman) and beat him senseless. Bloodied and bruised, Field left his hated home and his much-loved sister to fend for himself. He was fifteen years old when he became a member of the Bow Street Runners, London's ragtag prototype of organized law enforcement. When the Metropolitan Police Force was established in 1829, Field signed on. Its first commissioner was Sir Robert Peel, and the public, immediately suspicious of this new force, began calling the constables "peelers" in dubious tribute to Sir Robert. Since then, Field had risen through the ranks. He had solved some of the most notorious murders of his day. And then he'd been discovered by the wide-ranging novelist and commentator on London life, Charles Dickens.

The novelist had merely followed the inspector through night patrols of the city's most squalid and dangerous neighborhoods and recorded Field's interactions with the rogues and criminals he encountered. Dickens' "On Duty with Inspector Field," published in *Household Words* in 1851, created a sensation.

The inspector himself, however, couldn't understand it. "It's not me," he told his wife. The detective read and reread the account, baffled. "It's pure invention, it's not a bit like me!"

"Never mind, Mr. Field," she said. "It's made a famous man of you."

Jane Field's observation became even more true in the wake of the 1853 publication of Dickens' *Bleak House* and the appearance of the morally ambiguous Detective Inspector Bucket on the world's stage. Everyone knew the character had to have been modeled on Field.

Now, years later, the publican's son sat in the palace, arguing his position with knights of the realm. And then, shockingly, Prince Albert himself walked into the room, unexpected and unannounced, and Field saw his career coming to an abrupt end. He fell silent and stood with the other two men.

That's done it. I'm through. The wife is going to be upset, poor girl.

Field had caught glimpses of the Prince over the years. He remembered Albert as a strikingly handsome young man with almond-shaped, piercing blue eyes, a trim little mustache, and thick dark head of hair, erect of bearing and slender of build. Now the man before him, at age forty, was considerably altered: his hair thinning and combed over, he had sallow, puffy skin and a weary stoop. He still possessed the penetrating blue eyes, but what a contrast he made to his vivaciously plump and healthy Queen!

Prince Albert seemed to be studying Field as well. "Her Majesty is recovering from a grave shock," he said finally.

Commissioner Mayne and Sir Horace both bowed their heads, and Field followed suit. He had never heard the man speak before; he was surprised by the thickness of his German accent.

"Fortunately, she is endowed with great strength. *Unfortunately*, she has had to endure this sort of shock on more than one occasion in the past."

Am I supposed to apologize? No—don't speak unless he asks you a direct question. Please, God, don't let him ask me a direct question.

"Detective Field, as I saw this morning's events, you arrived late and you left early. Turned tail and ran, as a matter of fact."

Take me out and shoot me, please. Draw me, quarter me—anything but this.

"I was most distressed by what I observed of your behavior. Now, however, I see that you are quite literally covered in what I can only imagine to be blood. So there must be more to the story, is that so? You had reasons for acting as you did?"

"I did, sir. A common criminal, known to me, was planted in the crowd on purpose so I'd find him, sir. Or so I now believe. Thereby I was took out of the way, sir."

"If this were true, it would suggest conspiracy rather than lunacy," said Albert, glancing at Commissioner Mayne. "What leads you to believe this, Field?"

"Because of the bloke, um, individual, being found by myself moments later with his head halfway sawed off, sir."

Mayne cleared his throat and said, "Sir, if I may, we believe this to be an unrelated matter. We have the actual assailant under lock and key, sir. I assure you, the man is quite mad. He is incapable of conspiring with anyone, I would say, but he will no longer pose a threat to the Crown."

The Prince Consort's eyes flashed with sudden anger. "No indeed, Commissioner, nor will he be properly punished for his actions. He will be found 'innocent by reason of insanity' and cosseted in an asylum whilst you and I and all the world know he's anything but 'innocent.'"

Albert pointedly turned back to the inspector.

"Mr. Charles Dickens has written about you and your detective work, sir. Her Majesty and I have quite enjoyed his accounts of your manner of dealing with the criminal classes." The Prince's small mouth turned up in what the detective took to be a smile. "Mr. Bucket is a thoroughly unforgettable character. Not entirely savory in his practices but highly entertaining."

The little head tilt seemed to be working, so Field repeated it.

"Her Majesty saw you this morning, Field. Even in all the tumult and danger, Her Majesty took note of you. The Queen said, 'Oh, look, there's the Bucket fellow!' The Queen has a regard for your fictional self, and it caused dismay to see you run off as you did. I shall attempt to explain your actions as you've explained them to me."

The Prince moved toward the door. "It would be a shame to see the real Mr. Bucket fall from favor." With a tart nod to Commissioner Mayne and Sir Horace, the Prince was gone.

The commissioner turned to his subordinate. "Come along, *Mr. Bucket.* I've got a conspirator I'd like you to meet."

3

A turnkey led them through the crowded maze that was Newgate Prison. It was a clamorous place, a little city in itself, with guards leading shuffling knots of manacled prisoners to and from work details, and wives and children coming and going, bringing food and drink to incarcerated family members. Commissioner Mayne was speaking furiously above the din.

"As though little Stevie Patchen didn't have at any given moment in his miserable life a dozen enemies at the least, eager to do him in! Queuing up for the privilege! He was a two-faced, two-timing, lying, backstabbing son of a whore!"

Sir Horace Dugdale, following behind, made it clear by his placid demeanor that such language was quite inaudible to members of the royal household.

"The miracle is that it took this long for someone to go and actually do it!" continued Mayne. "Am I wrong, Field?"

"Of course not, sir," said Field in what he hoped were conciliatory tones.

The jailer stopped before an iron door, turned the key, and swung it open. A draft of cool, dank air swept out. The young man within, perhaps twenty-five years old, looked up from the bench on which he sat with his hands splayed on his thighs.

"I keep my mother's teeth in a jar," he said, his tone pleasant.

"Do you now," said Field. "Does she not need them?"

The young man smiled wistfully and shook his head. "Not where she is."

His bland hairless face was bruised and one ear was stained with dried blood; his clothing, too, had been torn and soiled in the scuffle during his arrest. The constant movement of his tongue within his mouth suggested a missing tooth.

"What's your name, lad?" said Field, gently.

Commissioner Mayne answered. "Philip David Rendell, six and twenty years of age, a bookkeeper until recently. Abandoned his position and his lodgings in Islington a month or so ago. Dropped out of sight altogether."

"Son," said Field, as though the commissioner hadn't spoken, "your name?"

"Philip, sir."

"Is your mother in heaven, Philip?"

The young man barked with sudden laughter. "Not her! She got herself into a cupboard and couldn't get out, the cunt!"

Mayne groaned while Sir Horace examined the ceiling.

"Why did you fire those shots this morning, Philip?" asked Field, unperturbed.

"Angel told me to shoot."

Commissioner Mayne snorted. "Perhaps it was a conspiracy of angels."

"What did the angel look like, Philip?"

"Eyes like coals, and the glory of the Lord shone round about him."

"Was he a big man, like me? Or a smallish one, like . . ." Field's eyes strayed toward Commissioner Mayne, but then he thought better of it.

"Tall enough," said Philip Rendell sternly, looking Field up and down, "but you, sir, are no angel."

"Too true," said the inspector, ruefully shaking his head, "too true. Where'd you get the gun from, lad?"

"Angel give it me." A truculent note had come into the man's voice. "See, there's a specter haunting us."

"Is there, now? Is the Queen a specter, Philip?"

"The *Queen*?" said the young man incredulously. "Not likely."

"What's the specter, then, lad?" asked Field, but Rendell put a finger to his lips and winked. "Did the angel tell you to put your mother in a cupboard, Philip? Did he tell you to take her teeth and keep them in a jar?"

But the young man had lost all interest in visitors evidently. He yawned wetly, leaned back against the wall, and closed his eyes.

Field turned quietly to his superior. "We might just check on the missing mother—you never know, sir."

"Actually, Detective Inspector *Bucket*, in this case we *do* know. Mother died in surgery at St. Thomas' Hospital two months ago. We believe the gun belonged to her late husband and is not of angelic origin. Now, is there any other line of inquiry you'd care to pursue with your conspirator?"

The inspector blinked rapidly, mortified. It wasn't often he allowed himself to be taken by surprise. He turned back to Rendell. "Angel have a name, Philip?"

But Philip's eyes were squeezed tightly shut. Field briefly considered picking the young man up by his ears and flinging him about the room but restrained himself. Sir Horace cleared his throat significantly and Commissioner Mayne said, not unkindly, "Charles, there really is no point."

Field leaned in toward the young man. "Philip, you missed the Queen. Shot twice and missed her twice. Why is that, do you suppose? You were very near to the royal carriage."

Rendell's eyes flew open. "Wasn't the Queen, fool!"

"Yes, it was, though, Philip. It was indeed Victoria, our Queen, at whom you fired two shots."

"You don't understand! Now the angel will be wroth with me! He has a flaming sword, you know!"

Field sighed and glanced up at his superior. Mayne, in turn, gave the jailer a nod, and the men filed out of the cell, leaving the prisoner alone. At the door, Field turned back. The bland-faced young man was staring at him, wide-eyed.

"Keep clear of his blade!" he cried. "Once cut, always kept!"

4

OXFORD

"A hat's shape is not the hat, nor yet is the color of the hat, the hat."

Samuel Wilberforce, bishop of Oxford, walked beside the Isis with one of his undergraduates, David Gates, a compact, fair-haired and earnest young man of nineteen. The bishop generally was able to convey basic philosophical precepts while thinking of other things altogether, letting his mind and eye wander, unimpeded by the pedagogical flow, which was, after all, to him, old hat. Not so young David, who strained to listen and to understand, his commoner's gown clinging sweatily to his shoulders. A summer storm threatened, the clouds massing and shifting greenly above Christ Church meadow, the sky swelling with heat.

The son of abolitionist William Wilberforce, Samuel had distinguished himself in the Oxford debating society, leaving university with a first in mathematics and a second in the classics, to begin life as a rural curate. The young Wilberforce quickly attracted attention through his writings, *Note Book of a Country Clergyman* and *On Correcting the Prejudices of the Lower Order of Farmers*.

He rose through the ranks to vicar and then to subdeacon. In 1841 Wilberforce was made chaplain to Prince Albert, and his future success was assured. He soon accepted the deanery of Westminster and the Bishopric of Oxford, becoming eventually a peer of the realm. At this time the so-called Oxford Movement was giving birth to itself, with Anglican intellectuals embracing High Church ritual and flirting ever more brazenly with the Church of Rome. Wilberforce himself was High Church but, as a cautious man, not too high.

"The size of the hat," continued Wilberforce, "the material of which the hat is constructed—these are not the hat. These, we say, are *accidents* attendant upon the hat; they do not constitute the *substance* of the hat." The bishop, glancing into the punt gliding slowly toward them on the river, took note of the young female passenger's pleasantly shaped bosom (*but the shape and size of her breasts are not her breasts*).

"Nothing," said Wilberforce a little distantly, "pertaining to the senses constitutes the substance of the hat."

"But, sir," said David, a scholarship student from Orpington, "are the senses to be dismissed altogether? Are the senses useless? Surely not."

Is that Conrad in the punt with the girl? No. Jenkins? Whoever he is, she's a delectable catch and seems to be enjoying her champagne.

"Sir?"

Wilberforce tore his eyes from the nearing punt. "Yes, Gates?"

"It just seems to me, sir, that the Church strains to redefine substance merely in order to justify the doctrine of transubstantiation. In order to get the true body and blood, we have to throw out common sense, which feels to me like the rejection of a great gift."

The imagined nipples of the young punt passenger were fading from the bishop's mind. *Tiresome young man.* Wilberforce rubbed his hands together in his signature fashion, as though washing them, preparatory to crushing his opponent. Because of this tic, he was widely known (behind his ample back) as "Soapy Sam."

"The body and blood are the gifts," said the bishop. "Compared with the real presence of the body and blood of our Lord, your common sense is a paltry thing."

There were running footsteps approaching from a distance, crunching on the gravel walk. The men looked up to see an undergraduate hurrying toward them, his black gown flapping behind. David involuntarily caught his breath; it was his friend from Jesus College, Jack Callow.

"I say, David, have you heard?" shouted Jack, and then he recognized the portly, jowly man at David's side. Jack abruptly slowed his run to a walk. "Sorry, my lord. Forgive me."

"Heard what, young man?" said the bishop. The two undergraduates stood flanking Wilberforce, glancing at each other awkwardly.

"It seems they've gone and tried to kill the Queen again, my lord. This morning, in fact."

David saw the color drain from the bishop's face and remembered that the man was, after all, an ecclesiastical adviser to Victoria.

"Sir," said David, "may I introduce my friend from Jesus, Mr. Jack Callow?"

Jack, tall, fine-featured, with dark tightly curled hair, smiled and bowed. The bishop's normally powerful voice faltered. "The attempt was . . .?"

"Unsuccessful, sir. Missed the Queen altogether."

"And the Prince?"

"As far as I've heard, sir, yes, thank God."

The bishop of Oxford closed his eyes, breathing heavily. David and Jack glanced at each other. "Perhaps, my lord, you'd like to sit?" said David. "There's a bench just here."

Samuel Wilberforce opened his eyes in time to see the punt with the young woman in it taking a bend in the river. A moment before she disappeared, the woman clutched the side of the punt, shuddered, and vomited over the side. Wilberforce's head swam.

"Sir?" said David, clutching the bishop's elbow. "Sir, you're not well. Jack, fetch assistance!"

"No," said Wilberforce, urgency in his voice. "I must return to my rooms. There are letters to be written, there are people with whom I must speak!" The man lurched forward unsteadily, sweat streaming down his face. David offered an arm, which the bishop grasped heavily.

"I say," said Jack, "that's a nasty-looking sky. We need to hurry along."

Wilberforce seemed to be looking into a great distance as he stumbled on.

"We shall be raised," he whispered. There was a flash of white light and a deafening crack of thunder.

"Raised incorruptible!"

As David and Jack struggled to help the bishop across Christ Church meadow, the heavens opened and the rain came down.

5

LONDON

By the end of the day, young Tom Ginty was ready to jump out of his skin. The man with the frozen smile was still there, somewhere, Tom knew it. It wasn't a matter of seeing the deep-set eyes he knew were watching him; instead, he *felt* them on his person, as real as importunate fingers, touching him immodestly, intimately, again and again. But as often as he'd wheel about to look, the sensation would vanish.

It was late afternoon and the sky was ominous. Throughout the market people were closing stalls and cleaning them, everyone eager to be off before the threatened storm broke. Tom filled two large pails of water from the pump in the center of the market and carried them on a yoke over his shoulders to the stalls where Jake Figgis awaited him impatiently.

"*You* took your time!"

"Sorry, sir."

Tom sluiced water over the butchers' chopping blocks. He scraped them with a blade and scrubbed them with a wire brush before sluicing them again. Jake, meanwhile, gathered the day's soiled rags and butchers' aprons into a bundle for the waiting washerwoman, a maiden of thirteen years who brazenly winked at Tom and made a flirtatious comment about his muscular arms and ginger curls before moving off, her barrow stacked high with the wash she'd be working on until dawn.

"Gentleman was askin' after you, Tom," said Jake, changing out of his work clothes and into his street gear.

Tom froze. "Wot?"

"Asked your name, said 'e was kin of your mum."

"A gentleman?"

"Tall man, big black eyes." Noting the look on Tom's face, Jake said, "Oh, you know all about 'im, do you?"

Tom shook his head.

"Never mind, 'e said 'e'd be back for you tomorrow."

Tom felt ice at his belly. "Did he walk like a lady?" he asked, his eyes wide.

"Did 'e *wot*?"

"Did the man sort of *skate* like?"

"Don't know wot you're on about, do I? Cheerio, Tom!" Jake chucked the boy under his chin and strode out into the evening.

From Smithfield Market to Cock Lane, where Tom lived with his mother above the Fortune of War, it was only a matter of steps. Tonight, though, it felt like a treacherous distance. Thunder rumbled, ever closer. The golden figurine of the chubby boy at the corner of Guiltspur and Cock, a commemoration of the Great Fire of 1666, was normally the welcome sign that Tom was home again; tonight it accused Tom of nameless sins for which he soon would be punished.

His mother, Martha Ginty, sat him down in the scullery with a glass of beer, a half loaf of bread, and a slice of cheese before hurrying back into the noisy, smoky Fortune of War. When she returned carrying a tray laden with empty tankards, Tom was staring, his food untouched. Martha anxiously clapped a hand to her boy's forehead.

"Do we have any gentlefolk for kin, Mum?"

"Not likely," said Martha. "Wot's wrong wiv you, then?"

"I don't want to go to the market tomorrow," muttered Tom.

Martha Ginty's laugh was a bark. "That's rich!" By the age of thirty-two, Martha had lost both her husband and her only other child, a girl, to typhoid fever, just two years earlier. She loved Tom, her firstborn, with a ferocity that almost frightened her. But for persons of their class, there were no days off work, sick or no.

Martha gave Tom a gentle cuff, which turned into an embrace. "Now eat up," she said, "and to bed with you!"

6

harles Field sat naked in the tin bath at the center of
Mrs. Field's kitchen, scrubbing himself with a coarse
brush. Jane Field, fair-haired, shapely, and some fifteen
years younger than her husband, poured another kettle of steaming
water into the tub. The inspector followed her with his eyes, marveling,
as always, that this beauty with cheeks like apples and a keen, often
frighteningly independent mind, was his very own wife. He had found
her in the Crimea five years earlier, one of Miss Nightingale's pioneering nurses. Field had been sent out to the famous hospital at Scutari on
a bizarre, highly secret mission. The peril from which he had rescued
Jane then had left its mark on her; it took persistence and time for Field
to win her confidence, and her hand in marriage, but if the inspector
was not invariably patient, he was always persistent.

"Used to be only the quality would try to kill a queen," said Jane.
"The nobility and such. It was all very aristocratic and accordin' to

form. Look at Shakespeare! Now you've got Islington bookkeepers having a go, what is the world comin' to?" She leaned briefly into the passage and shouted up the stairs. "Bessie!"

The Fields leased a house at No. 2 Bow Street, a down-at-heels red-brick structure just steps from where Mr. Field had begun his career with "the Runners." They shared it with a serving girl named Bessie and—to their unspoken sorrow—no children. Jane picked through the pile of her husband's discarded clothes with a pair of wooden tongs.

"Look at this shirt! Are you certain none of this blood is yours, Mr. Field?"

"My dear, I assure you it's Little Stevie's blood alone."

"We had boys in the Crimea who had no idea they'd been shot," she said. "There was one who thought he'd barked his shin when half his foot was off." She leaned out into the passage again. "Bessie! Where is that girl? Sent her out for chops a good while ago, I do hope she's all right."

Privately, Field thought it likely Bessie was doing all right by herself with a glass or two of gin on the way back from her errand.

"The bookkeeper said something about a specter haunting us," he said.

"A specter?"

Footsteps pounding down the steps from the street door announced the breathless appearance in the kitchen of Bessie, bearing small parcels done up in oily brown paper. She was twenty-nine years old, bug-eyed, warty, and, credible rumor had it, had never been kissed. Her apron was half-off and her bonnet half-on, hanks of her hair protruding from the bonnet like the many-headed Hydra.

"Bessie, there you are!" cried Jane.

"La', Missus, where should I be?" said Bessie in her habitually querulous tones. "If Missus sends me to fetch Master's chops, wot should I do but fetch 'em?"

Field could smell the gin from where he sat; could it be that his wife did not?

"There, there, Bessie," said Jane. "No harm done."

"Shall I *not* fetch 'em? Some might not, I s'pose," said the woman, on a rising note, with a hint of hysterics to follow. It was one of Jane Field's enduring delusions that Bessie was, in fact, a treasure and that the girl was at any moment liable to desert the household for a better position elsewhere.

"No, my dear girl!" cried Jane. "O' course you give satisfaction! Don't she, Mr. Field?"

"It's not unheard of," said that gentleman quietly.

"There's chops 'ere," said Bessie, "and a nice piece o' fish, but do I get any thanks for my trouble?"

"Nonsense, puss," said Jane, taking the parcels from her and sniffing each in turn. "Mr. Field met the Prince today, Bessie—Prince Albert, as ever was! Now what do you think of Master, and ain't you pleased to be in his service?"

"I 'ope I know my place," said the serving girl, "and any respect wot I owe the master."

Field pulled his knees to his chest. "Mrs. Field, if we could perhaps move things along? I've had rather a long day and I'm hungry."

"Of course. Bessie, take Mr. Field's soiled things and put them in the copper to soak whilst I get started on these chops—there's a good girl."

Perhaps they're right, thought Field. *Stevie had any number of mortal enemies. It all could have been a bizarre coincidence and Stevie's murder nothing to do with the insane man who tried to kill the Queen.*

The sizzle and smell of the frying chops comforted him. He closed his eyes and dozed.

LATE THAT NIGHT, the newly refreshed detective lay back in his bed, exulting in the comfort of the bedclothes. Jane yawned and settled in close by his side.

"I imagine," Mrs. Field said, "that poor deranged man was just one of them new communist fellows, that's all."

"What's that, my dear?" Field said.

"Well, it's their motto, isn't it? Or something like it?"

"What motto? Whose motto?"

"*You* know."

"I assure you, my dear, I have no idea."

"The communists."

"*Communists?* Mrs. Field, what's this about a motto?"

"They've got it printed on the broadsheets they pass out at market, don't they. "There's a specter hauntin' Europe!' it says across the top, big as brass. 'It's called communism!' Good night, my dear."

She passed quickly from consciousness to sleep, but Detective Inspector Field was suddenly awake and staring as lightning and thunder broke loudly over the city.

7

The lamps were dimmed; the royal servants banished. The two men stood at a wall of windows in the darkened room, watching the storm. Sudden, stabbing blue light created momentary vistas, disappearing in an instant. The lengthy silence between the men accentuated the sound of the rain pelting the windows and running in orderly channels across the roof beneath them.

"She is very strong." Prince Albert's voice was low. "I asked her if she would be able to sleep tonight, and she said, 'Why ever would I not be?'"

His companion, Sir Richard Owen, renowned professor of anatomy and one of the principal natural historians of the age, shook his head in wonder. A flash of lightning was followed almost immediately by a deafening peal of thunder: for less than a second, every tree in St. James Park was revealed.

"What can explain it? She is benevolent and good-hearted. As far as

I can tell, her subjects love her. Why should these devils wish to harm her?"

Sir Richard Owen pursed his lips and shook his head sadly, mutely grieving the inexplicable wickedness of the world.

"Of *me*," said Albert with a rueful laugh, "the people are not so fond."

A dissenting murmur from his companion: "No, no . . ."

"Owen, there are those in this realm who detest me, this is not a matter for debate. I am the foreigner, the German who stole their princess from them. I am the introducer of strange un-English ideas."

"Your Great Exhibition changed all that, sir," said Owen.

"Ten years later, does anyone care? Oh! how the great men opposed me and my exhibition! It was all a conspiracy to give away the secrets of British industry to the world! Because, of course, no one knows *anything* but the British, and the British have nothing to learn from anyone, *ever*!"

The Crystal Palace Exhibition of 1851 had been condemned from the pulpit. Members of Parliament had proclaimed their hope that it would fail. The aristocracy in particular had been skeptical; many of them, in fact, *did* loathe the German prince. He was stiff in society; his demeanor revealed the contempt he had for it. As it happened, the international display of technological advances had been a stunning success with the general public and with visitors from around the world. Millions had attended, the exhibition more than paid for itself, and in 1854 the entire massive glass structure was disassembled and moved from Hyde Park to Sydenham, south of the Thames.

"I understand, Sir Richard, that your monstrous lizards still inspire fear amongst the matrons of Surrey."

Owen raised his eyebrows and smiled modestly. "Indeed," he said. "There is even talk of erecting a similar menagerie in the Central Park of New York."

It was Owen who had coined the word *dinosaur* and who was the first to classify the gigantic fossil remains of the "terrible lizards," which were being discovered throughout the world. Both respected for his brilliance and feared for his competitive malice, Owen had a high fore-head, a prominent narrow nose, thin lips, and a wife and son whom he rarely saw. Critics said that Owen had never acknowledged his debt to Gideon Mantell, a self-taught scholar from the lower classes whose ear-lier work with fossils had paved Owen's way. It was common knowledge that Owen had viciously fought the presentation of the Royal Society's medal to Mantell for his pioneering work. The man had been cruelly disfigured by disease, then a carriage accident, and lived in constant pain; many were appalled when, following Mantell's death, Owen had the man's misshapen skeleton publicly displayed at the Royal College of Surgeons.

What mattered to the Prince, though, was that Owen had been a staunch supporter of his exhibition. Under Owen's direction, a sculptor had created massive full-scale models of a number of dinosaurs. At the exhibition's opening festivities, he had hosted a party entirely inside one of these models, a dinner for twenty-one guests—including Albert.

"If something should happen to the Queen," said Albert, abruptly, "what would become of the nation? Could Bertie govern?"

At last we come to it! The shooting today has put him in mind of mortal-ity and royal succession.

Owen had tutored the royal children when they were younger, and he considered the eldest boy, Albert, Prince of Wales and heir to the throne, to be dull, indolent, and vain. "With proper guidance, I believe he could, sir," he said.

"With guidance from whom, Owen? From you? Let us assume for the moment that both the Queen and I were absent from the scene."

"No, no, no . . ."

"One must have clarity, Sir Richard, and courage. Could our eldest son assume the throne and acquit himself honorably?"

Owen was silent and the Prince nodded grimly. "So, this is our dilemma. I plan to take the Queen to Coburg in September to visit my homeland. Must we take Bertie with us, to keep him in line?"

"I am sure it would be instructive for him."

"Perhaps we will send him to America. He's been invited often enough. He would need a chaperone, of course, and Bishop Wilberforce, alas, has risen too high in the world to be of service. We had a letter from him this afternoon, quite upset over the events of the morning."

"Of course, sir. So were we all."

"Wilberforce, too, expresses interest in the Prince of Wales." Albert gazed thoughtfully at Owen. "The bishop is going ahead with this debate at Oxford, or perhaps you were already aware of this."

"Indeed."

"Will Mr. Darwin participate?"

"It is uncertain," said Owen. "There is the matter of his health, you know."

"In any case Wilberforce will be going up against Huxley, God help him."

"The bishop of Oxford is quite a capable debater, sir. I shouldn't worry about him."

Albert snorted. "Worry about Soapy Sam? I certainly shall not!"

Owen stiffened. "I myself will be coaching the bishop for this debate in matters of comparative anatomy."

"Will you indeed, Owen! What is it you people have against Darwin?"

"I, sir? I have known Charles Darwin for twenty years. I believe I may say, in all modesty, that he looks up to me as a guiding light. I have nothing against the man."

"Do you not? You people came down rather hard on us when the Queen wished to bestow a knighthood on him."

"That, sir, was Bishop Wilberforce, not I. I believe Darwin to be a scholar and a gentleman who has simply drawn seriously mistaken conclusions from his rather admirable researches. Bishop Wilberforce is obliged, of course, by his vocation to object to the man's conclusions."

"Nothing to do with his vocation, I should have thought. Matter of science. Facts and figures, not religion."

"In this, sir, I am afraid we disagree. The lines between the two may *seem* to be parallel, but ultimately there is *one line* that intersects all others."

"Wouldn't think the Lord God Almighty needed Sam Wilberforce defending him, but then, he's got pluck. Wilberforce, I mean." The storm had lessened and the Prince turned again to the windows, looking out. "I intend to put Darwin's name forward once more, in the next Honors List. I mean to say, Her Majesty intends to do so."

"Indeed?"

"Indeed," repeated the Prince with the barest hint of an edge. "I am told he may be the greatest man of science these islands have produced since Newton."

"May I ask, sir," said Owen with an edge of his own, "who has compared Charles Darwin to Sir Isaac Newton?"

"You are not the only respected natural historian who dines with us, Sir Richard." He turned to Owen and added, "But you are one of the most esteemed." Owen acknowledged both the rebuke and the compliment with a slight bow.

"I've kept you late again, haven't I. But now you see the rain is stopping and you will have a better journey home." Albert pulled a hidden lever, and a butler appeared instantly. "Have Sir Richard's carriage brought round." The man inclined his head and vanished.

"Do you know," said the Prince, stepping out into the hall, "we interviewed that detective fellow today, the real Mr. Bucket."

"Indeed?"

"Detective Inspector Charles Field. I can see how Dickens might have become interested in the man—he *is* larger than life somehow. Even in person, the man seems like fiction." Albert moved crisply down the passage while Sir Richard hurried alongside. "Field thinks today's attempt upon the life of the Queen was not the work of a lone madman but part of a conspiracy."

"Does he now?"

"It seems there was a murder committed that is somehow connected." Albert stopped at the head of a grand staircase. "Here, my friend, is where we part company."

Owen seemed suddenly at a loss. "Ah, yes. A conspiracy, you say?"

"I do enjoy our little talks," said Albert, oblivious. "Even before

Owen could bow, the Prince Consort was walking away, his upright form receding down a long, flickering hall of gilt and glass. A footman nearby coughed gently. Sir Richard Owen turned and followed him down the steps.

IT WAS WELL past midnight. The rain had stopped and a wind had risen. The temperature was dropping and a half-moon was alternately revealed and hidden by ragged, fast-moving clouds.

The Royal College of Surgeons at Lincoln's Inn Fields was mostly dark at this time of night but far from empty. Row after row of mounted skeletons stared mutely at each other across the ages. Fetuses floated in countless glass vessels. In the cool vaults below, corpses lay waiting to offer up their secrets to the keen blades of the students and faculty.

The tall young man—a living specimen, known from childhood as "the Chorister"—glided up the staircase to the ground level. The night porter had given him the message that the professor had arrived and wished to see him, so Decimus Cobb had put down his instruments and made himself ready for the interview.

Tonight, the Chorister knew his mentor would speak of the day's failure, and he knew he would be scolded for it, but what was he to do? His master was determined to keep himself and his cohorts far removed from the work they had assigned him, so he had been compelled to recruit a deniable agent: the lunatic Rendell who, it transpired, could not shoot straight. If only they would give Decimus free rein! He wasn't worried. The professor would chide him but not overmuch: the older man feared his protégé greatly, and with good reason. (It was Decimus, in fact, who had boiled and boned the paleontologist Gideon Mantell and mounted his twisted spine for public view years earlier, when the anatomy student was barely out of his teens.)

The Chorister's dark deep-set eyes burned with fervor. He would deal with the butcher's boy who had spotted him tomorrow, one way or another. And Philip David Rendell, recently of Islington and currently residing in Newgate Prison—he would find a way of dealing with him as well. All *that* could wait until morning.

Lamplight through frosted glass splayed across the floor before him. Decimus paused. As always, the ambient odor of formaldehyde comforted him. He turned the brass knob on the door marked HUNTERIAN PROFESSOR, ROYAL COLLEGE OF SURGEONS and saw Sir Richard Owen, still wearing a damp raincoat, rise from behind his desk, a mixture of anger and fear contorting his face. Decimus smiled serenely and bowed. Then he froze.

Someone else was there. An old gentleman, florid face, bushy white hair and beard, head like a lion's, fierce and unforgiving.

Betrayed!

The Chorister's eyes flew back to Owen.

"Decimus," said Owen maliciously, "allow me to introduce Sir Jasper Arpington-Dix. He's the one actually running this show."

The Chorister was mute, his smile gone, a red heat filling his head.

"I'm not afraid of you, young man," said Sir Jasper. "I've dealt with worse than you, believe me. You're a means to an end, that's all."

Decimus Cobb went to the quiet place in his mind, a place where he could visualize the dissection of the man standing before him.

"None of that!" said Sir Jasper, as though he'd been listening to the Chorister's thoughts. "Sit!"

Decimus sat.

Sir Jasper limped around the desk, leaning heavily on his stick, until he stood directly over Decimus. "You've damn near given away the game, you know."

"*Conspiracy!*" said Owen. "I heard the word from the Prince's own lips!"

"Did you really find it necessary to cut your man's throat then and there, Mr. Cobb, moments after Inspector Field interviewed him? My house is close by, you see. I was watching. I found it curious. *And so did Detective Inspector Field!*"

Decimus considered the various implements he had secreted within his clothing. Some were spring-mounted; all of them were razor sharp. It had been years since anyone had dared to confront him like this. But the white-haired old lion was different; he actually *wasn't* frightened.

"I only employ effective tools," continued Sir Jasper. "Those who are not, I discard. Are you an effective tool, Mr. Cobb? Will you be?"

The Chorister found himself nodding. "Yes, sir," he said in a quiet voice.

"Do you give your word?"

And even as Decimus mentally sorted through the organs in the old man's body, he nodded again like a child and said, "Yes, sir. I give my word, sir."

"Good. Today was a setback, nothing more. We have just tonight received intelligence concerning the royal family's plans, and we foresee an opportunity arising in the autumn. Owen here tells me you traveled in Prussia when you were a young man."

Decimus' eyes rose to Owen's for one red instant and then fell again.

"Well," continued Sir Jasper, "you have from now until September to acquaint yourself with a particular locale in that region. I'll help you. Come—not so downcast, young man. This is good news—we're going to employ your considerable skills much more directly. Go now. Leave us. You'll hear from me."

Decimus rose as steadily as he could. He bowed to the two men and left.

SIR JASPER WORTHING Reynolds Arpington-Dix, riding home in a hackney coach, breathed deeply of the rain-freshened air. At age seventy, Sir Jasper was the latest scion of a family that had achieved prominence and great wealth two centuries earlier with the rise of the East India Company. Now all that and much more, according to Sir Jasper, was threatened.

Where had it all begun, this frightening decline? A dozen years earlier, in the late 1840s, Europe had been convulsed by revolution. Suddenly there was wave after wave of political uprisings—in the German states, in France and Italy. Sir Jasper, then in his late fifties, had worked at fever pitch to maintain the family fortunes, at home and in India. Now it seemed to him (and to many others) that rampant liberalism and radicalism threatened the established order and the very empire itself. Nothing was safe. There was even talk of dismantling the East India Company altogether and *giving the whole damned show to the natives!*

In 1859, however, a worse threat had arisen, one that outweighed all others by far. The very foundations of society were at risk, and immediate action was called for. Thus, Sir Jasper had convened a small but distinguished group six months earlier to address the situation. These men occupied the very highest echelons of commerce, the military, and the Church. Knowing his audience, Sir Jasper had laid out everything in *hypothetical* terms only. He would be the only person of his class who could be held accountable should the *thoroughly hypothetical* plan fail. If it was successful, history would never know of its existence. He had never even used the word *assassination*. Today, they had suffered a setback, granted. But they had just been given another means of skinning the cat, and skin it they would.

8

The morning was bright, brisk, and blowy. The heavy rains in the night had cooled the air and washed London clean—cleaner, at least, than it had been the day before. As Inspector Field strode along the Strand, there was a spring to his step and a sense of renewed possibility in his heart.

Now this is more like it, a proper June morning.

Although he'd heard of them, Field didn't know much about the political faction who called themselves *communist*. Now, thanks to his wife's conjecture, his interest was piqued. Weren't they the fellows who were blowing people up in Germany a few years back? Such folk would be antiroyal, doubtless.

The sight of his regular newsstand ahead of him gave him pause.

Best get this over with. After all, how bad can it be?

The first headline to catch his eye was relatively restrained. SHOTS FIRED! QUEEN UNHURT, proclaimed *The Times*.

Fair enough, fair enough.

Field's eyes moved to the larger, bolder banner of the *Daily Telegraph*:
MADMAN FIRES ON ROYAL CARRIAGE AS CONSTABLES LOOK ON!

The detective's buoyancy was fading. With dread in his heart he saw that the *Illustrated London News* was offering a large sketch on its front page. It appeared to be a caricature of himself—as seen from the rear—running, with coattails flapping. OUR POLICE IN ACTION!

Human nature being a mystery, it was the last of these publications that Field felt compelled to purchase. He fished in his pockets for a coin to give the newsboy, pulled out a sovereign, and stood suddenly motionless, staring at the coin. Mrs. Field must have transferred the contents of his yesterday's trousers into the pair she'd laid out for him this morning. The coin was stained a dry rusty color.

"Inspector Field?" said the newsboy.

Hatchet-Face could have come by the coin most anyhow in the course of a day. It don't necessarily mean a thing.

"Sir?" said the boy. "You want the paper or not?"

No. Stevie had been instructed: what to do and where to do it. And this coin here is what he got paid for it. I'd lay odds it is.

"Yoo-hoo, Mr. Bucket!" cried the newsboy, the twelve-year-old dripping with sarcasm. "Quite a nice likeness, don't you fink? Bottom could be a bit bigger, but then these artists got licenses, don't they?"

"Delightful child," said Field absently, laying a sixpence on the newsstand's wooden ledge. "Keep the change." He turned to find Constables Llewellyn and Kilvert just behind him.

"Sir," said Kilvert, "we've got someone at the station who might be able to assist us in our inquiries, sir."

"Is it the missing butcher?"

Kilvert sighed and said, "Right again, Chief."

"What do you know of these communist fellers, then?" said Field abruptly as he turned down Craven Street with his two colleagues in tow, a copy of the *Illustrated News* folded under his arm.

Kilvert looked sharply at Llewellyn. "Oh dear," he intoned.

"*Oh dear* what?" said Field, glancing from one to the other. Llewellyn was blushing.

"Land of my fathers, sir," said Kilvert, jerking his head in his partner's direction. "Llewellyn here is one of them!"

And the ruin of Charles Field's bright day was complete.

THE BUTCHER WHO had failed to bring the required pounds of flesh to No. 42 St. Albans the previous morning was sitting in a dingy room at the Metropolitan when Llewellyn and Kilvert ushered in Detective Field.

"His name's Merrydew," said Kilvert in a sepulchral tone. "Dennis."

Field looked him over. Not yet thirty years old, Dennis Merrydew had the beaten look of a man who believes fortune to be forever against him and likely would wear the same expression even when sober. The inspector adopted his approach accordingly.

"Hallo, Dennis," Field said, his voice a mix of commiseration and censure. "Rough night? I think you'll agree with me that you're a little worse for wear. Feelin' a bit queasy, perhaps? That's how it takes me, the mornin' after."

Merrydew swallowed and licked his lips and said nothing.

"My colleagues here say they located you asleep outside a public house early this morning, is that right?"

Merrydew's shoulders sank a little.

"Listen, chum," said Field with a wink. "I expect your head is splitting, but I'm in rather a hurry. 'I wasted time and now doth time waste me,' if you get my meaning."

Merrydew wiped his nose with his sleeve and coughed.

"That's Shakespeare saying the sooner you speak up brisk-like, the sooner you're out of here, right?" The young man nodded, wincing as he did so.

Field drew out a chair and sat opposite his subject; his colleagues remained standing, their eyes on Merrydew. "Where do you do your butchering, Dennis? What's your theater of operation, so to speak?"

Merrydew cleared his throat. "Smithfield Market," he said.

"Just so," said Field. "Something tells me, Dennis, that you met someone at the market yesterday morning, am I right? A stranger?" The butcher's face registered surprise. "Early this would have been. P'raps you're just arrivin' for work, or headin' out with a delivery, this bloke says howdy-do, offers to stand you a drink. An eye-opener, right? Where's the harm in that?"

Merrydew nodded hesitantly.

"That's it, lad! That's the spirit of cooperation! Well done!"

"He's been drunk ever since, Chief."

"Well, Officer Kilvert," said Field, never taking his eyes off the butcher, "it happens."

"Not to me it don't, sir," said Kilvert.

"No, Mr. Kilvert, of course not to *you*." Field inclined his head in Merrydew's direction and winked.

"A situation like that, Chief," said Llewellyn, "in my experience, could be a bit of fun or could be a situation where you get took advantage of, know what I mean?"

"He missed work, Mr. Field," said Kilvert indignantly. "He never showed up for work the whole day long, and him in the guild and all." He turned on Llewellyn. "That's not what *I* call a bit of fun!"

"Be fair, Kilvert!" said Llewellyn. "Can't you see the man's in pain?"

"Actions have consequences, Mr. Llewellyn!"

"Gentlemen!" said Field. "I think we all agree that the whole affair of yesterday morning was unfortunate. Am I right, Dennis?"

Merrydew nodded emphatically.

"How did the man get your apron off you, Merrydew?" asked Llewellyn suddenly.

"Your *butcher's* apron," intoned Kilvert.

"He *did* want your apron, didn't he?" said Field. "And your wheelbarrow?"

Merrydew hung his head. "Seems he did."

"Did he pay you for it?" said Llewellyn.

Merrydew's eyes darted from man to man. "Nah," he whispered.

"He's lying," said Kilvert.

"Now, now, Officer Kilvert," murmured Field.

"Sorry," said Merrydew. "I mean, he *did* let me have some coin for drink."

"How much?" said Kilvert.

"Don't remember," said Merrydew. "Don't remember much, to tell you the truth."

This statement produced an awful silence in the little room. Merrydew felt it and was alarmed. The three police officers looked at each other gravely.

"Uncooperative," said Kilvert.

"I thought we were getting on so well," said Llewellyn.

"Right," said Field, rising from the table. "I don't have time to waste here."

"You leave him to us, sir," said Kilvert darkly.

"Wait!" cried the butcher as Inspector Field opened the door. "Officers, please! What d' you want to know? I'm 'appy to oblige, if ever I can!"

Half an hour later the officers of the law had wrung Merrydew dry and sent him packing. They had a description, albeit a foggy one, of the man who had wrangled the butcher's apron and wheelbarrow in exchange for a day's drinking money.

The man was tall. Slender. A decent chap, never mind that he was well spoke. Yes, a gentleman, no doubt of that. Funny way of walking, smooth-like. As if he was on wheels or something. Good looking, fair-skinned, sandy-haired. And the darkest, deepest eyes you ever did see.

Did he have a name?

Cory something.

Occupation?

Merrydew had said he thought the man might have been a barber or a surgeon. Just a feeling he had.

A *feeling*? What sort of feeling would that be, Merrydew?

A smell of carbolic. And the man had showed him knives. A whole box of them.

Did he now? Thank you, Mr. Merrydew. Mr. Llewellyn will show you out.

When Llewellyn returned to the little office after ushering Merrydew out of the building, Inspector Field was gazing at the constable darkly.

"So you're a communist, are you? A bloody insurrectionist under my own command. A revolutionary, a bomb thrower."

"Sir, really, that's not us at all, we're just, you know, workers!"

"You're not a worker, you're a bloody policeman! I took you under my damned wing, lad, and this is how you repay me?"

"Please, sir! It's a free country, or so I'm told!" Llewellyn turned on his partner. "What have you gone and done? You prim little Baptist prig, turning the chief against me, and without cause!"

"There's been an incident," said Kilvert, ominously. "We've just had word."

Llewellyn looked from his partner to his superior.

"A demonstration outside Newgate Prison," said Field. "A show of support for Philip David Rendell."

"Solidarity, they're calling it," continued Kilvert. "Standing by the man who tried to kill the Queen."

"When a few of our lot moved in," said Field, "solidarity ran for the hills."

Kilvert's voice dropped to its lowest register. "Communists. Every man jack of them."

9

Charles Field, dressed as a laborer, stood among the massive columns before the British Museum, smoking a stubby pipe and wishing he'd chosen larger boots; these pinched. His target should emerge any minute now if the man kept to his daily pattern, which he was reputed to do. The man was a heavy smoker and perennially short on tobacco, according to Llewellyn, although the young Welshman claimed never to have met him but only heard him speak.

A museum guard was eyeing Field dubiously. There was a pushcart at the base of the steps, a hot-pie vendor. Field moved purposefully down the stone staircase, pulling out a battered old leather change purse as he went, to indicate his solvency. As he passed the guard, he deferentially touched his hat.

Nice, said the theater critic within him.

A workingman with money in his pocket, munching a pork pie,

viewing one of the monuments of his nation's glory—that's what he was. Not a policeman, not a detective inspector, lying in wait for a leader of insurrectionists. No, he was who he pretended to be; it was a point of pride with Field.

What a mark I would have made on the stage! Top tier! Amongst the very best of them, thank you very much!

Just then a stocky, striking figure in a rumpled old suit appeared at the top of the steps, polishing his spectacles and squinting in the daylight. Field had seen an engraving of the target (on file, supplied a few years earlier by the Belgian police), and Llewellyn had described the man to him, even as he deplored the whole enterprise as a waste of time.

Karl Marx was at this time forty-two years of age. The hair on his head had gone white, but his beard was still coal black and well kept. An improbably high forehead rose above a pugnacious brow and a squat nose. Officially unwelcome in Prussia, France, and Belgium, he had fled to London a dozen years earlier with his wife, Jenny, and their maid, Lenchen. In the years that followed, the couple had lost three of their five children (to pneumonia, cholera, and poverty). Marx had grieved for his children, lived financially off his friend and collaborator Friedrich Engels, and impregnated Lenchen. Marx told his wife that Engels was the father. During this time Karl Marx had also written works of philosophical and economic theory that would shake the world to its foundations and make his name forever famous.

Right now he was patting his pockets, in search of tobacco. Pigeons fluttered up into the gray London sky as Marx descended the steps distractedly. By the time he reached the bottom, Field had his tobacco pouch out and ready, nodding and smiling and touching his hat.

"Guv'nor."

Marx gave him a cool glance and passed on toward the omnibus stop in Tottenham Court Road.

Field hurried after, and when Marx stepped onto the rear platform of the waiting omnibus, the disguised policeman boarded, too. The 'bus was packed, as usual. The driver flicked his whip above the heads of the horses, the 'bus lurched forward, and Karl Marx fell backward into Charles Field.

"I beg your pardon," said Marx, looking Field up and down suspiciously. Field waved him off with a grin, as though he were perfectly delighted to be halfway crushed by strangers on 'buses.

"So," said Marx, "what do you want of me?"

At which point Field made a full confession: he had lain in wait for Herr Marx on purpose; he had heard the great man speak on a couple of occasions and had even got his hands on copies of the *New-York Daily Tribune* when Marx's articles were published there.

"I do not remember you," said Marx. "When did you hear me speak?"

"Let me think," said Field, slowly. "It was in the past year, o' that I'm sure."

"In Stepney, perhaps?"

Field had laid enough interrogatory traps in his day to be wary. "Stepney . . . does *not* ring a bell, Herr Marx, to tell you the truth, but then at my time o' life I'm sometimes hard put to remember me own address."

"Where *do* you live?"

"Blowed if I know!" replied Field, laughing. Marx looked at him a moment longer, then burst into laughter himself.

This time when Field offered his tobacco pouch, Marx accepted, and within moments the two of them were puffing congenially, clinging to the overhead straps with their free hands. Two female passengers seated beneath them waved the smoke away from their faces, but the men were oblivious.

"Your name, sir?" said Marx.

"Meadow," said Field. "Charles Meadow, sir."

"What, Mr. Meadow, is the state of your liver?"

Field looked at the great man blankly.

"Mine is a source of almost constant discomfort."

"You don't say, Herr Marx?"

"This entire month, it is for me almost impossible to work. I feel like bloody Prometheus."

Field cocked his head, his brow furrowed.

"The chap who gave the gift of fire to mankind?" said Marx. "And was therefore punished by Zeus by having his liver forever eaten by an eagle?"

Field sighed deeply. "See, this is why I like to hear you speak, Herr Marx. I am always eager to learn from my betters."

Marx drew at his pipe, regarding Field closely.

"This is why you read my essays?"

"To tell the truth, Herr Marx, I'm not much of a reading man."

"But you said you read me in the *Tribune*!"

"Oh! Yes, quite, but that's generally my helpmeet a-readin' them articles out to me, bless her old heart."

"So, a married man, are you then, Mr. Meadow?"

"Blissfully so, sir."

Marx sighed, staring over the heads of the other passengers. "*Ja*, so, me also," he said wanly. "Pure bliss, pure bliss." The omnibus was inching northward through heavy London traffic, with passengers boarding and alighting at every stop. "For how long have you been a communist, Mr. Meadow?"

"Well now, I can't say as I'm exactly a full-fledged . . . you know . . . one of you lot, not at this point, at any rate. I could be in time. I would say that currently, as of today, I'm more an interested well-wisher."

"I see. Then you are the enemy."

"Good God, no, Herr Marx! Please!"

Marx smiled and nodded. "We are at war, Mr. Meadow. Your good wishes are worse than worthless."

"Aha, well yes. Put it like that, I can see your point, Herr Marx. Given the . . . the war and all. See, I'm a slow man, I need things spelt out, in a manner of speakin'."

Marx jabbed him in the chest with the stem of his pipe. "Take this recent shooting at the Queen."

Field's heart quickened. "Yes, Herr Marx, wotcher think o' that now?"

"I think, what a pity no one ever shoots at cabinet ministers!" said Marx. "You've read my anti-Palmerston tracts, perhaps?"

Field shook his head.

"You must ask your blissful wife to read you my thoughts on the prime minister one day. The great liberal, the radical reformer, Palmerston? And how much better we all would be if he were dead and buried? *Ja?*"

"Yah," said Field. "But what about the Queen, then? Where do you stand on . . . well—not to put too fine a point upon it—shootin' the Queen?"

"A question for you, first, Mr. Meadow: are you fond of Primrose Hill?"

Field's mind raced. *Fond of Primrose Hill.* Was it a code?

"Not in particular, sir, although it's got its points, does Primrose Hill. I got nothin' *against* Primrose Hill, if it comes to that. Why do you ask?"

"Because, Mr. *Meadow*, that is where this omnibus is going."

"Ah, yes, of course."

"Do you really think I will confess assassination to you, an officer of the so-called law?"

"What? Herr Marx, that's not who I am—I'm a worker, like you!"

"I am not a worker, sir, I am a revolutionist. And this is my stop coming up. Detective Bucket, isn't it? My wife and I enjoyed reading about you in the Dickens, even if you *are* a counterrevolutionary and an enemy of the people."

Field's face slowly turned a shade of purple. "Think you're clever, do you?"

"I do indeed, Mr. Bucket."

"*I am not Bucket!*" shouted the detective, attracting the scrutiny of the conductor. Field lowered his voice. "You know I could take you into custody right this minute? Hustle you and yours onto a packet ship straight back to Germany?"

"Of course."

"Then, Herr Marx, talk to me. Open your heart. It will do you good, and to do otherwise would be sheerest folly on your part."

"Doubtless."

"So? Perhaps, sir, you would miss the checks that your friend Herr Engels sends you? If the postal authorities were to stop 'em?"

Marx's brow furrowed.

"Perhaps your good wife already knows who is the father of your servant's child?"

Marx shot Field a look of wide-eyed alarm.

"Oh, yes, our people know all about it. Maybe I'm not clever enough to fool you, Herr Marx, but we keep a close eye and I could cause you certain difficulties, I'm sure you would agree."

Marx looked off again and nodded slowly.

"Was your lot in on it?" asked Field. "Firing upon the Queen?"

The man was silent for some time as the 'bus crawled up the hill. "You feel it, don't you?" he said finally. "It's coming. *The Times* says this was a lone crazy man yesterday who tried to do this, but you don't believe *The Times*, do you, Mr. Bucket? No more do I. Because you can feel what's coming, too, just as I can, just as do thousands across Europe. The railroad, this remarkable new invention, you can hear it approaching from a long way off, *ja*? What you feel, Mr. Bucket, what you fear, what you hear in the distance, is the sound of the revolution that is coming."

"I'm a policeman, Mr. Marx. Not a fortune-teller, not a philosopher. I'm an uneducated man. But I've got a job to do and I do it, unlike some as I could mention, leavin' wife and children near penniless whilst he's off at some library. I arrest wrong-doers and turn them over to the magistrates. You say that makes me an enemy of the people, but there are many people who would say that makes me their friend."

Marx made sure his pipe was extinguished, gingerly dipping a thumb into the bowl.

"When will you wake up? You especially—a policeman, in your own subjugation, complicit. You feel inferior, speaking to me about 'your betters' and your lack of education and touching your cap to me—that was not *all* an act, Mr. Bucket, don't tell me it was. *Mein Gott*, you are the architect of your own pain! It is true, is it not? You rank yourself quite low on the scale of things. You serve your masters, hoping like a dog for a crumb from their table, or a pat on the head or a kind word. And when none of that is forthcoming, you simply try harder to please them. You poor man, how miserable your life is, and how alone with that pain you are. And when this dream nears its end, and you are about to wake to endless night, what then will you say of your life? That it was empty? Meaningless? Join us, Mr. Bucket. At least, sir, when you lie awake at night, as I know you do, think about it. Have a pamphlet."

Marx thrust a crumpled, soiled sheet of paper into Field's hand. Across the top Field saw the words A SPECTER IS HAUNTING EUROPE! He was speechless as the omnibus clopped to a halt.

"Listen," said Marx, lowering his voice, "do you think you could loan me a fiver, just until the end of the month?"

Field's head was spinning. "You want money from me?" he said, hoarsely.

"Even a quid would help, old man. I have mouths to feed. No? Never mind. My wife will be excited to hear I met you, Mr. Bucket."

Marx stepped down onto the street, turned, and waved up at Field with his pipe as the 'bus started up again.

"Old man, the Queen is irrelevant! Give me the man who runs his railroad over the backs of the workers who built it!" Marx aimed his pipe at Field, as though it were a pistol. "Put *him* in my sights, and—*bang*!"

10

Tom Ginty's mother, Martha, was jointing a chicken in the scullery of the Fortune of War when someone came kicking at the tradesmen's entrance. "Pull the bloody bell, can't you?" she cried.

"Martha!" The voice belonged to Jake Figgis. Martha put down the knife, wiped her hands on her apron, and moved to the door. Jake stood just outside, holding the handles of a wheelbarrow laden with freshly butchered meats.

"Where's Tom?"

"What do you mean?" said Martha. "He's with you."

"No he ain't."

"What?"

"Must run, I got this lot to deliver! Tell Tom to 'op it!" Jake lifted his wheelbarrow and moved off. Martha stood stock-still for a moment. Then she ran up a topsy-turvy series of stairs to the room at the top of the public house where she and her son lived. She flung open the door. She called his name. Surely he'd answer. He'd pop out of the corner cupboard, laughing. A bad joke, yes, but nothing more than that. He'd emerge from the blanket on the little pallet that soon would be too short for him. *Still asleep, Tom! At this hour?* Even though she'd seen him out the door that very morning, before the first rays of sun had penetrated the caverns of tottering tenements, even though she'd heard him say "Ta, Ma" over his shoulder, Martha waited for her boy to appear in that bare room to prove to her that God and his angels did, in fact, exist and Jesus did suffer the little children to come unto him.

ADDING YOUNG TOM Ginty to his collection had been the work of a moment. Rising before dawn, Decimus Cobb had chosen a priest's cassock and a broad-brimmed Roman hat. He'd be a country padre, pushing a barrow filled with burlap sacks to market.

Which is precisely what Tom had taken him for, in the short distance between the Fortune of War and Smithfield Market. A kindly, priestly smile in the morning darkness and a mumbled question. Asking directions, perhaps. Tom had leaned in closer, the better to hear the parson. A swish of black cloth, something moist over his nose and mouth, and then a quick glimpse of deep-set dark eyes, giving way to blackness.

A HISTORY OF the man eventually was pieced together from bits and scraps and much speculation. It is doubtless faulty, but it's all anyone has:

He was plucked from the streets some twenty years earlier, hollow-eyed and filthy, and placed in one of the new "ragged schools," created to deal with London's ever-growing population of destitute orphans. On his first day the matron stripped him and put him under the pump for a scrub. It took her some moments before she realized what she was looking at. Then she stood shrieking in the yard until the master came to see what was the matter. Whether out of compassion or curiosity, the master decided to keep the boy on. Since he had no name he cared to divulge, Master called him Will Tailor. After a largely mute first year the boy began to excel in his studies. He became ardently devout, committing to memory long passages of Scripture. A woman appeared at irregular intervals, who may or may not have been a mother, but she never stayed for long. His abilities and a soaring soprano voice won him a place at St. Paul's, where he had a superior education and a position in the choir until his voice broke at the age of fourteen. By then he had distinguished himself in the sciences. He liked to take things apart to see how they worked, especially living things, and he seemed not to mind that this stopped them living.

He was given a new name by the man who adopted him when he was still a choirboy. Artemus Cobb was a manufacturer of ladies' undergarments, and his whalebone corsets had made a wealthy man of him. The Chorister was twelve years old when he officially became Decimus Cobb and was moved into the single man's townhouse in Half Moon Street, off Piccadilly. Three years later his adoptive parent died from a fall in San Gimignano while visiting with his boy the monuments of Tuscany. The house in Piccadilly, with no family to contest it, seemed to become Decimus' property by default. Apart from a considerable stash of coins, which young Decimus had found hidden in the master bedroom, the corset fortune likely went to the Crown. To Decimus it hardly mattered; by then his sidelines were beginning to be highly lucrative. A professed desire to become a surgeon led to a scholarship, and his pious manner and studious ways had found favor in the Royal College of Surgeons, eventually attracting the attention of Professor Richard Owen.

Today, the grown-up Decimus was enjoying a cool, not-too-odiferous breeze off the river as he made his way from the market to Half Moon Street. Such a relief after yesterday's heat and the discord of the night before! He carried in one hand a compact wooden case, which he called his "kit." From his other hand swung a net bag containing bread, cheese, sausage, and a couple of hens. He had a hungry crew waiting at home, and food—offered or withheld—was one of the means he employed to manage them.

Oh, look! There's Mr. Dickens! Where is he off to now? Some theatrical business or other, I'll wager. A bony little man, really. Will he see me as he passes? Ha! Looked me right in the eyes! Wait until I tell the children!

This sort of thing was always happening. It's why Decimus loved living in the West End.

Tom Ginty opened his eyes experimentally. He saw nothing. He closed and opened them again and felt a surge of fear pulse through his body.

Please God, no, not blind, it's just a dark place, i'n'it, that's all.

The boy was horizontal. He raised a hand tentatively; it was stopped by a wooden surface less than a foot above his body. He moved it to his right and met another wall within inches. Fear threatened to overwhelm him.

Coffin.

He couldn't give way to terror or tears. He would think of sunlight and air. His mother's face, laughing. These were things that still existed; he just had to find them again, that's all. He would begin by breathing. In, out. In, out.

Inexplicably, he slept. His eyes sprang open again to pitch darkness and the sound of a key turning quietly in a nearby lock.

The light was searing when the lid above him rose. Tom struck upward, blindly, with all his strength. His fist barely brushed the hated face: the gliding man's head jerked backward with a surprised gasp. Tom set his legs in motion, scrabbling to find purchase, his fingers seeking the borders of the coffin. The lid began to descend.

"Not quite ready, are we," said Decimus in a sorrowful voice.

Tom roared inarticulately, frantically, as the lid came down on the fingers of his right hand, and the roar turned into a scream. The top rose up again by a couple of inches.

"Careful, butcher's boy, that's your cutting hand—mustn't do yourself an injury."

The boy thrust his fingers into his mouth, the lid fell again, and darkness was all.

PART II

11

As he wearily approached No. 2 Bow Street, Inspector Field found his maid of all work, Bessie Shoreham, in an agitated state on the front step.

Last bloody thing I need.

He hadn't slept the night before, or had dreamt he hadn't slept, hearing the onrushing iron wheels of the new railroad approaching at a frightening speed but never arriving, hour after hour. Then he was in a palatial home, walking behind a kitchen maid—or was it a cook?—who held something terrible close to her breast—what was it?—as she proceeded slowly from one corridor to the next. As slowly as she moved, he never could catch up with her. Somewhere a piano was playing "A Mighty Fortress Is Our God."

In the light of day, on the job, he had been frustrated in his ongoing pursuit of a headmaster, strongly suspected of poisoning his children's governess. Throughout the day Kilvert and Llewellyn had waited expectantly for their superior to tell them about his interview with Karl Marx. When Llewellyn finally cleared his throat and started to ask outright, Field had told him to *shut it* in a voice that had been audible throughout the station house. Now here was his servant, standing at his door, wringing the hem of her apron and dancing from one foot to the other.

"Master!" she shrieked.

"Hush, Bessie!"

"There's a woman!" she said, lowering her voice to a whisper loud enough to be heard across the road and jerking her head spasmodically in the direction of the house. "And a man!"

Field digested this useful information and hurried past her into his home, Bessie following him down the steps to the kitchen. Jane Field was pouring out cups of tea for a distraught-looking young woman seated at the table and a young man who stood nervously behind her chair. The woman looked up at Field hungrily; he'd seen her before somewhere. *A barmaid.* The young man's hands, clutching a hat, seemed to be stained a dull red. Field looked with raised eyebrows at his wife.

"Mr. Field," said Jane, "this is Martha Ginty and this is a friend of hers . . ."

"Figgis, ma'am. Jake Figgis, sir."

Detective Field waited for elaboration, but Mrs. Field was putting the kettle back onto the range, and neither of the strangers seemed likely to speak. Bessie brought her apron hem to her mouth and hissed through it, "It's about a boy!"

"Yes, that'll *do*, Bessie!" said Field with a little more heat than he'd intended. The servant huffed indignantly.

"Tea, dear?" said Jane.

"What's this about a boy?"

The woman at the table looked up at him, her eyes red. "My Tom never come home."

"Yes? And why are you here?"

"Neighbors said you were Mr. Bucket."

"I am *not* Mr. Bucket. Your neighbors were mistaken." Jane turned and stared at him darkly from the stove.

"You're the police, sir," said the young man named Figgis.

"Of course I am, but why are you here in my home?"

"Because of my boy, sir," said Martha Ginty.

"Has your boy committed a crime?"

"No, sir, never!"

"Then the police are not interested in him, ma'am! *I* am not interested in him!"

Bessie made a convulsive noise behind her apron, which might have been a sob, and the kettle began to whistle. Jane lifted it off the range and refilled the pot without taking her eyes off her husband.

"What Mr. Field means is," she said, "he needs more information before he can interest himself in the case."

"Case? My dear, what case?"

Jane sat down next to Martha and stroked one of her hands. "He's very clever, my husband. Once he knows the particulars, he'll set his mind to it and all will be well."

"Mrs. Field, there are hundreds of lads and lasses who go missing in London every year," said Field as reasonably as he could. "It happens all the time, every single day." He turned to Martha. "How long has your boy been gone?"

"Near two days, sir."

"Two days!" cried the detective. "Two days! He isn't even missing yet!"

"He is, though," said Martha Ginty with quiet fervor. "He's a good boy and works hard, but the night before he went missing he told me he didn't want to go to work."

"So he did a bunk, didn't he, Mrs. Ginty! I sometimes feel like doin' the same! Today especially!"

Jake Figgis cleared his throat. "There was a man, sir, askin' for him at the stall. Scared him, the man did. Tom tol' me about him, but I di'n't listen."

"What stall is this, then?"

"Smithfield Market, sir."

Field stared intently at the young man with the red-flecked hands. "A butcher's stall."

"Yes, sir."

"One of your colleagues is named Merrydew."

"Aye," said Jake with a wondering glance at Martha.

Field turned to the young woman. "You work in a tavern hard by the market, I believe," he said. "The Fortune of War, is it? You're a barmaid there?"

"Scullery, sir."

"Mickie Goodfellow's the landlord, isn't that about right?"

Jane beamed. "You see? Mr. Field is *that* clever, you wouldn't believe it!"

"Right," said the detective, drawing back a chair and seating himself at the table. "Tell me about this man who scared the boy."

"Tom said he moved funny," said Jake.

"Smooth-like," said Field.

"That's right," said Jake with rising wonder. "Like he was skatin', Tom said. I didn't notice it meself."

"You mean to say that *you* saw this man, too, Mr. Figgis?"

"Aye. Spoke to me. Said he was kin to Martha here, and where was Tom?"

"But he wasn't kin?" Field asked the woman.

"No, sir."

"Tall, fair-haired gentleman, was he? With deep-set eyes?" Jake nodded, and Field smiled for the first time all day. "Did he give a name?"

"No, sir. He were just about your height, sir, but his eyes is what struck you. Sunk in, they were."

"Let's all have something to eat, Mrs. Field."

"Bessie?" said Jane. "Fetch the cakes from the larder."

"And me not be there if my Tom comes home?" said Martha, rising. "You're most kind, Mrs. Field, and I thank you for it, but I've stopped away too long as it is." Jake stood and took her by the arm.

"You'll get your boy back, Mrs. Ginty," said Jane. "Mr. Field will see to that."

The others looked expectantly at Field, but he glanced quickly away, unable to bear the hope in their eyes.

"Mr. Field?" said Jane.

The inspector looked up. "D' you know a Cory? Or a Cory something?"

Martha and Jake shook their heads.

"What about medical men? Surgeons?" Jake glanced at Martha and she bit her lip.

"Not to speak to, no, sir," she said.

Touched a nerve?

"Not to speak to," repeated Field. "But in some fashion?"

"Lots o' folk come to pub."

"Is the Fortune of War especially popular with medical people, would you say, Mrs. Ginty?"

"With some, maybe," said Martha.

"That's odd," said Field. "I should have thought, with St. Bart's Hospital so close, the tavern would be overrun with doctors."

"Yes, sir."

She's coloring up to the roots of her pretty black hair, I wonder why.

"Ah, well," said Field, "we'll do what we can do, which I'm afraid is very little. If you think of anything further, Mrs. Ginty, do let me know. Good night, Figgis."

When they had gone Field sat at the table staring at his hands while Bessie and Jane prepared his tea. As the two women came and went, Jane glanced anxiously at her husband, knowing that something was troubling him. Perhaps he'd thought of something having to do with Mrs. Ginty's boy? Perhaps he already knew something, and it was too terrible to tell. Finally she stood behind her husband and put her hands on his shoulders. "Mr. Field?"

"Am I happy, Jane, do you think? Are *you*?"

"*What?*"

"Is my life miserable?" he asked. Jane took her hands from her husband's shoulders, suddenly hurt and confused. "Mr. Marx said it is," continued Field. "When we die, what will we say of our lives?"

A shrill voice from the door chimed in. "Won't be no time for talk," said Bessie, wiping her hands on her apron. "You'll be whisked to 'eaven or 'ell that fast, and for all eternity!"

Field was shouting. *"For God's sake, woman, was I addressing you?"*

Bessie shrieked and pulled her apron up to her mouth, giving way to cascading tears.

But the inspector's face had lit up suddenly. "The bloody apron again!"

"Language, sir!" said his wife sternly. "Language!"

Bessie was in full cry. Jane threw a protective arm around her bony shoulders and ushered her to the stairs, glowering back at her husband all the while.

"For shame, Mr. Field!" she hissed. "And no, your life ain't miserable, nor so I *thought*, sir!"

The two women disappeared up the stairs. Field took the stopper from a stone bottle and poured himself a finger of gin. "The killer brought it back," he said in wonder as he stirred a spoonful of sugar into the drink. "Nicked the apron in the morning, returned it when finished, and the boy saw him! Why in God's name didn't he stuff the bloody thing down a drain?"

12

Tom searched the darkness desperately for his mother's face. What would she do when he didn't come home at the end of the day? Had the end of the day arrived yet? Was it the same day or some other? If the sun neither rose nor set, would time stand still? He'd seen a madman once, crossing the market, his hair matted, gibbering to himself and swatting at the children who danced after him. Was that what was in store for him? Was he there already? If he had just a thimbleful of water, he could make a plan. Just a small drink and he would stop thinking all these thoughts, he would breathe again and hope.

I di'n't see nothin', he would say. *I don't care who you are nor yet what you done. I'd never split on you. Let me go an' you'll never see nor hear o' me again.*

Was he saying it aloud? His throat felt ragged, perhaps he was shouting. Maybe he had been screaming all along, the same things, over and over again for hours. Or days. Who could tell?

THERE WERE MUFFLED voices, very near. Something like hope filled him so abruptly it left him nauseated.

They've come, they're goin' to make an arrest, they'll be settin' me free, oh God please God please.

No. It was the hated voice, talking calmly. Even as Tom made lavish promises to the deity in return for deliverance, he heard other voices as well.

"I want to see!" A young girl?

"Careful," the hated voice was saying as the coffin lid edged up, "it bites!"

There was muffled laughter. Tom squinted as light penetrated the box.

"Ginger hair spells trouble, it never fails," someone cackled, an old woman, perhaps.

"Nonsense, Mrs. Hamlet," said Decimus. "Granted, he *has* been making a racket."

"What's his name?" This was the young girl again. Tom's vision was blurred. He saw indistinct faces peering down at him.

A gruff, gravelly voice responded. "His name is ''Nother Mouf to Feed,' that's wot it is, ain't it?"

"Well, that's less than gracious, Hamlet, I must say. We're not short of provisions here, are we? Not unless we've been disobedient."

"'Bedient." A male voice, adolescent, parroting.

"Who does all the cookin', then?" growled the old man. "Me and Missus Hamlet, that's who, but nobody cares about us and all our labors, no, not likely."

"Hamlet?" said Decimus sharply. "Shut it." A perceptible shiver of fear went through the room. Tom, squinting against the light, could feel it. "Perhaps, my dear Hamlet, you'd like to lodge with Mary Do-Not at the top of the house?"

Tom struggled to see the blurred gallery of faces that swam above him. As he later would learn, Decimus called them his children, although they ranged in age from young to old. They were servants one moment and pets another; they were subjects to be studied, court jesters, and tools. They were rewarded or punished according to their actions or their master's whim but probably no more or less severely than the below-stairs populations of many a London household.

The girl was ten or eleven years of age. Her name was Belinda, but Decimus called her Blinky. She helped the Hamlets in the kitchen and scurried about the West End running errands and thieving. Blinky often returned from sorties into the wide world bearing tokens of her private enterprise: handkerchiefs and other baubles. Her thin arms were circled by bracelets from wrist to elbow. She had a pinched, knowing face, large green eyes that twitched and fluttered, and she could move as quickly and quietly as a cat.

John Getalong (named, like Blinky, by Decimus) was a gangly youth of about seventeen years. He had survived a childhood bout of the pox, but the disease had ravaged his face and his mind. He was intensely loyal to the Chorister.

Mr. and Mrs. Hamlet were an elderly couple who looked (and smelt) like carrion birds. Both had hunched backs, beak-like faces, and nearly bald heads. They had come with the house. Because they had served his adoptive father when young Decimus entered the household, and had turned a blind eye to their master's use of the boy, Decimus punished them. For the first six months after his accession he kept them locked up in a stone shed in the garden, feeding them from scraps. When Decimus realized the two old vultures didn't mind this treatment and, in fact, preferred it to their usual workload, he released them to resume their labors.

Compared with the others who stared down on Tom, the hated man looked almost normal. As far as Tom was able to see, it was a handsome face, smiling with interest if not warmth. Tom started to speak, but his tongue was swollen and sticky; an inarticulate squawk emerged. He tried to lick his lips.

"Can he talk?" asked the girl.

Hatred flared up in Tom's heart, and he mustered his will. "I di'n't see nothin'," he croaked. "I don't care who you are nor yet what you done."

"Well, that's a relief!" cried Decimus with a laugh, which was echoed by his menagerie.

"I'd never split on you," said Tom. "Let me go an' you'll never see nor hear o' me again."

The others looked to Decimus to see how he would respond.

"Tom," he said finally. "You *are* called Tom, are you not? Tom Ginty? You live above the Fortune of War, I believe. I must say, your mother is most attractive."

Tom didn't respond; new avenues of fear were branching and spreading rapidly throughout his body.

"I saw her just yesterday. I can see her whenever I choose, do you understand me?"

Petrified, the boy managed to nod.

"Tom, what if there was a very bad, very powerful man and you had the chance of stopping him from doing great harm to the world? Would you do it?"

"Let me up."

"First answer my question, Tom."

Pox-scarred John Getalong said, "Question, Tom." Hamlet cackled with laughter and Mrs. Hamlet shushed him.

"Tom," said Decimus, "would you kill for me? If it was the right thing to do, of course."

Tom's mind raced but not quickly enough evidently, because Decimus sighed and said "How disappointing" as he slowly swung the coffin lid shut.

"No! No, no, no, no! I mean, yes, yes, I'll do anything, yes!" But it was too late. Tom went on shouting in the utter dark, alone again.

13

Field walked rapidly up Fetter Lane, toward Smithfield Market, his two constables hurrying to keep abreast of him. They were respectfully skeptical of the inspector's theory that the killer might have brought the butcher's apron, wet with Stevie Patchen's blood, back to where he'd got it.

"It's strange, I know," Field was saying. "How do you explain the missing ear? That's at least as odd, if not more so."

"Treasured memories?" said Kilvert. "Or a warning to others, perhaps."

"Maybe the killer was in a rage," suggested Llewellyn. "Maybe he was punishing Stevie and got carried away."

"But dressing as a butcher done up in blood means the killer knew all along he was going to do for Stevie, doesn't it," said Field. "We know the butcher's costume and wheelbarrow were took from Smithfield, and now the butcher's apprentice, I have no doubt, was snatched because the boy saw something."

The din of the market rose as the three men approached. For centuries prior this ground had seen more than the spilling of animal blood; it had been a frequent site of public torture and execution. In times gone by, men and women had been dragged here from the Tower behind slow-moving horses, to be strung up, half hanged, cut down, and quartered. Run-of-the-mill public hangings in London had been banned only recently (again, to a large extent thanks to the ubiquitous Mr. Dickens), but the seamier transactions of the market continued unabated. It was known, in fact, as a place where a man could sell his own wife if he was so inclined, typically to avoid the difficulties and expense of official divorce.

The three policemen proceeded into the heart of the market, quickly finding the butchers' stall in question. Dennis Merrydew blanched when he saw them and devoted his attention to dressing a lamb, but Jake Figgis touched his cap to Inspector Field and nodded respectfully.

"No sign of the boy?" said Field.

"No, sir. Nor yet the gentleman wot asked after 'im."

"Look at this, Mr. Field," said Kilvert, circling the stall and indicating a pile of bloody aprons and rags on the ground behind.

"You get through quite a load of this mucky stuff in a day?" said Field.

"When weather's warm, like now," said Jake, "it's all got to be washed regular or it stinks, sir." Field crouched to inspect the blood-stained fabrics.

"I don't know, Chief," said Kilvert. "It's a good half hour on foot from the Mall to the market. Seems a long way to go, does it not?"

"Unless our man had other business hereabouts," suggested Llewellyn.

"Figgis," said the inspector, "does the name Philip David Rendell ring a bell? Or Stevie Patchen?" Figgis shook his head. "What about you, Mr. Merrydew?"

"Nossir," said Merrydew.

"How do folk round here feel about the Queen? Anyone talk about topping Victoria?"

Both butchers looked scandalized. "Sir," said Merrydew, "anybody in the market whispered such a foul thing, he might get out with his skin, but he wouldn't find no work here, not ever again, sir."

"Right," said Field. "Never mind, carry on."

The three policemen moved on to the Fortune of War and waited respectfully as a funeral cortège processed out of the chapel next door and into the already crowded street. Once it had passed, Field and his men found the interior of the pub bustling with midday diners and drinkers. The landlord, Mickie Goodfellow, moved along the bar toward them, wiping his hands on a rag. He was tall and broad, a northerner with ruddy cheeks, black stubble, and a wide grin.

"Charlie Field!" he bellowed. "We've not seen you here for months! Got too famous for your old mates, didn't you."

"Still watering the beer, Mick?" said Field.

"Listen to the man!" said the landlord. "Slander! Perfidy!" Addressing the constables, he said, "To have a devil like this over you, you poor sods, how do you endure it?" As he spoke he pulled an ivory-handled pump, filling pint glasses one after another and shoving them in front of the policemen.

"Goodfellow here worked for my old man," Field explained to his men. "Always had his hand in the till, did Mickie."

"I'd never been paid otherwise! A nasty piece o' goods was his dad, God rest his miserable soul. Lord, what a temper! But *you* fellows must know that, I imagine, since he passed it on to his son."

Field stiffened. "No, he didn't." The two men stared at each other for an awkward moment. The landlord grinned again.

"'Course not, Charlie."

"You do a thriving business, Mr. Goodfellow," said Kilvert.

"I'd do a better if you'd drink the beer in front of you!"

"Thank you, no, sir. It don't agree with me."

Goodfellow's face registered shock. He turned to Field and cocked his head. "Where'd you find the undertaker?"

"We're here about Martha Ginty's son," said Field.

"Indeed? You got lunatics shootin' royalty, but of course a runaway 'prentice comes first."

Field's complexion darkened. "You don't change, do you, Mick?"

"Sorry, just jokin'! Poor Martha dotes on her boy. She's in a right state, and who could blame her? My wife has her up in our rooms; she's no good down here today."

"Any idea who might have snatched the boy?"

"You *believe* that story? Tom's a good lad, but come—he did a bunk, that's all."

"You reckon he'd do that to his mother? Run off, break her heart?"

Goodfellow had turned to watch two new customers, well-dressed gentlemen, moving through the crowd.

"Give it a day or two," said the landlord absently. "He'll be back."

Field followed Goodfellow's gaze. The two gentlemen glanced cautiously over their shoulders and pushed through a swinging door marked SALOON BAR. "You get medical men in here, Mick?"

"Fully half my custom, Charlie. God help us, but these physicians can drink! Makes you wonder, don't it."

"I'm looking for a tall man, sandy-haired."

"Thought you was lookin' for a boy!"

"Dark deep-set eyes. A surgeon, maybe."

"Narrows it down to two or three dozen, don't it."

"This bloke moves in a strange way, according to witnesses."

"Charlie, the *Lord* moves in strange ways. *Witnesses?* To what?"

"Her Majesty's government is looking for a tall blond man," said Field, slowly and deliberately, "who walks with a gliding motion, never you mind why. All I'm asking for, Mickie, is a little help."

"Charlie, there's a whole gang of 'em walks like they got wheels instead of feet—open your eyes! It's not the doctors, it's the holy men. You'll find 'em at St. Bride's, you'll find 'em at St. Paul's. It's some new damn religious thing they got going."

"*Religious?*" said Field.

"They call it High Church, Mr. Field," said Kilvert with distaste. "All the rage at Oxford."

"What's religion got to do with the way a bloke walks?"

"God knows, Charlie," said Goodfellow. "I don't."

Llewellyn put down his empty pint and started in on Kilvert's untouched one. "There's a good lad," said Goodfellow. "*You*, sir, are welcome to the Fortune o' War anytime, but leave these glum fellows at home, they're bad for business." The landlord continued in a lowered voice. "It's grand to see you, Charlie. But please do not come into my establishment, which I got by the sweat of my brow, askin' me to tell tales against my customers, 'cause of I won't do it, and that's flat!"

"A little less high talk from you, Mickie, or I'll start wondering what you got going in the Saloon Bar. Girls, is it? Gaming? Why does everyone look guilty who goes in that door?"

Field slid off his stool. He strode through the crowd and pushed open the swinging door into the Saloon Bar. It was populated by a decorous crowd; gentlemen, by the look of them, speaking in small groups, quietly nursing their drinks. The two or three who looked up revealed by their cool appraisal of Field that he was of a lower order and didn't belong with this lot—at least, that was how the inspector interpreted their glances.

Field let the door swing shut, turned back into the main room, and found Martha Ginty standing before him, desperation in her eyes. "He is my only child," she said.

The inspector nodded somberly, turned and left, followed by his men.

14

RICHMOND SPA

The man in the wooden enclosure shivered as he removed his robe. It was just after dawn and a clean, chill wind eddied in through the slats. Naked, he surveyed his own body, then sighed. For how many of his fifty years had illness come between him and his work, his family? The thought that he might have passed on his mysterious affliction to the child of his heart, that she— dearest of them all—should have received from him an inheritance that had proven fatal, was almost more than could be borne. Sitting on the polished wooden bench, he closed his eyes and was transported aboard ship again, as he had been twenty-five years earlier.

The seasickness was forgotten. The smell of wood and brine filled his nose; his ears exulted in the creak and groan of the vessel, gently climbing and descending, climbing and descending. Everything lay before him. Everything remained to be discovered, to be comprehended, to be known.

With his eyes still closed, Charles Darwin groped for the chain and pulled it, releasing from above forty gallons of ice-cold water to fall thundering down on his body.

Standing just outside the wooden booth, Thomas Huxley heard the cascade of water and the frantic gasps of the genius within. *How could a mind like his embrace tomfoolery such as this?* he wondered. Like Darwin on the *Beagle*, Huxley's four-year seafaring journey of discovery on HMS *Rattlesnake* in the Southern Hemisphere had earned him the respect of the scientific community. Initially skeptical of Darwin's theories, he had approached them gradually, but the publication of *Origin* had won him over wholeheartedly. Now this square-jawed, outspoken advocate was due in Oxford in a matter of days to hear an American deliver a paper on evolution's relation to social progress. It was widely known that the powerful bishop Wilberforce would be on hand to refute the professor and condemn Darwin's theories. With Huxley present, Wilberforce would not go unanswered.

"Are you all right in there, Darwin?" he shouted.

"I'm an old hand at the water treatment, Tom," came the still-gasping voice from the enclosure. "I won't be a moment."

The two men breakfasted in the sanitarium's communal dining room, the air filled with comfortable aromas of toast and marmalade, sausage and coffee. There were five other patients in residence, along with family members and servants. Darwin's eyes strayed often to one table in particular, where a young girl sat with her parents, delicately rapping an eggshell with a tiny spoon.

"Did you happen to see the essay in the *Edinburgh Review*?" said Huxley.

"When someone writes something truly nasty about me or my work, I can be sure that my dearest friends will send me copies."

"You do know who wrote it, don't you?"

"My dear Huxley, I'm certain that *you* do."

"It's not just me, Darwin. *Everyone* knows it's Professor Owen! It's cowardly!"

"How strange that a towering intellect like Owen, a naturalist superior to myself, by the way, should be envious of me."

"He's not your superior in any way. He's a vicious, mean-hearted sneak."

"His work on the chambered nautilus will live, I believe, forever."

"Chambered nautilus notwithstanding, if Sir Richard Owen sticks out his hawk-like head too far, I mean to hack it off." Huxley noted the anxious look on his colleague's face. "With a minimum of fuss," he added.

Darwin shook his head and sighed. He had put off publishing his revolutionary theories for years, wishing to avoid just the sort of tempest in which he now found himself.

"Sir," said Huxley, more seriously, "these scurrilous writings stir up the worst in people. They speak directly to the deranged and the violent amongst us. I assume the volume of threatening mail arriving at Down House has not diminished?"

"On the contrary. I do my best to keep it all from Emma, but I know she's seen and read some of the letters. I can't blame her being frightened."

A young woman entered the breakfast room and paused at the door. Reflexively, Darwin attempted to classify her: twenty-two or -three years old, lustrous brunette hair, healthy blushing cheeks. He quickly glanced over at the table with the little girl. The child's face lit up; the young woman crossed the room and kissed the girl affectionately.

Sister? Aunt? No, hired help, governess most likely, but much loved. How sick is the child, I wonder? She's just about as old as Annie was.

"Darwin?"

He wrenched his gaze away from the girl's table. "Yes?"

Huxley saw that tears stood in Darwin's eyes and made a show of taking out his watch and consulting it. "I must be getting on," he said. "There's no chance of persuading you to join me in Oxford, then?"

"None whatsoever."

"I'm told that Owen is holed up with Wilberforce in the bishop's palace, coaching the man on his science!"

For the first time that morning, an impish smile transformed Darwin's clean-shaven face. "I should like to be a dipteran on *that* wall."

Impersonating Owen's rapid speech and taut voice, Huxley said, "'*Wrong*, Wilberforce, *wrong*! It goes kingdom, phylum, *class*!'" Darwin and Huxley laughed. Darwin saw the little girl at the neighboring table staring at them, and he fell silent.

"I wish you all the best, Tom, and I shall await your report eagerly."

Which is untrue. All this clamor feels utterly trivial. After Annie, what does not?

"The little dogs have been nipping too much at your heels, my friend," said Huxley, rising from the table. "Your bulldog will set them to rights!"

After Huxley's departure, Darwin remained seated at the breakfast table for some time. The little girl and her family left. As the servants cleared away the debris all around him, Darwin was aboard the ship again, preparing fossil specimens he'd collected on a trip inland to show the *Beagle*'s young captain and Charles' friend for as long as the five-year voyage had lasted, Robert FitzRoy. He would present his treasures after their evening meal. He knew the captain would attribute his finds to the aftermath of Noah's flood, but that did not diminish his excitement. There would be one initial moment of wonder on FitzRoy's face, and that was what Darwin was so eager to see.

Seashells, FitzRoy! An ancient chambered nautilus! From high on a peak in the Andes!

15

OXFORD

Time and the elements had creased the face and burned it a permanent brick-red shade. A lifetime at sea had left him looking older than his fifty-five years, and bitter disappointment had carved its own story on the man's features. As he moved along St. Aldate's toward Christ Church College, he attracted stares. Under any circumstance he would have looked out of place here: a white-haired old sailor navigating an unfamiliar landscape of black-gowned, smooth-cheeked young Oxford undergraduates. But today Robert FitzRoy, long-ago captain of HMS *Beagle*, was carrying an enormous Bible, hugging it to his chest and muttering furiously.

He had been more than the pilot of that damned ship, by God! He was descended from royalty, fourth great-grandson of Charles II on his father's side (*along an illegitimate line, of course, but still!*). His mother was the daughter of the first Marquess of Londonderry and half sister of Viscount Castlereagh, by God!

FitzRoy had been assigned to the *Beagle* at the young age of twenty-six because its previous captain had blown his brains out in Tierra del Fuego. (*Good God, it makes a man think!*) It was a vital assignment: to chart the southernmost shorelines of South America. It was *his* idea to bring along a naturalist, no one else's. It would be pleasant, he'd thought, to have intelligent companionship on board, friendship being something that one couldn't afford to indulge with the junior officers, much less the crew. And it *had* been pleasant, for the most part. Darwin was three or four years younger than the captain, and FitzRoy had become quite fond of him, despite their occasional dustup. At the end of the five-year voyage, they had both been called upon to publish their observations. Darwin's were clearly tending toward blasphemy and attracted great attention among the scientific elite. FitzRoy's were ignored.

No matter. It wasn't too many years before he'd been appointed governor of New Zealand. Of course the Maoris had cut up rough, and understandably so, with the British stealing their lands from them at such a pace. FitzRoy had run afoul of everyone, both white-skinned and dark. (*Dismissed! Bastards might have had the grace to let me resign!*)

He had soldiered on. Weather! So much of trade and commerce depended upon it. Was there not a way to predict what tomorrow might bring? Indeed, FitzRoy was making real achievements in the new field of weather forecasting.

But for what am I truly known? For helping that man formulate his beastly heresies! Good God, it's almost more than a body can bear!

THE YOUNG DIVINITY student, David Gates, was hurrying to his tutorial when he saw the old man stagger and catch himself, leaning against the Gothic stone base of Tom Tower, Christ Church College. He was breathing heavily and clutching something to his chest—a large book, it seemed. David rushed forward to offer his assistance.

FitzRoy stared at the young man with alarm and suspicion. The folded barber's razor in his trouser pocket felt suddenly huge to him, an obscenity.

Don't be daft, thought the captain. *The boy can't see it, no one can.*

"Thank you, young man," he said, gruffly. "I'm quite well, there's no need." FitzRoy turned from David brusquely, rounded the corner into the passage, and thrust his head to the porter's window. "I'm here to see the bishop, the name's FitzRoy, Captain, retired."

From behind, David saw the porter's eyes flick dubiously over the man. *No greater snob on earth*, thought David, *than the porter of an Oxford college.*

"Excuse me, sir, but I'm on my way to see the bishop myself, might I escort you?"

"Just a moment, Mr. Gates," said the porter, "the bishop's tutorials have been canceled for the rest of the week, did you not get the notice?"

David blushed. He had spent the night sharing Jack Callow's narrow bed in Jesus College, passionately and without sleep. No, he had not picked up the notice that the porter was now plucking from David's own pigeonhole.

"Were you signed out at all last night, Mr. Gates?" asked the porter, but the old sea captain was already moving into the quadrangle, hugging his Bible, and David quickly followed him across the grass. The man was talking, to David or to someone unseen.

"I showed him every courtesy. I gave him the big cabin and took the smaller for myself. I was patient when he presented me with heresy; I explained to him his errors, but he wasn't having it, was he?"

"I'm sorry, sir," said David, "but who is this?"

The old man stopped and looked at David as though he were an idiot. "Why, Darwin, of course! They think it's enough to keep him off the list, but I say Darwin must die!"

"Good God, sir, that's dreadful talk! Are you speaking of *Charles* Darwin?"

The old man sagged, staring ahead in confusion. "Who is that man there?" he said in a suddenly frail voice. "What's happening?"

David saw with dismay that a Bulldog was dead ahead, emerging from the bishop's staircase and approaching them across the quad. The Universities Act of 1825 had created a force of constables empowered to act as academic police in Oxford. As such, this unit constituted one of the oldest and most powerful police forces in the kingdom. Its members soon became known as Bulldogs because of their propensity to latch on and not let go. This Bulldog, a thick fence post of a man named Smuts, was upon them in a moment. To David's astonishment he bowed to the sea captain. "The bishop and Sir Richard are expecting you, sir, if you'd like to come this way?"

"Why, yes," said FitzRoy. "Yes, thank you."

"Might I carry that for you, sir?" said Smuts, gently easing the huge Bible from the old man's grasp.

David, now standing alone in the Christ Church quadrangle, thought again of the old man's threats, and he was suddenly transported to his childhood. As a boy growing up in Orpington, the Darwin family were the "quality" whose big white house stood in the countryside nearby. David's father was a haberdasher; David and his younger sister, Rebecca, had become friendly with the offspring of their father's most illustrious clients, Charles and Emma Darwin. The Darwin children were imaginative and madcap playmates, and Willie and Annie Darwin were David's favorites. Their father was the genial man who, despite being sickly, seemed to have the soul of a child; he was often eager to play. But Mr. Darwin also had the extraordinary reputation as "the man who'd sailed round the world."

David Gates and Annie Darwin were the same age, and on Annie's ninth birthday he and his sister had been invited up to Down House for the party. The afternoon was a breathless blur of games and cakes. Out of doors there were footraces and hopping matches and, indoors, a crazy wooden slide that Mr. Darwin had fabricated was put in place on the grand staircase. As the children slid shrieking down the polished wood, landing atop one another at the bottom, Mrs. Darwin's eyes brimmed with mirth while Darwin himself whooped with laughter. And then Annie had taken David by the hand, pulled him into a cupboard, and astonished him with a kiss.

In the months that followed, David longed to be invited back to the exciting house on the hill and counted the days until Annie's next birthday. Then he heard she'd been taken ill. Eventually he learned that she had gone away with her father, although he didn't know where. When he finally heard the grown-ups saying that Mr. Darwin had returned to Down House, young David set out immediately to pay Annie a visit, uninvited and entirely without permission, walking miles across the fields, picking a handful of springtime blossoms on the way. A wreath of black crêpe was hanging on the front door. As it happened, it was not a servant who answered his knock but Mr. Darwin himself. It was the first time the boy had looked into the face of a grief that had no remedy, and he never would forget it. The memory of Annie Darwin became for David the emblem of all that was fascinating and mysterious and fun about the female of the species.

This old sailor he'd encountered was likely senile, and the threats he'd uttered merely harmless ramblings, but David needed to be certain. He owed it to Mr. Darwin. Certainly his tutor, Bishop Wilberforce, would be shocked when he heard what the old man had said.

16

LONDON

On the third day, the Chorister let Tom out of his coffin. The boy was soiled, starved, and too weak to stand. Decimus treated him with great gentleness, bathing him in the little enclosed garden behind the house with the help of John Getalong, who brought soap and buckets of hot water from the copper in the kitchen. They wrapped him in a thick towel and fed him a clear broth and afterward laid him in a bed softer than any Tom had known. When he awoke, Blinky helped Tom to regain strength in his legs, slowly leading him by the hand along the halls and up and down flights of stairs in the house, letting him rest and feeding him broth and then walking him again. Tom's first real meal was more substantial, and the fourteen-year-old fell on it ravenously: a roasted chicken and boiled potatoes. Decimus served the boy himself while Hamlet and Mrs. Hamlet looked on. Tears of gratitude filled Tom's eyes.

They put a chair for him in the garden. Sitting in the sun he felt his vision slowly return to normal, the blurriness of the first two days leaving him. Blinky sat at his feet, sometimes singing and sometimes chattering above the din of the London traffic, which penetrated to this tiny courtyard. She told him stories of her adventures in the big world and showed him her prized bracelets and timepieces.

"Tom," she said, going through a pocket in her apron, "there's something I want you to have." Blinky's hand emerged, holding a man's gold ring. "Go on!"

"No," he said.

"It's too big, see," said the girl. "When I put it on, it slips right off, but if you wear it, you'll think of me wherever you may be." She slipped the ring onto the ring finger of Tom's left hand. "It's like we're married, Tom, isn't it grand?"

Blinky had warnings for Tom as well. At the very top of the house, she told him, lived a woman who was all alone; it was forbidden to visit her.

"Do not!" said Blinky. "Do not try to call on Mary Do-Not! It's her name, see? Mary Do-Not!"

"She must be lonely," said Tom.

"Oh, very! She walks right here, in the garden, when she's allowed. I see her from the window. She sighs and wrings her hands like anything, but always when we're not here, always when she's alone. It's not safe otherwise."

"Not safe?"

Blinky shook her head and lowered her voice to a whisper. "She makes people perish."

"She does for 'em?"

"She doesn't mean to, she *likes* people! She can't help it, you see."

But *Tom* was safe. He was among friends, and Decimus Cobb was his kind and merciful benefactor. Only one of the voices in Tom's head was of a different opinion, and that voice—which whispered to him of his mother and their little room at the top of the Fortune of War—he must ignore at all costs.

Careful, Tom, or it's back in the box with you! Master always said it with a smile.

Master brought beautiful clothing home to dress Tom in, along with a small traveling valise. He cut Tom's hair and fitted him with a cap. The rest of the household applauded the new boy who stood before them, a gentleman's son, scrubbed and shining. And very early on the seventh day, the Chorister took Tom out to teach him to kill.

DAWN, OR JUST before. Tom held a basket of food for the prisoner, but the man was looking past him. "Been expecting you," said Philip David Rendell.

"Turn round, Philip," Master said.

Philip peered into the basket Tom was holding. "Sausage," he said, and then, looking up at Tom, "you're the new me." Dutifully, Philip turned.

Don't think about it, don't think about it.

Tom was sick in the street after they left the prison, but Master didn't scold. He gave Tom a linen handkerchief and walked off ahead, not looking back at him, not checking on him, but Tom didn't dream of running. He wiped his mouth and spat. The first rays of morning glinted off the tops of buildings, coloring them bloodred, but Tom didn't think about their color. Just minutes from where he stood was the familiar intersection of Giltspur and Cock Lane and the Fortune of War, but Tom didn't think about any of that either, not even for a moment.

Or it's back in the box with you!

The boy turned round quickly, scanning the street, and was rewarded by a glimpse of John Getalong, perhaps twenty yards behind, hastily turning from him and pretending to study a shop window. Tom, in turn, pretended not to see Getalong.

Tom followed Master through the awakening streets, all the way to No. 4 Half Moon Street. John Getalong arrived just minutes later with a bucket of oysters. Master took a plate of them up to Mary Do-Not and then returned, beaming with pride on all his children. Breakfast was festive.

INSPECTOR FIELD HAD been awakened by a hammering from below. He'd thrown on a pair of trousers and padded downstairs in time to see Bessie open the street door to Sam Llewellyn. An aureole of dawn circled the young Welshman's head. A brougham waited in the street beyond, the horse stamping. From the expression on Llewellyn's face, Field knew that someone was dead.

Minutes later, in Newgate, Inspector Field knelt in the cell beside the still form of Philip David Rendell. He lay curled on his right side, his knees drawn up, with his back to the door. The young man's eyes were open and staring. His hands were at his own throat. From between his clenched fingers there issued a flow of blood that had pooled across the cell floor. Where Rendell's left ear should have been was a glistening red hole.

"If it's here, I want it," said Field. Gingerly Llewellyn and Kilvert got down on hands and knees and began carefully searching the floor. The warder stood in the door, and behind him, a peering group of the morbidly curious. Field patted the body, which was still very warm, finding nothing. He delicately raised the checked napkin inside the basket at the body's side, revealing two sausages and a quarter loaf of sodden, red-stained bread. He set the basket down on a dry spot of floor and stood.

"You say a child brought this?" he asked the warder.

"A boy and a man, sir, first thing this mornin'. Man said they was from the mission. We get lots o' mission folk. Bring food to the prisoners, say a prayer, sing a hymn."

"What did they look like, then?"

"Tall man, fair hair, deep-set eyes; the boy's hair red or brown. Wore a cap. Maybe fifteen years old."

"They were here rather early for mission folk, weren't they?" said Field. "Before dawn, in fact?"

"I suppose you could say they were, sir."

Field nodded. "The man didn't slip you nothin' for your trouble, I imagine?"

The warder looked Field in the eye and said, "Nossir."

"Of course not," said the inspector.

"There's no ear to be found, sir," said Kilvert, still kneeling on the floor.

"Looks like he took it with him," said Llewellyn, standing.

Field addressed the warder again. "Close this door up and let no one in until the coroner's man gets here." The small knot of onlookers sagged in disappointment as Field made his way through them, followed by his men.

"Well, Tom Ginty's alive, anyway," he said to them.

"This is not the sort of man one would wish to work for," said Kilvert, "as Stevie Patchen and now Mr. Rendell might attest, were they able."

"He's bloody peculiar, I must say," said the inspector. "So determined to cover his own tracks and yet he leaves his signature when he kills. Still, this proves Rendell wasn't acting alone. He clearly had a confederate who needed to silence him, just like he silenced Stevie. Maybe now Commissioner Mayne will admit it's a conspiracy. Sam, have you got your source at the palace in place?"

"Yes, sir. A royal horse groom, a mate of mine, Peter Sims."

"A Welshman," added Kilvert.

"Peter will send me word double quick," said Llewellyn, "well before any move the royal family makes."

"Kilvert, what do we know about the late Mr. Rendell?" said Field as they passed out of the prison gates onto the street.

"Not much," said Kilvert. "Left his position and his rooms at Islington more than a month ago and for all intents and purposes disappeared."

"Friends? Associates?"

"Friendless, sir. Even from his school days as a scholarship boy at St. Paul's, mocked and derided. Strange boy, strange man."

"St. Paul's? He was a choirboy, then?"

"So it seems, sir."

"If Rendell was friendless much of his life, I suppose it's possible the killer knew him from choir school," said Field with a shrug. "A master, maybe, or one of the choirboys. Judging by Rendell's age, it would have been roughly fifteen, twenty years ago."

"It shouldn't be difficult to come up with a roster of St. Paul's boys and masters from 1840 to 1845," said Kilvert. "I'll see to it this afternoon, sir."

In time, the constable's promise would return to haunt the inspector.

17

OXFORD

From his place among the other undergraduates, David Gates watched them at the high table all through the meal. Bishop Wilberforce was conversing in a lively fashion with his guests: a sharp-faced middle-aged man with a beak-like nose—a scholar, perhaps?—and a ferocious-looking old gentleman with a bushy mane of white hair. The old sea captain who had said such disturbing things sat silently for the most part, his eyes darting over the assembled students and the magnificent trappings of the Great Hall of Christ Church College. Farther along the table, Henry Liddell, the dean, was deep in conversation with Charles Dodgson, the mathematics lecturer whom posterity would remember by his pen name, Lewis Carroll. The other senior scholars on the dais carried on volubly as they dispatched plates of kidneys and gravy.

What did his tutor's guests have in common? The sea captain clearly seemed out of place, but he'd been staying in the bishop's quarters for two days now, and each time David had tried to speak to the bishop he had been turned away. How could David let him know that he might be befriending a seriously deranged man?

After the pudding, the undergraduates all rose with a thunderous scraping of benches and remained standing while the great men processed out. Eventually David made his way through the exiting crowd.

"Dinkins!"

"Yes, Mr. Gates?" replied the head butler, a placid-faced older man.

"May I ask, Dinkins, who was that dining with the bishop just now?"

"Certainly, sir. My lord the bishop was hosting Sir Richard Owen, the natural philosopher, and Sir Jasper Arpington-Dix of the East India Company." Dinkins' face registered faint distaste. "And FitzRoy, sir. A nautical man."

"I suppose the bishop has gone on to the Senior Common Room with the other masters?"

"No, sir. The bishop's party will be taking their coffee in the bishop's study, sir."

David was pleased. The study was familiar ground to him; he met there weekly with the bishop. It shouldn't be difficult to call him out for a private word. David crossed the quadrangle and climbed the bishop's staircase. He entered the secretary's office, just off his tutor's study, unoccupied at this time of the evening. He could hear one of the guests, in the middle of a story. David would wait quietly for a lull in the conversation.

"Lancaster Castle is not a cheerful place at the best of times," said Owen.

Wilberforce stirred his coffee, a faint smile on his face, and said, "One thinks immediately of the Lancaster witches, in Elizabeth's time."

Sir Jasper Arpington-Dix lit his pipe and settled back into a creased brown leather armchair, his walking stick across his lap. "It's an ugly pile of rocks," he said. "Have you ever been, FitzRoy?"

The captain, perched on his chair as though it were a hard wooden church pew, seemed startled to be addressed. He shook his head.

"Ugly or not," said Owen, "it was a home to me at the time, a nineteen-year-old medical student assigned to the prison. The night in question certainly added to the castle's gloom and menace. A storm raged, the wind howled, it was snowing and sleeting, a perfectly dreadful night. The cadavers were kept in an upper chamber. I had taken note of the negro man who had been hanged that morning and was determined to have his head."

"Oh, dear me," said Wilberforce, "whatever for?"

"To study his brain, of course! Late that night, when the castle was asleep, I made my way up to the room at the top, my heart fairly stopping at every creak on the stair, every howl and whisper of the wind."

"Ghost story, is it?" said Sir Jasper.

"Rather more corporeal than spiritual, I should say," said Owen. "Anyway, once I'd located my fellow it was the work of only a few minutes to remove the man's head. My God, the thing was heavy!"

FitzRoy stirred suddenly. "They were *happy* to be slaves!" he shouted. "Told me so themselves!"

The other men glanced at each other. They were becoming alarmed by the sea captain's outbursts. He'd been increasingly difficult ever since they'd broken it to him that Charles Darwin was *not* expected to make an appearance in Oxford that weekend, that he would be absent from the great meeting where his work would be debated. It had been reported in the press that Darwin was still at Richmond Spa for his health.

"Who was this, FitzRoy?" asked Wilberforce gently. "Where was this?"

"Tierra del Fuego, of course! Where white men go to blow their brains out!"

There was an embarrassed silence in the book-lined study, broken by the tock of a great clock and the tinkling of a demitasse spoon against china.

"*At any rate*," said Owen finally, "I got the fellow's great noggin into the sack I'd brought for the purpose, flung it over my shoulder, and headed down. Once outside I found everything coated in ice and the night black as pitch. I had barely started down the steep road to my rooms in the town below when I stepped on a slick patch and went down hard. Whereupon the negro's head flew out of the bag and rolled all the way down the hill, me slipping and sliding after it!"

FitzRoy spoke up again. "'Are you *happy*?' I asked the natives. 'Working for your master? Yes, they said, we *are*!' But Darwin wasn't having it. Didn't matter what they said, according to him. Contradicted me in front of my own crew! I should have put the man ashore and left him there!"

Owen coughed and stood, moving to survey the bookcases, but Sir Jasper leaned forward toward the sea captain. "First things first, old man. We must get rid of the royal danger first, but by-and-by—"

"Careful, Sir Jasper," warned Wilberforce. "Mind how you go. I *am* not and *will not* be a party to—"

Sir Jasper ignored the bishop. "By-and-by, FitzRoy, we'll put that son of a bitch ashore one piece at a time, just you wait and see!"

"I mean to say," shouted the captain, "for God's sake, a man's not an ape!"

"Wilberforce," said Owen quietly, nodding toward the open door that led to the study's outer office. "There's someone there."

Wilberforce frowned. "Who is that?" he called. "Who's there?"

David Gates appeared in the door, ashen-faced. "I'm sorry, my lord. I had hoped to reschedule this week's tutorial, sir. I'll call again tomorrow." He made a slight bow to the four unsmiling men who stared back at him, then turned and fled.

David and Jack Callow sat wedged in among the crowd at the back of the Bear, the venerable public house that, although it had existed in one form and another since the fourteenth century, the two young men considered to be their own discovery and private domain. They had met and become friends in their first year up at Oxford. The two of them were scholarship students from small villages and exulted in the heady atmosphere of university life in which they found themselves, so different from what they had known as boys. They went for long walks and argued fiercely about a variety of topics: the doctrine of the Trinity, varieties of ale, and rugby football, which they both played avidly. Over the long vacation they had not communicated once. In the first week of their second year, and with a minimum of discussion, they had become lovers.

"If I catch the night coach," David was saying, "I should be able to reach Mr. Darwin by midmorning."

"You can't be serious," said Jack.

"It's mad, I know. But what if I do nothing and something terrible happens?"

"You're basing these wild assumptions on a couple of outbursts from a clearly deranged old man."

"I owe it to Mr. Darwin to caution him. I owe it to the memory of his daughter."

"If you're worried about this Captain FitzRoy, talk to the bishop."

David stared into his beer. He hadn't told Jack that he'd already tried to tell his tutor; he hadn't told him about the scene he'd come upon in the bishop's study. He was reluctant to come out and say he feared his tutor might himself be involved in a conspiracy to silence Charles Darwin. This was Bishop Wilberforce, after all—a leader in the antislavery movement, a decent Christian man and David's own tutor. And if he were wrong? He knew that if he were to make unfounded accusations against Wilberforce or his guests, he stood a real chance of losing his scholarship and throwing over his Oxford career for a future in his father's village haberdashery. He glanced up into Jack's concerned face and gave him a reassuring smile.

"I'll be back on the Friday coach, you won't even know I'm gone."

As David and Jack rose and made their way through the crowd to the tavern's door, the human fence post who had taken a seat near them when they first arrived watched them go. Smuts had removed the bowler hat that identified him as a Bulldog, but now he replaced it and made his way out also, hurrying back to Christ Church to make his report. Within the hour, a message had been dispatched by telegraph from Oxford to an address in London. Meanwhile, the night coach jolted David Gates, half dozing, along the dark country roads in a light drizzle.

LONDON

IT WAS NEARLY midnight. The young man from the Electric Telegraph Company hesitated, listening. Faintly, from within the house at No. 4 Half Moon Street, came the sound of a single voice singing, a woman's voice or a child's, high and pure.

Like from a church, thought the young man. *Holy.*

Even by day, the house at No. 4 had a shuttered aspect. Had it not been for the singing, the man from the ETC would have thought it abandoned. The streetlamp by the door was unlit. (The gaslight had been broken so often the lamplighter had stopped repairing it, never imagining that it was the householder himself who regularly disabled the lamp in the dead of night).

The young man on the step adjusted the strap of the large leather pouch he wore over one shoulder and tilted the envelope to catch the light from the lamp on the opposite side of the road. The address was correct, all right. Moreover, it was stamped URGENT: FOR IMMEDIATE DELIVERY. He pulled the bell by the door and the singing stopped.

Within, little bells rang discreetly throughout the house. Decimus Cobb was the only occupant still up and active, working in his private chambers at the back of the first floor, shellacking and mounting specimens. He frowned at the tinkling spring-mounted bell above the door and hastily reached for a cloth to dry his hands.

Two floors above, Tom Ginty lay on his narrow bed, watching the bell on the wall above the door dance and then fall still. John Getalong, in the next cot, snored without interruption. As quietly as he could, Tom got out of bed and moved to the shuttered window. The louvers were nailed fast, but he had already discovered one loose slat that he could shift to give a thin glimpse of the street below. Now he gasped at the sight of a uniformed man on the step.

Peelers! he thought with a surge of hope and then realized that if it actually *were* the police calling, they'd be coming for *him* as much as for his master. *A murderer, now and forever.* Maybe it wasn't a policeman. No, the uniform wasn't right.

In the entrance hall, Decimus stared through the peephole in the door and then, with a sigh, slid the bolt, released the latch, and pulled open the door narrowly.

"Electric Telegraph Company," said the young man. "Urgent for Mr. Cobb." Decimus reached for the envelope, but the young man withheld it. "Be so good as to sign for it, sir?" he said.

Decimus' right hand, behind the door, currently held a long, thin surgical knife. He stared at the delivery man for a moment. "It's late," he said. "Did you come out specially with this?"

"The ETC is open round the clock, sir. I got a half-dozen more to get out tonight."

Decimus nodded and was carefully lowering the razor-sharp blade into a leather sheath in his trousers pocket when he noticed the young man looking past him. Decimus glanced over his shoulder and saw on the little table near the door a bloodstained hand towel and the ear he'd been working on.

Careless of me.

He turned back to the deliveryman who was staring in confusion at the shiny pink twist of flesh.

"Strange to see it out of context, isn't it," said Decimus.

Two floors above, Tom saw the young man disappear into the house. He heard the door swing shut and the bolt shoot into place. Quickly Tom closed the louver and laid himself down, shutting his eyes fiercely, his heart sounding like a drum in his ears.

Despite his alarm, he must have slept because Master was there, shaking him awake and then going away. It was still full dark. The clothes he was to wear were laid out at the foot of his bed. John Getalong's bed was empty. Tom dressed himself and quietly descended the stairs to the kitchen where he found a cup of tea and a hard roll waiting for him. Mrs. Hamlet dozed on a stool in the corner. Master sat at the table, watching Tom. There was no sign of the uniformed man.

Tom sat. He blew on his tea and lifted it to his lips.

"The path is strewn with stumbling blocks," said Decimus. Tom put down the cup in alarm. "One obstacle after another. Why must people move about so? It's much better when they don't move. Drink your tea."

Tom quickly took a sip. It burned his tongue and his eyes watered. He ate a bit of hard roll, crunching down.

"What do we learn from the obstacles?" Master's eyes were more than ever lumps of coal, thought Tom. "We learn that the obstacles *are* the path. That the road *is* the journey. Shall I tell you a story, Tom?" There was a silence. "Tom?"

Tom nodded vigorously.

"Long ago, when I was about your age, there was a man who pretended to be my friend. He was not my friend. He brought me to Italy to improve myself, so I did: I flung him from a tower. He tried to take me with him over the edge, he grabbed for me, but I wasn't having it. I caught what I could of him and shook him free, shook him hard! Well, down he went. And there in my hand, what do you suppose I found? Tom?"

Tom shook his head.

"His ear was in my hand, Tom. Torn right off. And from that moment to this, *everything* has been so much better. I had all his gold in hand, so I continued the tour. Saw the world from Ghent to Petersburg, all before I was sixteen years of age. Did people raise eyebrows at this boy, all on his own? Let them. I was taken in charge by a presumptuous policeman in Bremen but not for long. Germany was a favorite. I lingered in Aachen, learning from a very fine surgeon there who taught me much but passed away abruptly. Alas. Where is he now? Tom, never collect too many souvenirs, you forget where you put them. Now finish your breakfast like a good boy."

There was a sound of a key in the lock and footsteps descending the stairs. John Getalong entered the kitchen and Master looked up at him with eyebrows raised. The young man's hands and face were dirtier than normal, and his trousers were wet and dripping on the floor. Tom thought he smelled of river.

"Right, then, that's done," said John. "Is there tea? I s'pose *he's* goin', not me."

"That's correct, John. You have had a long night; you owe yourself a lie-in."

Tom didn't want to think what Getalong had been doing in the long night. Tom cleared his throat and said, "Where?"

Master and John Getalong turned to Tom in unison, Master with a gentle, surprised smile and John with a jealous scowl.

"What's that, Tom?" said Decimus.

"Where 'm I goin'? Sir."

The master drew a slip of paper from his breast pocket and slid it across the table. Tom glanced down at it and up again at Decimus, his face flushing.

"Can you not read, Tom?"

"Nossir," he lied.

"Not to worry, son," said Master, taking back the paper and pocketing it. "You'll discover the where and the what soon enough."

Tom *was* able to read, though, thanks to the relentless drilling to which his mother had subjected him for years. He had seen, printed beneath the banner of the Electric Telegraph Company:

GATES DAVID 19 YRS FAIR HAIR NIGHT COACH TO D CURRENTLY RICHMOND SPA SMITE THE LOINS OF THEM THAT RISE AGAINST HIM

"Let John go," said Tom, and he knew at once he'd made a mistake. The master's face turned to stone. He jerked his head in Getalong's direction and John boxed Tom's ear so sharply, he nearly cried out.

"Eat," said the Chorister, so Tom pointed his face at his plate and ate.

18

RICHMOND

Decimus and Tom traveled through the night along the dark, damp roads in a one-horse gig, arriving in Richmond at dawn, long before the night coach was expected. There was time, Master said, to stretch their legs. Tom followed him into the churchyard, on a hill above the coaching inn. The grass among the graves was wet. As light began to touch the tops of trees, Master read the inscriptions on the stones: *Beloved wife and mother, 1819. Lamented only son, 1792.* Lux aeterna. *We really must teach you to read, Tom. Oh, here's a good one, dated 1770. Farewell, dear Friend, How doleful is the sound, How vast my Stroke, Which leaves a bleeding Wound.*

Eventually they took a seat on a bench outside the inn. There was a wan, middle-aged gentleman already there waiting for the coach. He had smiled and nodded politely, and Decimus had touched his hat to him. Tom had been instructed never to speak, never to reveal his rough

Cockney accent now that he was dressed as a gentleman's son, so he avoided the stranger's eyes.

The sun was burning away the mists, and the day promised to be fine. Tom wondered about Gates, David, fair-haired and nineteen, who was on his way this moment to meet D. Maybe Master would merely steal him, as he had stolen Tom. Maybe Gates, David, might become a friend of Tom's, an ally in the frightening house. On the whole, though, Tom thought not.

Master and the gentleman on the bench checked their pocket watches at the same moment, and they acknowledged this with a smile. "Seems to be late," said the man.

Don't talk to him, thought Tom. *Can't you see how dangerous he is?*

But Decimus did not look dangerous. He looked like a gentleman and he enjoyed playing one. After giving Tom a cautioning glance, he stood. "I'll see if they know anything inside," he said with a gracious bow and went into the inn. The man smiled at Tom.

Don't talk to me, please don't please don't.

"Hello," said the gentleman.

"'Lo," said Tom, looking away.

"It's the strangest thing," said the man. "I mistook you for someone I once knew, a young sailor I'd been thinking of, just this morning."

Tom stared straight ahead, willing the man to stop.

"I made a lengthy sea voyage some years ago, you see. Young Philip King and I had many profound philosophical conversations in the course of our travels. You look so much like him, I very nearly seized you by the hand when you sat down just now. It's not just the hair color you share, there's something else." Tom didn't respond. "Of course, Midshipman King would no longer be a boy but a grown man by now. Stupid of me."

Inside the inn the man behind the bar told Decimus that rain on the road had delayed the coach but not by long. As the Chorister turned to go, the barman said, "You know who that *is* out there, don't you? That's the monkey-man, Mr. Charles Darwin himself!" Decimus flushed red and waited for a moment to regain control of his breathing. Then he went outside.

Darwin looked up expectantly at Decimus, who smiled thinly and said, "Should be arriving any moment now, sir." Decimus had seen caricatures of Darwin in the press, of course. He had memorized artists' impressions, but the man in person bore little resemblance to any of them. There was an amiable gentility and a playfulness about the man's smile, which contrasted with his sharp, observant eyes. Decimus resumed his seat on the bench next to Darwin, with Tom on his other side. He could hear the heartbeats of both, having long ago learned to filter out his own. From Darwin's moderately paced pulse his ears moved on to other things.

Faulty plumbing there. I should like a look at that gallbladder. And the man's bowel! Peristaltic spasms. Turbulence. Parasites?

He thought of a tapeworm he'd once taken from the intestine of pretty young woman from Clapham. *Thirty feet long it was.* Decimus felt himself going red again and restrained himself with difficulty. Here the great man was, served up on a platter, and Decimus, forbidden to touch him! But was he? Truly? Decimus had such skills, he could bleed the man without his even being aware. In the confusion of the coach's arrival, who would notice the man growing pale and faint? Even when he collapsed, it would take time for anyone to discover the small puncture wound in the man's back . . .

No. Decimus would be obedient. He would stop young Gates—but how? How to prevent the meeting of David Gates, due to arrive imminently, and Charles Darwin?

"You're expecting someone, obviously," said Decimus.

"Our children's old nurse," said Darwin. "Miss Brodie left our employ some years ago and returned to her native Scotland. But she comes to us from time to time and we're always happy to see her. She's just been with my wife for a week, and now she's visiting the sick—*me!*"

Decimus looked off, up the road. Perhaps the story was true; perhaps the naturalist was unaware of Gates. There was a distant sound of hooves.

"For whom, sir, are *you* waiting, if I might ask?" said Darwin.

"Doctor. A specialist, come about my son. He's deaf and mute, you see."

Darwin's brow contracted. He looked at Tom and Tom looked away. "I'm sorry," said Darwin uncertainly.

There was a clop and a clatter, and a mud-splattered carriage came into view, followed by three barking dogs. The barman emerged from the inn, and the hostler and a groom bounded out from the adjacent barn. Suddenly the forecourt of the inn was filled with shouted greetings and orders, and the honking of geese chased by the barking dogs, and the snorting of four hard-ridden horses. An old woman in black bombazine was the first to be helped down from the coach, her arms clutching bundles and an umbrella.

"Brodie!" shouted Darwin joyfully.

"Look at you, sir!" she said. "You're *that* thin!"

"Brodie, Brodie, Brodie!" he cried, dancing the woman in a circle and causing several of her packages to drop to the ground.

"Nae, sir, leave off! These are straight from Mrs. Darwin, they'll be all mucky now!"

Decimus approached the carriage door. A portly bald man climbed out, rubbing the small of his broad back and shouting for someone to fetch down his bags from the top of the coach.

"And how *are* things at Down House?" Darwin was saying as he gathered up the fallen gifts.

"Well, everyone misses you, of course, sir, and Mrs. Darwin sends her best love, and so do the children. Horace says, 'Tell Papa to feel good and to come home again, soon as ever he can.'"

The portly man and the groom were helping a rotund woman down from the coach. When they were clear, Decimus mounted the step and looked into the carriage. *Empty.*

The old Scottish nurse was still talking breathlessly as Darwin engaged a boy to load her bags and the gifts onto a waiting brougham. "All my old friends at Down House and from Orpington came to see me, sir, including the vicar, and all of them so concerned about you, with your old ailment acting up and you becoming so very famous and the papers writing such scandalous things about you, it makes me that angry, I can't tell you!"

"There, there," said Darwin. "We'll have luncheon and a good long talk, shall we?" He turned back and said to Decimus, "Rotten luck, I'm afraid—looks like your man didn't turn up. Goodbye, now." He looked at Tom quizzically. "Goodbye, son."

Decimus watched Darwin put the old nurse into the carriage and climb in after her. A red heat filled his brain.

The fools sent him to the wrong place! Down House! That's where this Gates fellow was headed! To the man's own home, of course!

He grabbed Tom by his lapel and jerked him to his feet. "Come!" he snapped, and set off running for the gig, Tom racing behind.

DOWN HOUSE

EMMA DARWIN ROSE when the young housemaid ushered David Gates into a cluttered sitting room, her eyes narrowing, trying to recognize the boy he once had been. David took her extended hand and bowed over it briefly, his mind racing. It had never occurred to him that Mr. Darwin might be away.

Now what do I do? What do I say? I was a fool to come!

"Yes," said Mrs. Darwin, slowly. "I do remember you, Mr. Gates. You were little David, I can see it. The same age as our Annie. Come to the garden with me; it's a shambles in here, I'm afraid. We still have young ones, you see."

Her voice was neither warm nor cold. She led him through the house to the capacious gardens beyond, her arms folded across her chest, holding herself.

"If you've come to see Mr. Darwin, he's at Richmond, taking the cure. Are you here to see Mr. Darwin? I cannot imagine you're here to see me."

David searched for words, but before he'd found any, Emma Darwin was stooping to pluck a weed.

"Is your father well?" she asked. "I'm afraid I have never met your mother."

"My father is well, thank you, ma'am. My mother passed away some years ago."

"Ah." She found and pulled another weed. "I think I heard you were at Oxford."

"I am, ma'am." How was he ever going to bring up the fears that had set him traveling without sleep since the night before?

"Your course of study?" she asked, standing and flinging away the offending plants.

"Divinity."

Mrs. Darwin glanced at him keenly and then continued to walk.

"Such strange weather for June," she said. "The heat last week—or was it the week before?—fairly scorched half my garden, or so I thought. But then it cleared off and now I think it all just might survive. Do you remember Annie?"

"Vividly."

"The achillea is coming on, you see, and the lady's mantle. The early heat pushed everyone's schedule forward, it seems. Those delphiniums will need staking. Are you at all familiar with my husband's work, Mr. Gates?"

"I've read *On the Origin of Species*, or stumbled through most of it, rather. I couldn't claim to be familiar with it. I'm afraid it's rather a steep climb for me."

"For us all, one way and another. Mr. Darwin has been sharing his thoughts and discoveries with me for two decades now, whatever the cost to me personally. He was reluctant to publish, you know, and put it off nearly twenty years for fear of igniting all this . . ." She made a sweeping, hopeless gesture.

"I suppose it's because of *all this*," said David, "that I've come today, although I had hoped to find Mr. Darwin at home."

"Yes?" she said, striding on across the grass and leaving the gardens behind.

"His theories have distressed some persons, I imagine."

Mrs. Darwin's laugh was a single bark, mirthless. "You might say so, Mr. Gates," she said over her shoulder.

"Ma'am, I came in hopes of alerting your husband to the possibility that some persons in positions of authority may actually . . . wish him harm."

"I shouldn't be surprised. He gets the most dreadful mail."

She seemed to David to be remarkably unconcerned.

"Ma'am, in the past week I have heard, in my college's quad, and later in my own tutor's study, direct threats made against your husband's life and perhaps a member of the royal family."

"There's a strange combination. Who was making these threats?"

"Principally a retired sea captain named FitzRoy, ma'am."

"Oh, poor FitzRoy! He piloted the *Beagle*, you know."

"I am afraid I did not know."

"He has had a dreadfully hard life since then, and I understand that his first wife's death left him quite altered. They were friends, years ago, but Charles has had to break off correspondence with the man. I shouldn't worry about poor old FitzRoy, Mr. Gates."

"There were others at my college—at the House, you know—who seemed to tolerate his violent talk or perhaps even to encourage it."

"Oh, isn't there to be a great debate soon at Oxford? On the merits of my husband's theories?"

Is she not hearing me? Am I not being sufficiently clear?

"Yes, ma'am, tomorrow, in fact. Bishop Wilberforce will likely take on Mr. Thomas Huxley."

"That's right. Huxley wanted Mr. Darwin to participate himself, but Charles is far too ill."

"I am sorry to hear it, ma'am."

"I am not! Thank God he'll be well away from that circus! Anyway, it's no wonder you're hearing angry talk. My husband's work has got everyone in a state." She stopped before a neat gravel path that stretched on into the distance, bordering a stand of trees. "This is the Sandwalk. It goes on in a great elongated sort of oval. The Sandwalk is where Mr. Darwin walks and thinks, once in the morning and again in the afternoon. He's done it for years and years, when his health has permitted it. This is where he created his masterwork, and our misery."

"Misery, ma'am?"

"Mr. Gates, I believe my husband to be one of the greatest natural philosophers who ever lived. He is without doubt the kindest husband and father and the most decent of men. And I live in desperate fear for his eternal soul." She looked at David searchingly.

"Surely *you*, a divinity student, can understand my feelings?"

He didn't know what to say so he said nothing.

"If we are not created in the image of God, who are we? What are we? Accidents of nature?"

"I do not know, ma'am. I *believe* us to be God's creatures, however he created us."

She turned brusquely away from the Sandwalk and started back toward the house. "After Annie, nothing was the same. Mr. Darwin walks me and the children to the church and leaves us at the door. He shuffles about outside until the services are over. Me, inside; him, outside. Sums it up, really. Forgive me for speaking about such things; I never do. I don't talk about *her*, normally. We neither of us do. But seeing your face so unexpectedly brought many things back. I can't offer you lunch, I'm afraid. Nanny's due back with the children at any moment, and it will be sheerest pandemonium here."

"Ma'am, I was very fond of your daughter. It was a bitter loss for me as well, as young as I was."

She turned back and grabbed his arm suddenly; she spoke in an altered voice. "Tell me God's love is great enough, Mr. Gates. Tell me God's love is sufficient to embrace my dearly beloved husband for all eternity. Tell me!"

David hesitated. "Mrs. Darwin, I hope and truly believe it is."

She looked down at her own hand as though it belonged to someone else, gripping the young man's arm. She released it hastily, flushing pink in the face, and continued on toward the house.

"Goodbye, Mr. Gates," she said. She did not look back.

ORPINGTON

THE SIGN ABOVE the shop proclaimed GATES HABERDASHERY. Inside, David Gates' father was rolling a bolt of silk, and Rebecca was adjusting a boater on a hat stand when David astonished them by walking in.

"Hullo?" cried Mr. Gates.

"David, you've been sent down!" cried Rebecca.

"Becca! Of course I haven't been sent down, what a goose you are!"

She and Mr. Gates looked at him expectantly. "I just . . . I had some business in the area."

"You did?" said Mr. Gates.

David felt foolish under the intelligent observation of his sibling and parent. "There was a message I needed to deliver to Mr. Darwin."

"To Mr. Charles Darwin?" said Rebecca. "But he's away!"

"I know, Rebecca, I know that now!" Why had he stopped? He could have gone straight to the inn and had a bite to eat while waiting for the return coach.

"What message?" asked Mr. Gates.

"It was just . . . to do with a debate that's going to be held at the weekend."

"Well," said his father, finally beaming and pumping his son's hand, "this is an unexpected pleasure, I must say."

Rebecca moved forward, awaiting her turn, and then she was in her brother's arms, alternately hugging him and looking intently into his face. "You've aged," she said. "University is making you older. How is Mr. Callow?" Jack had spent a few days with them after Christmas and had made an enormous impression on Rebecca.

"He's very well, thanks."

"Do remember me to him, will you?" said Rebecca. "You won't forget? People always say they will and never do."

"Listen, Davy," said Mr. Gates. "I'll just shut up the shop, shall I?"

"Not on my account, Father."

"Nonsense. Have you eaten?"

"No, sorry, Father, I can't stay, I was simply wondering . . ."

"You mean you're turning round and going back, just like that?" said Mr. Gates.

"Yes, and Father, I was wondering if I might have a five-pound advance against next month's allowance?" David said in a rush.

Mr. Gates' face registered only the briefest flicker of disappointment. He was genuinely proud of his son, and deeply fond. "Yes, of course," he said.

Rebecca stared at her brother in silence.

"I thought I might travel a bit at the end of term. With Jack, you see."

Mr. Gates nodded, moved to the till, and punched it open, producing a merry tinkle of bells that sent spasms of guilt through his boy.

"It's too bad of you, David," said Rebecca.

"Now, Becca . . ." said Mr. Gates.

"But it *is*, Father. 'Thought I might travel a bit at the end of term.' Oh, why could I not have been born a man, *why*?"

"It's the strangest thing, Davy," said Mr. Gates, surveying the contents of the till, mentally calculating the impact of a five-pound diminishment.

"What's that, Dad?"

"Your stopping by today, when just this morning you had a caller here at the shop."

"A nice-looking gentleman and his son," said Rebecca.

"He said he knew you from Oxford, but he was under the impression you would be down here today. I assured him that you were away at university. But *here you were* all along! I hope I haven't done wrong."

"Did he leave a name?"

"No, he said it wasn't important, he was bound to catch up with you sooner or later. Here's that fiver, son. See that you make it last now!"

"Thanks, Dad. I will do. Must run." But he hesitated.

There was something in the faces of his father and sister that spoke of the limited margins of their lives, their loneliness and their yearnings. Impulsively, he threw an arm round his father's shoulders and drew him into a brief, awkward embrace. Rebecca offered a cold handshake, which David rejected, pulling her to him in a hug that lifted her shrieking and laughing off the floor. The young man hurried away then, the shop door's bell ringing after him.

The coach was already taking on passengers when David arrived at the Orpington Inn. It was bound for London, and then on to Oxford, making local stops all the way. It would be a long day, and David was already dizzy with exhaustion. Taking his seat, he nodded to the tall gentleman and ginger-haired youth who climbed up after him and took their seats just opposite. Despite the cramped quarters and the jolting ride, young Gates was soon asleep.

In London he swam briefly toward consciousness as the suburban passengers disembarked, all except for the father and son. New riders boarded and fresh horses were harnessed, and with that jingle in his ears, David Gates sank back into waters of profoundest sleep.

He awoke with an urgent need to relieve himself. His fellow passenger was speaking softly to the boy. The coach had somewhere taken on an elderly country woman. She held a walking stick with an ornamental brass eagle's head in one hand and with the other clutched a handbag in her lap, as if expecting it to be taken from her forcibly at any moment.

David squinted out the window at his side. They were on a country road, passing farmland; there was a low hill in the distance and a gray stone manor house on the rise. It was late afternoon, green and golden. He heard the *skitter-skeet* of a skylark and peered up into the blue, spying a hovering black speck far above. Gradually David became aware of what the father was saying to his son.

" . . . mainly those small animals that came readily to hand—mice, rats, the odd cat. Birds. One needs a good blade for such work, and I was a poor boy, Tom, I couldn't dream of walking into a shop and buying one. That's how, when I wasn't singing, I came to work for the barber. I was, oh! much younger than you are now. Not for sixpences, mind you, but for my first cast-off razor."

David wondered how much farther it would be until the next stop. He leaned back, willing himself not to think of his bladder but instead savoring the fresh country aromas of earth and grass, manure and blossoms.

"For the larger species—dogs, pigs—I needed more space, of course, and found it down along the river flats, where planks fished from the water became my operating tables and where my activities never raised so much as an eyebrow."

Operating tables? Activities? What can the fellow be on about? His boy looks like he's heard enough; his eyes have a glazed look.

"Eventually, of course, I moved on to the study of humankind and then my education truly began." The man suddenly looked up at David and winked.

Did that actually happen? No. A speck of dust flew into the man's eye, that's all.

The man was focused again on the boy. "Now, then, Tom—what's the great difference between a man and a beast? Between a boy and a brute, if you will?"

The lad's eyes darted from his lap to the man's face and back again.

He's frightened of his father.

"It's his brain, of course! His mind! His seat of reason! Just you open up a horse, as I did on a couple of occasions, or some other mammal, and look inside; then open up a man, as I have often done."

The elderly woman clutched her bag even more tightly and stared out the coach window.

"You'll find similarities of bone structure in all mammals," continued the man. "Of course you will. But between the two brains? No, Tom. Therein lies the great difference. Now try a monkey. Go on, I dare you! These transmutation fellows would have you believe the monkey's brain is just like yours or mine, only smaller." The man seemed to David to be breathing heavier as he went on.

"Stop, I know what you're going to say, Tom. You're going to tell me the brain's too difficult to examine."

Poor boy's face has gone white.

"Agreed. It's an advanced study, is the human brain. But take any human feature." He glanced up again at David and said, "Take the ear."

The man's gaze was singular, almost mesmeric.

"Unique. Exquisite. These evolutionists would have you believe we inherit the ear from worms or mollusks or from God knows where! That *Darwin* fellow claims we're all one big family. How many brains has *he* examined?" His voice was rising. "How many men or women has Prince Albert opened up? Not a single one? No, sir, of course not!"

David stared back at the man. He felt an unwelcome churning in his stomach and sweat running beneath his arms. They were very nearly at Oxford. Should he keep quiet?

"Believe me, Tom, I have delved into this matter deeply, and if Scripture isn't enough for you, all my research has shown me that species are immutable and fixed, ordained and predestined, now and forever, amen!"

"Excuse me, sir," said David, "did you stop at my father's shop this morning, asking after me? In Orpington, this would have been."

The man ignored him, addressing the boy again. "Why is this important, Tom?" The boy's eyes flew to David's face for the first time, imploring. "Well, for one thing, people need to know their place, don't they, Tom. Not get above themselves."

"Sir," said David, "have you followed me this whole time? Who sent you?"

"Just so with the beasts, Tom. It wouldn't do to have a dog or a baboon ordering us about, now would it? Tom? Would it?"

The boy shook his head, still looking at David.

"Of course not, it's just common sense!" In one swift motion, he grabbed the old woman's walking stick from her and rapped his own forehead sharply with the brass eagle that formed its head. "Dear God, it makes me angry!" he whispered.

He's raving.

The man turned to the woman and said, "Forgive me, ma'am. I am a warrior for truth. I do hope I can count on your support."

Stark, staring mad.

"You are right to be cautious, ma'am. You want to be careful of that bag of yours. The highway bandits along this road will slit your throat as soon as look at you."

What to do? What to do?

David reached forward to rap on the coachman's box. The crazy man leaned toward David. "Farewell, dear friend," he quoted. "How doleful is the sound . . ."

The heavy brass top of the walking stick caught David on an upward thrust beneath his chin, snapping his head back. He felt his mouth fill with blood and, from a great distance, heard the boy cry out.

"How vast my stroke . . ."

"Get help!" David tried to say to the boy, but it didn't come out right. He brought his hands up to shield his face.

" . . . which leaves a bleeding wound."

The next blow, to the side of the head, was the last. In the relative silence that followed, the elderly woman emitted a quiet high-pitched mewling as she stared blindly out the window. The clop of the horses' hooves continued steadily, unchanged. A stinging scent of urine suddenly filled the coach.

"Empty his pockets," said the man to the boy. When Tom didn't move, Decimus boxed his ear savagely. Tom went through David's pockets, emerging with a crumpled letter, a pocket watch, a few coins, and a crisp new five-pound note. Decimus took the watch, tore the letter in two, and tucked the five-pound note into Tom's jacket pocket.

"There's a good lad."

Decimus gently prized the bag from the old woman's hands. She never once took her eyes away from the fields outside. He took out a small wad of banknotes and handed them back to the woman.

"Hide these, dearie, I've no need of them."

He dumped the other contents of the bag on the seats and floor of the coach, and wrenched off the bag's handle. He let the bag fall and turned to the woman again. "A highwayman did this," he said. "Say differently and I'll come find you." She continued to stare, unseeing, out the window. Decimus opened the door a crack, and when the driver slowed for a curve just outside of town, he grabbed Tom and leapt, tumbling them into a ditch. As the coach moved on into Oxford, he and the boy brushed themselves off and walked after it, Decimus jauntily employing his new walking stick.

19

OXFORD

Jack Callow, awaiting David's return at the coach station, decided to step into the Gloucester Arms, just opposite, for a pint. He was standing at the bar reading a book when the stationmaster entered with a constable.

"That's him," said the stationmaster, and the policeman approached Jack with a grave demeanor.

"You were expecting a passenger on the afternoon coach, I believe, sir?" he said.

"I am, yes," said Jack. "Has the coach been delayed?"

"It has just arrived, actually. If you please, sir, what was the name of the party?" The man's manner was profoundly somber.

"The coach is here?"

"The party's name, sir?"

"David Gates."

"Did you know him well, sir?"

There was a sudden pounding in Jack's ears. He searched the face of the constable for even a trace of mercy and found none there. He rushed to the door of the pub and saw a knot of police and drivers surrounding a coach, and an elderly woman being led away, shrieking.

The electric telegraph sent word down the line to London: a tall man and a ginger-haired boy (as per the coachman's scant description of them) were being sought in relation to the bludgeoning death of an Oxford undergraduate. Inspector Field and his men arrived by the nine o'clock train, just as the nightly tolling of Tom Tower finished—101 peals for the scholars of Christ Church, among whom David Gates had proudly numbered himself. The London policemen soon stood round an examining table with the Oxford coroner and a young sergeant Willette of the Thames Valley Constabulary.

"Handsome boy," said Field, his hat in his hands.

"It took only two blows to dispatch him," said Willette.

"And you reckon this poor lad had been robbed, do you?"

When Willette didn't answer, the coroner did. "Oh, yes. Pockets emptied and turned wrong side out, a bit of broken watch chain. A letter torn up by the attacker, addressed to the victim from his father. Boy's name is David Gates. His people are down in Orpington, according to the letter."

"Which is where he was coming from, is that right?"

"Indeed. According to the people at the coaching station, Mr. Gates went down from Oxford yesterday and returned, or tried to return, today."

"What do you make of it all, Sergeant Willette?"

"According to the old woman who shared the coach, highway robbery. Nonsense, according to the coachman, who is quite certain he would have noticed had his coach been boarded by highwaymen."

"And yet he was unaware of the attack?"

"Completely. But he says it had to have been the two passengers who went missing, a man and a boy. They were already seated when the driver came on in London, so he did not get much of a look at them, except to note that the man was tall and slender and the boy, about fifteen years of age and ginger-haired."

Kilvert spoke up. "Surely the old woman can give us a better description?"

"A gibbering imbecile," said the coroner bitterly.

"She was unable," said Willette, "or unwilling, to talk about anything but her own losses. Her handbag emptied and her walking stick stolen, a family keepsake." He did a shrill impersonation: "*The one with the eagle's head wot was give me by the gaffer!*"

"This wound here on the left temple, gentlemen," said the coroner, "was made by something pointed and metallic, possibly in fact the beak or talon of an ornamental eagle."

"The poor fellow's still got his left ear, at least," said Kilvert quietly to his colleagues.

"Killer didn't use a blade," said Llewellyn.

"Different go-about entirely," Field said. "Perhaps it's two other blokes altogether and nothing to do with us. Let's have Mr. Callow in."

After a few moments, Jack was shown into the room. He had been asked to identify the body earlier. Now his handsome face was haggard, his eyes red. He moved deliberately to the table and stood for a moment in silence. He brushed David's cheek with the back of his hand.

"We need to ask you a few questions, son," said Field.

"Are you in charge here?"

"No, that would be Sergeant Willette. But I am an interested party. Inspector Field of the Metropolitan Police, London."

"What was the purpose of your friend's journey, do you know?" asked Willette.

Jack turned his eyes back to the still form on the table. "I thought he was being absurd."

"Mr. Callow?"

"David went off to warn Mr. Darwin about a threat to his life. I could have stopped him, I could have said *no*."

The others glanced at each other.

"Mr. *Charles* Darwin?" said Field.

Jack nodded. "David has known the Darwin family since he was a boy."

"*What* threat to Darwin's life?"

"David encountered an old man a few days ago at his college. A sea captain named FitzRoy. He told David that Darwin needed to die."

The coroner was shocked. "FitzRoy? That seems unlikely—he's the man who piloted Charles Darwin round the world!"

"Well, all I know is he's here in Oxford, staying with Bishop Wilberforce, David's tutor. Everyone is gathering for the meeting of the British Association tomorrow. I imagine that's why this captain is here, if he's connected with Mr. Darwin. David was keen to attend it himself." Jack briefly covered his eyes, then took a breath. "For him, Darwin's work didn't represent a threat. It seems odd to say it, perhaps, but David loved God. He wasn't put off by any surprises that the Creator may have had in store for him or the rest of us. That's how he put it, anyway."

"We'll need to talk with this sea captain," said Field to his men, "and the boy's tutor, and we'll need to interview Mr. Darwin, I suppose, at some point, and find out what young Gates said to him."

"He didn't say anything to Mr. Darwin," said the coroner. "It was in *The Times*— Mr. Darwin is not at home, he's at Richmond, doing the water cure. The boy made his journey for nothing."

Jack put his face in his hands and wept.

Field took Willette aside. "We may learn something from the family. You've notified them?"

"They arrive in the morning. Gates Senior and a daughter, I believe. As it was a lifetime's dream to get the boy up to university, their wish is to bury him here."

Sir Jasper Arpington-Dix struggled to sit up in bed. He was staying in college as a guest of the bishop and had retired early after lightly dosing himself with laudanum for his gouty toes.

"Who's there?" he said.

He could just make out the silhouette of a man, perched on a chair near the window. Sir Jasper groped for the heavy walking stick that always lay beside him in bed. It was gone. Fear brought him wide awake.

"Who are you?"

There was the scratch and flare of a phosphorus match and the lamp on the table by the window came to life, revealing Decimus Cobb. There were two walking sticks lying across his lap, one with a brazen eagle's head and the other Sir Jasper's own.

"Good God, how the devil did you get in here! How dare you! Get out!"

"He wasn't there."

"D' you hear me, get out!"

"He wasn't there," said Decimus again.

"Who wasn't? What are you talking about?"

"The student. You misdirected me."

"I don't understand."

"I had to find him on my own, miles from Richmond Spa. He went to the man's own home to talk to him, of course."

"Ah. The Gates boy. And?"

Decimus laid one of the walking sticks on the floor, stood abruptly, and swung the eagle-headed stick toward Sir Jasper's head, stopping just short of his skull. "I got him with this."

Sir Jasper blinked back tears.

"I met Darwin himself down at Richmond," said Decimus. "Sat close beside him. Talked with him. I could have dispatched him easily, but you have forbidden me. It angers me, Sir Jasper, do you understand? All this angers me profoundly."

It took a moment before Sir Jasper was able to answer; he knew his life hung in the balance. "I do understand. I am certain it must have been a trial to your spirits, old man. But don't you agree, Mr. Cobb, that rather than create a martyr, you should instead stop those capable of promoting him and his work throughout the world, now and forever? There's the *real* danger. At some future date, perhaps, you will be able to do what you will with Darwin, when he's become inconsequential."

Decimus seemed to ponder this.

"What did you make of Darwin, Mr. Cobb?"

"His bowels are troubled. The gallbladder is poisoned."

Good God, the man is positively bizarre.

Sir Jasper had met with Decimus several times at Sir Jasper's London house, discussing with him travel itineraries and the identities of like-minded allies in Germany and elsewhere. That Decimus was well and truly insane Sir Jasper had no doubt, but he was clearly very intelligent and passionate about his work.

"I do apologize for the mixup with the Gates boy, Mr. Cobb."

Decimus nodded.

"I didn't expect to see you in Oxford," said Sir Jasper.

"But you do. You do see me."

The old man hesitated. "I should have thought, given the death of the Gates boy, that you would go to ground. Lie low for a time."

Decimus lifted both walking sticks and eyed them narrowly, comparing their respective heads. "I have a greater sense of history than *that*, Sir Jasper. I am a part of it, and I make it."

"Of course, of course," said Sir Jasper wanly.

"You cannot have thought I would miss tomorrow's meeting, me or my boy."

"Well," said Sir Jasper doubtfully, "no, I suppose not. Your boy?"

"If he is to join me in making history, it will be a test of his abilities and his loyalties."

"Bumboy, is he?" Sir Jasper realized he'd made a mistake the moment the words left his mouth. "I beg your pardon, Mr. Cobb, I meant no offense. Back East it was . . ."

The Chorister leaned forward and prodded Sir Jasper's gout-swollen foot with the eagle's beak. The pain was electrifying.

"The gout is merely troublesome, Sir Jasper; it is not your real problem. The tumor in your neck is your real problem, but I could have it out in no time."

"What tumor?" said the old man as evenly as he could.

"You'll find out within the year, I imagine. That thyroid of yours is growing like a little squash."

Sir Jasper realized his brow was covered in sweat.

"To your slumbers, Sir Jasper. I'll let myself out."

A missile was flying through the air. Sir Jasper covered his head and then cried out when something hard hit his chest. He opened his eyes, gasping for breath. His own walking stick lay on his sternum. Decimus was gone.

MASTER CALLED IT Oxford. He had taken rooms at Mrs. Andrews' Guest House where there weren't any guests as far as Tom could tell. Mrs. Andrews, dressed in black, was a severe-looking woman of perhaps fifty-five or sixty hard years. Her narrow features were dominated by two hairy black warts, one emerging from her chin and the other from one side of her pointed nose. She had assisted at the dyeing of Tom's hair, jet black. There was a new suit of clothes for him: a broad-lapelled coat with tails, a gray waistcoat and trousers, and a wide-collared white shirt with a velvet cravat. A soft gray cap lay on the bed.

You're to be a choir scholar now, Tom, isn't that grand? I was a choirboy once.

They would attend a great meeting. Some of the finest minds of the kingdom would be there.

The whole world's buzzing about it, isn't it exciting? Here's history, and here you are, a little butcher's boy, part of it all!

After his hair was dry, Tom had been allowed to collapse on a pallet at the foot of the bed. Master had taken the bed for himself, fully clothed, but in the night Tom had awakened to see a figure, tall and naked, standing before the mirror above the basin. There was something strange, something wrong, and then Tom had seen. The boy had shut his eyes tight, hoping, praying he had not gasped aloud. He heard the man turn and then nothing. No sound, for one hour? Two? Tom slept.

In the morning the bed was empty, but Master was present below in the little parlor, drinking tea, dark circles beneath his deep-set eyes. Mrs. Andrews, with her pinched, starved look and her warts, set a plate in front of Tom. He hungrily devoured the roll and morsel of cheese. Before he'd finished eating, Master was off again without a word.

Tom quickly climbed the stairs to their rooms, knowing how foolish he was being. His heart pounding in his ears, he took the little pencil he'd found in a drawer and used it to write on the five-pound note Master had given him. It was perilous, it was wrong. Like the watch chain he'd taken from the nice young man on the coach and hid in his clothes, and the knitting needles he'd found in the old woman's handbag, thinking he might somehow put them to use. Just last night, when Master cut his hair, Tom had watched to see where he would put the scissors, and Master had seen him watching, he was quite sure. Foolish and dangerous, like the tightly folded five-pound note, hiding now in his waistcoat pocket. For whom was the note? For what reason had Tom put himself (and his mother, as Master often reminded him) at such risk? Looking into the chipped mirror above the bowl, Tom saw again the young man from the coach, saw the fear and confusion in the young man's eyes. And then he gasped, he couldn't help it: Master was there, in the mirror, standing in the door, wearing a black gown and staring.

"Come along, then, Tom," said Decimus, pulling a wry smile. "We've a busy day ahead." Master's features suddenly darkened. "What's that?" he said, pointing.

Heart racing, Tom looked down at himself, assuming the Master had detected the note in his pocket. Then he saw the ring on his left hand and felt a rush of relief.

"It's just Blinky's ring, sir. She gave it me."

"Did you copulate with her?"

"No!" shouted Tom, appalled. "No, sir, she gave it me, the ring, it was too big."

Master shook his head and said, "She's old enough, I suppose, but I don't like it when they move."

It took a moment for Tom to realize what Master was saying, and then he felt a rising wave of nausea.

"Never mind, I am setting you an examination, of sorts. Are you attentive? Do you listen and recall everything? Not everyone who answers history's call is fit for the task, don't you see?"

Tom didn't see and his face showed it, so Master crossed the room in two steps and slapped him, hard.

20

OXFORD

In the morning, Inspector Field stood in the porter's lodge at Christ Church College, enduring the disdainful scrutiny of the porter through his window. Black-robed undergraduates and dons were coming and going beneath the arch of the college's main gate, and a carriage was pulling up before it.

"Was the bishop expecting you, sir?" said the porter.

"No indeed," said Field. "This is a police matter that has just arisen."

The porter's frown deepened. He turned and spoke to someone behind him. "Mr. Smuts? Would you be so kind? This person wishes to speak with the bishop, says it's police business."

After a moment a door opened in the wall, and Smuts, the human fence post, emerged, clapping a bowler hat on his head. "I am the police here," he said, looking Field up and down.

"Delighted to hear it," said Field. "I am Chief Detective Inspector Field of the Metropolitan, and I am a policeman *also*."

"The bishop is fully engaged."

"My business is urgent, sir."

"Nothing I can do about that, is there."

"I can think of one or two things you *could* do right about now, Mr. Smuts, but never mind that." He raised his voice a notch. "Kindly let the bishop know that the London police request an audience!"

"Bishop's just coming, sir," said a passing undergraduate, nodding toward the quadrangle.

With a triumphant glance at the Bulldog, Field turned to see a stocky, gowned man in a priest's collar entering the lodge with a black-robed, beak-nosed man at his side. "Bishop Wilberforce?" said Field, and the two men paused.

"Yes?" said the bishop.

"We mustn't be late, my friend," said the other man, gesturing to the carriage waiting on the street.

"My lord, I am Inspector Field of the Metropolitan Police, and I regret to tell you that one of your scholars has suffered a grievous accident."

"Who is it? What sort of accident?"

"His name was David Gates, and I am sorry to say he was murdered, my lord."

The bishop stared. "Murdered."

The other gentleman murmured, "Dreadful, dreadful."

"Where?" asked Wilberforce. "When?"

"Yesterday afternoon, on a coach approaching Oxford."

"By whom?"

"We do not yet know, sir."

"Has Mr. Gates' family been told?"

"Yes, my lord. They are arriving this morning."

Wilberforce seemed genuinely upset. "Fond of the boy." He took a deep breath. "Sorry, Inspector Field, this is Sir Richard Owen."

Owen nodded and then laid a comforting hand on Wilberforce's shoulder. "My friend, this is a terrible shock. Nevertheless, we need to be going."

"One moment, gentlemen, please," said the inspector. "It seems young Mr. Gates was concerned about a guest of yours, my lord, a man named FitzRoy."

"Concerned?" said Owen. "In what way?"

"We understand Mr. Gates heard FitzRoy threaten the life of Mr. Charles Darwin."

Look at this, the bishop is going all white.

"FitzRoy is not well," said Owen. "The man's confused. Addled."

"You don't suspect *him* of this crime, surely?" said the bishop. "He was here with us all day yesterday."

"Nevertheless," said Field, "I wondered if I might have a word with the captain."

"But he is at the University Museum for the great meeting."

"Which is, my lord," said Owen, "where you and I need to be going without delay. If you will excuse us, Inspector Field?"

"Of course, gentlemen. I'll see you at the museum, then. My men are there already."

Owen's smile was acidic. He led Wilberforce through the lodge and into the waiting carriage. Field turned back to the porter. "Where is this museum?" The porter glanced uncertainly at Smuts, who stared, his arms folded across his chest. Field thrust his head to the porter's window. "Quickly!" he barked.

"In Parks Road, sir, at the end of the Broad."

Field strode out, shouting over his shoulder, "Thank you kindly, I'm sure!"

THE INSPECTOR, AS he walked, was all eyes and ears. It was the end of Trinity term and, as always at that time of year, there was a kind of frenetic madness in the air. Freedom was at hand. Undergraduates were giddy with it and, in many instances, drunk with it as well. The river teemed with punts. The romantic comedies of Shakespeare were performed by torchlight in the college gardens, and unscripted love affairs were consummated in the neighboring woods. The Bulldogs patrolled the streets with fierce countenances, dragging miscreants to justice, but the antic mayhem was rampant even so. Field walked to the end of Broad Street, past the soot-blackened busts of Roman emperors perched before the Sheldonian Theatre, their faces glaring fiercely above the heads of the current youthful populace into their own contentious histories.

As he turned off into Parks Road, a back gate at St. John's College opened on his left, and a stream of choirboys emerged, followed by their masters, all of them wearing long black robes. The sight left the inspector momentarily stunned: the masters all seemed to move on wheels instead of feet. The boys moved their legs like normal human beings, but the adults *glided*.

They dress alike, do they have to walk alike as well? This is religious somehow?

A large man fell into step on his right. "Oh, Mr. Smuts," said Field, "can you explain why these chaps walk like they're bleeding ballerinas?" Another solid, bowler-hatted man appeared at Field's other side. "Hullo!" said the inspector, and then turning to Smuts, "Are you not going to introduce us?"

"You do not belong here," said Smuts.

"Why would you say such a thing, Smuts? You are a warm and welcoming person, that's what you are!"

"University police are in charge here. You and your lot can hop it."

"Not going to do that, certainly, I've a sea captain to interview."

The Bulldog on his left laid a police baton across Field's chest, and all three men came to a stop.

"Mr. Smuts, tell your man to take away his stick."

"I think we'll lock you up, London. Just for the night, and then we'll put you on the first train out come morning."

The Bulldog holding the baton doubled over with Field's fist in his belly, gasping for breath. Smuts, drawing a truncheon from beneath his coat, was stunned to find his opposite hand cuffed to the wrist of his falling comrade, the two big men going down together in a grunting tangle. Field left the men thrashing on the ground and moved quickly across a broad expanse of grass toward the imposing University Museum.

LLEWELLYN AND KILVERT were already inside. The crowd was such that they had to edge up the staircase one step at a time toward the museum's upper gallery and the library where the meeting was to be held. The stone walls of the soaring neo-Gothic structure reverberated with hundreds of voices, all talking at once.

"Will you look at those great creatures, Mr. Kilvert!" said Llewellyn, staring down over the rail at the enormous fossil dinosaurs mounted below. "To think monsters such as these once roamed this very land!"

"I'll wager they were manufactured locally, Mr. Llewellyn. It's all a fraud." Normally the annual meeting of the staid British Association for the Advancement of Science caused barely a ripple among the public; today, it captured the attention of the world. The gathering was not a debate per se but a platform for the presentation of scientific papers. Everyone, however, knew that whatever papers were presented, there was only one topic this year: Charles Darwin's revolutionary theory.

Professor Perkins, secretary to the British Association, watched dumbfounded as the crowds poured in, filling the library to overflowing. The day was humid and warm, the temperature in the library was already rising, and Perkins, a slender, querulous bachelor, was inwardly fuming. If anything went wrong it was *Perkins* who would catch it.

Beside him, the graying, mild-mannered scholar from New York, scheduled to read an essay inspired by Darwin's theory, was quite giddy, thinking mistakenly that this multitude was gathering to hear *him*. Professor Draper glanced down at the pages he clutched in his hands and realized with horror that the ink was running here and there from his own perspiration. "Oh, dear me, my remarks!" cried Professor Draper. Perkins offered the American a baleful glance and turned back to the incoming throng.

"Orderly now, gentlemen and ladies!" he shouted. "Orderly! There will not be room to sit, most of you will have to stand! You young men there, drunkenness will not be tolerated! Hallo, may we have some quiet please! May we have some order!"

MASTER HAD TOLD Tom to watch and listen and learn. *Every word, do you understand?* What he must *not* do, however, is speak; no one must hear rough London accents coming from an Oxford choir-boy, after all! Master himself kept shifting through the crowded room, edging this way and that, until he seemed to find someone he'd been looking for, and there he stopped. This was a square-jawed man toward the front, with mutton-chop whiskers (Thomas Huxley, had Tom known it). He was one of the few who had a chair in which to sit. Master placed himself just behind the man. A white-haired gentleman finally stood and held up one hand.

It took some time, but John Stevens Henslow, Darwin's old mentor from Cambridge, finally was able to hush the room. He made a brief introduction and then Professor Draper from New York University began reading his remarks.

FIELD MADE HIS way up through the crowd, which spilled halfway down the staircase. Finally he reached the threshold, elbowed his way in, and surveyed the room. It was packed from wall to wall. The audience was mostly male, with a few scattered females, whose crinolines took up even more of the limited space.

" . . . seen in this light, as suggested by Mr. Darwin," Professor Draper was saying, "the progression of organisms is determined by natural law and not . . . Oh, dear me, what is that next word? I seem to have blotted it . . . Skipping down a bit . . ."

Get him off! cried a young male voice from somewhere in the crowd.

" . . . the question thus arises, are we merely a fortuitous congrega-tion of atoms?"

The inspector caught sight of Kilvert, who was quite near to the speaker's podium. On the other side of the room he spotted Llewellyn, who clearly had located the sea captain: a florid man in an old-fashioned naval uniform, clutching a huge book.

Field pushed into the crowd, making his way incrementally.

Professor Draper finally stumbled to a halt and was given perfunctory applause. The crowd was impatient for the main event to begin, and the botanist Daubney, who spoke next about the implications of Darwin's theory on the sexual reproduction of plants, was not it. The rowdier elements among them grew more vocal, and then a Reverend Dingle was called to the podium. Dingle gave the crowd a big-toothed grin and turned to a blackboard, carefully writing the letter *A* on one side and *B* on the other. He circled each letter and drew an arrow connecting the two.

"Now, then," he said in a thick Yorkshire accent, "let 'A' stand for the *man* and 'B' stand for the *mawnkey . . .*"

It was simply too much for the crowd. A group of undergraduate rogues began to chant, *Mawnkey, Mawnkey, Mawnkey, Mawnkey!*

They would not be stilled and poor Reverend Dingle had to stand down, still bravely showing his large front teeth and still clutching a lump of chalk. There was a moment wherein the entire crowd seemed to take a breath, and then a door opened at the end of the room.

Bishop Samuel Wilberforce entered and strode the short distance to the podium. He grasped it with both hands, looking out over the vast assembly, waiting for silence. He inclined his head respectfully toward the single row of natural historians and dignitaries seated before him, beginning with the venerable Henslow. He bestowed smiles upon Sir Richard Owen and Sir Jasper Arpington-Dix. He had wry grins for Thomas Huxley and, seated next to Huxley, Joseph Dalton Hooker, the botanist, Darwin's closest friend. Wilberforce evidently failed to notice Professor Draper from New York, the botanist Daubney, and the Reverend Dingle sitting before him, since he acknowledged none of them. When there was a complete hush, the bishop's eyes twinkled.

"Odd," he said, finally, his strong voice reaching without effort from the front of the packed room to the back. "I was expecting a crowd."

The assembly exploded in laughter.

The bishop clasped his hands before him and worked them as if washing them. "Is this what you came to see?" he cried, and laughter again surged through the crowd. A daring young man cried, *Good old Soapy Sam!* Wilberforce held up one hand, calling for silence and quickly getting it.

"I wonder," he said, suddenly solemn, "if you know whose passion and dream it was to see this great building erected? This museum, newly completed, which is and will be forever a monument to the pursuit of natural history and all things scientific?" He looked over the crowd, as if waiting for an answer. "Well, my friends," he said finally, "the University Museum had many dedicated patrons, thank the Lord, and with their permission and your forgiveness, I proudly confess to being prominent amongst them!"

Applause from the assembly.

The bishop looked down at Huxley and Hooker, shaking his head sadly, and then up at the crowd, his eyes blazing. "I am the *friend* of natural philosophy! I am the *servant* of science, not her enemy!"

Renewed applause and scattered shouts of *Hear, hear!*

Again Wilberforce raised a plump palm to quiet the crowd. "Why, then, as a friend and ally of science, am I here?"

"Why?" shouted a tipsy undergraduate, provoking a ripple of laughter.

"As a friend of science I am compelled to speak out against *bad* science! On this occasion I am here, not as a man of the cloth and a defender of the faith, but as a defender of fact over fiction—a fiction that has been inflicted, regrettably, on the public and the world of natural history by the amateur Charles Darwin!"

Tumult from the crowd: cries and shouts, applause and catcalls. *Hear, hear! Shame! Hear, hear! For shame, sir! For shame!*

Sir Richard Owen was beaming. His pupil was doing him proud. Owen turned to Sir Jasper, seated next to him, but found that gentleman staring at his hands. Somber? Strangely remote, in any case. He scarcely seemed to be listening.

A tumor within the year? thought Sir Jasper. *Nonsense! How could the man possibly know what is happening within my body? He made it up to frighten me, that's all. The man's a lunatic, I don't need him. I'll hire a professional to do the job. A German, perhaps, one of these anarchist chappies. Of course! And then I shall feed Decimus Cobb to the damned jackals. Oh, won't I just!*

"WE ARE NOT naive," Wilberforce was saying. "We know the earth is much older than we once believed. The advances and discoveries of the present century—some of them thanks to great minds here present"—the bishop bowed to Owen who acknowledged the tribute with a modest smile—"have taught us differently, and so we accept that which is undeniable. We are scholars. We do not test the truth of natural science by the word of revelation but the other way round."

"You *should* do!" cried Captain FitzRoy from the crowd, shaking his massive Bible before him. "You can test it *all*, right in here in the Book! Trust God, not men!"

The audience registered their alarm with anxious murmurs. The inspector pushed more urgently through the crowd toward the captain. *This fellow wants watching.* Then he spotted a young lad with jet-black hair, standing very near the sea captain, looking frightened. It struck Field that the boy's hair might be *too* black.

"This does not mean, however," said the bishop, ignoring the outburst, "that we do not point out *on scientific grounds* errors, when those errors tend to limit God's glory in creation or to gainsay all that which creation reveals to us of God himself. To both these classes of error, we think Mr. Darwin's speculations sadly tend. The simple fact remains: a rock pigeon is a rock pigeon and always *was* a rock pigeon!"

The crowd liked this and showed it by their applause.

THOMAS HUXLEY WAS fuming. It was Wilberforce's condescending demeanor that most infuriated him. Here was this unctuous man, this intellectual lightweight, calling Charles Darwin an amateur!

Something was brushing Huxley's left ear. He swatted it, thinking it to be a fly, and was shocked to find it was a man's hand. He swiveled and looked up into the deep coal-black eyes of the tall man who stood behind him.

"Did you just touch me, sir?" whispered Huxley.

"Forgive me, Mr. Huxley," murmured Decimus. "There's quite a crush."

"Oh, well, yes. You startled me, that's all." Huxley turned back to attend Wilberforce's remarks.

"Your children currently enjoy good health, I hope?" said Decimus quietly.

Huxley again spun round in his chair. "I beg your pardon?" he whispered. "Have we been introduced, sir?"

But Decimus had his eyes now firmly fixed on the bishop and appeared to be listening intently.

"*Sir?*" hissed Huxley.

The tall blond man with the dark eyes smiled, shook his head gently, and put an admonitory finger to his lips.

Constable Kilvert observed the entire exchange. His attention had been caught some minutes earlier by the distinctive eyes of the man standing behind the speakers' row. Now the man seated in front of him seemed flushed and agitated. Kilvert started to edge his way in their direction.

"MR. DARWIN CLAIMS to be a Christian," Wilberforce was saying, "and we take him at his word in this. We do not suspect him of being one who harbors secret doubts, hiding them from the world for fear of consequences. If his village vicar tells me that Mr. Darwin is rarely, if ever, to be found in the pew alongside his wife and children of a Sunday, surely it must be because of the vicissitudes of his health. We should *pray* for him; I know *I* do."

KILVERT HAD LEVERED himself through the crowd to the tall man's side. Their eyes met for a moment, and then Kilvert turned toward the bishop.

Something, he thought. *There was something just now, what was it?*

"The words graven on the everlasting rocks," said Wilberforce, "written in the earth itself, hill and dale, mountain and valley, are the words of God, graven by his hand. They are ours to read aright, to gain thereby wisdom and strength. Truly it is said, 'They that wait upon the Lord shall renew their strength, they shall mount up with wings like the eagle!'"

Land of my fathers, it's a bloody eagle.

Kilvert slid his glance sideways down the tall man's torso. His hands rested on the brass head of a walking stick. A brazen eagle's beak protruded between the fingers and one brass eagle's wing. Kilvert raised his glance slowly and found the deep-set eyes of the man upon him. The man glanced down, saw his own walking stick, looked up again at Kilvert, and smiled ruefully, shaking his head.

"Sir," said the constable quietly, "I am Officer Kilvert of the Metropolitan Police. I am going to ask you to step out with me. Quietly now—I'm sure you will want to assist me with my inquiries."

"What, and miss the show?" whispered Decimus genially. Kilvert felt the warmth of the man's breath in his ear and the pressure of the man's hand on his back. "I'll tell you anything you want to know, Officer, after this breaks up. You don't want to cause a stir, not in a crowd this size, now do you?" The man's hand remained warmly on his back.

The policeman glanced about at the dense crowd.

"Fair enough," said Kilvert. "We'll wait."

THE BISHOP WAS heating up for a big finish. He surveyed his audience, his hands clasped before him again, unconsciously washing each other.

"To oppose facts in the natural world because they seem to oppose revelation is but another form of *lying for God*. This, we reject. Nonetheless, how *are* we to respond, when Mr. Darwin openly declares that he applies his scheme of natural selection not only to the dumb animals around him but to man himself?"

At this, the well-known Cambridge economist, Henry Fawcett, blinded in a shooting accident, said to the man who stood at his elbow, "No, he doesn't!" Fawcett apparently was unaware that his voice was perfectly audible to much of the assembly. "Implied, perhaps, but nowhere does Darwin come out and say it. One of my young men read it aloud to me, word for word. I'll lay odds from all he's said that this man here hasn't even read the damned book!"

Wilberforce, who in fact had *not* read *Origin*, turned in a red rage upon the speaker but, seeing who it was, the cane and the smoked glasses, swallowed the rebuke that was on his lips.

"Now we must say at once," continued Wilberforce at an ever-rising pitch, "that such a notion is absolutely incompatible with the whole representation of that moral and spiritual condition of man which is the proper subject of natural history." He fairly glared at the crowd now, as if defying anyone there to contradict him. "Man's power of articulate speech; his gift of reason; his free will; his supremacy over the earth; his fall and salvation—all are utterly irreconcilable with the degrading notion of a brute origin for him who was created in the image of God and redeemed by the Eternal Son!"

So forceful was the bishop's rhetoric that there followed a stunned silence. He himself was pleased with the words that had come to him, and their passion, but the bishop also liked very much to be liked. He needed to lighten the atmosphere a bit; he needed, frankly, a laugh and decided he'd found one sitting in the front row.

"Mr. Huxley," he said in a humorous, cajoling tone, leaning forward with his elbows on the podium, "on which side *do* you claim descent from the ape? Your grandpapa's or your grandmama's?"

The hoped for laugh did not come. There was an intake of breath and, if anything, a deepening of the silence from the vast crowd. He had gone too far. The bishop's smile remained frozen on his face. He felt drops of sweat roll from armpit to hip. He noticed the tall man with the infinitely dark eyes standing above Huxley, and he thought, oddly, of death.

"Soapy Sam has just made my work a deal easier," whispered Huxley to Joseph Hooker at his side as he rose slowly to his feet. Huxley acknowledged the bishop with a bow. "If, my lord, I were forced to choose between having an ape for an ancestor or a man of great ability and influence who used his manifold gifts to introduce ridicule into a serious discourse, I should without hesitation choose the ape."

Sensation in the room.

Hear, hear! What did he say? Shame! Well done, Huxley! Well done!

From the front row Owen was hissing at the bishop. "Remember the posterior lobes, Wilberforce! Talk about the *hippocampus minor*!"

JOSIAH KILVERT HAD never felt anything like it. He was suddenly, inexplicably exhausted. Light-headed, he grasped the back of the chair before him. He saw that the tall blond man was observing him closely. With curiosity? Amusement? The policeman realized he was in danger of fainting. He summoned all his will to make his way out of the library, pushing himself through the crowd.

THE BOY WATCHED the goings-on with a dazed look. Field, standing unnoticed next to him, confirmed his suspicion that the lad's hair had been dyed black and had reddish roots below. He decided to take a chance.

"Tom?" he said quietly. The boy's whole body jolted; he looked at Field and then adamantly looked away. "You *are* Tom Ginty, are you not?" Tom shook his head almost imperceptibly. "Your mother is frantic, Tom. She came to me. Distraught, she was. She begged me to find you, and I did, didn't I?" The boy remained rigid and unresponsive. Field glanced over the jostling heads around him and saw Constable Llewellyn watching him. Field tilted his head in Tom's direction and nodded. Llewellyn nodded back.

"Point the man out to me, Tom," the inspector said into the boy's ear. "You can do it with a word, lad. A whisper. I'll see, I'll know. I'm a policeman, son. My men and I will take him in charge. We won't let him hurt you. You'll go home again. That's what you want, isn't it?" Field thought he saw the lad's eyes glisten, but he did not move.

HUXLEY HAD TAKEN over the podium and was hitting his stride.

"Bishop Wilberforce ended his remarks with several claims. He claimed that the brain of man is different *in kind* from the brains of primates. He said that the brains of men have these three unique features that set them apart from all others: a posterior lobe, a posterior horn, and the *hippocampus minor*. These distinctions are perhaps somewhat unfamiliar to the layperson."

A smattering of laughter spread through the library.

"I think it may be possible they are, in fact, unfamiliar to the bishop himself."

The laughter grew.

"I think it is possible that my lord is merely repeating by rote what he has been taught by the distinguished anatomist here present, Sir Richard Owen." Huxley paused for a moment, aware of Owen looking up at him with beak-like nose and lips compressed to invisibility. "However the bishop may have come by these assertions, they are simply inaccurate. Had I the ability here and now to dissect the brain of a gorilla before you, I could point out to you in its brain a posterior lobe, a posterior horn, and—ladies and gentlemen—a perfectly viable *hippocampus minor*. Professor Owen has simply overlooked them. He is mistaken in his researches. His argument, espoused many times in the past few months to refute Mr. Darwin's genius and repeated here by the bishop of Oxford, is based on error, pure and simple. Now, we all make mistakes, but the natural historian is obliged by his calling to admit them. We are all of us humbled by the unfolding mysteries of the natural world—and each of us, without exception, must pray for the courage to face a fact and own up to it, even though it slays us! Thank you."

There was thunderous applause as Huxley sat, but a man was shouting.

"No, no, no, no, no!" cried the erstwhile captain of the *Beagle*, dancing with rage, swinging his massive Bible before him like a scythe, pushing toward the podium. "Follow the ways of God, not man!"

There were shouts throughout the library. A woman shrieked and an undulating wave convulsed the crowd. Someone was down. Perkins cried from the front, "Order! Order! There's a lady fainted, make way!"

Inspector Field knew this much: such was the size of the crowd, chaos had to be averted quickly or disaster would ensue. He grabbed

Tom by the wrist and dragged him toward the fallen lady, and Llewellyn approached from his side. They found the woman cradled in a sitting position by a female companion, who fanned her ineffectually with one hand.

The inspector turned to the boy. "Tom, I need to help this lady. You stick close to me and we'll see you safe home. All right?"

Tom barely nodded.

Field released the boy's wrist, stooped with Llewellyn to get the woman's arms around their shoulders, and the two men hoisted her up. At the podium, Perkins was red to the top of his balding crown. "Ladies and gentlemen, open a path there! Make way!" The crowd inched apart before the policemen as they shuffled with their burden toward the library doors, the boy in the lead. Field saw the tall man at the door before he made the connection. The man seemed to be beckoning them on, but no, it was Tom Ginty who sped up, leaving them behind, pushing through the throng to the man at the door with the deep-set eyes.

"Tom!" cried the inspector. "Stop!"

The man glared at Tom, then looked fiercely up at Field. A moment later he and the boy were gone. Field cursed savagely under his breath. The crowd was applauding the policemen, but to Field it sounded like a chorus of condemnation.

The inspector and Llewellyn emerged from the library onto the gallery with the woman draped between them; she was beginning to revive.

"You there!" cried Field to a knot of undergraduates who were among the overflow crowd. "I'm a policeman—you lot look after this lady, she's fainted."

As soon as Field and Llewellyn had passed off the woman to other hands, the inspector started down the staircase, shouting over his shoulder, "You check the gallery floor, Sam!" He didn't even notice Kilvert sitting at the top of the steps, but Llewellyn did. He was leaning against the stairs' balustrade, his cheek pressed to the marble.

"Josiah?" Llewellyn knelt beside his partner. "What's wrong? What's happened?"

Kilvert saw the hills of his boyhood, a vast chorus of Welshmen arrayed on them, singing. He was there with them, he was a boy again. He tried not to look at the mounted fossilized creatures on the museum floor below. They had taken life and were moving, their stone bones clanking horribly, their grotesque faces turning up toward him, their empty eye sockets gleaming with a red malevolence.

"Josiah!"

Kilvert's skin was paper white. He was singing in a faint voice.

Now by my faithful hound I'm led,
I wend from door to door . . .

Llewellyn stood and shouted down the stairs. "Mr. Field! Come quickly!" Field stopped and turned at the bottom of the steps. He saw the expression on Llewellyn's face and raced back up the steps.

Proclaim how Wales has fought and bled,
In tales of old time lore.

The hole at the back of Kilvert's coat was so small they didn't notice it, but when they got his jacket off they saw the back of his shirt was red and running. In a moment the men had shouldered their comrade and were carrying him down the stairs, his feet slapping the steps. They pushed through the museum's doors into the sunlight.

The two university Bulldogs whom Field had encountered earlier were waiting. The inspector had time to say, "Get him to a doctor!" before the first baton struck him a glancing blow to the skull. Llewellyn took the whole weight of Kilvert as Smuts' truncheon felled Charles Field like a toppled tree.

21

Jack Callow sat in the front pew of the St. Cross church, his elbows on his knees and his head in his hands. The closed wooden casket stood before him, resounding in its silence. The verger, a corpulent red-nosed old man, watched the undergraduate from the back of the church, rubbing his hands together to warm them.

Jack was twenty years old, and lost. His people were comfortable country gentry, and handsome Jack, who excelled at both sport and study, had grown up his family's shining star. There was nothing he could not do; this was received as plain fact in the village and among the neighboring farms. But had he ever possessed a sense of purpose or direction? Jack wondered. He hadn't anticipated the jolting, white-hot force that had brought him together with David Gates in their second year; he certainly hadn't looked for it. Now, it seemed to Jack, that it was gentle David who knew who he was and why, who believed in things with enough conviction to act upon them. And now David was gone and, with him, all sense of meaning.

He heard footsteps on the stone and a rustle of fabric. Miss Rebecca Gates, David's sister, stood above him. Jack leapt to his feet, but she motioned him to sit again.

"My father is at the hotel, sleeping," she said. "Cold in here, is it not. The stone saps the heat right out of one." Rebecca moved to her brother's casket and laid a hand on it. After a long moment she sat in the pew beside Jack.

"My beloved brother is not here," she said, looking at the coffin. "He is with God."

"Oh, Miss Gates . . ."

"Please, don't let's speak. Just for now." Jack nodded.

From the back of the little church the verger watched the two of them keeping vigil. When they finally left, he stepped out and stood in the door, wheezing in the sunlight. He was a lonely man whose life, when sober, was spent in silent observation. Now he watched the young woman and the young gentleman walk away wordlessly toward the long grass of the University Parks.

A SMALL POSTDEBATE gathering was held in the bishop's study at Christ Church. There were cold meats, and drinks in abundance.

"So you think I came off well, did you?" the bishop asked of the room in general. He was drinking port, and his eyes had acquired an unaccustomed luster. "I rather *thought* I did, but then, one never knows. The blind chap threw me for a moment, that Fawcett fellow. Why the devil is it, the blind never seem to know how loudly they're speaking?"

Sir Jasper, seated in a leather chair with a cigar in one hand and a whiskey in the other, seemed to have cast off his earlier glum spirits. He thrust the cigar in Wilberforce's direction. "My dear man, you spoke with eloquence and passion. Huxley and Hooker? Dry as dust!"

The bishop beamed, but Owen snorted. "How dare Huxley question my work!" he said. "Ridicule, from the likes of him!"

"Never mind Huxley, old man," said Sir Jasper. "He's nothing and no one."

"I'll make him pay. Before I'm done, Huxley will pay."

Captain FitzRoy watched them all, silent and abstemious, glowering from a deep chair, his large Bible on his lap.

"After today, gentlemen," said Sir Jasper, "Darwin's *bulldog* can bloody well scamper off with his tail between his legs! What does the common man care for *lobes*, front or back? Not a blessed thing!"

"But the science behind our argument is vitally important, Sir Jasper," said Owen heatedly. "Why, the posterior horn represents . . ."

"No, it don't. Don't represent a damned thing to the common man, old boy, and he's the chappie I care about—he's the one who will nip Darwinism in the bud. There's only *one* posterior horn that matters to the average fellow, I guarantee it!" Sir Jasper's bawdy laugh quickly became a smoky cough.

Owen moved away, muttering in disgust, but Sir Jasper struggled to his feet and followed him. "Owen, old man," he said confidentially. "I've had a revelation. Change of plan."

Owen glanced nervously at the others in the study, but Sir Jasper shook his head and put a finger to his lips.

"Different scheme altogether," he said in a low voice. "I'm going to engage a German to do the job, on his own turf."

"What?" whispered Owen.

"You can tell your man to stand down, with our thanks, of course."

"You're joking. *You* tell him!"

Suddenly FitzRoy stood. "Cowards," he said.

"Oh, dear God," said the bishop.

"Appeasers!" cried FitzRoy. "Blasphemers!" The captain was red in the face. "You are not defenders of the faith, but deniers!"

"Get him out of here, someone," said Owen.

"Huxley made mincemeat of you, Bishop!" cried FitzRoy. "Mincemeat, do you not understand? And Darwin, whatever his errors, is worth ten of any of you!"

"I cannot abide this," muttered Wilberforce, massaging his temples.

"Listen to this," said the captain, taking a creased, stained envelope from his Bible and carefully extracting a yellowed sheet. "He wrote this to me, oh so many years ago now: 'My dear FitzRoy, I hope you will not forget to send me a note telling me how you get on. If you do not receive much satisfaction for all the mental and bodily energy you have expended in His Majesty's service, you will be most hardly used.'" He looked up. "He was my friend, you see? Not my enemy."

"Get him out!"

"'God bless you! I hope you are as happy as, but much wiser than, your most sincere but unworthy philosopher, Charles Darwin.'"

Tears streamed down FitzRoy's face. He tucked the letter into his Bible and hoisted it. "We had such times together. *Now* look what's become of us."

"Captain, a word." FitzRoy glared as Sir Jasper approached him. "You might just set that Bible down, old man. Do yourself a favor." Sir Jasper's eyes twinkled as he draped an arm around FitzRoy's neck. "Don't worry, we'll have it sent on."

"What?"

Sir Jasper was leading him gently toward the door. "You're leaving us, sir. As soon as ever you can. *Now*, in fact."

FitzRoy's glare moved to Owen and Wilberforce. "I shake the dust from my feet. I don't know why you asked me here, and I don't know why I came."

"No more do we, Captain FitzRoy, no more do we," said Sir Jasper. "Off you go now, you queer old thing. You're not wanted here. Nor anywhere else, as far as I can tell."

FitzRoy threw off Sir Jasper's arm and left. A collective sigh of relief went round the room.

SAM LLEWELLYN SAT next to the bed in the Radcliffe Infirmary, staring at the unconscious form of Josiah Kilvert. The two sisters on duty bustled quietly up and down the ward, glancing often at the policeman keeping vigil. One of them—Sister Claire, it was—actually laid her hand gently on his shoulder at one point. Llewellyn looked up, gave her a wan smile and resumed his watch.

The doctor had been fascinated by the wound. Llewellyn had told him that Kilvert, before he lost consciousness, whispered something about a hand on his back.

"'Nothing sharp,' I think he said, Doctor, when I asked him."

"That doesn't surprise me. The region of the back hasn't many nerve endings, relatively speaking. Far fewer, say, than the hand or the foot. If I were to stick you square in the back with an ice pick, you'd feel a blunt sensation rather than a pointed one. What interests me about the wound is its precision. It's so clean and economical; it looks like the work of a professional mortician."

"Will he live?"

The doctor hesitated. "His pulse is not encouraging; his heart may have been weak to begin with. Nevertheless, he just might make it. I can't really say, son."

That was nearly two hours earlier. Llewellyn felt utterly at sea. He realized how much he depended upon the vinegary soul who lay there with paper-white skin.

I love the man, that's all, isn't it. He's a brother to me.

As the minutes dragged on, Llewellyn stared at Kilvert's still form and gradually began to doze. He was awakened when Sister Claire touched his shoulder again. Llewellyn leaned back in his chair and covered his face while she closed Josiah Kilvert's eyes and drew the sheet up over his head.

"WHAT DID YOU tell him?" said Master yet again. "I saw you talking, what did you say?"

"Nothing!"

"Liar. How else did he know your name?"

They were in the guest house; Mrs. Andrews was packing their things.

"It was a policeman, wasn't it?" said Master.

A blush suffused Tom's freckled face and Decimus laughed bitterly.

"I can always tell. What did he say to you? Answer me, or I'll have your tongue out!"

"He said my mother came to him; she sent him to find me and he did."

Master looked to the heavens, breathing heavily and shaking his head. Then he spoke to Mrs. Andrews in an urgent undertone. She took Tom out to the pump in the yard, stripped him, and washed the black dye from his hair, the black running in streams down his naked body while he shivered with fear. When she'd dried him off, she took him inside and gave him clothes that were made, he realized, for some kind of servant. She pulled a rough cap down over his wet hair, which was now an indeterminate, dirty color.

At the train station there was a bustle of people coming and going as the light failed. An Oxford fog was drifting in, and the lamplighter was summoning an indistinct glow from one lamp to the next along the platform. Decimus propelled Tom furiously before him: a prosperous gentleman with a recalcitrant servant. The London-bound train slowly entered the station, its headlamp lighting up the pendant fog. Expelling gusts of steam, the locomotive came to a halt. Decimus pushed Tom up the steps and onto the train, propelling him down the corridor and into an empty compartment. He thrust the boy onto a seat and sat close to him.

"Do you still not comprehend the opportunities I'm giving you? To be my protégé, my inheritor?"

The voices of other passengers rose just outside the compartment door. Decimus suddenly produced one of the knitting needles Tom had taken from the old woman's bag and pressed it to the boy's throat. "Say one word to anyone and I'll push it right through." The needle vanished; Master unfolded a newspaper and pretended to read as a middle-aged couple entered the compartment. A whistle blew and the train groaned into motion. As the train slowly accelerated, the fog pressed against the window, swirling, and Tom thought he might be drowning.

• • •

LONDON

It was raining. The household in Half Moon Street was waiting for them, it seemed. John Getalong opened the door wordlessly, and Belinda stood just inside, silent and watchful, her hair every which way, as though she had been pulled recently out of bed and sleep. Hamlet and Mrs. Hamlet stood at the top of the kitchen stairs, staring. There was a warm aroma of cooking from below, roasted fowl, perhaps.

"Children," said Decimus, letting Getalong help him off with his wet coat, "did you miss me?"

Each of them nodded solemnly.

"It feels as though I've been gone a month or more."

"Water's hot, sir," croaked Hamlet.

"And supper on the hob!" cried Decimus. "Mrs. H., it smells delicious."

"Who heated the bath, then?" grumbled Hamlet. "But do I get any thanks?" His wife jabbed him savagely in the ribs, but Decimus appeared delighted.

"You melancholy Dane, I've missed even you!" His face abruptly assumed a sorrowful expression. "Tom here will *not* be joining me for my homecoming meal, alas. He is, I'm sorry to say, a liar and a thief. Nevertheless, we don't turn on our former friends; we strive to improve them, do we not, children?"

The assembly nodded their heads, all eyes on Tom. Getalong chuckled aloud and then coughed to cover it.

"Tom will be staying on the top floor with Mary Do-Not, in hopes that she can correct his ungrateful ways."

Blinky gasped.

"If he is able to rejoin us at some point, so much the better. If he is not, well, let that be a lesson to you."

Tom, the wet dripping off him and chilled through, was determined not to show his considerable terror.

"Off you go, Tom! Three flights up, then the little steps beyond. I can trust you this far, can I not? You won't compel me to lead you by the hand?"

Tom shook his head.

"Knock thrice and then once again. Mary loves a surprise, and tonight you're it." Tom set his face toward the darkness above and began to climb. The image in Tom's mind of Mary Do-Not had assumed grotesque proportions. She was a monster. A witch, a hag, a cannibal.

It's me or her i'n'it. Right, no holds barred, then.

He knocked three times and then a fourth. After a silence he heard a rustle from within, a chair scraping, and footsteps. He clenched his fists and the door opened.

She was tiny. No more than five feet tall. A year or two older than Tom, perhaps. She wore a frilly pink-and-white dressing gown, which she clutched modestly about her throat, and pale pink satin slippers on her feet. Flaxen hair peeked from under a pink-and-white nightcap. She was exquisite, a china doll. There was a quick tentative smile and then a ducking of her head.

"You're new, aren't you." The voice was high and soft. "You're to stay, then? Like the other one?" She looked over Tom's shoulder and down the dark staircase. "I don't have much to offer. They below haven't sent much up today or yesterday. Has *he* been away? The bread is dry, I'm afraid, but I have a cheese on the shelf there, still in its paper, and you're welcome to it. Goodness, you're wet through. Well, come along!"

Tom took a deep breath and walked in. The garret was long and narrow and lit dimly by candles. At one end was a divan beneath the eaves. At the other was a small bed, done up in lace and frill. There were two windows. Before one of them was a table with an ink pot and quills and a prodigiously tall stack of paper. It was all neat as a pin.

"What is the o'clock, do you know?" she said, closing the door. Tom's fists clenched again. "I promise myself that I will keep faithful track of the hours, and then, like that, they've got away from me once more. I'm working, you see. He below keeps me well supplied with ink and quill and paper—I have no complaints in *that* regard. I should have put numbers to the pages, but then, if I'm honest, when I began I didn't *know* I was beginning anything, I didn't know I would be here such a long time or that I would be writing quite so much. So it is, the pages, like the hours of the days and nights, come and go unremarked by me, unnumbered, unnamed. If I should ever upset the pile, God forbid, I should have a difficult time putting them together again in the way they should go!"

Mary Do-Not laughed a little tinkling laugh, but then her smile vanished.

"Poor boy, do you mean to fight me?"

Tom didn't know what to say. He glanced down and saw that his fists were still fiercely balled and his feet braced.

"You're frightened. They have told you things about me." She sighed and moved to the window before the desk. She laid her palm against the rain-spattered, night-blackened pane. "For years now people have said the unkindest things." She turned back to Tom, tears in her eyes. "Does it seem fair to you?"

She began to pace. "You would never know it today, but I come of respectable folk. *Do-Not!* My name is not *Do-Not*, certainly. It is *Withers*. My mother died of the fever when I was a child, but she and Father were in service in a fine household and much appreciated, everyone said so. Father saw to it his girls were able to read and write and do their sums, and I learned so much from Cook, who taught me all I know of the kitchen. Life was *good*. But things can go so badly, so quickly. Remember this, young man: life can and does change in a moment, in the twinkling of an eye."

Tom looked at the tiny, pacing figure intently. She had just put into words the bitter lesson Tom had learned only recently; it was as fresh and sharp as a knife. He nodded fervently, but she didn't notice. As she moved, the candles made her shadow long and short by turns.

"After Cook died, I became kitchen maid to the new cook and worked as hard and well as ever I could. In just a matter of months, though, many of the family sickened and several perished, one after another. Father died. To my horror, our household broke up. I feared I would starve. Then young Mr. Thomas of our first household got me placed in another, thank God. This family was not a happy one, but I am a hard worker and gave satisfaction, I like to think, before they fell ill. I took a position with another family after that, but it was no good. The typhoid galloped over the land and took so many."

Mary paused again before the window, brushing the tears as fast as they came.

"All I want is to go back into service. To be placed with a good master and a kind mistress and a household of children—oh, it would be heaven. But no—people decided that I was a pariah, that *I* was the bringer of misfortune! Absurd! Then he below heard of me and took me in and I was thrilled for a time because I thought I was to cook for the house and make myself useful." She shook her head, drying her eyes with a square of linen. Her voiced hardened. "Instead, I am closeted here, almost always alone. My food comes up on a tray from below and my slops go down in a pot."

Confused as Tom was, he was struck through the heart by the young woman's pain, and her beauty. While Tom stood dumbly, Mary took a towel and a white bedcover from a wardrobe and laid them on the divan. She retraced her steps, this time carrying a porcelain chamber pot from the wardrobe and sliding it beneath the long couch, blushing, with her eyes demurely averted. She said she regretted she had no dry clothes suitable for a young man but laid a red silk robe with the other things on the long couch and then seated herself at the desk, leaving Tom to himself. He was shivering.

"Is the door not locked, then?" he said.

"No door is locked save his. But no one moves in this household without him below knowing of it. Everyone here is a spy. Everyone."

She picked up the quill and dipped it in the ink pot. "Dry yourself or you'll be ill. Sleep. I'm going to work for a bit." She looked up at him. "What is your name?"

"Tom. What do you write, Miss Withers?"

The quill already was moving across the paper. "It is a history of the world."

Tom pulled off his wet clothes and wrapped himself in the sheer scarlet robe. He sat on the divan, watching Mary write. He found himself nodding with exhaustion. He swung his legs up, pulled the thin white blanket to his chin, and slept.

PART III

22

OXFORD

The fog thickened in the night and settled in to stay. By morning the bells of the university town, ringing their changes, were muffled by the dense wet air. Charles Field awoke in a cell with an aching head and possibly a broken rib or two. There was a man standing on the other side of the barred door, looking at him.

"Good morning, Inspector Field. It's *me*, Sergeant Willette."

Field nodded and lights flashed painfully through his skull.

"You have caused quite a stir, I must say. Are you in much pain?"

Field shook his head no and wished he hadn't.

"You're being released into my care. There's some paperwork to be got through first. Your constable Llewellyn is making a statement, he'll be along."

"Constable Kilvert?" His lips were swollen; his speech was thick.

"Llewellyn is here, sir."

"Kilvert?"

Willette hesitated. "Your superior, Commissioner Mayne, has sent word. I'm to send you packing, sir. You're to desist in your activities and return to town. It seems the commissioner had a strongly worded note from the Earl of Derby, Mr. Field. That's the chancellor of the bloody university, in case you were unaware."

"Where is Kilvert?"

Again there was a moment's pause. "It's because of that situation, sir, that I'm inclined to defer Commissioner Mayne's directive, at least temporarily. This is, in fact, *my* patch, not his. I'll give you a day, Field, if you want it."

"Kilvert?"

"I am very, very sorry, sir."

Field dropped his head into his hands. There was a jangle of keys and the squeal of the barred door swinging open. The inspector looked up and saw an elderly jailer and, beside him, Sam Llewellyn, looking ashen.

"Josiah is on his way to Kidwelly, sir. His people will be waiting for him at the station."

"Did he speak . . . ?"

"Sang or whispered a song or two. I don't think he knew he'd been stabbed."

Field nodded. He started to stand, then sat again, grasping his side. As he gingerly explored the painful area, his fingers discovered something in a waistcoat pocket.

"What have you got there, sir?" asked Llewellyn.

Piece of paper, neatly folded. No, it's a five-pound note, that's what.

Field opened it. An unschooled hand had written in pencil on the bill, carefully folded it, and tucked it into his waistcoat while they were together in the library.

Missus Andrus, it said. Just below that was scratched *Gates*.

"This is from our boy, Tom," said Field, giving it to Llewellyn. "Let's get moving."

"Now?" said Willette. "Sir, the police surgeon is going to patch you up before you go anywhere."

"The lad considered these three words sufficiently important to risk his life, not to mention sacrificing a great deal of money. There is no damn time to waste!"

"Fortunately, Field, I am in a position to insist."

The inspector submitted himself to the ministrations of the surgeon and emerged with an array of sticking plasters about his head. With the assistance of Sergeant Willette, they discovered there were currently two Mrs. Andrews residing in Oxford: one who was nearly ninety years old and living with her daughter; the other, the owner of a guest house. But that lady, according to the woman who kept a shop next door, had closed up the night before and gone off. Where, the shopkeeper had no idea.

"She stopped her eggs again," said the woman, "that's all I know. Mrs. Andrews is always going off, she's forever stopping 'er eggs, the witch."

"A witch, is she?" said Field.

"Everyone says so, and not just along of them warts she's got sprouting out her nose and chin. She's a witch to her core, she is. Mean as a snake!"

Llewellyn put his elbow deftly through a glass pane in the front door of the guest house and let them in. They found, in a bedroom above, a pair of boy's dress trousers with their pockets inside out and a boy's waistcoat with its small side pockets sliced open. A single knitting needle and a thin watch chain lay on the counterpane. In the little court behind, they found a still-moist stream of blacking, which led from the pump to the drains.

"I don't like the slit pockets," said Field.

"The boy was in trouble," said Llewellyn, and Field nodded grimly.

"Strange sort of guest house Mrs. Andrews keeps," said Sergeant Willette, turning the pages of a large register. "No entries more recent than October of '59."

"Perhaps she has an independent income," said Field. "Let's tackle the bishop, shall we?"

"Bishop *Wilberforce*?" said the sergeant. "What exactly is it you are investigating?"

"The links of a chain, Sergeant. D' you want to come along?"

"Sir," said Llewellyn, "the service for the Gates boy is about to begin. I wonder if I might attend, sir. I know Mr. Kilvert intended to do so."

"Yes, yes, you go on. Sergeant Willette and I will interview the bishop."

"Thank you, sir."

"When you've paid your respects, see if you can find where Captain FitzRoy has got to. Then don't wait for me—get back to town and onto that groom of yours at the palace. I don't want the royal couple to move an inch without we know about it."

"Yes, sir."

Sergeant Willette looked sharply at Field. "Is this something to do with the recent attempt on Her Majesty's life?"

"Quite possibly, Sergeant. Off you go, Sam."

AT CHRIST CHURCH, Sergeant Willette overcame objections at the porter's lodge and ushered Field into the vestry, where Bishop Wilberforce was dressing for the morning service. Wilberforce was aghast at the sight of the bruised policeman.

"Inspector, whatever has befallen *you*?"

Field thrust his face into the bishop's. "This is nothing. Other folk who come a-nigh you and your friends seem to die violent deaths, so we'd like to know what's going on and who's responsible."

"What in heaven's name are you talking about?"

"Inspector Field," said Willette, "if I might?" The sergeant interposed himself between the detective and the cleric. "According to the porter, you've had friends staying here during the past week."

Wilberforce's hands were working each other. "Not *friends*, exactly. I wouldn't describe them as *friends*, Officer." Field darted a sharp, triumphant glance at Willette, his eyes gleaming. "Colleagues, perhaps," continued the bishop. "Acquaintances."

Field was nose to nose with the bishop again. "I'm not in the mood, your Reverence, for the parsing of words. Three blokes ate, drank, and slept in your quarters for the past week, and while that may not amount to friendship in your world, it's enough to make you a person of interest in mine!"

"Are you mad? What are you talking about?"

"One of them *acquaintances*, FitzRoy by name, told young Mr. Gates that he desired the death of Charles Darwin. Soon after, David Gates is found with his head bashed in. And now there's my own man, a respected and valiant officer of the Metropolitan Police, killed dead at the museum whilst you're going on about the natural order of things. When you wish to make a clean breast of it all, your lordship, I will be entirely available."

Field turned and left the vestry. Willette made a bow and followed him out. The bells ceased ringing, and within the cathedral the processional began, the white-robed boys and men moving down the central aisle behind the crucifix, wreathed in clouds of fragrant smoke from the censer, which swung in front.

The bishop managed to get through his homily, which was, in fact, devoted to extolling the natural order imbued by the Creator to all creation. Throughout, his eyes kept straying to the bandaged interloper who had managed to seat himself among the undergraduates, just above the choir. Visible below the bandages on his head, the inspector's eyes, resolute and implacable, were locked on Wilberforce.

The bishop ended his sermon and took his seat. The voices of the choir made the high, vaulted arches ring.

All things bright and beautiful,
All creatures great and small,
All things wise and wonderful,
The Lord God made them all.

The bishop's glance moved to the inspector, who stared back, unblinking. Wilberforce closed his eyes in fervent prayer, but when he opened them again the inspector was still staring. All right, he would speak with the officer after the service. He would be forthright. After all, he had nothing to hide. He knew nothing of any killings, certainly. Surely it was not conspiratorial to oppose Darwin? It was not a crime, surely, to have interceded with the Queen about a knighthood for the man?

Perhaps, the bishop reflected, he would *not* mention that to the policeman. It was confidential, after all. Between him and his monarch. It belonged to the past. He closed his eyes again.

The rich man in his castle,
The poor man at his gate,
God made them, high or lowly,
And ordered their estate.

At the finish of the hymn the policeman's eyes were still on him, as he knew they would be. Try as the bishop might to quell them, it was of no use. The tears came coursing down his face and would not stop.

23

LONDON

Tom Ginty opened his eyes. Muffled cries from the street below suggested that it might be morning, or nearly. He lay still, covered by the thin white blanket the china doll had given him, which he saw bore a stencil in one corner that read ST. BARTHOLOMEW'S HOSPITAL. He knew that name. St. Bart's was just round the corner from the Fortune of War. Tom looked up at the young woman.

She sat at the table, holding in her right hand a quill pressed pensively to her lips. Her nightcap was off, her golden hair spread over her shoulders. Had she been sitting so all night, had she not slept? Tom peered down the room. No, there was a distinct dent in the pillow, although the bedclothes were crisp and taut. Suddenly Mary stirred and looked at Tom. She smiled and bent over the page again, her quill scratching on.

Tom pulled the scarlet dressing gown close about himself.

"If I'm here long enough," said Tom in a voice still thick with sleep, "I could do up the numbers."

"I beg your pardon, Tom?"

"I could put numbers to your pages."

Mary gazed at him thoughtfully. "If you're here long enough, that would be very nice. I began with Genesis and from there I'm trying to find my way to the present age, so you see it's a long road I'm on."

Tom nodded vigorously and Mary resumed her work.

"Him below sent another up to stay with me," she said. "His name was Rendell. I did not care for him; I was frightened the whole time he was here. He was mad, I'm quite sure of it. I believe the master thinks of it as a test to stay with me, though for whom I'm not sure—for the guest or for me?" She laughed her barely audible tinkling laugh and Tom's heart raced.

"Master is mad, too, Tom, I'm sorry to say." Mary dipped her quill in the pot and wrote briefly before pausing again. "You should know," she continued, not looking at him, "he thinks you're likely to take sick and die up here."

From where he sat, Tom reached for the cheese in the cupboard.

"I do know that, Mary," he said. "You do not astonish me in the least." He broke the cheese into two large pieces and ate his half ravenously.

At the same moment, on the foggy street three stories below, the master stepped into a hansom cab, wooden kit in hand, looking brushed and scrubbed and shining. "Lincoln's Inn Fields, driver," he said briskly. "Royal College of Surgeons."

FIELD CAME DOWN from Oxford on the early train. His first stop was an address in the Mall given him by the bishop, the town residence of Sir Jasper Arpington-Dix.

Fancy that. It was just round this corner that little Stevie Patchen got his throat cut for him and his ear took off.

The servant at the door surveyed Field—his clothes disheveled and torn, his head bandaged—and informed him that Sir Jasper was out.

"Be so good as to tell Sir Jasper that a policeman is calling." Field brushed past the butler and into the marble hall. "Tell him that my lord, the bishop of Oxford, sent me."

"Sir," said the butler, "I must ask you to leave immediately."

"Ha! I see someone lurking in the library. Is that you, Sir Jasper?"

Sir Jasper emerged, leaning on his stick and limping. "Police?" he barked. "What do I care for the police? What's Wilberforce been telling you?"

"A law unto yourself, are you, sir?"

"In the Punjab you had to be."

"We are in *London* currently, but don't let's quibble over details. I remember you, sir. From the great debate. You were there up front with the toffs. As was a tall fair-haired man who stuck a thin blade into one of the Metropolitan's finest men and killed him dead. You wouldn't know anything about that, now, would you?"

"Not a thing. Get out."

"Eyes like the darkest abyss. I suspect the same fellow of putting a fatal dent in the head of an Oxford undergraduate by the name of Gates."

"What's that to me? Now get out, or do I have to complain to your superior, Sir Richard Mayne?"

"Friend of yours, is he?"

"Bosom."

"Lucky you. Philip David Rendell—ever heard of him? Tried to shoot the Queen a few weeks ago?"

"Lewis?" said Sir Jasper to the servant. "Show the man out. Summon the police if you need to."

"Ducks, I *am* the police!"

Sir Jasper turned and went back into his library, slamming the door after him.

With an aggressive smile, Field seized the butler's hand and pressed a calling card into it. "I'll call again."

His next stop was Lincoln's Inn Fields and the Royal College of Surgeons.

"You remember me, don't you, Professor?" said Field.

Sir Richard Owen sat behind his desk, his hands in an attitude of prayer, finger-tips touching his pursed lips.

"Indeed."

"The bishop was kind enough to sit down with me after Sunday's service. He was distressed, sir. He was agitated, he needed to unburden his soul. So we had ourselves a chin wag."

Owen regarded him in stony silence.

"Wonderful stuff, natural philosophy. The evolutionists versus the . . . whatever you lot call yourselves. If I was to have another life-time offered me, I don't know but what I'd seriously look to pursuing the untold mysteries of the natural world."

"And what did my friend the bishop have to say?"

"Oh! *You* know, this and that. Good God, the man can talk once he makes up his mind to do so. Sir, do you recall me telling the bishop about the tragic death of one of his students, David Gates?"

"I do."

"Did you ever clap eyes on the chap?"

"Not that I know of."

"Odd. Young Gates was hanging about the bishop's study just days ago whilst you were reminiscing—this, according to the bishop, you understand—reminiscing humorously about a negro's head you once removed and stole. That would be the young Mr. Gates. Subsequently dead of a blow to the skull."

"Ah, yes. I did just glimpse the young man."

There were three knocks at the glass door of the professor's office and then a fourth a moment later. Field saw reflected in the cheval glass near the fire a tall shadow on the frosted door pane, but Owen made no move to respond.

"Don't mind me, Professor," said the inspector. "Do go ahead—I'm perfectly content to wait."

Owen remained where he was, but Field noticed a flaring of his nostrils and a quickening of respiration. Field rose and moved to the door.

"Please," said Owen, "do not disturb yourself!"

"No trouble at all, Professor."

Field seized the knob and pulled the door open. There was no one there. He quickly stepped out into the corridor, looking from one end to the other. A short bald man was walking slowly away, a stack of ledgers in his arms.

"You, there!" shouted Field. The man stopped and turned, revealing a neatly trimmed graying beard and thick spectacles.

"Sir?" replied the man, looking puzzled.

"Did you not just now knock at this door?"

"No, sir."

Field looked up and down the hall again and then realized that Owen was standing directly behind him in the door.

"That will do, Harris," said Owen, and the man with the ledgers continued on his way. "Mr. Field, what precisely is your business here? Is this an official inquiry?"

"Call it whatever you bloody well like."

"I *beg* your pardon?"

"One of my best men was cut by someone who knew how to cut. Punctured and drained of blood. Killed dead by someone, Professor, with the skill of a surgeon. I'm guessing that you know very well who I'm talking about."

"Do you realize who I am, Officer? Do you know with whom I am in daily intercourse? Commissioner Mayne, for one."

"Good Lord, how that man must get around—*everyone's* mad for him! So. How would you go about draining a living body of blood? You *are* a surgeon, I believe."

Owen surrendered a brief acidic smile. "I am an anatomist. As such, I have extensive surgical experience. Vast, I should say. But I am not a surgeon, Mr. Field."

"It's *Detective Inspector* Field, actually."

"It is for now."

The inspector put his face close to the professor's. "'Do you think I'm easier to be played on than a pipe?' That's Shakespeare, sir."

Field turned brusquely and walked away down the corridor, Owen staring after him. Finally he turned back into his office. After a moment a communicating door near the bookcases opened and the Chorister entered.

"Ah, yes," said Owen. "Decimus."

Decimus inclined his head toward the outer door. "Mr. Bucket needs tending to."

"You recognized him, did you?"

"At Oxford. He came close."

"Never mind, I think we can manage the man, thank you. Mr. Cobb, you have been, if I may say it, somewhat *too* active of late."

Decimus stiffened.

"Am I to understand that you . . . interfered with a policeman?"

"One of Bucket's men."

"Good God. Were your actions concerning the policeman *strictly* necessary?"

"The man saw and recognized the instrument used on the student, Gates."

Suddenly Owen was shouting. "And whose fault was that? Whatever possessed you to hang on to the bloody walking stick? Surely you could have thought of a safe place to stash your damned *instrument*!"

Decimus smiled. "I can indeed, sir," he said, his eyes suggestively running up and down the professor's body. Owen's heart raced; he softened his tone.

"In any event, we have determined, Sir Jasper and I, that our aims will be best served by taking a different course. We wish to thank you for all your help, of course."

Decimus stared, unmoving and expressionless.

"I didn't intend to raise my voice, Mr. Cobb. The detective's visit was upsetting."

Still Decimus said nothing.

"Very well, then, Mr. Cobb," said Owen.

"Germany?" said Decimus softly.

"No, sir," said the professor, as firmly as he could. "No longer on."

"Sir Jasper agrees?"

"This, my dear man, is his decision."

"And you concur, Sir Richard?"

Owen took a deep breath and said, "Yes."

"I will need to speak with Sir Jasper."

"Mr. Cobb," said Owen, "I'm confident the Royal College will continue to rely upon your . . . remarkable skills, as it always has done. Likewise St. Bart's and St. Thomas'."

Decimus ignored the suggestion. "We had discussed admonishing Mr. Huxley."

"No! I mean to say, there's no need, my dear man. I may have spoken rashly."

"But I have a plan, sir."

"Not necessary, thank you."

Decimus fell silent again.

"Thank you, Mr. Cobb. That will be all."

The clock on the mantel tick-tocked with agonizing slowness before Decimus finally turned and left the Hunterian Professor of Anatomy to contemplate his own transgressions.

ALONG THE RIVER Thames, the ebb tides each day brought forth swarms of ragged creatures who waded into the filth and sewage exposed by the receding waters, searching for anything of value that might be salvaged and sold. *Mudlarks*, they were called. Many were children. Not surprisingly, they stank.

One of these, a small boy called Button, opened his eyes reluctantly, awaking to a new day on the riverbank. Button was roughly ten years old, skinny, short, and cross-eyed. His hair was a tangled, matted mess. He yawned and turned over in the barrel that had been his bed in the night, surveying the prospect before him with a sigh. Fog clung to the river's surface. The tide was receding, but who could spot a treasure in the muck, if there were any, with the fog hanging so low? Button considered having another go at sleep, but an uncomfortable vacancy in his belly sent a stronger signal to his brain. The boy crawled out, had a stretch and a pee, and waded in.

He moved slowly and cautiously. The Thames was dangerous and unpredictable. Where there were shallow waters yesterday, a treacherous underwater ditch may have opened today. Riverboats, large and small, were out there, somewhere, but entirely invisible. In a fog like this noises could be misleading, sounding close at hand when their source was actually far off, and distant when they were looming dangerously near. As Button's feet stirred the fetid river bottom, gulls swooped and dived, screaming just above his head.

His foot struck the leather pouch before he'd gone five yards. Coated in slime, it had lodged against a rotted spar on the bottom. Groping about, Button found that the pouch had a handle or strap. He seized it in one hand and grabbed the body of the pouch with the other, gently easing it free from the jagged wood. The boy did a preliminary grope inside. It was heavy, filled with silt and muck and some wadded, muddied papers at the bottom. Button drew a sudden breath and abruptly stood upright. The ship's spar had also caught a man. The hand, which seemed to cling to the splintery wood, looked more or less hand-like, but the mass of swollen flesh it led to, floating sluggishly near the surface, was a bloated parody of humanity. The head lolled, bobbing slightly in the shallow water. An eel had attached itself where the left ear used to be. The insignia on the distended jacket was still visible. Button couldn't read, but he had seen these same words before, on the facade of a massive building off Moorgate Street: ELECTRIC TELEGRAPH COMPANY.

"Blimey," said Button.

He looked round furtively, made certain he was curtained from view by the fog, and then quickly started going through the bloated corpse's pockets. He considered himself a businessman. He liked to think he knew to the farthing what he was apt to get for the merchandise he flogged riverside. He knew all the potential buyers by name: the low-life receivers of scavenged or stolen goods who would in turn sell them to others, who would sell them to others still. The merchandise, if it had any genuine worth to begin with, would rise in price and respectability with each sale. Button knew the large leather pouch he'd pulled from the Thames signified, by his standards, a life-changing fortune. For this reason, the boy made the bold and foolish decision to eliminate the middlemen.

He cleaned the wad of soggy, muck-smeared blue papers that he had taken from the bottom of the pouch, wiping them with a rag. These he hid in a tin box beneath his sleeping barrel. Then he eased the big leather pouch into the filthy cloth carry-all he wore when scavenging. He moved furtively inland with his leather treasure hidden in the bag, searching for a pump in a quiet back street. He found what he wanted in the stable yard of a small priory in Southwark. The fog was now his friend, shielding him from covetous eyes. Button cleaned the pouch with assiduous care, using the water sparingly, daubing at the leather with a bit of cloth, all the time trying to decide how much his asking price should be. When he was satisfied with the merchandise, he put *himself* under the pump and had a good scrub. The dense fog had lifted only slightly by the time Button crossed the river and presented himself at the imposing front door of the Electric Telegraph Company, Nos. 12–14 Telegraph Street, off Moorgate.

The uniformed doorman, without even seeing what Button had in the bag, slammed shut the big brass door. Button made his way round to the tradesmen's entrance and gave the porter there a peek at the contents of the carry-all, whereupon he was yanked into the building and shoved into the porter's small office. Before he knew what was happening, a trio of terrifying, black-frocked businessmen had appeared and were staring at him, talking in rapid whispers among each other. Button soon was pulled from that office and marched up two flights of steps into a room so large it staggered him. The ceiling, high above, was a series of massive skylights. Below, the room was filled with women seated at high benches, row after row of them, all of them bent over polished wooden boxes that clicked and chattered incessantly. Beneath the sound of the clicking was the low murmur of women's voices. There was a high platform in the middle of the room where a solitary man sat, overlooking all.

While his precious leather pouch was passed from one fierce man to the next and closely examined, one of Button's captors strode off to the high platform. The solitary man, after listening for a moment, looked up sharply. Mr. Apfel, manager of the Moorgate branch of the ETC, climbed down from his perch and soon stood over Button, eyeing the boy darkly. Apfel was florid and well fed, with neatly trimmed whiskers and pomaded wavy hair. He pinched the bag's opening and turned back the top lip, examining through thick spectacles the numbers embossed just inside.

"How did you come by this?"

"Seven pound, not a shilling less," said Button, his good eye fixed boldly on the wavy-haired man, while his wandering eye seemed to seek a way out.

Apfel adjusted the glasses on his nose and looked down on the boy incredulously. "What's that you said?"

"I want seven quid for it," said Button, thrusting forth his chest. "You know it's worth ten."

Apfel nodded, seeming to ponder the offer. Then he backhanded Button, knocking him to the floor. The chattering of the machines continued, but the women's low voices were suddenly stilled.

"Go out into Moorgate Street," said Apfel to one of the men, "and fetch in a policeman. Do it quickly, please, the girls have been disturbed."

A black-frocked man quickly made for the stairs as Button struggled to his feet, his fists clenched for battle. "I got friends, you know," he said with murder in both his good eye and his bad.

"No, you don't," said Apfel, and Button knew the man was right.

STEAM ROSE FROM the tub in the kitchen at No. 2 Bow Street. Jane Field dabbed at her husband's head with a hot, wet cloth, removing bandages as gently as she could.

"He was my right-hand man," said Field. "He was a pillar."

"Poor dear Mr. Kilvert," said Jane. "Whatever will you do without him?"

"I do not know, my dear. It is a loss I cannot yet fathom."

"You're all the colors of the rainbow, Mr. Field."

"It was entirely my doing. I sent them on ahead. Why didn't I keep us all together? Why did I not have a plan? I had none, Jane, and now my friend is dead."

"You did your best, Charles. You always do."

"He was with me from the beginning. He saved my life more than once. I'm not . . . Jane, I'm not clever like Mr. Bucket. I wish I was. Oh, God, I wish I was."

Field wept then, and Jane let him. When he was done, she gave him a thick towel, and he stepped out of the tub.

"You have yourself a lie-down," she said, "and I'll bring you up a nice cup of tea."

Naked and dripping, Field climbed the stairs, dabbing at himself with the towel.

There was a shriek as he passed the ground-floor landing. Field turned and saw Bessie Shoreham just behind him, one hand covering her mouth and the other holding up a brown envelope.

"Go away," said Field, glistening.

"But, sir!" she cried, waving the envelope above her head. "This just arrived by messenger for Master!"

"Do go away! *Now!*"

Bessie dropped the envelope on the landing and fled.

A little more than an hour later Charles Field awoke from a light doze. He ached in every part of his body. He noticed a teapot and a plate of biscuits on his bedside table and an envelope lying on the tray. He reached for it as his wife entered.

"Tea's cold, I'm afraid, dear—you were asleep by the time I brought it up."

"Never mind, Jane, I'm feeling better for having rested," said Field, opening the envelope with a thumb.

"I found that on the landing," said Jane. "Police commissioner's seal."

The message inside was brief.

Report to me directly. If it is at all possible for you, assault no one on the way. It will give me great pleasure to sack you in person. Yours, et cetera.

"Dear?" said Jane. "What is it?"

Field forced a smile as he climbed out of the bed. "Duty, Jane. Duty."

THE MAGISTRATE HAD to lean well over his bench to see the diminutive Button standing below. Button glared up at the judge, his intended ferocity mitigated by the wandering eye. Mr. Apfel of the Electric Telegraph Company stood nearby, impatiently awaiting justice.

"As I understand it, Mr. Apfel," said the magistrate, "the boy tried to sell some of your own property back to you."

"That's right, sir."

"He is rather a small boy, Mr. Apfel, wouldn't you say?"

Apfel shrugged, as if to say the size of boys was not a subject within his purview.

"What I am wondering is, why you didn't merely take back your fine leather bag and boot the lad out the door?"

"Sir, the bag was assigned to one of our deliverymen who went missing days ago."

"And . . .?"

"He's gone, sir! Vanished! One of our best men!"

The magistrate leaned back in his chair. "You suspect this boy . . ." The judge leaned forward over his bench again. "You say your name is Button, son?"

"Wot they all call me," said the ten-year-old.

"Yes. Mr. Apfel, you suspect Button here did away with your man?"

"Given how vicious these wastrels can be, I'd say it's entirely possible! In any event, *who* did it is not my concern, sir, it's *yours*."

"Indeed." The judge peered down at Button. "Where'd you get the bag, boy?"

"River."

"Ah, yes."

"The man was *already* drownded when I found 'im, sir, I never touched the man."

There was a sudden stillness in the room. "The man?" said the magistrate.

"He were swelled up, *that thick*!" said Button, extending his arms. "So you see, I didn't nick the thing at all, it's *mine*! How much do I get for it?"

In the course of the afternoon it was a question raised time and again by young Button, who was forced to lead a crew of constables to the site on the south bank of the Thames. Even as the police officers, with kerchiefs tied round their mouths and noses, used grappling hooks to haul the telegraph deliveryman to shore, the boy kept shouting.

"You see? I di'n't *steal* the bag, I *found it*, so it's mine!"

Something was wiggling about the corpse's head.

"Are you stupid, is *that* it?" shrieked Button.

The eel detached itself and snaked off, revealing a gaping left ear hole.

"Crikey," muttered one of the men.

"If I di'n't *steal* it, it's *mine*, all right?" Button's high voice was growing hoarse. "How thick *are* you lot, for God's sake!"

24

Sir Richard Mayne, seated behind the great desk in his office, studied his senior detective's battered face with interest. Field stood opposite, his hands clasped behind his back, staring over his superior's head out the window behind, wary of making eye contact, wary of the anger he felt simmering beneath his surface.

"Have you lost your mind?" asked Mayne. "Is that it?"

"Not yet, sir. Not altogether, in any case, I hope."

"Look, you simply cannot go messing about with people of this rank and caliber, Field! The chancellor of the university wants me to bring you up on charges! I mean, what in God's name do you think you are doing?"

"We lost Kilvert, sir."

"*Lost* is the appropriate word, I would say. I hold you responsible for a good man's needless death, Mr. Field."

Since the inspector was of the same opinion, he said nothing.

"Come, Charles," said the commissioner in a gentler tone, "I am as cut up about Kilvert as the next man. So find his killer and bring him to justice, and leave the gentry alone!"

"And if the gentry are involved? There's a connection here, sir, if only I could see it. Patchen, Rendell, Gates, Kilvert. The Queen."

"The *Queen*, oh yes!" The commissioner shook his head and sighed. "Charles, you have your strong points. I hope you'll not take it amiss if I say that you didn't get where you are today by *thinking*, and this is no time to begin."

Field felt the heat rise to the top of his head.

"Stick to what you know best, Charles. Intimidation. The strong arm. Putting the fear of the hangman into the heart of the wrongdoer. This is your métier, my good man."

Field forced himself to think of his wife and count ten. "Your note said I'm sacked."

Commissioner Mayne thought for a moment. Field had won acclaim for a number of successful prosecutions over the years. The Palmer poisonings had caught the imagination of the country a decade earlier. Field's protection of Lord Lytton and his theatrical production, *Not So Bad As We Seem*, from the wrath of Lady Lytton had won favorable attention in aristocratic circles. The public knew nothing of the entire Nightingale affair, thank God, but Field's work there had been impressive and wide-ranging, to say the least. Overriding all these considerations was the most salient argument in Field's favor: if Mayne dismissed him, the commissioner would be known to the nation as the man who had shown *Inspector Bucket* the door. No, it was impossible. He would have to consider mollifying responses to Sir Richard Owen and the Earl of Derby.

"You do have *legitimate* irons in the fire, don't you, Inspector Field? Ordinary criminals and the like? Apprehend them. Bring them to justice. This is all we ask of you."

"I'm not sacked, then?"

"No, Charles, you're not sacked," said Mayne with an indulgent, avuncular smile.

"And if I take and pitch you out that window?"

The commissioner was silent for a moment. "It was Dickens did this to you," he said at last. "Gave you ideas above your station, didn't he."

"Dickens? Not him, sir. I'd say the greater influence on my current thinking would be Mr. Karl Marx."

"Karl Marx? Indeed."

"Indeed, sir. Herr Marx urged me personally to stop waiting beneath your bloody table for the bleeding crumbs to fall."

"*Personally*, I see. Because of your celebrity, I imagine."

"Shall I open the window first or leave it as it is?"

"Get out."

"Right, then."

Field turned and left, stumbling down the stairs and out into the street, the folly of what he'd just done to himself rolling over him like a crushing wave. Oblivious to carriages and horses, he rushed across the road toward the Eagle and Child. Just coming out of the public house was a thin man with a broad expanse of forehead, bun-shaped wings of hair on either side of his head, and a beard like a tangled wire brush.

"Inspector Field!"

"Mr. Dickens!" said Field, trying to gather his wits. "How do you do, sir?'

"I'd do a damn site better if you'd stop passing yourself off as one of my creations!"

"I . . . I beg your pardon?"

"Everywhere I go I hear stories of you cashiering on my good name. Mr. Bucket is an *invention*, do you understand? An invention! He's a character whom I created! I mean, for God's sake, have you nothing better to do than to leech off my fame?"

Before the inspector could take in what the great novelist had said, Dickens was gone, Field staring off after him. He couldn't bring himself to walk into the Eagle and Child. It was as if the entire world had witnessed his public shaming. Never mind that what the man said was blatantly untrue.

It is *untrue, isn't it? God help me, it* is *untrue, it has to be!*

He couldn't go home, he couldn't face his exquisite, innocent wife after what he'd just done to their lives. He couldn't go back in and apologize to the commissioner, he couldn't return to the building that had been his home for so many years—the best part of his life, the very best. He had exiled himself to the void, with no one to blame but himself.

Inspector Field started walking.

AFTER SEARCHING ONE public house after another, Llewellyn finally discovered Field in the Fortune of War, standing unsteadily at the bar. A nearly empty bottle of whiskey stood at his elbow. Field's head jerked up when Llewellyn said his name.

"Hallo, Sam," he said.

"What have you gone and done, sir?"

Field shrugged and smiled wanly. "Temper got the better of me. Drink?"

"What about Josiah Kilvert's killer, then? What about all of it? You're just walking away?"

Mickie Goodfellow approached with a freshly pulled pint of beer. "How d'you do, Officer? Our friend here has had a few—I'll trust you to keep him in line."

Goodfellow set the glass before Llewellyn and moved off, down the bar.

"Like you asked, I tracked down FitzRoy," said Llewellyn. "Works on the Board of Trade doing weather forecasting, went direct from Oxford to the Channel Islands."

"If that nutter is calling the weather, it's no wonder they always get it wrong."

"Very amusing, Mr. Field. Then I had a word with Peter Sims, our friend in the royal stables. Sims says the royal couple are off to Germany come September. You see, I was engaged doing my job as per your requests, sir, and in the meanwhile setting up a fund for Josiah's aged parents. So what am I supposed to do now? Do you not know that *I'm* going to catch it because of what you done? Everybody knows that Llewellyn belongs to Field—the bloke who told the commissioner to stuff it!"

"Line them up, Sam, the corpses, one by one. Stevie Patchen. The shooter, Rendell. The young student, David Gates. Josiah Kilvert. They have a story to tell us, Sam. They're fair desperate to tell us how they all link up to the plot against Her Majesty the Queen, or they'll never have no peace."

"You're drunk, Mr. Field."

"Start with Kilvert. Up front in that library they're arguing for and against Mr. Darwin's notions, do we come from monkeys or not. In the middle of that, Kilvert must have spotted our killer. What would make Kilvert so certain of his man? What did he do or say to him? Kilvert must have posed such a threat to the man that he had to top him then and there. And why is the killer at this debate in the first place? What's the link? That's the problem."

"Your problem, the way I see it, is how are you going to feed your wife and keep a roof over her head now you've lost your position!"

Martha Ginty slammed a tray of empty glasses on the bar. "He says he's seen my Tom. So where is he? He's the police—why don't he bring me back my boy? If this is the police, what good is the police?"

Goodfellow moved quickly along the bar. "All right, Martha. That'll do. You heard what the officer said: he had your boy by the hand, but he went off. If Tom wanted to come, he would have come, but he didn't want to, did he?" She glared at her employer and the policemen. Then she pulled off her apron, threw it onto the bar, and pushed her way out of the tavern.

"Well," said Goodfellow, "at least I'm shut of Martha Ginty. She's gone off her nut, you ask me." He leaned across the bar. "Listen, old friend, if you ever find yourself in a bind, you come to me."

"I'm not in a bind."

"I'm just saying, as the proprietor of a public house hard by Smithfield, I could use a good man. A guard, like. A protector. These are dangerous times."

"You want to engage me?" said Field, incredulously.

"I pay well, Charlie. Far better than the Metropolitan, I think you'd find."

"When all the rivers in all of hell are crusted over with ice and adorned with skating fairies, I'll be sure to knock you up for a position, Mickie."

Goodfellow colored. "See, this is why you find yourself in a bind, old friend, no matter what you say. You've an irritable nature." Goodfellow moved down the bar again.

Llewellyn shook his head in disgust. "He's right, you know. Does Mrs. Field know what you've done?"

"Sod off," said Field, suddenly dangerous. The two men stared at each other for a long moment; Field was the first to look away.

"I'm a bloody fool, Sam. Always was. No better than my old man, and *he* was no good whatsoever. I always needed someone to think well of me 'cause *he* bloody well wasn't going to. I had to go and be a big man, I had to win praise and accolades. And then, out of the blue, Mr. Dickens put me in his magazine. And then look: he's put me in a book! I thought, *I've done it!* I'm bloody marvelous, am I not! I've got the blessing of the greats! I'm a man of stature! Well, the joy of that particular lie lasted all of an hour, didn't it. Who was I kidding? I was forever waiting for the honors to roll in, and they never did, at least not the way I thought they ought."

Llewellyn snorted. "Stop, sir, you're breaking my heart."

Inspector Field was staring off. He held up one hand. "Wait a moment."

"Why should I?"

"Dear God, it's so bloody simple," said the inspector, finally. "Waiting for the honors to roll in, that's it exactly."

"What's simple, sir?" said Llewellyn with barely suppressed impatience.

"I come from the lower orders, that is understood by all. Not the lowest; you'd have to go back to my grandfather for the *lowest*. He was a night-soil remover, did you know that, Sam? One shilling per stinking cesspit. Did you know that they set me to working with him when I was a boy? One summer I chucked it, ran to the countryside, hid in a hay mow. Farmer found me in the morning, took pity, let me stay. Let me work with him and his dogs, tending his sheep. It was bliss. I never loved anything like I loved them dogs. Then my father showed up and dragged me home. *Why?* He didn't *want* me.

"Never mind. You could say my father's rise to running his own public house was nothing short of a miracle, really. And then *I* went and edged up a rung from *him*, didn't I, when I became a constable. Promoted to detective. Then chief of detectives. Still and all, I got about as high as I could possibly go, given what I come from. And that ain't particular high. Just ask Sir Richard Mayne, commissioner of the Metropolitan, if you're unsure of that."

Llewellyn sighed deeply and shook his head.

"You seem impatient, Mr. Llewellyn. Am I keeping you?"

Field poured the last of the whiskey into his glass.

"Now, forget my old man. Forget the night-soil remover. Start over. Say I come from a monkey. And so did you. And Commissioner Mayne—him, too." He looked around the tavern. "And so did every bleeding body on the whole earth come from monkeys, and those monkeys come from God knows what—fish? Worms? Who benefits, Sam? Who gets hurt? Who likes it, and who don't?"

Llewellyn shrugged.

"I'll tell you who *don't* like it: the merchants who run the bleeding empire don't like it, not one bit. It puts every man on the same level as them, see? The rich, the poor, the light-skinned, and the dark. The bishops don't like it, nor the lords, because if Mr. Darwin has his way, where's the control? Who's in charge, who's on top and who's not? Bad for business, Mr. Darwin's notions are. But for blokes like me and you? Well, even a policeman can dream, can't he? It's not flattering, perhaps, having an orangutan as your forefather, but there's a kind of hope in it, don't you see? Last I checked, there weren't no *quality* monkeys, nor were there lower-class ones."

"And?"

"Crash, boom, Mr. Darwin brings it all down. Rule Britannia and the lot. Brings it down harder and more thorough than Mr. Marx ever dreamt in his darkest revolutionary dream."

"So why kill the Queen? Why not kill Mr. Darwin?"

"The book's out, ain't it. Nothing to be done about the book, that horse has bolted, there's no locking the stable door *now*. So what's the call to action? What's so urgent? We only just *assumed* it was the Queen who Philip Rendell was aiming for, Sam. He even *told* me it wasn't, and I didn't listen. I'm guessing the Queen don't know Darwin from Adam's off-ox. But Albert? Lover of natural philosophy and all things scientific? He's Mr. Victoria, ain't he. And even if his good wife don't care about Darwin's monkeys, Albert does. All the Prince has got to do is put a word in her ear. Round Christmastime."

"Land of my bloody fathers, the Honors List," said Llewellyn.

"The Honors List."

"Sir Charles Darwin."

"Come the New Year, that's it exactly, lad. Knighted by Her Imperial Majesty, Darwin and his theory given the blessing of the Crown. There'd be no putting *that* genie back in the bottle, not ever."

"Damn it, sir, you've got to apologize to the commissioner! You've got to get your position back!"

"I can't do that, Sam."

"They'll kill him, sir! Or the two of them together, him and the Queen both! You can't leave me holding the bloody bag!"

"I wonder, is someone grooming the Prince of Wales even now? You might look into that, Sam."

"Get stuffed, sir! You think I won't be demoted now, with you having got the sack? I won't be following no lines of inquiry. I'll be back where I started, or worse. But when Albert gets himself topped, it'll all be down to me and my incompetent ways, I'll be finished!" Llewellyn turned and pushed his way out through the crowd.

"Sam!"

Field watched Llewellyn go, and Goodfellow watched Field.

When the inspector arrived home that afternoon, having rehearsed his terrible confession, he found his wife in the kitchen, weeping silently. She was flanked by Martha Ginty and Bessie Shoreham, both of them glaring at him. The admission clearly was not needed; everything was known. He wished he were more sober, but not by much.

"I'll find another position, Mrs. Field," he said.

"A man's already been to make a list of the furniture," said Jane wonderingly. "And the landlord, giving a warning. Does somebody hate you so much, Mr. Field?"

It *was* remarkably fast work; premature, in fact. Clearly, someone's malice was behind it; Sir Richard Owen, most likely. Or maybe it was Sir Jasper Bushy-Beard.

"I'm very sorry, my dear. You have the keys to the household box; there should be enough coin in it to keep you for at least a bit. I will find work, Jane. I will provide."

He turned and left the house.

25

Blinky stared at the door set into the kitchen wall. The dumbwaiter was descending, she could hear it in the walls. It was the wrong time of day for it. The shelf always went up to the top of the house at midday, laden with food, and came down again with empty platters in the evening. Night slops arrived each morning, and Blinky was summoned to deal with the covered pot and its contents.

Blinky glanced round the kitchen. Mrs. Hamlet was sleeping on her usual stool in the corner. Hamlet himself was absent. The girl moved quietly to the dumbwaiter. Furtively, she grabbed hold of the knob, slid the door up, and there, all by itself on the shelf, was the ring she'd given Tom.

Her ten-year-old heart raced. She stared at the little circlet of gold, trying to make out what it could mean. That it was a message for her, there could be no doubt.

It meant he loved her as she hoped he might.

It meant (*no please no*) he did *not* love her.

It meant (*oh dear God no*) that the woman above had done for Tom and this was all that was left of him. Blinky snatched the ring and shut the door.

"Wot's that, then?" the voice behind her croaked. Blinky froze. How could she not have smelled Hamlet before she heard him?

"Mouse," she said.

"*You're* a mouse. Where?"

"Gone."

"Give us a cuddle, then," breathed Hamlet through the blackened stumps of his few remaining teeth.

"Mrs. Hamlet!" Blinky cried.

The woman in the corner woke with a snort, her bonnet askew. "What? Where?"

"I'll get you," whispered Hamlet venomously in Blinky's ear.

Mrs. Hamlet, coming into focus, shrieked at her helpmate. "You! Goat! Get your stinking hooves off the girl!"

"I'll give you to the master," hissed the old man quietly.

"And you, you little hussy," shrilled Mrs. Hamlet, "stop pawing at 'im, can't you?"

Hamlet whispered. "He'll have your ears off, girlie, and everything else as well!"

Mrs. Hamlet bolted off her stool and charged across the kitchen, grabbing what there was of her husband's long greasy locks and jerking hard.

"Aow!"

"Come along, goat," she said, dragging him toward a door leading off the kitchen into the back garden and the shed, which was where the couple slept. Belinda knew what *that* meant. The old buzzards' yells would change to shrieks and moans of greater intensity but equal rage, and then they would sleep.

Master was out, and John Getalong, as far as she knew. The house was quiet.

"THE GIRL IN the kitchen can help us," Tom was saying. Mary Do-Not stood at the soot-smeared window, staring out at the vague shapes of rooftops and chimney pots. Tom knew he had taken a risk, sending down the ring. He hoped his message, if it reached Blinky at all, would give her the courage to climb the stairs to the forbidden room at the top of the house.

"She can let me know when it's safe to go. Give me a signal, like. They can't all be watching *every* minute. If I can once get to the Fortune of War, my mother will fetch the Worshipful Brotherhood. The butchers won't be afraid of Master. They'll come, the butchers will set us all free."

The young woman sighed. "If you manage to go from this house, Tom, I promise you, you will never come back."

"I will do, I swear!"

Mary shook her head adamantly.

"We can take my mother and go where Master will never find us, Mary. We got family down in Dorset, he'll never know where we got to."

"You are very young," said Mary, tracing letters on the window with a finger.

"I'm not afraid. I'd do anything for you, Mary."

She turned and looked at him with a sad smile.

"Can you get me a position in service?"

Tom didn't have an answer; he wasn't entirely sure what was meant by the phrase.

Mary pulled out the chair and sat at her writing desk. "Did you know, Tom, that the Flood carried camels to these shores, riding on the rooftop of pharaoh's house?"

"What?"

"Camels. Those few that weren't on the ark, I mean. And when the Romans arrived, centuries later, they found all these camels here in England, and they thought nothing of it—it looked just like home to them!"

Tom looked at her blankly.

"So you see, Tom," she said, gently, "you may think you understand a thing when really you don't. In point of fact."

The boy was silent, trying to work out what he'd just been told. A dropping, hopeless feeling at his belly said it was all an elaborate version of the word *no*. "What happened to the camels?" he said finally.

"*I* don't know, Tom," she said. "Died out, I suppose."

A noise in the wall startled them both. The dumbwaiter was rising up from far below. It was making more racket than usual, starting and stopping in jerks. Tom and Mary stared at it in suspense. There was a final thud, near at hand. The boy took a breath and lifted the door.

Blinky, her small form squeezed onto the shelf and still gripping the rope, looked out at him fearfully. Her eyes darted to Mary and back to Tom.

"Was you wanting me?" she whispered.

CHARLES FIELD HAD heard of priests being defrocked. He thought he knew now what they felt. As an officer of the law, he had been a man set apart. Like a priest, he had been the human representative of a force that transcended the individual. He had communed with the mystery and majesty of the law, which in turn had endowed him with authority and power. Now he was bereft.

Also, he was hungry. He fingered the coins in his pockets, regretting the expense of the bottle of whiskey earlier in the day, as well as its aftereffects. He stopped at a public pump, laid his top hat carefully to one side, and put his head under. Having thus refreshed himself he continued on his way to the row of insurance companies whose granite faces frowned implacably over the City.

In 1860 there was still no public fire brigade in London. Firefighting was a privately owned business affair run entirely by insurance companies. Each company supported its own brigade: horses, wagons, pumps, and men. Their sole purpose was to save the companies having to pay out claims. A fire might break out in a building near one of these private fire brigades, but if it was not insured, never mind the shrieks and cries of those within, the firefighters would not stir. Even so, the insurance companies' fire brigades were overworked. London was densely built, accidental fires were frequent, and arson was a big business. This is why the companies also employed individuals who acted in investigative and enforcement capacities, and as spies. Mr. Field thought he would be able to obtain such a position without delay.

In this, he was mistaken.

From one establishment to the next he was warmly greeted and firmly rejected. He was well known to many of the security men of the insurance industry—they had often worked together to achieve convictions. But he was better known as Inspector Bucket.

"My dear fellow," went the refrain, "you're not fit for a position like this—you're famous! Everyone knows *you*. For this sort of work one has to be *unknown*. Why ever did you give up being a policeman?"

Thank you very much, Mr. Dickens! Cashiering on your fame, am I?

After being turned down by a half-dozen companies in quick succession, Field made his way to Newgate Prison.

"Charlie!" said an old friend there. "Are you mad? You can't be a prison guard—you're responsible for a good portion of Newgate's population being here! Don't go looking for death, man, it will find us all soon enough!" South of the river he had a similar reception at the prison in Horsemonger's Lane. Footsore and very hungry, he made his way back across the river as the light began to fail. He ate a penny pork pie standing at the bar of a down-at-heels pub, pondering his options. To go home without having secured a position was not one of them.

As he continued walking through the gathering dusk, he saw a theater marquee being lit by a jolly-looking little man on a ladder. The bill featured *A Life for a Life, or The Burden of Guilt* and an act called the Four Mowbreys. The actors within would be dressing and painting themselves for the evening's performances.

I could have been a Mowbrey.

Field sighed and walked on to the Fortune of War, his feet like lead. He paused before the door.

What fates impose, Field recited inwardly from his store of memorized Shakespeare, *That men must needs abide.*

He pushed resolutely into the tavern. Mickie Goodfellow was in the middle of the evening rush, but he stopped when he saw the inspector. He moved to him and leaned across the bar to hear him above the din of the public house.

"What do you pay?" said Field.

Goodfellow burst into laughter. "I love this man!" he said to the heavens. "Do you hear me, God? It's love!"

"How much?"

"Blimey, you are going to make me regret my generosity, are you not, Charlie Field? I will pay you *twice* what you was paid as a peeler, how's that? I've a sweet little bedroom for you, just one flight up, and you'll be free to spend one night each week with that ravishing wife of yours."

"I'll need an advance."

"Good God! Two weeks' pay in advance, Charlie, I'll have a lad bring it direct to your wife this instant. Can't say fairer than that, can I?"

Field finally nodded.

TOM GINTY'S HOURS of freedom had gone horribly wrong. He, too, had sought salvation at the Fortune of War. But the giddy elation he had felt as Belinda slipped him out the back garden and as he raced, a free man, through the streets of London toward Smithfield, had vanished. He had been told at the tradesmen's entrance that his mother was no longer employed there, nor did she any longer live in the room high above. A bundle of her clothing and linens, tied up in the kitchen, proved it. She had just walked off, according to one of the scullery girls.

"She say where she was going?" Tom had asked.

"She said nothing whatever! Gave no notice, just waltzed out the door and left me with a whole morning's washing up to do! Where'd *you* get to, then? You didn't half break her heart, you know, running away like that."

He flushed, realizing what his mother must have thought. Tom had abandoned her. Gone off and joined a world that had altered and tainted him to such an extent that he would never be fit company for her again. The boy found himself homeless and motherless in one go.

Tom knew Jake Figgis lived nearby, but where? He had no idea. There was no one to whom he could turn. He considered chucking the lot. He could lose himself in London, scavenge some sort of work, and never think about Master again or the house that held Master's people and all his nasty secrets. And if he did?

Mary Withers will think what Mum thinks, that I run out on her. And she'll be right.

Tom hesitated for a long moment, torn. And then, almost against his will and certainly against his better judgment, he resolved to return to Half Moon Street and the china doll who lived in the attic. He would have to wait until morning; there would be no getting into the house unnoticed at this time of night. He would sleep rough, in a doorway or under a bridge, and hope that Master and everyone else below would assume that he was still above in the garret. Tom set out looking for a spot in which to kip. He would set Mary Withers free. He would get her out all on his own.

26

In little more than a week at the beginning of July, Police Constable Sam Llewellyn had lost his partner, his famous chief officer and his standing within the Metropolitan. "The Darwin conspiracy" was the sarcastic name given in the department to Charles Field's final pursuits with the force. The investigation was over. According to Llewellyn's superiors, Josiah Kilvert had been murdered at a crowded public lecture, most likely by a pickpocket he was about to apprehend. The young scholar, David Gates, had been robbed by a common highwayman and bludgeoned to death. Philip Rendell had added his name to the list of lunatics who had tried and failed to kill Victoria. *He* was subsequently the victim of a typical prison murder. Field had been attempting to connect events that were wholly unrelated.

Llewellyn found himself on a foot patrol of the south bank with a junior constable named Crawley. Crawley was young and wide-eyed to an irritating degree as far as Llewellyn was concerned; the lad was in a perpetual state of morbid excitement. It seems a Frenchman had been found garroted in a Park Lane hotel; Crawley had learned the grisly details from one of the other recruits and was sharing them with Llewellyn as they walked.

Then he launched into the story of another recent murder; a man had been pulled from the Thames, just about *there*. A small boy had discovered the corpse and stolen what he could from it. *Fellow had been with the telegraph company. One of his ears was sliced clean off.*

"What's that you say?" said Llewellyn suddenly. "The chap's ear was off?"

"That's what they tell me."

"Eaten away?"

"Sliced off is what they told me, but of course I wasn't there, was I. Mr. Llewellyn! Hi, Mr. Llewellyn, where are *you* going?"

Despite the heat, Llewellyn ran. He wasn't sure why, but he felt a surge of urgency. At London Bridge he hailed a hackney cab to London Hospital, expense be damned.

After dropping Inspector Field's name, he found the chief coroner willing to talk to him. Thomas Wakeley, Esq., was in motion, walking briskly along a corridor, with Llewellyn trotting alongside. *Oh yes, the river corpse. It was only a few days ago, after all. No, the fellow hadn't drowned; there was no water to speak of in the lungs. Ear surgically removed. Cause of death, well, that had taken some searching, hadn't it, given the state of the body and the minute size of the fatal wound: a precisely aimed puncture of the heart's left ventricle. Death would have followed quickly. The fellow's possessions? Couldn't say. Might be with the police still or returned to the telegraph company.*

When the constable called at the Electric Telegraph Company, Mr. Apfel was not disposed to be of assistance. *The entire affair bungled by the Metropolitan, as per usual. Theft of company property and murder of company personnel, but what do the police and the courts offer me? A shrug, little more. No, Officer, of course the pouch was empty when that deranged wastrel found it—it had been in the river for days! A list? Mr. Llewellyn, or whatever your name is, there happen to be strict laws governing the privacy of communication via the electric telegraph. You certainly may not have a list of the telegrams the deliveryman was carrying that night!*

At New Scotland Yard, Llewellyn found two of the men who had helped fish the corpse ashore. They said the hooligan who had discovered the body was a mudlark called Button who lived in a barrel on the south bank.

As he picked his way carefully along the slimy sand and slippery, rubbish-littered stones of the Thames' south bank, Llewellyn wondered how long it would be before he got himself dismissed from the Metropolitan. He took off his woolen tunic and carried it, his shirt clinging sweatily to his back. The shoreline was strewn with debris. There were any number of broken barrels. Llewellyn peered into each one. Most were skeletal, consisting of hardly more than a few shivered staves. From a couple of them, the beady black eyes of crustaceans peered back at him. It was slow work.

"Wotcher think you're a-doing?"

Llewellyn stood up from the barrel he'd been looking into and turned to see a short, ferocious-looking boy glaring up at him with unfocused eyes and balled fists. His hair was tangled and filthy. The rags in which he was dressed were barely hanging on to his skinny frame. In contrast to his dirty skin, his teeth and disconcerting eyes shone a brilliant white.

"Mr. Button?" said Llewellyn.

"Don't you Mister *me*! Clear off!"

"Just *Button*, then. All right? I'd like to talk with you if I may."

In the end, after enduring a diatribe on injustice and the incompetence of the police, Llewellyn was able to induce the young businessman to retrieve a mass of sodden papers from a tin box hidden beneath his barrel. They cost Llewellyn several shillings of his own money after an extended period of haggling.

The constable, heading toward his chaste bedsit in Pimlico at the close of day, was aware that he smelled of his afternoon's endeavors. He resolved to ask his landlady to prepare him a hot bath and to have his uniform thoroughly sponged and brushed. Whenever the Metropolitan sacked him, he was determined to look his best.

THE GOUT WAS acting up again. Sir Jasper slowly made his way up the marble staircase of the Athenaeum Club to the dining room above. Sir Richard Owen, climbing one step at a time at his side, fairly radiated impatience.

"I believe I have things well in hand," wheezed Sir Jasper. "One of my shipper friends in Hamburg has put forward a young anarchist for the task, and I think he'll do." Sir Jasper paused yet again, one hand clinging to the iron rail, the other clutching his stick. "My friend had one of his spies stand drinks for the chappie, and the report is he'd do the deed gratis."

Two other members, Charles Dickens and his close friend, the artist Augustus Egg, overtook them on the stairs and quickly disappeared above. Owen watched them trip rapidly up the steps with barely concealed irritation, which delighted Sir Jasper.

"You've called off your man, I trust?" said the latter.

"*My* man?" said Owen. "Decimus Cobb was *your* man until recently. I believe he has been in *your* home *at your invitation*. He's never been in mine."

"The fellow's a lunatic. Doesn't know what he's talking about. Suggested I had a tumor! Infernal cheek. Saw my man in Harley Street. Said it was a load of rubbish."

"By the way," said Owen, "Officer Field is no longer a problem. I used my influence to have him dismissed from the Metropolitan Police."

"Really? Odd, my Fleet Street friend, reporter chappie, told me the man was dismissed for gross insubordination. Nothing to do with your influence."

Owen's lips disappeared. Lunch was going to be an ordeal.

TOM APPEARED AT the glass-paned door giving onto the kitchen garden just after dawn. Blinky threw the bolt and let him in. "Where are all the butchers?" she whispered. "You said you was bringing butchers."

"Never mind the butchers, Blinky. Are the stairs clear, you reckon?"

"Call me Belinda."

"What? Why?"

"It's me name."

"It is? All right, Belinda, are the stairs clear?"

"No one about. Where were you last night? I waited."

"Master's out?"

"I think so," the girl whispered vaguely. Exasperated, it finally dawned on Tom that she might fancy him. There was nothing for it but to hope there were no watchers and no Master nearby. He took the stairs two at a time as softly as he could, three flights up, and then the small steps to the attic door, with Blinky—Belinda—pattering after him.

Tom knocked three times and then once more. There was no answer. He turned the knob and pushed open the door. There was no one there.

"Mary?" The garret was deserted.

Tom wheeled on the girl. "What's this, then?"

"Dunno, Tom!"

He ran to the wardrobe and flung open the doors: no clothes. The top of the ink-stained writing desk was bare. Tom pulled out the drawer: empty. The history of the world was missing.

"She took her book with her, Tom," said Decimus, standing in the door. Blinky shrieked.

"Please don't do that, dear. It goes right through my head."

"What have you done with her?" said Tom.

"I did what *you* couldn't do, certainly. I found her a position. She's been placed with a fine family. I'm confident she'll give every satisfaction. When I came to give her the good news about the position—this was soon after you left yesterday, Tom, with little Blinky's help—Mary told me all about you and your aspirations."

"I don't believe you."

"Young love et cetera. The thing about women, Tom, is that one must give them what they want or it's simply *not on*, isn't that right, Blinky? Mary wanted work; I found her work. I myself prefer a woman who wants nothing, but that's just me."

Mary Do-Not's words came back to Tom. *Everyone in this house is a spy, Tom. Everyone.*

Decimus moved to the dumbwaiter, both Tom and the girl shrinking from him involuntarily. He slid open its door and looked in. "Long way down," he said. He closed the door again and turned to the young people.

"You're a slow learner, Tom. We're going to have to get serious about your studies. Hey, ho, I've gone freelance!"

Tom looked blank.

"Doesn't know what I mean, never mind. We've got work ahead and some traveling to do, and you'll need to acquire much more knowledge than what you appear to possess. Take inspiration from Mary Do-Not, Tom. There's a girl with vision! I believe that wherever she goes, for as long as she lives, she will be writing and rewriting the history of the world."

He glanced briefly at the girl. "Would you like me to drop little Blinky down the chute, Tom? Didn't think so. Come along, then."

Decimus left the room and started down the stairs, and after a moment, his shoulders sagging and his head down, Tom followed.

27

BUCKINGHAM PALACE

Albert was reviewing a tall stack of dispatches, and his wife, seated at the adjacent desk, was reading and writing letters. The evening meal was long over and Victoria was barely suppressing her yawns.

"Vicky does *not* answer one's questions," said the Queen. "It is most frustrating." Princess Victoria, their firstborn and favorite child, had two years earlier married Crown Prince Frederick of Prussia. "In my letters I tell her to answer questions briefly and in the order one asks them, but she *will* neglect to do so."

"Indeed," murmured Albert, not looking up.

The Queen had had their two desks moved together years earlier. Her husband possessed firm ideas about the duty owed by the monarch to her subjects and her empire, and eventually he had been relatively successful in imparting them to the Queen. The tempestuous early years, when young Victoria was fond of society and dancing until dawn, had passed long ago. Her early rejection of his attempts to be the head of the household had given way to unstinting respect for her Prince and a love that bordered on adoration.

In return, Albert was mindful of his duty to his wife and Queen, and to his adopted nation. He felt a profound gratitude to Victoria as the mother of their children. The fact that she had borne nine of them was proof, he felt, of *his* commitment, as well as hers.

Victoria turned to the second page of the letter she was reading and shook her head. "Naughty Vicky! She's painting in oil again, never mind the sound advice you gave her, my dear. An amateur's oils will *never* stand up to an *artist's* and will only *suffer* by comparison, so why put oneself in such a *position*? And what does one *do* with the product of one's labors? Watercolors can be kept so *nicely* on a mantel or a piano, strewn casually for the visitor to come upon and discover with delight."

A massive ornate clock ticked sonorously. The Queen's quill scratched along a fresh leaf of paper with frequent, emphatic underlinings. She stifled one yawn after another and then said, "Perhaps I'll finish in the morning." She looked fondly at her husband's balding head, still bent over the dispatches. "*Bist du nicht müde?*" she said gently, speaking as she often did in her husband's native tongue.

Albert looked up and offered an affectionate smile. "*Ja, so, meine Liebste,* perhaps I am tired." He swept a hand above the papers on his desk. "If everyone is not very careful, very delicate, there could be in America a war within the year. But what does Mr. Palmerston care for delicacy or caution? *Nothing at all!*"

"Whoever is going to war with America?"

"Other Americans," said Albert gloomily.

"I must say, little Bertie seems to be acquitting himself well in the United States."

"*Miracula miraculum,*" muttered the Prince.

"I'm certain that it's due, however incomprehensibly, to the Americans' astonishing fondness for my unworthy self."

Victoria waited for Albert to agree, but he continued reading silently. "In any event," she said finally, "you can prevent war in the morning."

She rose and waited. After a moment the Prince obediently closed a folder, straightened the stacks on the desk, and stood. The Queen started for the door, which a servant was already opening.

"My dear?" said Albert.

"Yes?"

"Do you know the man Sims? One of my grooms?"

"I believe I do. Welsh. Nice-looking boy, *very* well mannered."

The servant was still holding open the door. "Leave us, will you?" said Albert, and the servant disappeared.

"He's become very attentive, Sims. Oddly so. I feel that I'm being *watched over.*"

"Yes? What is this about, Albert?"

"That's what I was wondering, *meine Liebste.* So this morning, when we were riding in the park, I asked him about it. He feigned not to understand me, but I pressed him. 'You seem to be on guard every minute, Sims,' I said. 'I cannot make a move but you're there at my elbow, so to speak. It is distracting and disconcerting.' 'Well,' he said, 'one hears rumors.' '*What sort of rumors?*' I said."

"You're frightening me."

"In the end, I had it out of him. The whispers he had heard concerned a threat against my person, and the whisperer had been a member of the Metropolitan Police."

"Against *you*, Albert? Surely not."

The Prince shrugged. "Sims claimed not to know anything more specific."

"The young man is entirely mistaken, of course," she said somewhat archly. "It is *I* who must bear the constant threat of annihilation. The harsh spotlight of the world, for good or ill, is directed at *me*, and I must endure its glare as befits a head of state."

Victoria turned rather grandly and put her hand to the door, which was opened instantly by the waiting attendant. "Yes, my dear," said Albert, following in her wake, "I am sure you are right. Still, I might have a word with this policeman, whoever he is."

• • •

IN TIME, CHARLES Field learned the real reason he'd been taken on at the Fortune of War. This was a public house that sold, with great efficiency and remarkable profit, much more than food and drink.

Field had returned home for an evening with his wife, the night after he was first enlisted by Goodfellow. He had not been pleased to discover that Jane had taken in Martha Ginty and was housing her in the empty nursery, but he didn't want any unpleasantness to interfere with their night together, and besides, it was all his fault in the first place, wasn't it. Jane was already wide-eyed with the first pay packet she had received. In the morning she had packed him a small trunk filled with clean clothing, an extra pair of boots, a razor, hairbrushes, and other necessaries. Field quietly retrieved his pistol from its hiding place and stashed it in the trunk as well.

Two weeks went by with Field in residence in the public house, wandering about the place, vaguely eyeing the clientele and wondering what in God's name he was doing there. He had broken up two fistfights and escorted five or six inebriated patrons from the premises in all that time. Goodfellow would wink at him from behind the bar and tell him what a grand job he was doing and Field would move off again, more baffled than ever. His pay packets were delivered directly to No. 2 Bow Street. Jane had never seen money like this. Perhaps Mickie Goodfellow truly did not know how much (or rather, how little) a chief of detectives earned. Or maybe he knew it very well and wanted to ensure that his new man would not be likely to leave. Field was earning nearly three times his old wage; he'd be mad to give it up.

In the third week of July, during a morning lull, Goodfellow had suggested they sit down together for a drink in the saloon bar.

"Any word from your old mates in the Metropolitan, Charlie?" asked the publican.

"Not to speak of, Mick," said Field, sipping his beer.

"Not even that nice young chap, the Llewellyn boy?"

Field said nothing.

"Well, I call that a shame. If this is what years of hard work and loyal friendship get you, what's the point?" Goodfellow took a draft of beer while Field eyed him silently. There were two others in the saloon bar, gentlemen talking quietly at a nearby table; a third now entered and joined them, carrying a half-pint of stout from the main bar.

The publican saluted the newcomer from his table. "Good morning, Mr. Wells!"

"Morning, Goodfellow," said the gentleman with a quizzical glance at the inspector.

In response, Goodfellow gave the man a nod and a wink, to Field's confusion. The gentleman glanced at his two companions and then said to Goodfellow, "Have you got anything for us, then?"

"I do indeed, Mr. Wells. We're having a very productive week. I'll be with you gentlemen presently."

Goodfellow turned to Field. "All's well at home, Charlie? Good, good. You're not finding your new duties overly taxing, then? Shouldn't think so. The pay's decent, anyway? Right, that's what I like to hear."

Field stared at him. "What's going on, Mick?"

"Progress, Charlie. Discovery. Knowledge. Understanding. These are exciting times, my friend, and you and me—we're a part of them."

"What's going on, Mick?" said Field again drily. He noticed the table of gentleman had grown to four, and they were all watching him and the publican.

"When history sets down the chronicle of our age," said Goodfellow, "our names will be writ large as two who helped mankind advance."

"Wake me, won't you, when you've run out of gammon?"

"Now what did we say, Charlie?" Goodfellow wagged a finger in Field's face. "We're going to be agreeable, right? Respectful. Decent. All right, Charlie?"

"You know *me*, Mick."

A spasm of irritation crossed Goodfellow's face, and then the man nodded ruefully and chortled. "I do indeed, Charlie. Intolerable man. Always was, always will be. Come along, then!"

Goodfellow rose, nodded to the gentlemen, and led the way to a door marked GENTS, which had a yellowing, fly-specked handwritten notice attached: *Not in service.*

The publican unlocked the door and led Field and the others into a dank stone corridor leading, one would have expected, to the jakes in the courtyard behind the pub. He paused at a door in the wall on his right and produced another set of keys. Unlocked, this door opened into an unlit room. It was surprisingly cold. Field heard the retort of a gas jet being lit and became aware of a sweetish, sickly odor. A slowly rising glow illuminated the room.

There were sturdy wooden shelves attached to three of the four walls of a modest-sized room, one set of shelving mounted a few feet above the other. On the floor beneath, large blocks of ice nestled in beds of straw. The shelves themselves were roughly three feet deep, more than large enough to hold the bodies. The corpses, male and female, young, middle-aged and old, were naked. Field guessed there were perhaps twelve of them.

The gentlemen fanned out through the room, examining the bodies with appraising eyes. Several had a tag affixed to a toe. Field approached one—a male, gaunt and old. The hand-scrawled label read *Chapel*. He moved to the next corpse, a female, perhaps thirty years of age when she died, he guessed, and read the label: *Tailor*.

Field looked up at Goodfellow.

"Will Tailor's the chap who brought that one in," said the publican. "The digger gets his pay, see? The tag is his invoice."

For years medical students had been allowed to dissect and study only the bodies of executed criminals. As many of these as there were at the beginning of the nineteenth century, the number was still far too small to satisfy the demand. The Anatomy Act of 1832 relaxed the strictures to a degree, allowing the aspiring vivisectionist to dissect the bodies of paupers and others who died in the workhouse, as well as the corpses of those few who chose to donate their earthly frames in the interest of science. But demand was rising to an unprecedented degree, and there were simply too few bodies to go around, hence the body-snatching industry.

A favored technique involved the nocturnal digging of a relatively small hole near the top of the burial site, descending and opening that end of the coffin and pulling the corpse out headfirst. Less dirt was disturbed this way, and the diggers' tracks could more easily be covered. Sometimes the entry hole would be dug several feet from the grave so as not to attract notice. A tunnel was constructed, and small adults or sturdy children were sent down to open the box and haul out the body. All of this had to be accomplished as soon after the burial as possible for obvious reasons, especially in the warmer months. The situation got so troublesome that families would post guards to watch over their loved ones' plots during the first critical days.

The snatchers called themselves *resurrectionists*. They were always busy.

"So?" said Field. "Am I supposed to faint now, Mickie? Turn purple? Arrest you? I am no longer a policeman, if you recall." Field turned to the others. "You gentlemen would be from St. Bartholomew's Hospital, I assume? Convenient for you, just steps away. I work for this gentleman now, I do what he tells me. You've nothing to fear from me."

Goodfellow put an arm warmly around Field's shoulders. "That's me old mate, I knew you'd come through."

"But honestly, Mick, this is much ado about not so much, ain't it? All right, it's a bigger operation than any I've seen. Granted. But for the most part the Metropolitan has been turning a blind eye to you resurrection fellers for years. To protect this, you needed to hire *me*?"

Suddenly there was a deep rumble and then the sound of a pipe organ playing, very close, very loud. Solemn music. The medical men seemed uninterested; they returned to their examinations of the bodies. Field looked to Goodfellow for an explanation, but the publican merely put a finger to his lips, his eyes closing, seeming to relish the music. It rose in volume suddenly as double doors in the fourth wall swung open and a buxom woman entered, pushing through black velvet curtains. She was dressed in deep mourning: bombazine and crêpe and layers of veil.

"Reverend Carmichael's outdone hisself today," she said to Goodfellow in hushed, pious tones. "They can't hardly see for cryin' in there."

"Mrs. Carmichael," said Goodfellow, "allow me to introduce Charles Field. Charles, this is Mrs. Carmichael of Shepherd's Rest."

The woman lifted her veil, revealing copper-red hair and full coppery cheeks. She dipped and winked. "Pleased, I'm sure."

There was a rattle of wheels and a bier and coffin appeared through the black velvet, pushed by two tall young men. They also were dressed in mourning, with tall hats draped in crêpe. "Quick now," said the buxom woman, "or I'll know the reason why!"

The dirge finished and the organ took up an energetic recessional hymn. The two boys unscrewed the coffin and opened the lid. In a single motion they hoisted the body out of the casket and onto an available shelf. The deceased appeared to be a male in his twenties. The boys rapidly unbuttoned the grave clothes and stripped the corpse, throwing the clothes into the open coffin. Mrs. Carmichael drew a burlap bag from between blocks of ice and lifted it with effort into the casket. She situated the weighted bag, draped the clothes anyhow over it, and shut up the whole affair. The lads screwed down the lid and assumed their positions, one on each side, just as a glorious head of flowing silver hair appeared from between the velvet curtains. The Reverend Carmichael smiled benevolently, nodded, and disappeared. Adopting a solemn demeanor, the boys slowly pushed the bier back into what Field realized was obviously the chapel next door to the Fortune of War. The woman sighed piteously and followed them out. The entire operation had taken less than two minutes.

"Right," said Field to Goodfellow. "Like a night at the fucking ballet. You did well to hire me, Mickie. For this you'd be hanged."

Goodfellow beamed proudly and took Field aside. "We all get paid twice, see? Once by the family of the deceased and then by the customers who buy the bodies. I wish I could take full credit for it, Charlie, but that belongs to another. It was all in place, set up by him, as is the reverend's landlord. All I had to do was say *yes*, which I did, and quick."

"What's in the sacking?"

"Scraps from the butchers in Smithfield. Creates an authentic air after a few days, if the grave is dug shallow, which it generally is these days, times being what they are."

"And the clothes?"

"The law says if you leave the grave clothes, the crime ain't so bad. Take the grave clothes and you're much likelier to hang, don't ask me why."

One of the medical men looked up from the pitiably vulnerable form of the young dead man. "Consumption," he said with a bored shrug.

"So, here's the matter, Charlie," said Goodfellow. "You're one of us now, ain't you? A peeler comes sniffing about, you direct him elsewhere. If need be, you offer him a little incentive in the way of pounds, shillings, pence, right? Nothing excessive, but you know what I mean. And if you ever was to get a demented notion in your head to peach, well, these fine gents here is all witnesses to you being up to your neck in it. So let's all be friends and not even dream of spoiling a very good thing. All right?"

To what have I sunk? A bleeding body-snatcher's pimp.

"Charlie?" said Goodfellow, in a warning tone.

"I'll be back," growled Field. He pushed through the pub and out into the street, gulping for air. If there had been a miscreant's head to crack, it would have helped. But no—*he* was the criminal now. He'd put himself forever beyond the pale, on the other side of the law, and for what?

Without knowing where he was going, he found himself minutes later taking the steps of St. Paul's two at a time and felt a degree of relief as soon as he plunged into the cool dark vastness within. The cathedral was nearly empty but a service was in progress; a Eucharist sung by the choir of men and boys.

Whatever am I doing here?

He made his way to the very front pew, and when the pew opener seemed to suggest that he did not belong there—at least not without first making a substantial payment—a single murderous look from the former policeman was enough to dispel any difficulties.

God judgeth the righteous, intoned the choir, *and God is angry with the wicked every day.*

If he turn not he will whet his sword; he hath bent his bow and made it ready . . .

As THEY SANG the words of the psalm, the men's and boys' attention was fully fastened on the choirmaster. The purity of the boys' voices stung Field's eyes, and he bowed his head.

He hath also prepared for him the instruments of death;
He ordaineth his arrows against the persecutors . . .

Whatever had they done with that list of St. Paul's choirboys that Mr. Kilvert had put together? Kilvert had been eliminating names too recent or too old to have been in the choir alongside of Philip David Rendell, leaving some half-dozen or so possible names. And then they'd had word of David Gates' murder and that line of inquiry had been set aside, forgotten. They had made the disastrous journey to Oxford from which Josiah Kilvert had not returned.

Among the children, one voice dominated. Field picked out the singer: somewhat taller than the others, blond, his face a picture of rapt intensity. Twelve or thirteen years old. Field tried to imagine the boy's eyes deeper and darker.

I was a reproach among all mine enemies but
especially to mine neighbors, and a fear to mine acquaintance:
They that did see me without fled from me.

The killer who eluded him had perhaps stood right there, had perhaps sung these very words. Field thought it possible, anyway. How did a child become a monster?

I am forgotten as a dead man out of mind:
I am like a broken vessel.

There was no comfort for him here. Field rose, opened the door to his pew, and sped up the aisle, the choir's voices hurtling after him.

28

St. Thomas' Hospital, just across London Bridge, had been in operation since the twelfth century, when Augustinian monks began to offer care and shelter here for the sick and homeless in the name of the martyred Thomas à Beckett. Shut down for a time in the sixteenth century by the English Reformation, it eventually reopened with a similar name but a new Protestant dedication, to St. Thomas the Apostle. By the Victorian era it had become a medical training center and a lying-in hospital for expectant mothers. This very year, 1860, Florence Nightingale had founded her famous school for female nurses here. The St. Thomas' operating theater was among the oldest in Europe.

In this venue Decimus Cobb was unknown, but a surgeon calling himself William Tailor, who resembled Decimus in every detail, was a highly respected figure. When Tailor presented his young apprentice, the sisters were in a flutter to make Tom feel welcome. Surgeons were still considered members of the working classes in that they labored with their hands; even so, it was considered generous of Tailor to bring in this poor, quiet Cockney boy and teach him skills that would allow him to better himself.

In a world without anesthesia, the success of a surgeon was measured by his ability to cut, saw, drill, amputate, and sew *quickly*. Dr. Tailor enjoyed a reputation at St. Thomas' and elsewhere as one of the fastest. He was even known occasionally to *sing* as he worked: sacred music, in a beautiful countertenor voice.

Tom was not afraid of blood; he was a butcher's boy, after all. He had experience with knives. He knew how to cut through flesh, muscle, tendon, and bone. He even had experience with the screaming, which was a regular feature of the daily drill at St. Thomas'. Pigs produced similar sounds when the knife went in.

To begin with, Tom merely observed the goings-on, standing at attention on the risers of the operating theater with Decimus at his side, Decimus watching Tom watch. The boy saw ulcerous growths removed; he saw a man's skull drilled into and a gush of clear fluid shoot out; he watched a goiter the size of a melon cut from a woman's neck. After a week, Decimus left Tom on his own in the observers' gallery while he himself went to work with blade, drill, and saw. He *was* remarkably fast. He used his own tools, some of which he had invented himself. In his hands, they were a blur of brass and silver, splashed with scarlet. He worked so rapidly that there were instances in which the patient did not cry out at all. One man, whose lower leg Decimus had just taken off—closing the wound and sewing up the stump with great speed—urged Cobb to go ahead and get started. When Decimus told him his ordeal was already over, the man wept with relief and gratitude. The Chorister looked up at Tom, cocked his head, and winked.

Eventually, Tom took his place with the others on the operating room floor. There were always helpers needed to hold the patient still and this was young Tom's first job. Some of the patients exhibited remarkable strength as the knives penetrated their flesh, but Tom was a strong lad himself and up to the task. He spoke little, did as he was told, and observed everything closely. The sisters clucked over this "pair,"

as they came to be known: the young ginger-haired Cockney and his
brilliant master.

In time, after arduous instruction, Tom was placed in charge of his
mentor's kit while he operated. When Decimus called for a tool, it was the
boy's responsibility to place it instantly in Master's waiting hand. The first
time he'd reached for a razor-sharp knife that Decimus had demanded,
the rage that lived somewhere within him had risen to his throat, but he
quelled it and, with only a moment's hesitation, gently laid the tool handle
first in his master's hand. Tom was a good and obedient student.

One day Tom stood by with surgical thread and needle, ready to pass
them to his master after he'd finished taking off a farmer's gangrenous
foot. One helper held down the man's upper torso while another leaned
on the farmer's legs, pressing them to the operating table. Tom heard
the amputated foot drop into the bucket on the floor. He extended the
needle and thread, but Decimus didn't take them. Instead, he wiped
his hands on his apron.

"You finish him up, Tom," he said. "I must run." Decimus turned
and left the operating theater. Tom saw the farmer's eyes widen in fear.
Without thinking, the boy frantically sought open tubes and tied the
slippery things shut; he folded the flap of flesh and skin the way he'd
seen Master do it; he plunged the surgical needle in and out, drawing
the sutures as tightly and as quickly as he could, desperate to stem the
flow of blood coming from the wound.

Then, somehow, it was over. The farmer was still living. The others
round the operating table clapped Tom on the back. His life as a surgeon had begun.

Decimus took his pupil from one hospital to another, introducing
him to the routines at St. Bartholomew's, the City Hospital, and the
College of Surgeons. Other days, Tom was left alone at Half Moon
Street, where he continued to occupy the attic room. Decimus had
supplied him with several books of engravings, illustrating locales and
architectural sites in Germany. He was to memorize everything he saw:
the size and shape of certain grand homes and palaces, as well as palace
grounds and surrounding countryside. He was given illustrations of

a variety of royal carriages to study. Tom still maintained the fiction that he was illiterate, but when Master was away, he would study the accompanying texts. Belinda would sit on the floor, chattering or singing liturgical responses (learned from Master) in a clear, high voice.

In his attic retreat, Tom continued to sleep on the divan; to Tom, Mary Do-Not's bed was still a shrine and not to be defiled, despite her treachery.

MARY DO-NOT, NÉE Withers, had fallen in love with the family with whom she'd been placed, almost from the first. Cook treated her well enough, and Mrs. Huxley was the perfect mistress. Mr. Huxley had frightened her to begin with, but then she saw that despite his intimidating brows, he was the gentlest of men, one who loved his wife and adored his children. There was just enough space in her tiny room at the top of the house to continue writing, when she was not too exhausted, her history of the world.

But in only a matter of weeks, a fearful shadow had fallen over the family. One of the children was sick. Little Noel, aged four, was Thomas and Henrietta Huxley's firstborn. Now Noel was not seen outside of the nursery. Doctors arrived at all hours and left looking grim.

Please God, no, not again, not the typhoid, they'll think it's me and send me away.

Mary prayed when she rose before dawn. She prayed while she worked and when she collapsed into her narrow bed at the end of the day. She prayed without ceasing.

JANE FIELD WAS growing ever more concerned about Martha Ginty. It had been a sudden impulse that prompted her to invite Martha to move in; perhaps it was because Martha had lost her child while Jane never had the child she had so badly wanted.

Martha was installed in the nursery and usually proved to be a great help about the house and a sympathetic companion now that Mr. Field was working away from home. Bessie Shoreham was implacably jealous, but Martha was a down-to-earth workingwoman who did her best not to give offense. But some days a crazed light would come into her eyes and she would go out into the streets carrying a large sign she had lettered herself, looking for her boy.

HAVE YOU SEEN MY TOM?

14 YEARS GINGER

BUTCHER PRENTIS

TELL ME NO. 2 BOW STREET

On these days there was no talking to Martha. She would speed through the streets at a furious pace, thrusting her sign into people's faces and shouting. *Have you seen him? Tom Ginty, he's my only boy! Have you seen my Tom?*

She became a recognized figure, one more London madwoman. Eventually she would tire herself out and return to Bow Street, the light gone from her eyes. Jane wasn't certain Martha knew where she had been or what she had done.

SAM LLEWELLYN HAD not been dismissed from the Metropolitan Police. Neither had he been reassigned to the detective division. By early August it was clear to him: foot patrol was his lot. Llewellyn could only hope his disgrace was a passing thing. In the meantime, he would pursue his own investigations. On the hob at his landlady's he had dried the sodden papers he purchased from Button and flattened them under a brick in his room. When he spread them out to examine them, he found three telegrams and a column of addresses. Names flanked each of the addresses. The names were either ticked or not. For those that were ticked, the deliveryman had entered the o'clock.

Llewellyn quickly examined the telegrams. Each was a single page, folded in thirds, with the address on the top fold. The constable ran his finger down the list. Sure enough, there were no ticks beside the addresses of the telegrams in his possession. Three names had checks beside them. Three others on the list were unchecked. A Mr. McBride off Curzon Street. Mr. Cable in Hertford Street. Mr. Cobb nearby in

Half Moon Street. Had these telegrams floated away in the Thames? Had they been delivered, but the young man merely neglected to check them off? Or was he unable to do so? Could it even be so simple that the first unticked name on the list, McBride, was his man? Llewellyn could almost hear Inspector Field's derisive snort. *Human beings*, the inspector always said, *almost never make it easy for a bloke.*

From the addresses it was clear that the man from the ETC had been assigned a patch of London running adjacent to Green Park, with Piccadilly as its southern margin and Curzon Street at its northern boundary. There was nothing for it but for Llewellyn to knock on doors.

His first stop, Mr. McBride, turned out to be the manager of the Mayfair Chapel, known as a center for clandestine marriages among the upper crust: a venue with a dubious repute and no great fondness for the police.

"A telegram?" snapped McBride when the porter summoned him to the door. "We receive telegraphic communiqués on a regular basis. To which telegram do you refer?"

"It would have arrived Thursday last, sometime after ten p.m.," said Llewellyn. "Might someone else have accepted it? A caretaker, perhaps?"

"There's no one here at that time of night, Officer. A bizarre inquiry. Good day." And shut the door in Llewellyn's face.

Hertford Street, No. 6, Mr. W. Cable. A Georgian townhouse in a pleasant leafy street. Shuttered up. The front step unswept, unwashed. Llewellyn knocked and listened at the door but heard nothing from within. He knocked again with the same result.

The constable continued on toward No. 4 Half Moon Street, a short walk away. According to his list it was the residence of Cobb, Decimus. Llewellyn passed by it on the opposite side, observing. Like the Hertford Street address, it was shuttered, bottom to top. Not painted anytime recently. The streetlamp shattered. Llewellyn crossed the road and walked back toward No. 4 again. The day was warm, and beneath his heavy tunic he was sweating. Was that singing he heard coming from within the house? A woman, perhaps, or a girl singing a church tune? He climbed the steps and rang the bell.

29

The singing stopped as soon as the constable pulled the bell. Llewellyn waited. He could hear movement within No. 4. Then the door opened.

The figure before him was outlined by the darkness behind. The skin was white, the hair pulled back tightly, the clothing a dull black. She had a narrow, severe face. Two moles sprouted tufts of black hairs, one on her nose and another on her chin.

Llewellyn belatedly realized he wasn't prepared with a story.

"How do you do, ma'am? I'm Officer Llewellyn of the Metropolitan, and I'm looking for . . ." He gingerly took the torn sheet of blue paper from his tunic pocket and consulted it. "Looking for Mr. Cobb of No. 4 Half Moon Street." It was hard not to stare, the moles were almost comically prominent.

"What for?" said the woman.

Charles Field had drummed it into his men: *Don't answer*

questions, ask *them. Don't talk, let* them *do the talking. Above all, don't explain!*

The woman's deep-set eyes bored into him.

"Well," he explained, "it seems someone's been intercepting of messages sent by the Electric Telegraph Company. Making off with them. It's like interfering with the mails, you see. Now, Mr. Cobb was sent a telegram"—he consulted the paper again, hearing his former superior's voice shouting in his ears, *You'll be singing a bloody aria next!*—"not long ago, a Thursday it would have been, and the Metropolitan wonders did he receive it?"

"You've got his name on a list?"

"Is Mr. Cobb in, ma'am?"

"He's gone."

"Is that so? When do you expect him?"

"Wouldn't know."

Llewellyn peered past her into the gloom of the hall. He thought he heard someone weeping.

"Perhaps I might leave my card so Mr. Cobb can get in touch when he returns?" The constable brushed right past the woman, drawing one of his official calling cards from his tunic. He placed it on the little table by the door, looking about him, his eyes adjusting to the dim light. There was a stale, cooked cabbage smell in the air and another odor he couldn't place. There was a closed door beyond the small table and a straight-backed wooden chair, a hat rack on the opposite side of the hall, and a flight of stairs before him.

Llewellyn caught his breath. Two figures were sitting silently on the staircase; a gangly teenaged boy, staring at him with tears streaming down his face and a girl of ten or so. The lad's face was pockmarked and dirty, and the tears made rivulets through the grime. Llewellyn turned to the woman, raising his eyebrows.

"Their master's gone off abroad," she said. "Nobody knows when he'll be back."

A voice came back to him. It belonged to the shopkeeper in Oxford, the neighbor of the guest house that had no guests. *She's always going off, she's always stopping her eggs. She's a witch to her core, and not just along of them warts.*

Llewellyn struggled to hide a surge of fear. Could this be the elusive egg-stopping Oxford landlady, warts and all? He decided to take a gamble.

"Well, Mrs. Andrews, when you do hear from Mr. Cobb, have the goodness to let him know that the Metropolitan wish to speak with him."

There was a silence.

"What did you call me?"

Got it in one, didn't I. Lucky me.

The youth on the stairs stood. "Get out," he said.

The girl beside him blinked rapidly. On impulse the constable spoke to her. "Traveling on his own, is your master?"

"Taking *him* with him, ain't he," the girl said tearily.

"Taking who, miss?"

"*Get out!*" shouted the boy, descending the steps, glaring savagely, his fists clenched.

This is why a policeman needs a partner.

Llewellyn started backing as resolutely as he could past the woman to the door, feeling the hostile presence of the house swelling until he could barely breathe. The boy advanced on him, fishing for something in his pockets. "You will convey my message, then, Mrs. Andrews?" continued the constable, mastering himself. "Let Mr. Cobb know that Officer Llewellyn wishes to speak with him urgently." His hand found the doorknob behind him. "In fact, for anything he has to say, I'll be *all ears.*"

He stumbled awkwardly out the door and flung it shut. Out on the street Llewellyn walked briskly away, gulping for breath. He had located the man, he knew it!

Now what?

His exhilaration was punctured in an instant. There was nowhere he could go with his information. Already on shaky ground with the Metropolitan, if he were to reintroduce his disgraced superior's "Darwin conspiracy" he'd be laughed into the streets, or worse. Llewellyn was halfway across Green Park when he realized there was only one person who would believe him and understand the importance of his discovery: Charles Field.

THE DOOR JUST off the entrance hall swung open, and Decimus Cobb stepped out of the library, sliding something brass and barbed into a thin leather sheath, spring-loaded into one sleeve. He was followed by Tom, who carried a large traveling case at the end of one arm and Master's kit at the other.

"A cheeky constable," said Decimus. "Very. I saw him at Oxford. One of Bucket's men."

"He saw *you*, you mean!" hissed Mrs. Andrews.

The Chorister ignored her. "John?"

Getalong approached his master hesitantly.

"John, you neglected to destroy the contents of the messenger's pouch, didn't you?"

The youth hung his head.

"You make me tired, John. I'm actually sick of the sight of you. It will be a relief to be far, far away from you for a long time. Are you *whimpering*?" The boy shook his head. "You had better not be. Nor you, little Miss Blinky!" The girl hiccoughed and sniffed.

Decimus turned to Tom. "All right, then?"

Tom nodded.

"Didn't hear you."

"Yes, sir."

"Good. We're off to parts distant, children! Isn't that wonderful?"

The children stared at him mutely with glassy eyes.

"Your enthusiasm overwhelms me."

Decimus suddenly stomped several times on the floor. Turning to Mrs. Andrews he said, "Whatever has happened to the Hamlets? Are they dead?"

"Getting there."

"When they *do* go, Mrs. Andrews, kindly remind Getalong to empty their pockets before sending them downstream." Decimus arched his eyebrows at John Getalong.

The woman glared at him. "Is there anything else you'd like from me whilst you traipse round foreign parts? I don't think so!"

"Careful, now, Mrs. Andrews. Just because Tom and I are going away doesn't mean you are on holiday, my dear."

"You got peelers ringing the bell, calling me by name. You got this boy here, this Tom—his mother is a madwoman, did you know that? She goes about with a great sign, 'Have you seen my Tom, call at No. 2 Bow Street!'"

Decimus looked sharply at Tom, but the boy's face betrayed no emotion whatsoever.

"I don't like that," said Decimus. "We can't have her parading about with a *sign*. Approach her, Mrs. Andrews, if you will. Speak to her. Tell her about the son *you* lost when he was but a boy. You do, after all, have *that* in common. Remember? Offer your pretty bosom for her to cry upon, go with her to Bow Street, and persuade her one way or another to give up her sign-carrying ways."

"Oh, yes, your majesty!"

"And if you *don't*, my dear, no matter where I am or how far away, I'll *know*. I'm like God that way."

"I won't be around, Decimus. I'm clearing out."

"Where you choose to lay your warty head is your concern, my dear, so long as you accomplish the very important tasks I've assigned you. Leave even one undone and you won't like the consequence, I promise you."

"The police will be back!" she said shrilly. "Wot am I to do with them?"

Decimus flushed red. "How the devil do *I* know, Mother! Must I think of absolutely *everything*? Come, Tom, I can't bear it here another moment. We have one quick social call to make, and then we're off!"

BEFORE THEIR RELATIONSHIP had soured and his mission had been terminated, Decimus had been a guest several times in Sir Jasper

Arpington-Dix's home overlooking the Mall, receiving instruction concerning his assignment. The butler, opening the door to him now, knew him by sight. The servant feared the tall man with the sunken eyes even more than he feared his master, although he couldn't say why. *Something about the way he looks at you.* The butler admitted Decimus and Tom without question and without first asking his employer if he was in, hence Sir Jasper's surprise when he found the pair in his drawing room.

The butler watched from an adjoining room through a generous keyhole. He heard the man with the disconcerting eyes say something about Germany and then Sir Jasper shouting angrily. The boy stood mutely at the tall man's side, holding a wooden case. Strangely, the visitor began talking about a tumor, or so the butler thought; the man's voice was low and even.

. . . has by this time grown too large to be removed without dire consequences to the patient . . .

The boy laid the case on a side table and opened it. Sir Jasper rang for his servant furiously. The butler decided not to hear the bell. The lad gave the tall man an apron, which he looped over his head and tied about his waist. Sir Jasper was red in the face, shouting for his manservant to come at once.

When the boy gave the man something sharp and shiny from the box, the butler stood and walked quickly toward the rear of the house and the tradesmen's door. As he slipped out, he thought he heard singing. The butler tried to maintain his dignity as he hastily crossed the Mall, dodging carriages. He kept up a rapid pace as he entered St. James' Park. He had family in Wiltshire. They would take him in, at least for a time, he was almost certain of it.

THE BODIES ACROSS the passage from the Fortune of War held a fascination for Charles Field. As the room's protector, he now possessed his own key to the place, and he would look in from time to time as Mrs. Carmichael and the youths went about their work. The corpses came and went at a brisk pace not only because it was necessary they do so—flesh being what it is—but because there was no shortage of supply *or* demand. Field would return to the pub ruminating on the brevity of life and the common lot that awaited all. He carried with him the copy of *Origin* that he'd purchased, and when he had nothing else to do—which was often—he would read, standing at the bar, struggling with the text. He'd have a drink. And then another.

If I understand what Mr. Darwin is saying, a creature will do anything at all in order to survive. And every creature that does make it does so because some other creature don't. Everything and everyone at war all the time, just to keep the show going, and it's been a very long-running show indeed. Look at it that way, nothing matters, really. Not being a policeman nor working in a pub nor fencing the odd corpse. Look at it another way, of course, it makes every second we got desperate precious.

Someone at his elbow was talking.

"Hello? I say, Inspector Field?"

Field looked up from his book and tried to focus. He'd had more whiskey than he'd intended.

"It's Sergeant Willette, old man, of the Thames Valley Constabulary."

"Oh, yes," said Field without enthusiasm.

"I came to town on purpose to find you, but you took some finding, my friend."

Field looked away and nodded. "Drink?" he said.

"Stout for me. You've had a change in situation."

Field motioned to one of the barmen. "Pint of stout for the gentleman."

Willette looked about the smoky pub, filling up at the end of the afternoon. "Forgive me, Field, but what in the name of God are you doing here? If I may ask?"

"I don't believe you may, sir."

Willette nodded. "Fair enough, I suppose."

"What's on your mind?" said Field guardedly, watching Mickie Goodfellow who was serving at the other end of the bar.

The sergeant took a sip from his pint. "It's that guest house in Oxford we looked into together. I've kept my eye on it ever since. The proprietress never returned. That got me wondering if it was because she knew the police had called, so I looked a bit further. Town records show the house is owned by a Mr. Donnelly Andrews, a church organist who went to London one day six years ago and never came back."

"So his wife started taking in lodgers?" said Field.

"Never had a wife. According to those who knew him, Mr. Andrews was not at all in the marrying way, if you take my meaning."

"So who is Mrs. Andrews? A relative?"

"No one knows, but I doubt it. When she failed to return, my boys and I had another look round. In a little room at the top of the house we found an old wardrobe, a smallish one. Crammed inside was a middle-aged woman. Fully dressed. Her skin was like leather, like one of the mummies at the British Museum."

Field nodded. "How many ears had she?"

"How extraordinary you should ask! Her left one was off, and her teeth were in a glass jar, perched neatly on her shoulder."

"Good God. I wonder if it could be Philip Rendell's mother. Cause of death?"

"Not readily apparent, but the coroner is looking into it. Philip Rendell—isn't that the chap who shot at the Queen?"

"It is, it was," said Field with growing excitement. He suddenly felt keenly sober.

"Charlie?" said Goodfellow, standing just opposite them, a glint in his eye. "Everything all right?"

In an instant the inspector recalled his altered state. There was no *we* in his life anymore, no team of fellow officers, and nothing to investigate. Only things to hide.

"That's right, Mick. All is well. Sergeant Willette, may I introduce my old friend, the landlord hereabouts, Mr. Goodfellow." The two men shook hands over the bar. "Willette's with the Oxford police."

"I'll tell you what, Sergeant," said Goodfellow in his most genial manner, "the best decision I ever took was to tempt this man here away from the Metropolitan and into my employ. The town's loss is my gain, don't you see? I'm making him a full partner in all my enterprises. Mr.

Bucket is getting stinking rich at my expense, he is." He reached across the bar and gave Field a playful punch to the jaw.

Field bore it, expressionless.

"Sets his teeth on edge," chuckled Goodfellow, "to be called Bucket."

"The inspector created quite a stir on my patch not long ago," said Willette. "Everyone's still talking about him at Oxford."

Field was very still, staring off above their heads.

"Good Lord," said Goodfellow, seeing Sam Llewellyn make his way through the crowd to the bar. "You might have warned me, Charlie, that you were hosting a bloody policeman's convention!"

"Chief!" said the constable urgently. "I've found him. *And* Mrs. Andrews."

"I say, well done," said Willette. "Who's *him*, though?"

"How do you do, Sergeant," said Llewellyn. "Mr. Field, I'm quite sure our man's name is Cobb. Decimus Cobb at No. 4 Half Moon Street."

"What's all this?" said Goodfellow, all geniality gone.

Field finished his whiskey.

"Nothing to do with me," he said, pushing away from the bar.

"But, Chief . . ."

"I am not your chief," said Field evenly. "I am nothing to you, nor you to me." He turned and edged through the customers, disappearing into the saloon bar.

A moment later, Charles Field stood in the ice-cooled darkness of the room behind the funeral chapel, trying to breathe. When he was in trouble in the past, he would turn to his wife for answers. Now there was an endless, ever-changing row of corpses between him and Mrs. Field. Between him and the rest of the world.

There was a popping sound and the gaslights slowly rose in the room.

"Is that you, Mr. Field?" said the copper-haired woman. "I had just now put this light out. Come to see our newest arrival, have you?"

"No, Mrs. Carmichael, I have not."

"Oh, but he's a dear old thing, just in. Look at that head of white hair and that bushy white beard—positively aristocratic. Must have perished on the operating table, his throat is newly stitched up, you see? And they've patched over this ear."

Field slowly approached the bench where the elderly naked body lay.

"From the expression on his face," said Mrs. Carmichael, "he did not enjoy his surgery very much, but that's not to be wondered at, is it? Gout, you see, they had his toes off."

"Who brought in this man?" said Field quietly.

"Will Tailor, him and his lad. They just now left. Mr. Field, what are you doing? *You can't go in there!*"

Field yanked the black drapes aside and thrust open the door into the funeral chapel. He took in the sight of Reverend Carmichael dressed in his smalls, sitting at the pump organ, looking shocked. Then Goodfellow burst into the chapel, shouting.

"*Charlie!* You listen to me!"

Field pushed open the front door and ran out into the road. Both Giltspur and Cock Lane were crowded with street traffic: horse-drawn carriages, cabs, and individual horsemen.

Sir Jasper had to have been brought on a cart.

Giltspur led north, past St. Bartholomew's Hospital to Smithfield Market, perhaps a hundred yards distant, and south to Holborn, the area's major thoroughfare. Cock Lane was narrow and nearly choked with traffic; Field saw no cart down that way. He chose to walk south on Giltspur, moving briskly along the middle of the road toward Holborn, weaving in and out among the carriages. He realized that Sergeant Willette was trotting up abreast of him, followed by Llewellyn.

"I say, Field," said Willette, "what's going on?"

"Sergeant," said Field, "would you kindly turn round and head up toward Smithfield? Just in case I'm wrong? We're looking for a cart big enough to hold a coffin, or at least a corpse, driven by a tall slender man and a boy of about fifteen, ginger-haired."

"Same pair as you were looking for in Oxford, is it? What do I do if I find them?"

"Stick with them but not too close."

Willette turned and headed toward the market.

"Llewellyn, you come with me. Cobb, did you say? Not Tailor?"

"Back when I was nothing to you, nor you to me, I believe I did mention a Mr. Cobb."

Suddenly Inspector Field was running. "There he is!"

Llewellyn caught a glimpse, some distance ahead, of a cart moving toward Holborn, a tall slender figure driving the horses and a smaller figure sitting next to him. Llewellyn took off after them, dodging in and out among the horse-drawn vehicles while Field fought his way up the other side of the road.

"Whistle, Sam!"

The constable found the silver pipe in his tunic pocket and blew. The driver and his passenger glanced back over their shoulders, revealing the faces of a grizzled old farmer and his petite, elderly wife. The pair made the turn into Holborn and disappeared.

A sick feeling lodged in Field's belly.

Willette.

Field reversed direction, running north, and Llewellyn ran after him. Up ahead, just short of the market, Field saw a group gathering about a single figure who was shouting and pointing; it was Sergeant Willette, beckoning them urgently. The crowd arrayed itself in a discreet circle around the policeman, staring at him.

"Come along, Field!" cried Willette. "They've just gone round there, the man and the boy, off toward Long Lane, I'd say. On foot, you see? Here's their abandoned cart. The tall blighter struck me from it, or I'd have had him! Who is he, anyway?"

Willette didn't seem to realize that he was bleeding profusely from the left side of his head.

"You can still get them, Mr. Field! Go, go, go!"

In the distance the inspector saw the tall blond man making his way smoothly through the crowded market precincts and, with him, the boy he recognized as Tom Ginty. The man glanced back over his shoulder, offering an indelible view of deep-set eyes, mesmerizing even at this distance.

"Never mind *them*, old fellow," said Field to Willette, drawing a handkerchief from a pocket. "Let's step round to St. Bartholomew's, shall we? Get you looked after?"

Llewellyn was already at Willette's right side, taking him by the elbow.

"Why? The man knocked me down, that's all." He put a tentative hand to the side of his head. "Good God."

"Come along, sir," said Llewellyn. "Just lean on me, if you will."

"What's happened to me?" Willette stared at his left hand, which had come away covered in blood.

"Here we go, Sergeant," said Field, folding the handkerchief into a compress. "The hospital is just along here."

"Good God, the dirty blighter took off my ear," said Willette, then fainted dead into Llewellyn's arms.

Around the same time, at the Royal College of Surgeons, Sir Richard Owen waited impatiently. He'd had a message declaring that Sir Jasper Arpington-Dix had urgent business with him and was on his way. That was hours ago. Owen irritably passed the time by opening the afternoon post.

Methodically he scanned the letters and assigned them different piles, to be read and dealt with later. He came to a small parcel done up in brown paper. A lovely mother-of-pearl box was within. Owen frowned, perplexed, and took up the wrapping again. There was no return address. He cast aside the brown paper and lifted the lid on the box.

A normal thyroid gland has roughly the figure-eight shape of a butterfly. This one was swollen; a cancerous growth had grotesquely distorted its normal symmetry. Owen shoved the box away from him on the desk, stifling the wave of nausea he felt. In so doing, he caught sight of the accompanying note.

Sir Jasper is indisposed. Yours apologetically, Decimus.

Sir Richard Owen leapt to his feet but it was too late: he was sick all over his fine mahogany desk.

30

Sergeant Willette had lost a great deal of blood, as well as most of an ear, but the physicians who treated him at St. Bartholomew's were confident of his recovery. It was nearly dusk when Field and Llewellyn, both of them stained with the sergeant's blood, entered the Fortune of War and moved through the crowded room to the bar. Mickie Goodfellow watched them approach.

"Careful, Charlie," said Goodfellow.

"Will Tailor is, in fact, a man named Cobb, is that right? Does business with you regular?"

"Keep your voice down!"

"You got his name writ on little tags in the back room, tied to people's toes."

"You split on me, Charlie, I split on you, that was our deal."

"That deal only worked as long as I cared, which I don't no more. You lot ain't resurrectionists only, you lot are putting people to sleep!"

Two constables entered the pub and made for the bar. "Good God," said Goodfellow. "You'll regret this, Charlie, I swear."

"We have an officer at St. Bart's," said Llewellyn, "wounded by your Mr. Cobb. It was the doctors who sent for the police, not us."

"So, Mick, you can tell us all about him fast," said Field, "or I can take the constables back to meet your latest, a knight of the realm, cut to bits."

Goodfellow hesitated.

"I'll do it, I swear!" said Field. "Who's Cobb to you?"

His eyes on the approaching officers, Goodfellow spoke in a low voice. "Surgeon. With a sideline. Insane. I can't cross him, Charlie. It'd be worth my life. I never told you nothing, right?"

"Go on."

"He owns this whole show, Charlie. The chapel? Shepherd's Rest is his. Then he bought me out, didn't he. He took over the pub, Charlie, he's my bloody landlord."

"You son of a bitch. You had me working for him."

"You oughtn't to cross him neither, Charlie. He's death dressed up like a man."

"How d' you do, Mr. Field," said the older of the two constables.

"Passable, Mr. Peale," said Field. "Listen, there's a house in Half Moon Street we need to visit, and fast."

"Who's this *we*?" said Constable Peale. "I believe you left the Metropolitan, sir."

"So you'll have all the glory, won't you, Peale. You and your young partner here can make the arrest. And Mr. Llewellyn, of course. It's capital offenses, multiple murders, all yours."

"I dunno," said Peale doubtfully.

"You can't be seriously considering of it, Mr. Peale?" said the younger constable. "This man here's a laughingstock at HQ!"

"You'll go far, lad, I can see that," said Field. "What's your name?"

"Quinn."

"Look here, Constable Quinn, we'll clear it with your precious HQ first, right? Who's in charge of the detectives now?"

"Abercrombie, sir," said Peale.

"God help us. Well, we'll pay him a visit, lay it all out for him."

"He'll be happy to see *you*, Llewellyn," said Quinn. "He's just sacked you, you know, when you weren't to be found yet again. You're out of the Met."

"Shite!"

"Pity," said Field, nodding. "Still, too late now, isn't it, Sam. How about we call on this house in Half Moon Street and tell Detective Abercrombie later? Mr. Peale, are you with us? Constable Quinn? You can come along, or you can run along, it's up to you. I'll be back directly."

Field went to the staircase behind the bar and disappeared up the steps to his little room on the first floor. When he returned a couple of minutes later, he had the pistol, which few knew about, secreted within his coat. Quinn was gone; Peale and Llewellyn remained. Field nodded. "Let's go."

AFTER A LONG wait, the door at No. 4 Half Moon Street was opened by a hunched old man. He looked the policemen up and down in silence.

"We're from the Metropolitan Police," said Field, looking over the man's stooped shoulders to the dim recesses of the ground floor.

"What d' you want?"

"Is your master in? Mr. Cobb?"

"Which one?"

"You tell *me*, ducks," said Field.

The ancient servant's mouth grew wide, revealing a few black stumps. Field realized with an unpleasant shock that this, for the old geezer, was a smile.

"Mr. Cobb the First, weren't *he* a pretty one," said the relic.

"I'm sure he was, Mr. . . . ?" said Field impatiently.

"Hamlet."

"Hamlet?"

"Hamlet."

"Right, I've heard of you. Kindly let Mr. Cobb know the police would like a word."

"He's dead."

Field restrained himself. "Sorry, I shouldn't have been so bleeding obtuse. The *current* Mr. Cobb, if you'd be so good."

Old Hamlet sighed.

Constable Llewellyn was shouting. "Where's Mrs. Andrews? Where's the old woman with the warts? Where are the children I saw here just hours ago?"

Instead of answering, Hamlet groped for the chair that stood against the wall and sank down onto it, his grizzled head flopping back, looking to the heavens presumably. Field followed the old man's gaze.

"Oh, dear God."

John Getalong might have been a pockmarked angel looking down on them, suspended in the dim air above their heads. The rope he was hanging from was tied to a railing on the landing. Field took the stairs two at a time, although he knew there was no need for haste. Without touching anything, he made a cursory examination. "The lad did this to himself, I'm afraid," he said.

As the only currently legitimate member of the Metropolitan present, Constable Peale was quietly dispatched to fetch in a coroner. Field drew the pistol from his inside pocket and motioned Llewellyn to one side of the door closest to them. At a nod from his chief, Llewellyn turned the knob, flung the door open, and Field plunged before him into the room. A dull glow from the streetlamp on the opposite side of the road touched bookshelves, small tables, a globe. A clock ticked.

"He ain't in there," said the desiccated old man, still sitting just outside the room. "Cut you into little pieces if he was." He started to laugh, choked noisily, and fell silent. Field lit the gas sconce on the wall. The books stacked on end tables were atlases. Most featured German duchies and principalities.

"Royal family off traveling soon, you said, Sam?" said Field.

"To Germany in little over a month, according to Peter Sims."

Downstairs in the kitchen they found an old crone who looked disturbingly like the ancient man who'd let them in. She was sitting on a stool against the wall, shaking her head.

"It's all broke up now," she said without prompting. "Nothing's the same since he took in the new boy."

"Is that the boy, hanging in the hall?"

"No! That's John Getalong, of course. Idiot boy devoted to Master, and Master broke his heart again and again."

"Where is Cobb?" said Field.

"They're off abroad, ain't they."

"But we saw them just hours ago in the Smithfield Market."

The crone shrugged.

"Why would your master be going abroad?"

"Oh, yes," cackled the old woman. "Master tells *me* everything."

"Where abroad?"

"I dunno. Across the water. The witch is gone, too, God knows where."

"This witch, her name is Andrews?"

"Scum. She's the one who sold the choirboy to the first Mr. Cobb all those years ago."

"Sold?"

"Always wondered what Mr. Artemus paid for him. He was no bargain, mind you, not at any price."

"Is there anyone else in the house?" asked Llewellyn.

"Dunno. The little hussy may still be about. Master sent Mary Do-Not off as kitchen help to folks he wanted to punish."

"Mary *what*?"

"'Do-Not,' Master called her. He gives us all names, you see. That one upstairs weren't born a Hamlet, believe me, nor yet was I Mrs. Hamlet when he led me from the altar, curse the day."

"To punish, you say?" said Field.

"She's got the evil eye. Wherever Mary Do-Not goes, they sicken and die." She shook her head mournfully. "What's to become of me? Hamlet will be dead soon. Where's the food to come from? And the coals? How am I to eat?"

The men left her rocking on her stool and moaning. On the first floor they found the two doors off the landing locked.

"Here's where the odd smell's coming from, sir," said Llewellyn. "A mix of scents."

"Eau de cologne and carbolic? Let's put our shoulders to it, Sam."

"No, sir! If it's true I'm no longer in the Metropolitan, that would be breaking and entering, and I wish to avoid Newgate even if you're determined to end up there!"

Field, muttering, turned his back on the young man.

"What's that you said, Mr. Field? If you've something to say to me, say it!"

"Never mind!" growled the inspector as he started up to the next floor. The rooms off this landing were unlocked. The first contained two cots and a few bits and pieces of boys' clothing, some larger, some smaller. The wooden louvered blinds were nailed shut. Field thought-fully fingered a single slat on one that was loose and could be lifted to give a glimpse of the step below. The second bedroom on that floor looked as though it had been recently vacated by a woman in mourn-ing: there were long black hat pins scattered on the floor, black ribbons at the bottom of a wardrobe, and a torn black veil.

At the top of the house the men found the tidy room with the femi-nine bed and the divan and the austere desk between them, stained here and there with ink. The grime on the windows had been rubbed repeatedly by someone wishing to see the outside world.

Llewellyn stooped to look under the bed and came up with a sheet of crumpled foolscap. He smoothed it out, brushed off the balls of dust, and read aloud: "'From 1577 until 1580 Sir Francis Drake circumnavi-gated parentheses sailed round end parentheses, the globe.' A young person's writing, female most likely. She blotted it and discarded it."

Charles Field was on his hands and knees, peering beneath the divan.

"Hullo!" He got to his feet, holding aloft a boy's stocking trium-phantly. "Here he is, Sam! This right here is Tom Ginty, I just know it is, the little wanker!" He stared at the sock, suddenly somber. "He's only a boy, Sam. He's been too long with that bloody monster. I mean to find him and get him back to his mother if it's the last thing I do!"

Llewellyn cocked his head, listening. "What was that?"

"What?"

Llewellyn put a finger to his lips. He moved quietly to the dumbwaiter set into the wall, listening. He grabbed the handle and shot the door up. A pair of frightened eyes stared out, blinking rapidly.

"What in God's name . . .?"

The eyes of the girl in the box filled with tears.

"Hullo," said Field. "How long have you been in there, then? Can't be comfortable. Climb on out, we don't bite. Let the handsome young man help you."

"Can you find Tom?" she whispered.

"I . . . I certainly can."

"He don't care for me, but I care for him, see?"

"What's your name, dear?"

"Belinda."

"Well, Belinda. Men can be hard to fathom. Same with women, if you think about it. From the male point of view, difficult to decipher. Mysterious." Field winked kindly at the girl and a smile flickered briefly across her face.

"Do you actually ride up and down in this thing?" said Field, and the girl nodded proudly. "Astonishing. Well, you just climb into Officer Llewellyn's waiting arms there, and let's get you out of here and off to my good wife's."

Llewellyn smiled and nodded, trying to appear as harmless as possible. Belinda blinked doubtfully from one to the other.

"Wait a moment," said Field to Llewellyn. "This thing opens onto each of the floors below, don't it. Sam, she could ride it down to the rooms in question and unlock 'em from inside, don't you see?"

"Inspector, for Christ's sake!"

"It wouldn't be breaking and entering, then, would it!"

"*She's a child!*"

"*I know she's a child!* I know that!" He took a breath and turned back to the girl. "Sorry, my dear, I am a hasty man. Forgive me."

"Locked, anyways," said the girl. "Tried it once when he was away."

"Well, aren't you a marvel of resource and invention. My good wife will love to meet you."

After a moment the girl hesitantly started to inch her way out of the tiny cubicle. Just then there was a hammering from far below on the street door, followed by footsteps in the hall and shouts.

"Field! Mr. Field, do you hear me?" The voice was arch, like a headmaster's.

"Bloody hell," muttered Field, "it's Abercrombie himself. Don't he have better things to do?"

"Mr. Field, show yourself!"

The inspector stooped to the blinking face in the dumbwaiter again. "Belinda, I want you in my home, in the care of my good wife, before this day is done. Would you like that?"

She nodded tentatively.

"Good. You know your way round this house pretty well, am I right?" Belinda nodded again. "Is there another way out besides the front door?"

"From kitchen. Out the garden."

"Right, then, go there. Mr. Llewellyn and I are going down to talk with some gentlemen below and we don't want you mixed up with them. You lower yourself quietly as ever you can and scarper, right? Wait for us at the reservoir in the park—all right?"

The girl nodded. "Here we go," said Llewellyn, slowly shutting the dumbwaiter door on her.

He and the inspector clattered down the stairs, past the floor with the locked doors, past the hanging body of John Getalong. They found Detective Inspector Abercrombie and Constable Quinn staring up at the corpse. Constable Peale stood uneasily by the door. Hamlet, still seated, seemed to sleep soundly.

"Impersonating an officer of the law," said Inspector Abercrombie, addressing Field in a deadly tone. "Trespass. And now, in flagrante delicto, with a hanging corpse on premises where you have no legitimate business."

"It's all quite dreadful, I agree, sir."

"And you, Llewellyn! Such an able young man to have squandered your promise on this lunatic, I simply do not understand it!"

"Lunatic's a bit harsh, don't you think?" said Field.

"I should lock you up. I really should. Who is this fellow, hanging here?"

"Member of a household that you urgently need to look into, sir."

"Oh, do I."

"The head of which household is, we believe, leaving or about to leave the country with the intent of intercepting the royal couple in their upcoming travels, sir, and doing them to death."

"Still spreading your conspiracy theories, are you?"

"The man's name is Cobb. He's killed several persons that we know of."

"We think he killed Kilvert, sir," said Llewellyn.

Constable Peale cleared his throat. "Sir?" he said. "The old man, sir."

Abercrombie turned. "What about him?"

"He appears to have expired, sir."

"*What?*"

"Dead, sir."

Field touched Hamlet's throat. "Good Lord, so he is. 'Now cracks a noble heart.' That's Shakespeare, Abercrombie."

"Get out."

"Abercrombie, I implore you to rise above your plodding, dull-witted ways . . ."

"Get out, Mr. Field! Take your fool Welshman with you! I will be pleased if I never have to clap eyes on either one of you again! Out!"

Field and Llewellyn, free of the house, hastened along Half Moon Street toward Green Park. "Can't believe he let us off like that," said the inspector. "I wouldn't have done, I'd have locked us up for a few hours at least, teach us a lesson."

Llewellyn did not deign to reply.

It was dark now, but the lamps were lit and there was a moon. Belinda sat on a curb at the western end of the reservoir, a wooden case on her lap. Traffic was thinning; she looked very small and very alone.

"Well done, Belinda!" cried Field as they approached her. "Look at this, Mr. Llewellyn—she's even packed a traveling kit for herself!"

Belinda shook her head, her eyes darting around nervously.

"Not mine," she said.

"What isn't? What's wrong, dear? You're out of that house and you'll never have to go back, I promise."

"I stopped for it on me way down," she whispered, indicating the case. "Dumbwaiter door wasn't locked this time."

"This is from your master's rooms?" said Llewellyn.

She nodded, her face screwed up with fear.

"Would you like me to take it from you, Belinda?" said Field.

"There's lots more boxes like it," she said, relinquishing the latched wooden case to the inspector. "I just took the one." She was trembling.

"I see," said Field. "Did you look inside?"

She nodded, tears starting down her cheeks. Field offered his hand and she took it, standing.

"It's got bits in it," whispered the girl. Field nodded somberly.

"Let's go say hello to Mrs. Field, shall we? Won't she be surprised! You can show her that lovely bracelet if you like."

She touched the gold-link bracelet on one wrist and looked up at Field gratefully.

"We will let Officer Llewellyn carry the box." The inspector passed the box back to the constable. "We won't even think about it no more. All right, Belinda?"

The girl nodded and the two of them started walking, hand in hand, followed by Llewellyn with the case.

"Before you know it Mrs. Field will have set something tasty to eat before us. You all right back there, Sam?"

Llewellyn nodded grimly.

A rapidly approaching carriage swerved toward them and clattered to a sudden stop. "There she is!" cried a woman from within. "Belinda?

Precious? What have they done to you!" A streetlamp caught the woman's luxuriant coppery hair, blossoming out from under her bonnet.

"Who's that?" said Field. "Mrs. Carmichael?"

The dignified silver-haired gentleman holding the reins shouted, "Despicable men! Vile! Get them, boys!"

The few passersby watched with interest. Two lanky youths leapt down from the carriage. One slashed at Field's face with a stiletto while the other tore Belinda from him and swung her up into the carriage. The Reverend Carmichael caught Llewellyn around the neck with his riding whip and pulled him to the paving stones. There was another crack of the whip and the horses jolted forward. Field tried to grab hold of the rig, but a blow from a cosh wielded by Mrs. Carmichael knocked him to the ground, unconscious. The carriage sped into the night.

WHEN THE AMBUSH struck, Llewellyn realized in an instant that they were not up against a sole madman but concerted enemies. Mr. Field had been right all along. Llewellyn flopped over onto the wooden case and lay there covering it until he heard the carriage clattering off. When all was quiet, he got to his feet, clutching the box with one hand and gingerly touching his neck with the other. He approached Field, who lay motionless in a pool of lamplight, and knelt beside him.

"Hi! You there!" A constable was approaching quickly.

Who knew how wide this conspiracy was? How far did it reach? Into the Metropolitan Police itself? Llewellyn stood and walked at a sedate pace into Green Park.

"Is that you, Llewellyn?" the constable shouted after him. He blew his whistle, and Llewellyn stepped up his pace, turned the corner round the reservoir, and broke into a run.

But where to? This will never do.

He gradually slowed to a walk again, glanced casually over his shoulder and assured himself he was not followed. He found a bench beneath a gas lamp and sat. He would ignore the pain running round his neck from the whiplash. He would take time to see what he had on his hands. He set the case on his lap and opened it.

He was not surprised by the ears; he had expected these. It was the other "bits" that provoked a sharp intake of breath. Mr. Cobb's tastes were eclectic. The specimens were each mounted under little glass squares. The glass squares were mounted on cream-colored mats; one per mat in some cases, two in others. The mats were attached to the case by wire rings. Orderly. Scientific. A fine hand had labeled each; a flowing black script on the cream-colored boards.

A withered nipple. An ear. What seemed to be a portion, perfectly preserved, of a young person's lips: pale, cracked, pursed.

Llewellyn slammed shut the case and took deep breaths. He would not be sick. He would think and act. He headed on foot toward Pimlico. The case at the end of his arm felt heavy as lead.

Whatever am I doing?

He had openly antagonized his superiors at the Metropolitan Police. He was hardly in a position to stop this madman, much less to protect Albert and Victoria. It was a hopeless tangle. He shifted the case from one hand to the other. Doing so brought to mind its contents.

Never mind hopeless, Sam Llewellyn. The man who filled this case and others like it must not be allowed to walk the earth. All there is to it, really.

Tom Ginty was surprised to find he did not feel sick in the least. His master was off, walking up and down the deck of the little steamer as it rose and plunged with the waves. Tom stood at the bow, clinging to the rail. From the atlases he'd studied, he roughly knew the course the ship would take across the North Sea to Ostend. He knew the streets of the town ahead of him—those nearest the harbor, anyhow—and the roads that led to Antwerp. Many maps lived within Tom's head.

For now, though, there was no land in sight. Under the moon the steel-colored sea merged into a steel-colored sky without a join. There was no past and no future. Tom closed his eyes, letting the wind lift his hair and breathing deeply the sharp salt tang of the air.

PART IV

31

When Charles Field regained consciousness, a constable was taking him in charge. His head throbbed, his vision was blurred, and Sam Llewellyn was nowhere to be seen.

"Had more to drink as was good for you, am I right, Mr. Field?" said the policeman. "Do you find it wearying at all, sir, living up to your reputation?"

When the officers at the station found the pistol in Field's pocket, their mood shifted; he was no longer a joking matter. Furious, Field called for Detective Abercrombie, who finally appeared and obliged the inspector by having him locked up for the night. He was led off, shouting about a girl named Belinda and the Shepherd's Rest chapel by the Fortune of War.

The next morning, with a parched mouth and spots swimming before his eyes, he called from his cell until he was hoarse. At length

Abercrombie approached with Police Commissioner Mayne himself, both of them regarding him—he felt—with pity and disgust.

"Show us," said Mayne. "Come along with us to this pub and this chapel and show us the hidden room and all the corpses."

With a swimming head, the inspector crossed town in a carriage with the senior policemen. He asked them what they'd done with Sam Llewellyn, but they seemed not to know what he was talking about. At the Fortune of War Field stumbled dizzily on the threshold and nearly fell. Mayne and Abercrombie exchanged meaningful glances.

Mickie Goodfellow greeted the police officers cordially enough and led them through his establishment.

"Decimus Cobb owns it all," Field said, his voice cracking. "It's his game, start to finish."

"Is it now, Charlie?" said Goodfellow. "And who is this Cobb when he's at home?"

"The man who owns you, Mickie—that's who!"

Goodfellow smiled compassionately and shook his head.

"Take us to the gents!" cried Field hoarsely, realizing how ridiculous he must sound. "Take us to the room!"

Goodfellow shrugged indulgently and led them to the door in the saloon bar marked *Not in service*. The publican was saying something quietly to Commissioner Mayne; Field strained to hear.

" . . . took him on for old times' sake but had to dismiss him, poor man, he was drinking up all my stock . . ."

Goodfellow led them down the brick corridor and into the chapel's back room. It was brightly lit. Rows of shelves ran round the room, on which sat funeral urns and buckets of flowers, sprays and wreaths. Two tall young men were arranging a large bouquet; they registered surprise at the interruption but bowed to the visitors gravely. Field felt he was underwater. Sounds were muted and motion was unnaturally slow.

The Carmichaels entered and greeted the officers respectfully after their fashion, the reverend, reserved and dignified; Mrs. Carmichael, effusive and beaming.

"Where is she?" rasped Field, his voice nearly gone. "What have you done with the little girl? I'll walk away, I'll forget about the bodies and all the rest of it if you just let me have the little girl again!"

"What little girl is this, then, my dear?" said Mrs. Carmichael sweetly. Field tried to strike her, but Goodfellow grabbed him and held him back.

"Good God, Charles," muttered Commissioner Mayne.

"Poor man," said Goodfellow. "He's far gone."

The figures in the brightly lit room spun round and round, looking at him with distaste.

"Go on, Field," said Mayne. "Get out."

And then he was crawling out of a hogshead. It felt like dawn, or nearly. He was somewhere in Smithfield, he thought. He found a pump, stripped to his smalls, and put himself under it. Bruises on his head came alive under the streams of icy water. He sat on the ground, dizzy with hunger. To an old woman who was passing with a bulging sack of bread, he said, "Mother, give us half a loaf. You can see I've had hard times."

She passed him by, then stopped and turned her toothless, creased face to him. "Do you mean to teach *me* about hard times?"

"Forgive me, Mother."

She lowered her sack to the ground and fished a half round from it. "Thank you," said Field humbly.

"Don't drink," said the old woman. "Look after your wife and children." She hoisted the bag and moved on. He bit into the loaf and ate ravenously, even as tears came streaming down his face.

Belinda. Tom. Josiah. Sam.

He dried his face and dressed himself. From Jake Figgis at the butcher's stall he got a cup of tea.

"Bless you and your wife for taking in Mrs. Ginty, Inspector," said Jake. "She's that troubled in her mind, along of her boy gone missing."

"I had her boy and lost him. Whatever you do, don't bless me."

And then Field began to walk. He walked from the Fortune of War to Green Park, scanning the ground for even a hint of little Belinda. He walked back again, along a different route. And to the park again, searching for the girl and for everything else he'd lost. Between Charles Dickens and Charles Darwin, Field was no longer certain who he was. Clearly he was not the clever detective Dickens had drawn. Was he no more than a fortuitous collection of atoms?

Perhaps not even fortuitous, if it comes to that.

Again and again, he crossed the town. It was very late when he finally presented himself at No. 2 Bow Street. Jane opened the door to him in her nightclothes. Field stood empty-handed and silent before her. Without a word Jane led him up to their bed where he slept like a dead thing.

OXFORD

SAMUEL WILBERFORCE WAS a quivering jelly by the time Richard Owen arrived at Oxford in answer to the bishop's urgent bidding. Wilberforce's normally ruddy complexion was ashen. His reedy voice shook and his hands trembled as they clasped each other. Owen suggested they walk together along the Isis.

"Why me?" said Wilberforce. "I've never even met the man."

"When did it come?"

"Yesterday. I was never a party to any conspiracy!"

"Now, now, Wilberforce . . ."

"I was *not*! I never knew what you and the others were getting up to and I never wanted to know!"

"Don't shout, man. People are looking."

Fog and morning rain had given way to cool September sunshine. The grass in Christ Church meadow glistened.

"From where was it sent?"

"Ostend. 'What's this,' I thought—a parcel from Belgium."

"So he's already launched himself," muttered Owen.

"I have former students throughout the continent; it's not unheard of for one of them to send me a little gift, a token of gratitude or affection. It never occurred to me not to open it. Oh, God, I feel sick, even now!"

"Steady on, Wilberforce."

"It's no wonder poor Sir Jasper hobbled so. The toe in the parcel was three times the size it should have been. 'Sir Jasper would send his regrets if he were able, full stop.'" The bishop stopped and put his hands on his knees, taking deep breaths.

"Calm yourself, Wilberforce."

"*Calm* myself? I'm in fear of my life!"

"Mr. Cobb has gone out of the country, anyway."

"Stop!" The bishop looked about guiltily and then lowered his voice. "No names! I will hear no names!" They walked on in silence for a few moments. "Who *is* this man? Some sort of assassin?"

"You know very well he is an assassin, Wilberforce. Your hypocritical posing is wasted on me."

"Damn you, Owen! You're an arrogant prick! Everyone knows it, everyone agrees. No one can *bear* you actually, did you know that? No one!"

"When you've done with your childish taunts, my lord bishop, perhaps we can discuss a strategy."

"Here is my strategy: I am finished with you! You may consider our acquaintance to be at an end!"

Owen sighed. "Tiresome man. Well, let it be as you wish. You will be discreet, my lord? Thoroughly so?"

"Of course. What do you take me for?"

A flock of starlings swooped and dove in the distance.

"We will watch quietly, then, as events unfold," said Owen, looking off at the birds. "Perhaps he will be apprehended."

"Pray God they hang him on the spot!"

LONDON

THE HUXLEY HOUSEHOLD was once again in a state of profoundest anxiety. At the beginning of the summer, the little boy, Noel, had recovered from whatever childhood disease he had suffered. The visits from the physicians had ceased. Thomas Huxley and his wife had rejoiced (and so had Mary Do-Not, née Withers).

Now, though, the doctors were back. The nursery again became a sick ward. People talked in whispers, and the servants put down straw in the road outside the house to quiet the wheels of the passing carriages. Noel Huxley lay gravely ill and his parents were distraught. Mary, going about her duties, renewed her prayers for the little boy's recovery.

And then—Mary called it answered prayer—Cook reported that the doctors were saying it was the scarlet fever that laid the boy low—*not* typhoid at all! No one could accuse Mary of somehow bringing the typhoid into the house, because it wasn't there! The girl was very sorry for the little boy and his parents, but there was a voice deep within her that was singing for joy. Her history of the world made wonderful progress during late-night writing sessions; it leapt forward. By the time the four-year-old died, she was up to the beheading of Charles I.

Less than a week later, though, Cook herself took to bed with a high fever and stomach pains. A swath of rose-colored spots spread across her abdomen. The next day her fever was even higher. Mary quietly packed her clothing and her pages. She stole a quantity of cash from the household box and slipped out in the dead of night.

NEAR OSTEND, BELGIUM

TOM DIDN'T KNOW whose grand country house they were staying in, and, of course, he didn't inquire. From the elegant bedroom he'd been assigned, he heard voices in the night. The servants spoke German, never mind that Master called this place Belgium. Tom was learning words. He surprised himself and those around him by how quickly he was able to understand short phrases and to repeat them.

But the big thing was the horse. Master said she was to be his! Standing before her, Tom was suddenly reminded of his first journey, when he was eight years old. They called the place Dorset. His mother and father were there, and sister Lily, aged six. Uncles, aunts, cousins. But mostly he remembered the horse! She was a brown mare called Julie. His father put him in the saddle and walked alongside, one hand on Tom's ankle, talking quiet to Julie. *How did you know to talk to horses, Dad?* It was the good time, the best, before the sickness came.

"Tom," said Master, bringing the boy out of his memories, "what will you call her?" A groom helped Tom up into the saddle.

"Lily."

Day after day he rode. He was up before dawn with the staff. At first he rode with the groom; soon he rode alone. He rode over the wet meadows as the sun rose. A saddle, he felt, was the place on earth where he most belonged: the strong chestnut flanks between his legs, the sweat and smell of the hide, the rhythms of the different gaits jolting his body, the dizzying speed and the heart-pounding thunder of the hooves.

In no time at all Tom on his chestnut could ride better than Master on his jet-black horse; Master generally stood in the stirrups, rather than sit, as if always ready to leap.

32

LONDON

At No. 2 Bow Street, Bessie Shoreham left the gentleman standing at the door while she went to confer with her mistress. Eventually she returned, dipped a curtsy, and said, "Lady of the house begs pardon but says Master is laid up ill."

"Kindly tell the lady of the house that my errand with her husband is of the greatest urgency, or I wouldn't press the matter."

Once again Bessie made the trip from street door to her employers' bedchamber and back with a refusal. Finally Charles Field himself descended the stairs in a dressing gown and a temper.

"Listen, you. If you want to take me in charge, have the goodness to wait a day, will you? For old times' sake and for all I done for the Metropolitan? I've been long gone from my good wife and I've been unwell. Surely Commissioner Mayne can wait one day more to see me in custody!" Field was just a few steps from the gentleman when he stopped. "Good Lord, who are you?"

The gentleman smiled. "We *have* met, you know, Inspector Field."

"Shoot me for a fool, you're Sir Horace Dugdale. From the palace."

Sir Horace bowed.

"I beg your pardon, sir," said Field.

Jane stood on the staircase above her husband, and Bessie with her. Martha Ginty had come up from the kitchen below and stood staring at the visitor.

"Well," said Sir Horace, cheerily, "hullo, all!"

Jane and Bessie curtsied.

"Now that we've cleared up the mystery of my identity, I hope I can prevail upon you, Inspector, to accompany me, unless of course you truly *are* too ill to attend the Prince."

"The Prince," repeated Field.

"His Royal Highness summoned your colleague Llewellyn to the palace early this morning, and the constable already has told us quite a tale."

"Summoned my Sam Llewellyn to the palace? His Highness did?"

"He is most eager to speak with you as well, Inspector Field."

"You understand, sir, I am no longer a detective inspector, I am no longer with the Metropolitan Police."

"Nonsense. You were reinstated this morning. Commissioner Mayne is currently mulling an appropriate rise in your wages and, I imagine, an apology."

Field stared in confusion at the man from the palace.

"The Prince, by the way, is unaware of your brief sabbatical from the force. I see no reason to disturb him with the knowledge of a minor contretemps that is now well behind us."

"Come along then, Mr. Field," said Jane. "We'll get him dressed and brushed up for you, sir, if you just give us a moment."

"By all means," said Sir Horace.

Field indicated a chair by the door, wishing it weren't quite so shabby. "Do have a seat, sir."

Suddenly Martha Ginty took a step forward. "Have you seen my Tom? Tom Ginty, ginger hair."

"I have *not* seen him, ma'am, but I do believe I have heard of him. The butcher's apprentice?"

Martha nodded eagerly.

"I assure you, ma'am, we all are concerned about your boy. We shall do everything we can, one way or another, I promise you."

Whatever that meant.

Sir Horace ushered Field into the Prince's study. Llewellyn was already there, smiling wanly, and a young man whom Llewellyn introduced as his friend, *the Peter Sims I told you about, sir*, a groom with the royal household. In response to Sir Horace's raised eyebrows, Peter said, "His Highness stepped out soon after you left, sir." The groom tilted his head in the direction of a communicating door.

The courtier crossed the room, tapped gently on the door, and opened it. Moments later the Prince Consort entered and sat behind his desk.

"Detective Inspector Field," said Albert, "how good of you to come."

Field, utterly bewildered, tried to indicate with a nod and a deprecatory smile that he had been only too happy to rearrange his schedule.

"Sims here suggested not long ago that a friend of his—a member of the Metropolitan Police—suspected a plot was afoot against my life and so forth. When I could find the time—this morning, in fact—I invited this man in to enlighten me, and he turned out to be *your* man, Mr. Field. I confess I was somewhat skeptical. But Llewellyn asked for and received a separate interview with our friend, Sir Horace. It seems he possessed evidence that he wished to share with *him* but not with *me*. Well, fair enough, I suppose. When I returned from my breakfast, Sir Horace assured me that the matter was of the gravest urgency. Is that fair to say, Sir Horace?"

"Yes, my lord. Although I have yet to see any evidence of a broad conspiracy amongst the notables of the land, as Mr. Llewellyn has suggested, I *can* confirm that one is dealing here with a profound criminality."

"Mr. Llewellyn?" said the Prince. "You have a question?"

"Only this, sir," he said. "Begging your pardon, Sir Horace, for interrupting, but Inspector Field has been right about this all along. If we got no conspiracy amongst the notables, we got no reason to be sitting here today—we'd merely have a devil who enjoys cutting people up, and sooner or later we'd run him to earth." He turned to the Prince. "Forgive me, sir, but it's the way I see it."

"According to Mr. Llewellyn," said Albert, turning to Field, "you have put forth several names—names of persons not unknown to myself and the Queen, persons we might even consider to be friends—who may be participants in this plot."

"Yes, sir," said Field.

"And this hostility, this alleged conspiracy is all because of my esteem for the work of Mr. Charles Darwin?"

"We believe so, sir."

"Extraordinary. I fervently hope you are mistaken, Mr. Field. But woe betide you if you are; this would be a fearful slander on your part." Albert pursed his lips. "He . . . cuts people up, you say?"

Field bowed his head in mute affirmation.

The Prince turned to Llewellyn. "The evidence you did not wish me to see had to do with this?"

"Your Highness, yes, sir."

The Prince sighed. "Well, Inspector Field, what would you suggest?"

Field cleared his throat. "You are planning a trip, I believe, sir?"

"Indeed, to my homeland."

"Cancel it, sir."

"You are joking?"

"Can you believe, sir, that I would make light of such a situation? Cancel it."

"Impossible."

Llewellyn was alarmed to see his superior's face redden.

"Sir," said Field, "the killer is, we believe, already on his way to Germany or is there already, just a-waiting for you. Cancel your travel plans now and I'm confident this man will return to these shores. He will pursue you here—this one's not the sort to give up and go home, sir. But it will be much more within the grasp of the police to catch the bugger, individual, here on home ground."

"The Crown will not cower, Mr. Field. *I* shall not cower before a threat of this sort. The planning for this journey has been extensive and has taken up much of the past year. The Queen has prorogued Parliament and signed a new copy of her will. Three heads of state and their respective courts await us. My own daughter awaits us, and the grandchild whom we have never seen. We shall be making this trip."

"Yes, sir."

"Have you ever traveled on the continent, Mr. Field?"

"I have, sir."

"A holiday, perhaps?"

"Police work, sir."

"The Nightingale affair, Your Highness," murmured Sir Horace.

Albert's brow furrowed and he glanced uneasily at the inspector. "Ah, yes. Well. Here is what we will do. You will accompany the royal party on its journey to Coburg. Llewellyn and Sims, you also. Now listen to me. Under no circumstance are you there to protect myself. It is Her Majesty the Queen whose safety you are to ensure. This is how I will explain your presence to the Queen and the court. Do you understand? Good."

The news that the royal party would embark in only fifteen days put Jane Field into a state. There was so much to prepare, so many things to attend to! She dispatched Mr. Field to the barber, and Bessie cleaned and pressed his best clothing. Jane bought him new boots, and since Llewellyn had no woman in his life, she did the same for him.

Police Commissioner Mayne seemed to have no memory of the recent unpleasantness between himself and Inspector Field. Field was and always had been his chief of detectives. Abercrombie was transferred to Norwich.

Field issued orders and they were obeyed. A watch was to be placed on No. 4 Half Moon Street. A small girl named Belinda, a resident at this address, was missing and needed to be found; she had information pertinent to the case. An older woman at Oxford calling herself Andrews was of interest to Field: a Sergeant Willette of the local police would keep her guest house under observation. When Field asked for his pistol back, Commissioner Mayne grudgingly acquiesced. The only request that the commissioner flatly refused was to alert law enforcement in the royal party's destination, the kingdom of Saxe-Coburg; the palace had been firm on this matter. But Commissioner Mayne was quite willing to authorize the inspector's raid on the Fortune of War and Shepherd's Rest.

The chapel was shuttered; the Carmichaels were gone. Field dispatched two officers to search the building while he bearded Mickie Goodfellow in his tavern.

"I'm telling you, Charlie, I have no idea where they went! They must have gone in the night, I didn't hear nor see a thing."

"What about the little girl?"

"For the last time, Charlie, there wasn't no little girl! Not that I saw, anyways. Come, Charlie—would I lie to you?"

Field stared at the publican. "In the old days I would have followed my impulse to pound your face to a jelly, Mick. Those days are behind me."

Goodfellow grinned indulgently and shrugged.

"Officer Llewellyn," said Field, "take him away."

"What? Whatever for?" Llewellyn quickly snapped handcuffs on Goodfellow's wrists. "On what charge, Charlie? You can't do this! I got rights!"

"Yes, I can, and no, you don't."

With Goodfellow gone, Field returned to the chapel. His men had found nothing to indicate the whereabouts of the reverend or his wife, but one of the constables put a paper tag and a bit of string in the inspector's palm.

Will Tailor, the tag read.

The other officer had found a fine gold-link bracelet in the back room. The last time Inspector Field had seen it, it had been on young Belinda's wrist.

NEAR OSTEND

"WAKE UP, TOM."

Tom opened his eyes and saw Master's face just above his. Master held a candle and seemed to be studying him. *Help me, God.* In his mind Tom gauged the distance between his bed and the window. It was still full dark outside.

"The skull comprises interlocking plates. Elegant, secure, unmoving. Not like the mandible, is it, Tom? The jaw is *always* moving. Chew, chew, chew, talk, talk, talk."

Dear God above, help me.

"Can I trust you, Tom?"

The boy managed to nod.

"Your riding clothes are laid out for you. The next stage of our journey begins."

Decimus turned and left the room. Tom blinked back tears. He had just now pissed himself, but perhaps they would not be coming back here, so this one crime at least would go undetected.

For the next week, Master and Tom rode horseback at a desultory pace, stopping at small inns for the night. If the village had a telegraph office, Master would step into it for a minute or two. Had Tom thought about it, he would have guessed Master was expecting messages, or sending them, but he made sure he didn't think about it.

Out in the countryside they shot quail and hare for practice, and for practice of another sort, Tom skinned and boned them. Master gave Tom a variety of instruments and showed him how to work them. There were several blades on springs, which could be hidden about the body. There was a shiny brass garrote that operated like a noose when you pulled the cord back sharply. Lily was magnificent; she and Tom grew close in a remarkably short time, and the boy's skills as a horseman grew as well.

Master was alternately silent and talkative. "I have people everywhere, Tom," he said at one point. "Allegiances shift; loyalties cannot be relied upon. I have learned to spread wide my net. There are many of us who feel the threat posed by this Prince and the demon he champions.

They see the need for action, they see the need for a warrior of my abilities. When you are disappointed by one Arpington-Dix, Tom, you turn to the next one, in a manner of speaking."

One night they stayed in a town called Sint-Niklaas, and Tom nearly thought about Christmas before he caught himself and stopped thinking altogether. Master spoke in low tones with a serving girl that night, the one who had brought them sausage and potatoes for their supper, and then the two of them disappeared. When the girl didn't reappear in the breakfast room the next morning, Tom didn't think about that either.

THE ISLE OF WIGHT

ON THE EVE of her departure for the continent, Victoria hosted a small dinner at Osborne House, the residence in the Isle of Wight that Albert had designed and built for their private use. It had rained heavily all day, and even among this distinguished company there was an unmistakable air of damp. The conversation did not sparkle. After dinner the Queen retired early and Albert asked one of the guests to join him in his study.

Again the lamps were extinguished and the servants sent away as the Prince sat down in the dark with his old friend, Sir Richard Owen. Again rain slanted against the windows, as it had three months earlier, when Owen last had dined with the royal family. The two men sat in silence for a long moment, listening to the rain and sipping the fine whiskey that was shipped by the barrel for the Queen from her beloved Scotland.

"Do you ever wonder, Owen, about the paths your life did *not* take?" said Albert finally. "I do, from time to time. Had not fate and circumstance thrust me into all this, who might I have been? *What* might I have been? Do you ever so speculate?"

"No, sir, I must say I do not."

"It follows, then, that you have no regrets?"

Owen's smile was perplexed. "None that I am aware of."

What the devil is he getting at?

"I believe, had things been different for me, I should have been a serious student of natural philosophy instead of merely an ardent amateur. I have been rereading your writings, Owen. A remarkable body of work, going back decades now."

"I am flattered, Your Highness."

"I often examine that exquisite chambered nautilus you were so kind to give me—how many years ago was it? That shell alone presents a world of mystery, does it not? Back and back and back it goes, chamber after chamber. And so, confronted by such mystery, I read and ponder and struggle to understand."

"Whenever do you find the time?"

"Life is short and uncertain, Sir Richard, I *make* the time."

Is there an edge to his voice?

"It seems to me, sir, that your thinking on a number of matters has undergone changes over the years, yes?"

"Indeed, to be a man of science is to be continually learning anew, sir, discovering and unfolding the wonders of the natural world."

"Quite so. Earlier in your career, for instance, I think you stood firmly with the Frenchman Cuvier, did you not? Species may have gone extinct, but they were created separately and intact by the Creator."

I see, it's about Darwin again.

"I stand with no man, Your Highness. I'm a follower of knowledge, not men."

"Yes, yes, yes, yes," said Albert, impatiently. "I am asking you about your current position on species mutation, sir. It seems to me it has changed over the years. *Evolved*, if you will."

He's openly hostile, he's angry.

"Well, sir?" said the Prince. "You now acknowledge a *sort* of mutation, do you not? Or do I misread you?"

"My researches into the comparative anatomy of vertebrates have enlarged my understanding, certainly. I believe now that there exist archetypes from which variations may occur, as the twigs of a tree emanate from the branches, imitating and enlarging upon the shapes that precede them."

"Variations *occur*, precisely! *How?*"

"The archetype is of divine origin, of course. The variations are occasioned by divine intervention."

"So, Sir Richard, evolution is *God's* invention! God *nudges* creation from time to time, and so we get mutation of species!"

"As you acknowledge, my lord, these are complex matters for even the most ardent of amateurs." Owen realized that he'd said the wrong thing; the Prince was quietly furious.

"Do you not imagine, Owen, that if Charles Darwin had not existed, *you* by now would have reached the promised land yourself, in a manner of speaking? It would be you who had rightful claim to the most significant discovery since Newton. Since Galileo, since Archimedes. Already you were on the road toward it, *ja?* You were getting there. If it hadn't been for Darwin, the evolution theory would be *your* claim to eternal glory. But since it is Darwin's, not yours, you are compelled to declare it false and reject it."

Owen's face flushed.

"Poor Sir Jasper Arpington-Dix," said the Prince out of the blue. "I am told by the police they suspect murder."

Dear God, he's telling me he knows. He knows everything.

"They say whenever dismemberment is involved," continued Albert drily, "foul play is suspected. I am so happy you were able to spend a few moments helping this ardent amateur understand the great matters of the world, Sir Richard. Good night. And goodbye."

HE SAT AT the desk in his little guest room, quill in hand. He would place an advertisement in the Ostend newspaper. And in the papers of neighboring towns. Sir Richard Owen, his face white with terror, his hand shaking, wrote out the message.

Choral Master: Nothing is secret that shall not be made manifest, neither anything hid that shall not be known and come abroad. Repent and return.

33

Her Majesty the Queen and her entourage boarded the royal yacht at Woolwich on the evening of the twenty-second of September. The *Victoria and Albert* was a steam-powered, paddle-wheeled palace. Her long, sleek hull was a gleaming black with rich gold trim. The two massive paddle wheels were discreetly enclosed amidships; the smokestacks were taller by far than the highest masts in the harbor, and the staffs bearing the royal banners were higher still. There was a pavilion on deck for royal dining, and below decks were accommodations that emulated on a smaller scale Victoria's other homes. Farther sternward were the mess and quarters for servants and crew.

This was to be a family trip, not a state visit, so Albert kept the number of passengers low. There were six close friends who already had endured royal entertainments and were not likely to kick up a fuss at the discomforts of further travels with Her Majesty: bone-chilling cold because of Victoria's hatred of heated rooms and, in the evenings, flickering candlelight because Victoria considered gaslights to be a decadent modernity. The bare minimum of personal attendants were aboard, a little over a dozen for Victoria and Albert together. The Queen's personal physician, Sir James Clark, was on board. In addition, there were the equerries and the palace grooms, Peter Sims among them. And a shipboard crew of 240.

The royal couple dined with their guests not on deck this evening but in the saloon below. By the time the yacht weighed anchor around 3 a.m., bound for Antwerp, most everyone was asleep. But not Charles Field or Sam Llewellyn. They lay awake in hammocks, suspended one above the other.

"Crikey, Mr. Field," said Llewellyn in an awed whisper. "Will you look at us?"

The inspector allowed himself a smile in the darkness. "There's one thing to say for impersonating Detective Bucket, Sam. He does move in exalted circles."

Around 4 a.m. the royal yacht hit a brief patch of weather, and the policemen were sick by turns.

"Why does it pitch so?" gasped Field. "It's the Queen's own boat, for God's sake. I didn't think the Queen's own boat ought to be subject to pitching!"

LONDON

IT WAS ONE of Martha Ginty's bad days. Jane Field had noted her agitation at breakfast, Martha muttering to herself, seeming to be in a world of her own. When later in the day Jane found her missing from the house, she went looking for her.

She did not have far to search. Martha was sitting on a bench near the local pump, her large sign leaning against her knees, deep in conversation with an old woman. The woman was dressed in black; her black-plumed hat was a forest of long black hat pins.

"Mrs. Field," cried Martha, "I have wonderful news! This lady says

I needn't worry about my Tom no more, I needn't go about with my signs, searching him out! He's gone and made something of himself, she says!"

"Is that so?" said Jane, glancing dubiously at the woman and wondering how it would affect a person to go through life with two such prominent facial warts.

"Well," said the old woman, "if it's the same lad I'm thinking of, it is."

"But it must be!" cried Martha. "How many ginger-haired Toms who were 'prenticed to the butchers of Smithfield could there be?"

"Where is he, then?" asked Jane.

The woman in black shrugged. "Abroad."

"Gone abroad," said Martha, "to study with a surgeon, Tom is."

"Which surgeon is this?" said Jane. "I was a nurse, you see—I may know the man."

The woman stared for a moment and then said, "Tailor."

Jane felt a distinct tingle just below her sternum. Her husband had told her everything he knew about the case that so bedeviled him, including Sam Llewellyn's description of the lady on Half Moon Street, warts and all. When he said the murderer Cobb's other name was Tailor, she hadn't connected him with the St. Thomas surgeon known for his speed and skill. Now she did. Good Lord, she actually had *seen* the man herself on several occasions!

"This is wonderful news indeed," said Jane evenly. "Come along home, both of you, and you can tell us all about it, Mrs. . . . ?"

"Miss Coffin. I don't want to be a bother."

"A bother! Not likely, not when you bring word of Martha's Tom. It's a pity, though, the boy don't write a note to his mother, don't you think? Letting her know the good news himself, instead of leaving her half-mad with grief?"

"As I understand it," said the woman with the warts, "the boy can't read or write."

"Oh, no, no, no!" said Martha. "I taught him his letters when he was a boy. Tom reads ever so well."

The woman's eyes narrowed.

"Well, come along, then, both of you. We'll celebrate with a nice bit of cake I've got put by."

The woman looked uncertain.

Martha spoke up. "Miss Coffin lost her position in the medical man's household, Mrs. Field. It was along of the surgeon moving off to foreign parts with my Tom."

"In that case, Miss Coffin, you *must* stop with us! I won't take no for an answer."

"I'll need to collect my things."

"Excellent. No. 2 Bow Street, we'll be expecting you." There was a glitter in Jane's eyes. She had always envied the role *Mrs.* Bucket played in helping Mr. Bucket unravel the Dedlock mystery.

She took in the murderess herself, didn't she? Kept her as a lodger. Well, here's a chance to do the same for my *Bucket!*

ANTWERP

CHARLES FIELD AND Sam Llewellyn spent the day in their cubicle, recovering, as the royal yacht crossed the North Sea. At dusk the *Victoria and Albert* churned up the Scheldt estuary and finally dropped anchor. The policemen emerged from their small cabin, feeling hollow but improved, and made their way to the stern, where they leaned on a rail and stared. Antwerp lay before them, its harbor lighting up, lamp by lamp, spreading amber dimples across the black water. They would stay aboard with the royal party for the night and disembark in the morning to continue their journey by train.

"I do believe travel suits me, Mr. Field," said Llewellyn.

"Never you mind what suits you, Sam Llewellyn. We are not on holiday. If our fellow does for the Prince on our watch, there'll be no one to blame but you and me."

At the same moment, Tom Ginty and his master stood with dozens of other local sightseers who had gathered on the quay, looking out at the royal vessel, lit by a thousand lamps, sleek and regal.

"Magnificent," said Decimus. "Isn't it grand, Tom?"

Tom nodded. They could hear piano music coming from the royal yacht. They even could hear, once in a while, a sprinkle of genteel laughter.

"Look, there at the stern!" whispered Decimus. "If it isn't our old friend Detective Bucket and the other one, the cheeky constable!"

Tom had already spotted the man who had gripped his arm in the Oxford library and spoken to him of his mother.

"You know why they're here, don't you?" whispered Master. "It's along of us! Look how high you've risen, Tom—that the mighty should tremble before you!"

Tom nodded again, staring intently at the two policemen across the water.

"If only one could set the whole thing alight," said Decimus, "imagine how it would burn!"

THAT NIGHT AFTER the evening meal, the policemen and Peter Sims were summoned to attend the Prince in the saloon. The three men brushed themselves up, combing hair and mustaches, and Sims led them forward toward the royal suites.

"Perhaps we'll even learn where we're going and when!" said Field. "A plan, a plan, my kingdom for a plan!"

"Please, sir, hush," said Sims, "begging your pardon."

"Pardon granted, young Sims," said the inspector, and then in a stage whisper to Llewellyn, he said, "'So wise so young, they say do never live long.' That's Shakespeare, Mr. Sims. For nigh unto two days now, I've either been kicking my heels or sicking up in a pail, what we need is a *plan*!"

Someone behind a door coughed and Field was silent for the rest of their transit through the yacht.

The three men, admitted to the saloon, stood in the door, momentarily dazzled. Before them was a vast semicircular room paneled in maple, the pale golden wood lit by dozens of flickering candles. The carpet was a vivid crimson and the built-in banquettes were done in bright green silk. An ebony piano gleamed in the distance. A porcelain heater, its tiles painted with red and pink roses, stood near the long oblong oak table, which dominated the room. And there, seated at the head of the table and staring intently at them, was Her Majesty, Queen Victoria.

She motioned to Albert, standing above her. The Prince leaned forward and she whispered in his ear. He nodded and murmured.

Opposite the royal couple stood Sir Horace Dugdale and another man, dapper and goateed, also staring at the policemen.

The Queen cleared her throat. "Does Mr. Dickens tell you in advance what he has in store for you, Mr. Field?"

Field's mind raced. "Your Majesty?"

"One hopes one has not seen the last of Mr. Bucket," continued Her Majesty.

"Oh. Yes, ma'am," said the inspector. "No, ma'am."

Victoria nodded at the young groom. "Sims," she said, and Peter Sims bowed deeply. She glanced at Llewellyn appraisingly, then braced her hands on the table to rise. Albert pulled back his wife's chair and helped her to her feet, and a lady-in-waiting appeared from the shadows, adjusting the Queen's voluminous skirts.

"Do you really believe one is in danger, Mr. Field?" said the Queen.

"All will be well, Your Majesty, I'm certain."

"Your certainty may be misplaced, you know. We have been given ample reason to beware 'the arrow that flieth by day' and 'the pestilence that walketh in darkness.' Stop that," she said abruptly to the lady-in-waiting. "You're pinching."

With a great rustling of silks Her Majesty moved toward the door while Field and his men made way before her. She paused at the threshold.

"This is a simple family journey, Mr. Field. We trust you will not make a nuisance of yourself."

And she was gone. Field realized he hadn't been breathing for some time.

"Men," said the Prince, gesturing, "be seated."

Hesitantly, Field, Llewellyn, and Sims took the seats indicated. Just then another man entered the saloon, handsome, distinguished-looking and tall.

"Ah, Ponsonby," said Albert. "Good, we can begin."

"Good evening, sir," said Colonel Henry Ponsonby, equerry to Prince Albert and private secretary to the Queen.

"Colonel Ponsonby and Monsieur Kanné"—the dapper man inclined his head—"allow me to introduce Field and Llewellyn of the Metropolitan Police."

"Actually, sir," said Ponsonby, "I am acquainted with Detective Inspector Field already."

"Indeed?"

The colonel lowered his voice. "The Nightingale business, sir."

"Yes, of course," said the Prince with sudden distaste.

"Good to see you again, Field," said Ponsonby.

"And you, sir."

"Well, then," said Albert, "we have rather a complex schedule of travel ahead of us, Inspector Field. Monsieur Kanné here, who makes our arrangements, has worked it all out for us. If you would, monsieur?"

Joseph Julius Kanné laid out the itinerary in a crisp Gallic accent. In the morning Her Majesty would cross Antwerp by brougham to the train station, her guests following in similar carriages, with some of her entourage making the journey in a diligence. Others would board Her Majesty's tender yacht, HMY *Fairy*, and follow along down the Rhine. At Mainz they would again resort to horse-drawn coaches, transferring to a different train line. Here the Queen would board a railway carriage on loan from the Grand Duke of Hesse-Darmstadt, traveling just one stop to Frankfurt, where another change would be necessary. From Frankfurt they would proceed in the King of Bavaria's railway carriages, which they would keep all the way to Coburg, although there would be some complicated switching at Lichtenfels to a different railway line.

Kanné looked up from the itinerary beaming, as though anticipating applause.

"Well, that's all quite completely calamitous," said Field. "Her Majesty and the Prince are exposed again and again to risk. Let me see that itinerary, sir, if you please."

Kanné cast an affronted glance at Sir Horace. "Kindly oblige the inspector, monsieur," said that gentleman. With an ill grace Kanné slid the ornately illustrated page across the table to the inspector.

"Good Lord, why is the thing written in French?" cried Field.

"It is customary," replied Kanné icily.

"Well, it ain't *my* custom. Kindly copy it out in English, sir. No need to illustrate it, plain black and white will do. Three copies, if you please, before you retire for the night."

Kanné fairly staggered, so profound was the affront. Llewellyn and Peter Sims watched the Prince apprehensively but were relieved to see the corners of His Highness's mouth twitch and his eyes dart to Colonel Ponsonby with a twinkle.

"Who is familiar with this route and this timetable besides ourselves?" asked Field. "Let me guess: everyone, including the King of Bavaria's aunties."

"This is outrageous!" cried Kanné. "For a journey to be successful it is *essential* that everyone along the way know the details!"

"I'm sure that's how our assassin views it as well, sir. He's committed all this to memory, no doubt." Field sighed. "No changes are possible, I imagine?"

"I'm afraid not, Inspector," said Ponsonby. "Not at this late date."

"No, of course not, it's only the monarchy at risk. Well, we'll want tall men. If you would, sir, give me a list of the four tallest men in the crew and I'll have a private interview with 'em early tomorrow morning before we disembark."

"Is the man mad?" whispered Kanné.

"Shouldn't you be copying out my itineraries, sir?"

"I . . . I . . ."

Albert nodded. *"Merci bien pour tout, Monsieur Kanné. Bonsoir!"*

Kanné bowed stiffly and left the saloon.

"Whenever and wherever Her Majesty and the Prince move,"

continued the inspector, "from ship to shore, from coach to coach, and from coach to train, the tallest amongst us will surround them—we'll form a very palisade of flesh, gentlemen, but with as little ado as possible. What you'll be looking for is someone trying to get close enough to use a blade; our man is a wizard with a knife. Even if he's armed with a pistol, he'll try to get near to his target to ensure success. In either case, gentlemen, our duty will be to interpose our own bodies. He's a tall man, beardless the last we saw him, slender, with memorable eyes. He likely has a lad with him, curly ginger hair, although both may have altered their appearances considerable.

"The boy, in particular, presents a problem. He was an innocent, we believe, took by the assassin months ago and kept all this time. Who is he now? Does he represent a menace also? I don't frankly know what to expect from young Tom Ginty. Well, my lords, I need to confer now with Mr. Llewellyn. I'll have further instructions for you all in the morning."

He passed the ornate itinerary across the table to Sir Horace and was about to rise when he caught himself.

"I beg your pardon, Your Highness—may I?"

"Detective Field," said Albert, "a nautical expression comes to mind. You'll want to mind how you go, because you are *sailing close to the wind*."

"Yes, sir. Sorry, sir."

"Bright and early tomorrow, then," said the Prince.

"Thank you, sir." He bowed, then suddenly held up three fingers. "The itinerary, black and white and in English, three copies to our cabin tonight, please. Peter, you may retire for the night. Sam?"

With that he strode from the room, followed by Llewellyn, who blushed to his scalp.

MASTER WAS OFF to see about the horses. Tom stood before the glass in the room at the inn, washing his face in the basin. The fine clothes he had been given at the country house were packed into a rough satchel. In their place he wore long brown trousers of a coarse fabric and a loose gray blouse with a red scarf knotted about his neck. Master had shaved Tom's hair close to his scalp. Tom ran his hand over the fuzz on his skull and put on the soft flat cap given him by Master.

But here he was: Master, standing silently in the door, reading something. He, too, had altered his appearance. The two of them had arrived at Antwerp in the garb of a well-to-do Englishman on holiday with his son. Now they were poor but respectable artisans, a tinker and his boy, traveling the countryside, sharpening knives.

Master approached Tom at the basin. "You never learned your letters, is that right, Tom?"

Tom shook his head, his heart suddenly pounding.

"So you wouldn't know what it says on this paper." Master held the telegram before Tom's eyes:

WITH BOYS MOTHER FIELDS WIFE THE BOY CAN READ WRITE

Master thrust Tom's head into the basin and held it there. Tom struggled fiercely, but Master was very strong, circling his torso with one arm and holding the boy's head underwater with the other. *Must inhale, must inhale.* But then Tom was free, snorting water and mucus, struggling to breathe again, and Master was leaving the room.

"We leave in ten minutes," said Decimus.

34

ANTWERP–FRANKFURT–COBURG, GERMANY

Their early start quickly evaporated. Charles Field's team of oversized crewmen stood ready to surround Albert and Victoria and usher them from the deck of the yacht to the open launch, which would ferry them to the quay, but it was all taking forever. Field was learning how very inconvenient it was to be royal. Everything was cumbersome, everything encrusted in ceremony and circumstance; nothing was simple or easy.

And then a ladies' maid thinks she's left Her Majesty's brushes on board, and a shriek goes up from staff, but no, she's got 'em after all, bloody hell.

Finally Her Majesty and His Royal Highness were seated in the launch, headed to shore. Field himself stood with the crewmen encircling the couple, trying to keep his balance, eyeing the crowd on the quay. Awaiting the royal couple was the Queen's beloved uncle, Leopold, King of the Belgians, along with dozens of local dignitaries, a cheering crowd, and a marching band. When the launch docked,

Albert handed the Queen up to Colonel Ponsonby with a look of warm concern in his eyes.

He's fond of the girl, ain't he, thought Field. *It's no wonder they have so many royal offspring.*

A cheer went up from the people as Victoria successfully entered the ornate brougham. Albert's foot was on the carriage's lowest step and his hand on the golden rail by the door when a fearsome volley of gunfire sent dozens of gulls screaming into the sky. Field leapt up behind the Prince, clinging to the carriage and blocking Albert's body, the two of them in an awkward, spooning embrace.

"Get *in*, sir!"

Field, pistol in hand, looked back over his shoulder, scanning the crowd.

"The Belgian militia is saluting Her Majesty, Mr. Field," said the Prince with a flicker of a smile. In the square just above them Field saw a line of uniformed men with wisps of blue smoke about their heads.

Victoria leaned forward, looking at Field curiously. "You will become accustomed to the salutes," said the Queen, "as we go along."

"Thank you, ma'am," said the inspector. "Sorry, ma'am."

He dropped down from the carriage as a second volley of rifle fire exploded in the crisp morning air, and the royal party was off at a stately pace. Charles Field, thoroughly abashed, trotted behind.

Meanwhile, Sam Llewellyn hurried through the crowd toward the diligence, which was taking some of the entourage to the train station. The inspector had dispatched him and Sims to prowl the harbor since dawn, in plain clothes, to search the gathering crowds for the man with the dark eyes and the boy.

"Come along, Peter," cried Llewellyn over his shoulder, unaware of the tall blond man who followed him only a step behind. "We don't want to miss the 'bus!"

"Never mind *Peter*," said the man, overtaking the constable and pressing the barrel of a pistol into his back. "*You* come along and don't make a fuss." The accent was German. A second man appeared on Llewellyn's right and linked his arm through the constable's. In moments they were off the main square and in a narrow cul de sac. Peter Sims was there soon after, in the custody of two others.

"You are English," said the first man.

"Certainly not," said Llewellyn, "we're Welsh! Who the devil are you?"

"What do you do here? What is your business?"

"We are traveling with Her Majesty the Queen," said Llewellyn. "How dare you interfere with Her Majesty's party?"

"Is that so? And what do you do for Her Majesty the Queen?"

Peter Sims was ashen-faced but defiant. "We are grooms, if you must know."

"The two of you have been since early morning in the harbor, here and there and everywhere."

A light dawned. "Oh!" cried Llewellyn. "You're policemen! So am I!"

"First you are a groom, then you are a policeman? What next will you be, *Englischer*?"

"No, I really *am* a policeman. *He's* a groom."

The first blond man nodded soberly and doubled Llewellyn up with a fist to his belly. The interrogation had begun.

Their abductors *were*, in fact, policemen, of a sort. The Police Union of German States, *das Bund*, had been formed in response to the popular uprisings of 1848. It was one of the first cross-border alliances among policing bodies and involved primarily the suppression of political dissent. The union embraced the principalities of Sachsen, Prussia, Hannover, and Bavaria and extended all the way to Austria. The group spied, shared information, confiscated political materials, and enforced newly minted laws regulating and effectively strangling freedom of assembly and speech. This particular unit of the *Bund* had no legitimate business within the sovereign kingdom of Belgium on the twenty-fourth of September 1860, but the union did not much bother itself with the niceties of law.

At the train station, while Field looked out over the crowd in vain for Llewellyn and Peter Sims, a band played "God Save the Queen" and then "A Mighty Fortress Is Our God." Again, the transfer of the royal party proceeded much more slowly than Field would have liked for safety's sake, but in this case, with his own men unaccounted for, he was grateful for the delay. He saw the royal couple safely seated in their resplendent private railway car and actually ventured to address Her Majesty, suggesting Her Royal Highness might wish him to draw the blinds. (He did not add that this would hinder an assassin from firing on her or her husband through the window. It was, in any case, moot; the Queen did not deign to hear the suggestion.)

When he returned to the station platform, Sir Horace motioned to him. There was a blond man at his side and others approaching.

"Detective Field," said Sir Horace, "allow me to introduce Hauptmann Dieter Klimt, an officer of the law. He has recovered your people."

Llewellyn and Sims appeared, in the custody of a small cadre of men. Field noted a thin trickle of blood running from Peter Sims' right nostril.

"These two," said Klimt, "have been cleared for passage into the territories of the German Police Union."

"What did you do to my men?"

"We had to establish their bona fides, you understand."

"I'll rip your bona fides clean off, mate, how would that be?"

"Mr. Field!" said Llewellyn. "Stop! He's got news, news that will interest you!"

"Detective Field," said Klimt, "your man says you are here to protect the Queen of the *Englischers*. We applaud you! We ourselves are chasing an anarchist, which is also fine, yes?"

The train's whistle blew.

"What's your news?"

"I have long wanted to meet you, sir, ever since I was reading "On Duty with Inspector Field" long ago. So here is a happy accident!"

"What's your damn news?"

"Two, three nights ago, the *Polizei* in a small town of the Belgians, Sint-Niklaas, they found a girl. Dead, of course. We know this because many *Polizei* tell us things, even the Belgians. It meant nothing to us, but your fellow says to us you are seeking a man who takes from people their ears, and from this dead girl her ear had been taken. Another happy accident, yes?"

"Good God."

The train's whistle gave three short blasts.

"We must be getting along," said Sir Horace.

"How far from here is this town?" said Field.

Klimt shrugged. "A few kilometers, not far."

"I'm sorry, Detective Field," said Sir Horace, "but there's no more time."

"Sir," said Field, "send His Highness back."

"*What?*"

"If Her Majesty must, let her go on, but send the Prince back on the yacht, tell everyone it's down to his health, tell them anything you like, but get him away, sir!"

"You must be mad," said Sir Horace. "This trip is all about the Prince!"

"Dear God, which of us is mad? Your Prince is being hunted by a man who lives to kill. He's brazen and he's unstoppable. Do you actually care for the safety of His Highness?"

"Keep your voice down, Mr. Field. You are profoundly insolent!"

Sir Horace turned and strode to the train.

Klimt laid a hand on Field's shoulder. "We, too, are hunters, Mr. Bucket."

"My name is Field," he said, shaking off Klimt's hand.

"As you and your retinue continue on in splendor, we poor Germans must seek our unwashed anarchist, but now, also, we will hunt your strange *Fetischer, ja?*"

"My what?"

"This man has a *Fetisch*, surely, Mr. Field."

"Did the police in St. Nicholas identify a suspect?"

Klimt pursed his lips and tilted one hand this way and that. The train's whistle blew loud and long.

"Sir," said Llewellyn, "we really must board now."

"How was he traveling, Herr Klimt?" asked Field. "Do you know?"

Klimt shrugged, as if to say, *Who knows how these dismembering killers get about?*

"Was he alone, Klimt? Was there a boy with him? What name was he using?"

"*Auf wiedersehen*, Herr Bucket! In Frankfurt perhaps our path will cross! Or somewhere! Later or sooner, *ja*?"

Peter Sims hurried on ahead. Llewellyn threw an arm round his superior's shoulders and firmly turned him toward the train. Moments later the train bearing the Queen of the English chugged out of Antwerp at a stately speed.

The countryside beyond the train's windows was flat and featureless. White gulls dotted the shorn black fields, and for a time the air spoke of the sea. A fog tumbled in, causing the slowly turning windmills to fade and vanish. The sky grew leaden, matching the spirits of the policemen. They sent Peter Sims, shaken by his encounter with the Germans, to the rear of the train to join the other palace staff while they patrolled the train from one end to the other.

"Decimus Cobb comes all this way pursuing the Prince," said Field, navigating the narrow corridor with difficulty, "but takes time off for a spot of fun with a local girl? Either he's so confident of his plan he can allow himself a capital crime that's got his signature writ all over it, or it means he don't have a plan, he acts on impulse, he's out of control."

"Perhaps the one don't rule out the other, sir. Remember all those books in his library, sir—the maps of Germany and all. That says planning."

"Of course it does," said the inspector dismally. "And Sir Jasper What's-It, cut to bits on the parlor floor, seems to say impulse."

Field paused at a window just as the fog shifted, revealing for a moment the Rhine and then hiding it again. "The Queen's other boat, what do they call it, the royal tender? She's sailing down the river along of us, is that right?"

"I expect the *Fairy* is well ahead of us by now. She got an early start and no delays." Llewellyn touched his temple gently and winced.

"How's your head?"

"As thick as you always said it was. Peter Sims got the worst of it. Sir, I wish Peter was with the horses on board the tender. He's a stout lad, you couldn't want a better, but he's a farm boy at heart. This show ain't for the likes of him."

The two policemen moved from one car to the next and found themselves in the clamor of the galley, where staff were busily preparing the royal luncheon; there was an aroma in the air of roast beef and panic. In the next compartment two young women were taking a tissue-wrapped gown from a trunk while a third heated an iron on a small stove. The train passed cities glimpsed through intermittent fog: Cologne, Bonn, Wiesbaden. Finally they came to a halt in Mainz.

Under Field's watchful eyes and surrounded by another *palisade of flesh*, the royal party crossed the town by coach without incident and were settled comfortably into the Duke of Hesse-Darmstadt's borrowed train for the brief ride to Frankfurt. Another marching band awaited them on the platform there, a clutch of dignitaries, and a milling crowd. With growing anxiety, Field watched the light fail as the band played one number after another. Finally, Victoria, Albert, and their entourage stepped down onto the platform to the cheers of the crowd and proceeded to waiting coaches. A teenaged boy, only feet from the Prince, pointed something directly at Albert's head as he passed. Field engulfed the lad in a crushing embrace, wrenched the pointed object away from the terrified boy, and discovered it to be a little Union Jack on a wooden stick.

They would spend the night in Frankfurt, at the Hotel d'Angleterre, before resuming their journey. The city itself seemed to pay scant attention to the procession of the English monarch to the hotel; the horse traffic was thick and the merchants and businessmen of Frankfurt had other concerns. At the hotel, though, the reception was elaborate and the speeches long-winded.

Field and Llewellyn were given a small room opposite Her Majesty's. Staff labored on for an hour or two after the entourage retired, but finally the gas lamps in the corridor were dimmed by half and all was quiet. Field and Llewellyn stood guard by turns, two hours on, two hours off. They discovered the creaks, knocks, and other unaccountable noises that grow loud when all other sound ceases. At 2 a.m., with Llewellyn on duty, the newly installed hydraulic lift clanked to life and rose to the entourage's floor, where it stopped. Llewellyn warily approached the ornate cast-iron cage. He turned the knob and flung open the door. It was empty. He shut the door, listened for a moment, and then walked back to Her Majesty's door. With a clank and a whir that caused Llewellyn to jump, the lift came to life again and sank inexplicably from sight.

There was no other disturbance until a little after 4 a.m. Field was standing guard. Suddenly he heard footsteps running up the staircase at the end of the corridor. The inspector put his hand on the pistol in his pocket, but it turned out to be a breathless aide-de-camp whom Field recognized.

"I need Ponsonby or Dugdale," said the aide. "There's been a death in the family."

"This is Ponsonby's chamber," said Field. The man knocked until the door opened to admit him. In a matter of minutes, Colonel Ponsonby, in dressing gown and slippers, was rapping at Victoria and Albert's suite.

Soon the gaslights were turned up full and members of the entourage were coming and going, speaking in hushed tones as the word spread: Prince Albert's stepmother, the Dowager Duchess Marie, had died. A night-piercing shriek went up from the floor below, but when Field rushed to investigate, he found it to be one of the young serving women he'd seen earlier, unpacking royal dresses.

"Dear God," she wept, "Her Majesty is going to need full mourning! Her and the entire court! Where is it to come from? However am I to manage it?"

Dawn brought much coming and going in response to the royal bereavement. The train's departure was put back two hours. Proper mourning attire for the entourage was sent for by telegraph. In the meantime, black armbands were being sewn and distributed to the men, and black veils found for the Queen and the ladies. A revised protocol was hastily put into place. Military salutes along the rest of the route were canceled and the marching bands banished.

By the time everyone had been transported back to the train, Field and Llewellyn were bleary with exhaustion. A woman in the train's galley gave them steaming cups of tea and rounds of buttery toast, which they consumed gratefully. While they ate and drank, the policemen were unaware of an exchange taking place on the platform between Colonel Ponsonby and Major Davenant, the head groom. It seemed one of the Queen's horses, newly arrived at Frankfurt on the *Fairy*, had gone lame.

"Suzette seemed to be fine yesterday, sir, aboard the tender. We took all four horses off and stabled 'em here overnight, and this morning we made the unhappy discovery."

"Why are you telling *me* this, Davenant?" said Ponsonby. "Monsieur Kanné is in charge of travel matters."

"He's gone off, sir."

"What do you mean, he's *gone off*?"

"Left his position, sir, or was let go by Sir Horace, depending who you talk to. Just last night. He's on his way back to London, I heard, in a right huff."

"Well, what the devil am I to do about it?"

"Permission to replace Suzette, sir? I didn't know who else to turn to."

"Well, of course you must replace her!"

"Also, sir, can I have Sims back, sir?"

"Peter Sims? Whatever do you mean, *have him back*?"

"He's always off with these detective fellows we're not supposed to know about, but I need him, now the second groom's done a bunk."

"The second groom has *done a bunk*?" repeated the colonel with rising heat.

"He's been off the drink for near a year now, sir, but I fear someone may have led him astray."

"Good God, Davenant, your entire department needs setting to rights, and I mean to see to it the moment we're home again!"

Thus did Peter Sims resume his normal duties with the royal horses and carriages. He was, in fact, the groom who tended the new mare, a beautiful chestnut named Lily, for the remainder of the journey to Coburg. The young man who had brought her forward at the Frankfurt stables was taken on by Davenant as well. Not only was he an English boy, but he had a smattering of German, and that was bound to come in handy.

35

The fog was gone. The air was crisp and autumnal and carried a scent of apples. Despite the sad news of death in the night, a feeling of excitement grew among the train's passengers, from the Queen downward. In just hours they would be in Albert's homeland. Even the two weary policemen harbored renewed hope: soon their royal charges would be within doors and less exposed to public view.

A dispatch bag of mail had caught up with the royal party at Frankfurt, and its contents were distributed throughout the morning as the train made its way along the banks of the river Main. Amid the dozens of official letters and personal posts was one addressed to Detective Field in the familiar hand of his wife's. He opened it, frowning, and read the brief note twice.

"Good Lord, my good wife is now *housing* Mrs. Andrews! And

belatedly realizes she is acquainted with Decimus Cobb from her nursing days!"

Field passed the letter to Llewellyn. When he'd read it, he shook his head. "This *Miss Coffin* is clearly the Andrews woman. Why would Mrs. Field invite her to stop in your own home?"

"She is trying to help, Sam. God help us, she's playing at being Mrs. Bucket."

"It's no accident the old witch turned up, chatting with Mrs. Ginty—she sought her out, sir."

"Of course she did. Mrs. Field thinks *she's* the spy, whereas I rather think it's the other way round. *Now* what do I do?"

There was a rap on the compartment door and Llewellyn opened it to Sir Horace Dugdale. "His Highness the Prince wishes to speak with you, Detective Field." Gone were the amiable tone, the genteel smile. Sir Horace turned brusquely and led the way up the corridor while Field hurried to follow. Albert was in a compartment fitted out like an office, going over documents with Colonel Ponsonby, all the men wearing black armbands.

"Ah, thank you, Sir Horace," said the Prince, looking up. "You and Ponsonby may leave me alone now with Field."

The inspector stood at attention as the other two men left the compartment, sliding shut the door behind them.

"So, Inspector?" said the Prince.

"May I offer, sir, my condolences on your loss."

"Yes, yes, yes, thank you. Have you anything to report to me, Mr. Field?"

"A few days before Your Highness arrived at Antwerp we believe our man was in a town only a few miles distant."

"What makes you think so, Inspector?"

Field raised his eyes and stared above the Prince's head. "He did a mischief there."

"A grave mischief?"

"I am afraid so, sir."

"Involving someone connected with me?"

"No, sir. Involving someone of no importance. Except of course to her family, her parents, a young man perhaps, a child."

"An innocent victim."

"It seems so, Your Highness."

"And the people who set this monster on," said Albert with rising heat, "are respectable. Known to me. Friends, even, of mine, of Her Majesty. Please, Mr. Field, tell me that Bishop Wilberforce is not truly mixed up in this, as your man suggested. The Queen is very fond of him, and, in a way, so am I."

"I interviewed the bishop at length, sir, and I think he lives in a world of words. I believe he was genuinely horrified to learn that words might have consequences in what most people would consider to be the real world."

"Not complicit, you think?"

"No, sir."

Albert sighed deeply and looked out the window at the passing landscape. "All this to stop us bestowing an honorific on Mr. Darwin! How can it be? Do his theories truly pose for these people a threat of such magnitude that they would stoop to any depth in order to suppress them?"

"If I may, sir, I've read Mr. Darwin's book, and although I didn't entirely follow it, I can see how it would have a leveling effect if it was to catch on. It's destabilizing of the established order, if you get my meaning. Dangerous, sir, even to monarchs."

"*Especially* to monarchs, I suppose. All things in flux, ever changing, the only hierarchy being that of survival. But thereby making possible, nonetheless, 'endless forms most beautiful.'"

"Yes, I was took by the phrase, too, sir. Saved it for the last, didn't he, Mr. Darwin."

"You are a surprising policeman, Field. Mr. Dickens did well to choose you for his model."

"No, he didn't, sir, if you'll forgive me. I am a very ordinary policeman. Mr. Dickens invented the Bucket fellow. Made him up out of whole cloth."

"Perhaps, Field, this *invention* is not so uncommon. Perhaps, sir, *Prince Albert* is an invention, too. From the whole cloth, as you say." The Prince suddenly pointed up, out the window. "Look there. We are passing the Schloß Marienburg."

Field stooped and peered up at a massive walled castle. Below, the greenish-gray river was spanned by an arched stone bridge.

"This is Würzberg, Inspector. Here were many women burned at the stake. Six hundred and more, in perhaps five years. Old bishop Adolf presided at the fires. They called it 'the burning times.' These were, of course, women who had entered into contracts with the devil, as one will do when pressed, or so I'm told."

The train rounded a bend and the fortress was gone.

"I am a God-fearing man," said Albert. "A devout man, if I say it myself. But according to these people, I have contracted with the devil and so I must burn. How many other lovers of knowledge would they send to the pyre? And in the meantime, we risk the monumental work of Darwin being dismissed for another generation. Perhaps for two generations. What a loss that would be! It is not acceptable, Mr. Field. As to the great men who conceived this plot, my ministers and I, in absolute secrecy, will find a way to make them pull their heads into their shells, like the great old tortoises of the Galápagos."

"Ah, sir, the Galápagos!" Field's eyes shone. "He had me on the edge of my seat there, did Mr. Darwin. I wished I was there with him."

"In the meantime," continued the Prince, "find this fiend and stop him, Mr. Field. We must expect great things from even the ordinary policeman. Good day."

"Excuse me, sir, but there's one thing more. A confederate of this evil man, a woman, has insinuated herself into my own home. I believe my wife to be at risk."

"Why did you not say so at once? I will have Ponsonby send a detachment of the Horse Guard immediately to apprehend this person."

"I beg your pardon, sir, please do not."

"But if your wife is in danger . . ."

"Sir, *so are you*. I believe we must tread softly, especially if this woman has been placed in my household as a spy. If that's the case, she must have a means of communicating with the man who menaces you. That could reveal him to us. Or she could expose *us* to *him*, you see. It's difficult to know what to do."

The Prince stared at the policeman. "You want to go to her," said Albert.

"She is the light of my life, sir."

"I understand you."

Field sighed. "May I send Mr. Llewellyn back to London to look after this matter?"

"Of course, Mr. Field. Have Monsieur Kanné attend to his travel arrangements."

"Mr. Kanné is gone, sir."

"Gone? Nonsense."

"Dismissed, I was told."

"That cannot be. Monsieur Kanné is indispensable; the Queen is devoted to him. No one could dismiss Kanné except Her Majesty. Godspeed, Mr. Field. May God protect your wife and protect us all from the *burners* of the world."

Within the hour, Sam Llewellyn's gear was packed and ready for the return trip. When the royal train switched tracks at Lichtenfels, he would disembark and catch the first train running back to Frankfurt.

"This is madness," said Field. "After coming all this way."

"I know, sir," said the young constable, locking his trunk. "I never got to see you in a riding habit."

"Very amusing. Remember the drill, Sam. It's a two-man job. Mrs. Andrews knows you. The moment she sees your face, Miss Coffin goes up in smoke and Andrews will try to bolt."

"I remember the drill, sir. Who do you suppose sacked Mr. Kanné?"

"I make it out to be either Ponsonby or Dugdale."

"Never!"

"Who else has the rank? I will be eager to see who is now in charge of making travel arrangements for the Prince."

"Hard to believe, sir, that someone right here, in the innermost circle, might be a part of the conspiracy," said Llewellyn as the brakes squealed and the train began to slow.

"'I follow him to serve my turn upon him.' That's Shakespeare, Sam."

The train's whistle blew and it juddered to a halt. "I don't like leaving you on your own, sir."

"No more do I like it, Sam. Convey my regards to my wife, Sam, if you will."

"I will, sir."

"Take care, son."

"And you, sir. Good luck!"

The inspector watched his constable cross the platform and disappear into the little station, feeling a pang.

The switching process was laborious. The train reversed, exhaled gusts of steam, and then crept forward again. Field moved along the corridor from one car to the next. The door to the monarch's compartment was open and Field caught a glimpse of Her Majesty chatting with her longtime physician, Sir James Clark. Albert sat close beside her, the two of them holding hands as she spoke.

"Vicky tells me the baby is a perfect *lamb* and has my Albert's beautiful eyes. Of course, you were *there* at the birth, Sir James—is it true about the baby's eyes?"

The royal surgeon smiled and shook his head in silent wonder at the beauty of the infant's eyes.

Field moved on, then paused before a window in the corridor. The train was moving slowly out of the station, leaving the tiny town behind. There on a country road was a man on a black horse, trotting alongside the train, just keeping pace with it. He was a tall man. He stood in the stirrups. From his garb he looked to be a workingman or an artisan, but his impressive horse and even his neatly trimmed blond beard seemed to speak of a higher station. His infinitely deep eyes were fixed on the royal carriages.

Field ran back to the coupling between the cars and stood between them in the open air. The horseman was not more than twenty feet from him, now looking off into the wood, opposite the rail line. Field had only ever seen Decimus Cobb twice: first, at the great Oxford debate, and then again when the man was halfway across Smithfield Market.

Field put his hand on the pistol concealed in his coat. The horseman looked back at the train, saw Field, and lifted his cap to him with the flicker of a smile.

Dear Lord, it's him.

As Field drew his gun, the train picked up speed; the horseman fell behind. Cursing, Field ran back into the next carriage and sped the length of the corridor, forced to stop at one point for a lady-in-waiting and her voluminous dress to pass him, his pistol hidden again. Then the inspector hurried to the next coupling.

The horseman had spurred his stallion and was gaining on the train. Field braced himself against the carriage and took aim.

"Decimus Cobb!" he cried.

The train jolted, slowed suddenly, and the horseman passed the policeman, grinning back at him over his shoulder. Field sped forward once more. He reemerged onto the coupling. The train was drawing abreast of the rider. Field half-squatted to retain his balance and leaned against the carriage.

He's had his warning.

As the rider came directly into range, not a dozen feet from him, Field slowly squeezed the trigger. The explosion sent crows screaming up from the branches of the trees. A cloud of smoke hung where Decimus Cobb had been a moment earlier. Field stared in disbelief, watching Decimus wheeling his mount from the road, plunging into the woods and disappearing.

THE ROYAL TENDER steamed serenely up the Main, her paddle wheels steadily churning the murky waters. Tom drew the brush down over Lily's flanks, again and again, whispering into her twitching ears.

"You wasn't made for boats, was you? No more was I. Soon we'll be off it, girl, with sod beneath us and fresh grass."

The horse's great brown eyes turned anxiously on Tom.

"Don't ask me, Lily. I got no more idea nor you. I'm in harness, too, see."

"Young Thomas!" said Peter Sims.

Tom whirled about and stood at attention, blushing. "Yessir."

"It's near time, boy, let's look lively there." A chorus of snorts and whinnies arose from Lily and the three other royal horses traveling on the *Fairy*. Peter moved from horse to horse, nodding approval.

"Well done, young man. Already you're an improvement over the old sot you replaced. Still, be on your toes, Master Thomas. It's kings and emperors from here on out, nothing can go amiss."

"Yessir."

"You sound London-born, boy. However did you come to end up in foreign parts?"

Tom remained silent.

"There's a story there, I see," said Peter, "but leave it. We're docking in a few minutes and we've got to be ready to spring."

The *Fairy*'s horn blew just then.

"Stand to, Thomas! Here we go!"

SERVANTS SCURRIED UP and down the train's corridors bearing trunks. Valets and ladies' maids busily dressed and coiffed their masters and mistresses. Orders were shouted and countermanded; the train's whistle began blowing at regular intervals. The town of Coburg drew near. On the hill above it stood a massive fortress. From its ramparts trumpets blasted a royal welcome.

Inspector Field found Sir Horace Dugdale moving along the crowded corridor with Sir James Clark.

"Sir Horace, may I have a word?"

He nodded. "Clark, you go on, I'll catch you up in a moment. Yes, Mr. Field?"

"Sir, we need to keep the royal couple out of sight, in closed carriages from here to the castle."

"Not possible."

"Sir, the assassin is *here*, showing himself brazenly. The situation is now urgent, don't you see?"

"What do you want *me* to do about it? *You* are here, are you not? Do your job!" He turned and hurried down the rapidly filling corridor.

Field made his way through the rising chaos in the train corridor until he came upon Colonel Ponsonby, to whom he quickly related his news.

"I *thought* I heard a shot," said Ponsonby, "but I just took it to be a hunter in the woods."

"Sir, there *is* a hunter in the woods and we know who he's hunting!"

"Well, I don't know what's to be done about it at this point, except to remain vigilant. This thing's in motion, Field, there's no stopping it. Our people will dress you for the banquets and all the rest of it, by the way. Your own clothing won't do here, you know. Now if you'll excuse me . . ." Ponsonby hurried off, leaving the inspector fearing he'd made yet another mistake, sending his best and only man away just when he needed him most.

It was Albert's brother, Ernest, Duke of Saxe-Coburg and Gotha, and Albert's son-in-law, Frederick, Crown Prince of Prussia, who somberly greeted Victoria and Albert at the station. The marriage of Frederick, or Fritz, to Crown Princess Victoria—Vicky—had been arranged entirely by the Queen and Prince Consort and was one of their greatest triumphs. Handsome Fritz had been presented to Vicky at Balmoral when she was sixteen years old. They were betrothed on the spot and married two years later. Uniting these families would, in Albert's opinion, help moderate the traditionally militaristic Prussia once the old emperor died and bring its interests closer to those of the United Kingdom. Vicky was very much her father's child: intelligent, interested in the sciences and arts, and concerned, at least in theory, for the welfare of the common people. In Fritz, they found her perfect match and the anomaly Albert had been hoping for: a progressive Prussian.

Charles Field, still wearing his own unacceptable clothing and feeling not only out of place but also quite powerless, struggled to keep as close to Albert as possible during the short journey to Ehrenburg Palace. There, the Princess Royal, wearing a long black veil and mourning clothes, awaited her parents on the steps. Field pushed forward, eyeing the gathered crowd anxiously while the Queen fell on her daughter's neck, weeping copiously. Then the inspector was swept on in an irresistible stream of pomp and glory.

36

LONDON

The installation of Miss Coffin into the household at No. 2 Bow Street seemed at first to ease Martha Ginty's agitation; it was as though the newcomer provided a connection to Martha's son and a ray of hope that he would someday return to her. For Bessie Shoreham, however, the new presence was an outrage, especially since Bessie was forced to share her chaste pallet at the top of the house with *the old hag*.

"Missus, it's not fair!" hissed Bessie. "And them pins! They're every-where! Turn over in bed and they're like to run me through!"

Jane let her servant know confidentially that there was a reason behind it all: the two of them were going to act as real-life detectives, just like Master.

"This is a great secret between us, Bessie. We're *watching* her, do you understand? But quietly. No one's to know, not Martha, not nobody!"

"I don't want to be no 'tective. I did used to think I give good service, but I see I was wrong." For once, though, Bessie's tears were of no avail. Mistress was determined to be as sly, resourceful, and heartless as her husband.

Miss Coffin claimed she did not know where her former employer and the boy had gone off to, but the day after she moved in, Jane cautiously followed her and saw her pause at a branch office of the Electric Telegraph Company. The close-set eyes turned to scan the street behind, but by then Jane was ardently studying a shop window. In the reflection she saw the woman duck into the office.

Sam Llewellyn, meanwhile, on his reverse journey, found that travel *without* royalty was much less comfortable but somewhat quicker. He would be on the cross-channel steamer in another day, sooner than he'd expected. He stared out the train window at the flat, featureless landscape. Fogs crouched over the valleys; the river ran alongside the train, vanishing and reappearing like an apparition. What would he find at No. 2 Bow Street, he wondered. He'd bring with him one of his mates from the Metropolitan, now that his stock had risen in those quarters. He'd station the other constable on the opposite side of the front door, to catch Mrs. Andrews if she bolted.

The air grew chill as the day wore on.

Joseph Julius Kanné, until recently the Queen's travel arranger, had progressed even faster than Llewellyn. He arrived at St. James' Palace in a righteous Gallic rage. "I am dismissed!" he cried. "I serve at the pleasure of the Queen, or so I thought, but now? It seems I can be sent down by a lackey!"

One of those in range of his remarks was a head butler who nodded sympathetically while wondering privately if he might possibly seek promotion to Kanné's post. He might not have a goatee, for God's sake, but at least he was English! He'd pen a note and send it along in the pouch; he had a beautiful hand, everyone said so.

NOT A HALF mile from the palace, Mary Do-Not, née Withers, dipped her quill and wrote by candlelight. After leaving the Huxley home, she returned to Half Moon Street and was shocked to find the house boarded up. Making her way round to the back, she found her way into the house from the little overgrown garden, terrifying Hamlet's widow, who stood trembling with a candle and a knife.

"Put a light on, can't you?" said Mary.

"There was peelers watching for a time," said Mrs. Hamlet, "and then they put boards over the door. I daren't light the gas."

So No. 4 now had a population of two. The money Mary had taken from the Huxley household box was enough to keep the two of them alive. Mrs. Hamlet was terrified of Mary but had no choice but to take her bread. Mary added further chapters to her book and waited. She was confident Master would send for her; he had promised she had roles to play that history would long remember, and Mary was devoted to history.

AT THE ROYAL College of Surgeons, Sir Richard Owen canceled an afternoon lecture and walked round the square to his home, glancing over his shoulder repeatedly. He told his manservant he was ill and retiring for the night, and did not wish to be disturbed, even by his wife. He locked his bedroom door and took a telegram from an inner pocket with trembling fingers, reading it yet again:

BUT LOT'S WIFE LOOKED BACK FROM BEHIND HIM
AND BECAME A PILLAR OF SALT. CHORAL MASTER

IN OXFORD, BISHOP Samuel Wilberforce puzzled over a telegram *he* had received. It asked him to use his influence to assist a worthy young woman to secure a position in service with one of the nation's first families. The sender promised she would perform her duties ably, but the bishop was confused. *Which choral master?* he wondered. *I am acquainted with several.*

Elsewhere in Oxford, Sergeant Willette had a round-the-clock watch placed on old Mrs. Andrews' vacant guest house. At the constabulary, he conducted extensive research into the practices of the "resurrectionists." In fact, on the subject of body snatchers in general, and those who might be connected with Decimus Cobb in particular, Willette was becoming something of a fanatic.

There was a knock at his office door. Hastily, he adjusted the black silk cloth that he now always wore round the top of his head, angled down on the left side, covering the livid, angry confusion of cartilage and skin where his ear used to be. He put the looking glass into a drawer and said, "Come."

It was his young aide. Evidently a new party was moving into the guest house abandoned by Mrs. Andrews.

"Four adults and a child, sir. It won't be a guest house no more, according to the shopkeeper next door. They're making a funeral chapel of it."

Willette nodded and put on his hat. "Let's have a quiet look, shall we?"

37

COBURG

Charles Field had been dressed soon after his arrival in Coburg by a valet traveling with the party, a wry young Cockney named, memorably, Sheldon Olderwiser. The somber clothes *almost* fit him, although the inspector might have wished for a bit more fabric in the leg and a bit less fabric round the middle. Field and Olderwiser would share a tiny bedroom one floor above Her Majesty's suite during their stay in Ehrenburg Palace.

As soon as he was presentable, Field took up his position just outside the Queen's chambers. He could hear her voice, excited and imperious as she was being dressed for dinner, and Albert's voice, measured and calm. Then Field heard a hushed exchange from a nearby staircase. He stood sharply at attention.

It was Crown Princess Victoria and her husband, Prince Frederick, who appeared at the top of the stairs, followed by a nurse with a writhing toddler in arms. The royal couple were whispering urgently in German, oblivious to the inspector. Fritz seemed to be proposing something that Vicky adamantly opposed. Finally Fritz nodded in capitulation, and Vicky told the nurse in English to stand the little boy on his feet.

Field's intake of breath was involuntary; he could never bear to see injured children. The Prince and Princess turned on Field, surprise and outrage on their faces, and the nurse quickly pulled the toddler's sleeve down over his malformed left arm, which hung from him, limp, blue, and lifeless. The inspector had no idea what to do or say.

Finally Vicky spoke. "The fool of a surgeon did this to our son with his forceps. The Queen and Prince Consort are not to know just yet. Is that understood, whoever you are?"

"Ma'am," said Field, bowing, "of course."

Field was then forgotten; the Princess Royal turned back to the nurse. "*Halten Sie immer seine Hand*" she said, then caught herself and spoke English to the woman. "Never let go his hand, Mrs. Hobbs, never!"

The nurse took the toddler by his maimed hand and led the way into Victoria's chamber. A joyous cry went up from the Queen and the door was shut.

IT WAS KNOWN as the Hall of Giants. The immense naked figures circling the room held brightly burning candelabra at the ends of their muscular plaster arms. The lavishly sculpted ceiling, erupting with baroque effusions, rested on the Giants' heads. The hall was packed with eminent diners: an empress, an emperor, the families of two royal houses, high military officials, dignitaries, churchmen, and courtiers. The din was astonishing; it seemed to Charles Field that everyone talked at once.

The assemblage wore mourning, but the sea of black was enlivened by a glittering of jewels. Field stood at attention, as instructed, against the wall immediately behind Her Majesty, his eyes scanning the crowd. Victoria chatted in German with her son-in-law's father, Emperor Franz Joseph, seated on her right. Albert was on her left, with his beloved Vicky at his side and his much loved (but remarkably dissolute) brother,

Ernest, flanking her. It was the first meeting of Queen Victoria and Franz Joseph, and the banquet was followed by many toasts to the emperor and empress, their offspring, and the union of the families.

At one point in the long evening, Olderwiser passed by Field and winked. "When do *we* eat?" whispered the inspector. The valet pursed his lips, shook his head, and quickly straightened Field's collar. "It's been a long bloody day. I'm hungry!" Olderwiser chuckled and moved on.

The Ehrenburg stable hands and the visiting grooms supped early and well in a common mess. After their meal, Peter Sims and Tom Ginty retired to the small stable where the Queen's horses were housed, adjacent to the larger palace stables. They saw to their four charges, and then Peter stepped out *to have a drink with some of the lads*, leaving Tom to make up a pallet on the floor for his bed. He was just settling down for the night when Master walked in, kit in hand. Tom jumped to his feet, his heart racing. Master nodded at the boy and moved purposefully to Lily. Tom took an anxious step forward. Master opened his kit and took from it something that he offered the horse from his palm.

"No!" cried Tom, leaping to the horse's side and thrusting his fingers into her mouth. He pulled out a large lump of rock crystal. He sniffed it.

"Eat it," said Master. There was a click and the tip of a blade lay against Tom's throat. "Eat it."

The boy put the huge lump into his mouth, his eyes watering.

"You see? It's a sweet. You disappoint me at every turn. Why would I wish to harm Lily? I went to trouble enough getting her where she is, and you with her. Do you think Master is a bad man, Tom? Is that it?"

The knife point pressed on his Adam's apple. The rock crystal in his mouth was large enough to interfere with his speech. "No," he struggled to say.

"Did you know, Tom, Mrs. Andrews is concerned about your mother? Says she's lost her mind. She's keeping an eye on her. Surely you recall Mrs. Andrews' warm ways?"

Tom barely nodded.

"Keep it in mind. You remember the schedule, Tom?"

He nodded again. The lump filled his mouth, dissolving slowly into a syrup. "In three days' time," said Decimus, "you travel to the Prince's boyhood home in the hills. That is, unless I choose to make my move sooner, in which case I imagine the journey to Rosenau will be canceled." Something like laughter came from him.

The sugar was like having a small brick in his mouth; the boy fought a rising panic.

"I will be back with instructions as my path is revealed to me."

A door opened, Peter Sims came in, and the knife at Tom's throat disappeared with a click.

"Hallo, Thomas," Peter called out. The horses stirred and greeted him in turn. Peter approached, casting an eye over each animal as he moved through the stable. Finally he saw Decimus.

"Who are you, then?"

Decimus was examining Lily's teeth and barely looked up. *"Ich bin der Tierartz. Wer sind Sie, mein Freund?"*

"What's he say?" said Peter with a little slur.

"'E say . . ." Tom spat out the sugary lump. "He says he's the animal doctor."

Decimus turned from the horse and smiled at Peter, patting his wooden kit. *"Ich werde wieder in drei Tagen,"* he said, walking to the door.

"Thomas?"

"He says he'll come again in three days."

Decimus nodded briskly and was gone.

Victoria was the tourist and Albert her tour guide, showing her locales connected sentimentally with his boyhood. They were accompanied by Vicky and Fritz, as well as Albert's brother, Ernest, and his long-suffering wife, Alexandrine. There was resistance, at first, to Inspector Field tagging along for these outings. Ernest eyed him darkly and Vicky protested to her mother. Oddly enough, it was the Queen herself who seemed to be Field's defender. The inspector witnessed a whispered exchange (in German) between mother and daughter and distinctly heard the words *Mr. Bucket*. Field rode up front with the coachman, Peter Sims.

"How are you getting on?" whispered Field.

"Very well, sir, thank you. Sorry to see our friend Mr. Llewellyn leave us."

"You and me both, lad. That's a nice-looking mare, the chestnut."

"Lily is new to us, sir. She's a lovely beast indeed."

The inspector nodded, scanning the paths and surrounding woods for a fine black horse and a tall rider who stood in the stirrups.

They visited an old church Albert had attended as a child. They found a favorite overlook of Albert's youth, offering views for the Queen and Vicky to sketch or paint. Everywhere they went a local dignitary or cleric was awaiting them with a prepared speech. Inspector Field wondered at the patience the Queen displayed for the endless speechifying.

On the second day the family drove up to the massive fortress, the *Festung*, which glowered over the town. Victoria and her entourage were led through the ancient stone stronghold by Sir Horace Dugdale and Duke Ernest, who was in the process of restoring it. The Queen was rapturous with it all, from the parapets and their stunning views, to the exquisite wooden marquetry chamber, to the room where Martin Luther had been hidden for a month in 1530. Luther's patron, an ancestor of the Saxe-Coburg line, had tucked him up here, fearing his young reformer might otherwise be burned at the stake for his radical notions. Finally the royal party descended to the *Festung*'s dungeons.

As the royal visitors moved through the cavernous room, Field noticed an ancient wooden door on the left swing inward. He paused for a moment to see who would emerge. No one did. The party was ahead, gathered round one of the various instruments of torture on display. Field hesitated, then walked back to the open door.

It was entirely dark within; a mossy draft eddied out. The inspector was about to turn back to the group when a voice came from the darkness.

"Sir, a word."

Field's hand went to his breast pocket, but he was unused to carrying his pistol and realized with a jolt that the gun was still in his trunk.

"Who is that?"

Silence.

He hesitated a moment further, then stepped into the dark passage. "Who just spoke?" Silence. "Mr. Cobb, do I have the pleasure?"

He heard no other sound but the soughing draft and the voices of the entourage behind him. Field took another step and blundered noisily into a helmeted mannequin in full body armor, throwing his arms round it in a clanking embrace to keep them both from falling. The passageway, barely lit by the faint light from the open door behind him, seemed to be littered with many such things: suits of armor and weapons that hadn't been put on official display. He strained to see. And then, from behind, came a rusty squeak. He turned in time to see the massive door swing lazily shut, plunging him into utter darkness. Field groped his way as hastily as he could, back toward the door.

It was locked. Field swung round, putting his back to it. He could imagine it closing on its own with a draft of air but was quite certain the door had not bolted itself.

He spoke to the darkness. "Was it the boy just did that, Mr. Cobb? Young Tom?" A possibility suddenly occurred to him. "Or is it Sir Horace Dugdale, your particular friend at court?" *Of course.* Sir Horace, who had been present months ago when all this began and when Field had first uttered the word *conspiracy*. "He *is* the bloke who just shut and bolted this door, is he not? Was this planned in advance, me trapped in here with you, or is Sir Horace, like you, a creature of impulse and opportunity?"

Did he hear breathing? Surely his own eyes soon would adjust to the darkness, putting him on an even footing with Decimus. Somewhere there was a metallic click. "'How now?'" said Field. "'A rat?' That's Shakespeare, Mr. Cobb." The inspector gingerly took a step toward his fear instead of away from it, which had been his agonizing practice since childhood.

"Where is the boy? Where is Tom, Mr. Cobb? Have you taken off his ear and used him yet?"

Yes, there was someone breathing not far from him.

"A German policeman told me they found a dead girl near Antwerp with her left ear off. Ring a bell at all? He called you a . . . Well, it was a foreign term, so you can take it for what it's worth, but this German said you had yourself a *fetish*. Is that what you have, Mr. Cobb? Peculiar cravings? When tossing yourself off, I mean."

"I had intended," said a disembodied voice, "to make you a generous offer."

Suddenly Field smelt a man's breath, inches from him in the darkness.

"I bled your man," said Decimus finally, "the thin, bony one."

It took Field a moment to master himself. "So you did, and I mean to see you hanged for it."

"You put him in my hands, Mr. Field. And now you have delivered Constable Llewellyn to my care. He will soon be in London."

A worm of fear wriggled in Field's gut.

"You had this information from Sir Horace Dugdale, I imagine."

"I have sent instructions to Mrs. Andrews and she is awaiting him at No. 2 Bow Street. You have put your wife and your constable at great risk needlessly. You could ensure the safety of both, you know. Even now."

Field tried to control his breathing.

"Oh, yes? And how would I do that?"

"What do you care about these people? What do you care about the Prince? You might continue as you are, standing guard, following him about, looking a bit ridiculous in hand-me-down clothing, but when he dies you can say, *almost* honestly, that you did your very best to protect him. You could even say, *I told you so*. Could you not do that, Mr. Field? To protect those about whom you *do* care?"

He could do, and he knew it, but he forced the thought from his mind. "*This* is your generous offer?"

"Not to mention," continued Decimus, "preserving your own life, of course."

"So I *am* right, it *is* the Prince you're after. What do you care about Albert, Mr. Cobb, if it comes to that? You could as easily go home as me. Indulge your fancies and your knives until you and me meet up again and I get your neck into a noose. Or do you, too, have a bone to pick with Mr. Darwin? What is it about Darwin and his theories, Mr. Cobb? Why would you fear them so?"

Field sensed movement and stepped back. The blade caught the palm of his left hand with a slashing motion. A red rage filled him and he thrust his right hand out, grabbed blindly, and was rewarded by a high-pitched scream.

Damn me, it's his prick I've got hold of and the bloody thing is stiff! Well, of course it is, the bastard was about to cut me up!

With a sharp cry Decimus wrenched himself out of Field's grip. Footfalls followed, blundering at first, and then running, turning off into another passage, and another, and finally passing out of hearing. Field flailed about, searching the air about him, until he laid hands on a long shaft. He carefully fingered the end of the pole and found an ax head there. With the ax he turned back to the locked door and split it in three blows.

The royal party had moved on, but a castle retainer was there, looking horrified at the shattered door and the bleeding man with the battle-ax who emerged from it.

"*Was haben Sie getan?*" said the servant in a whisper.

"Did you lock this door a few moments ago?" Holding his bleeding hand with his other, Field made the motions of a man throwing a bolt.

The servant, petrified, nodded. "*Ja.*"

Field inspected his left hand. It was bleeding profusely but not deeply cut. The servant turned and walked quickly to the exit, looking back over his shoulder in wide-eyed terror.

Field made his way as unobtrusively as he could do out of the fortress. The royal party had indeed left without him, so the inspector walked back to the Ehrenburg Palace. He was relieved to find Sheldon Olderwiser in the palace kitchens, just finishing a cup of tea. Olderwiser was less concerned about Field's cut hand than scandalized at the state of his clothing.

"D' you think it's easy outfitting a man of your dimensions, Mr. Field?" The valet briskly bound up the inspector's injury with a kitchen cloth. "Now it's up to me to get you clothed again, just when I've got to get the Prince ready for his travels."

"What travels?"

"Himself, his son-in-law, and his brother are riding to Gotha tonight. Got to arrange for their stepmama's burial, don't they."

Field swore. "Where is the Prince now?"

"Lunchin' with Her Majesty in the Marmorsaal. Hi! You can't go in there looking like that! Let me find you a clean shirt, anyway. Mr. Field?"

The luncheon party was just breaking up when the inspector reached the colonnaded, vaulted dining room. He stood with head bowed respectfully as the Queen passed, chatting with her daughter, but he caught Albert's eye with a meaningful look. The Prince paused.

"Yes, Mr. Field? Good Lord, what have you done to yourself?"

"Sir, a slight cut."

Victoria paused and turned.

Field lowered his voice. "You travel tonight, sir, I'm told. Your Highness, allow me to accompany you."

The Prince glanced at his wife.

"But you are here to protect the Queen, Mr. Field. I expect you to remain here with Her Majesty."

Victoria laughed. "My dear," she said to her husband, "Mr. Field is always and *forever* under foot. Let him protect *you* for once, and give us poor *ladies* a single night's *respite!*"

THE ATTACK, WHEN it came, was swift.

There was a chill in the late September evening air and the three passengers in the coach—Albert, Ernest, and Fritz—were well wrapped up, conversing softly as the horses clopped out of Coburg. Field, his hand freshly bandaged, sat in front with Peter Sims, scanning the road ahead. About three miles from town the road narrowed, approaching a railway crossing, the trees drawing in on the Coburg side of the train tracks and opening up again on the opposite side.

"The barrier's down," said Peter, slowing the horses, "but where's the train?" Field strained to hear the sound of an approaching locomotive, but there was only the evening chirp of crickets and the murmuring voices of the princes in the coach. Field jumped down onto the road. He approached the little hut where the crossing keeper was housed while on duty. It was empty.

Field turned and saw a strange man climbing onto the Prince's carriage.

"Oi, Cobb!"

Field sprinted. The man on the carriage step raised a pistol and the inspector hurled himself through the air. He caught flying hold of the man's legs just as a volley of gunfire exploded. The man spun violently, taking the inspector with him to the ground.

Men were running from the woods toward the coach, shouting, and the horses were rearing, Peter Sims struggling to control them. Inspector Field sat up, wiped some wet matter from his eyes and realized it was the assailant's brains. A stocky blond man stood above him.

"Mr. Field, it is a good job we didn't shoot *you*!"

Field got to his feet.

"You remember me, of course—Hauptmann Klimt? Of the German Police *Bund*? Your comrade, Mr. Bucket, your comrade!"

Field looked down at the body. He got to his knees and put his hands on what was left of the assailant's head, turning it this way and that. There seemed to be fragments of a red bandana around it. It was certainly not Decimus Cobb. Field went through the dead man's pockets, empty except for a few pfennigs and a quantity of coarse black tobacco. He stood again and approached the carriage.

Albert was staring at him, ashen but jubilant. "It is over, then!" said the Prince. Klimt stepped up and bowed.

"My lord," he said, "it is indeed, sir. I am Hauptmann Dieter Klimt of the German Police *Bund*. We have followed for days now this anarchist assassin, from Hamburg to this very spot, acting on information we had some weeks ago. We are hunters, like my good friend Inspector Field, and here we are at the end of the hunt!"

"You have our gratitude, Hauptmann Klimt, you and your men."

Albert looked to Field, beaming, the color returning to his face.

"We do not know who he was," said Field. "We do not know who put him onto it, if anyone did. We know nothing, but I am quite unhurt, thank you."

Field turned brusquely and walked away, feeling the anger course through him and trying to quell it.

"Mr. Field?" said Albert, stepping down from the carriage and following him.

Field whirled on him. "It's not him, sir! Do you understand? It's some other bloke. Nothing is *over*, nothing whatsoever!"

Ernest and Fritz climbed out of the coach and approached gingerly, eyeing the bloody corpse.

"Albert, let us thank God for our deliverance," said Ernest, "but on no account must anyone know of it. My own position here, yours, Fritz's . . ."

"I must agree," said Fritz. "If my esteemed father, the emperor, were to hear of this assassin from Hamburg, I fear all our efforts toward unification will have been in vain."

"And the three of us, saved by members of the *Bund*?" added Ernest. "Amongst the people, Albert, they are *despised*. No, no, it will not do."

Albert nodded slowly. "For Her Majesty the Queen it would be the ruination of this entire journey, which she has so deeply enjoyed. And, to be frank, Victoria would not approve of any assassination attempt in which she was not the target."

"No one must ever know," repeated Ernest.

"My lords," said Klimt, "my men and I can make it disappear, all of it."

The Prince nodded. "Do so, then. And let us continue to Gotha."

Ernest and Fritz returned to the carriage. Albert regarded Charles Field appraisingly. He saw a man covered in blood and gore, just as he had been the first time they met, months earlier. "Mr. Field, you will need a change of clothing and we haven't time for that now. I won't require your services tonight, but I do thank you for all your efforts."

Field said nothing. Albert's eyes moved reluctantly to the corpse and then returned to the coach. "Sims, you are quite well?"

"Quite well, thank you, sir," said Peter.

"We'll be off, then," said the Prince.

One of the German policemen raised the barrier at the crossing and the carriage moved on into the evening. While Klimt's men went to work, digging a grave, Field stood staring after the royal coach. The snort of a nearby horse jerked him out of his dark reverie.

Field moved toward the sound, on the wooded side of the tracks. "Who's there?" Field entered the wood and stopped. He heard the horse walking away, fallen leaves crunching beneath its hooves. "Is it you?" The inspector walked briskly into the wood, accelerating, dodging trees and stumps, but it was dark and getting darker. "Halt, damn you!" He ran, nearly weeping with rage and frustration. Finally his toe caught on a root and he fell hard. The hoofbeats faded into the night.

38

LONDON

It was early evening when Bessie Shoreham emerged unsteadily from the tavern with her head held defiantly high. It was all a lie, no doubt about it. This detective nonsense was just a ruse her mistress was employing to replace her with that Miss Coffin, the old hag. As Bessie walked home, tears rolled down her cheeks. What could she do to make her mistress care for her again?

In a flash of unaccustomed ingenuity, Bessie had an idea, the possession of which was such a novelty it left her breathless. She would go along with the lie and be the very best detective she could be! She would spy upon Miss Coffin's every movement! And then came the sign that her idea was indeed a good one.

There she is now, the witch!

The woman's dull black clothing rustled drily as she walked. She clutched a fold of paper in one of her knobby hands. She, too, appeared to be heading back to Bow Street. Bessie hurried slyly after her.

With Mr. Field away, Jane most often ate in the kitchen with her *menagerie*, as she privately called them. Tonight's supper was a peculiar affair. As "Miss Coffin" cooked the meal of boiled mutton, Bessie never once took her eyes off her. While she always before had only scowls for the woman, tonight she never stopped smiling. Bessie had been so excessively helpful that Coffin had been obliged to tell her to *clear off.* Bessie had lumbered up the four flights of stairs then, to her room, but when she returned for the meal, she was all smiles once more. Grinning, she watched Miss Coffin's every forkful, from plate to warty mouth, every sip of beer, and each dab of napkin.

"What are *you* lookin' at?" snapped Miss Coffin finally.

At this, Bessie put on an enormously shrewd face, laid one finger alongside her nose, and said, "You know better than me, dearie."

"Bessie," said Jane, "that is hardly gracious."

Bessie nodded at Jane and winked confidentially. "No more is it."

"Are you drunk again, or have you lost your mind?" said Miss Coffin. She turned abruptly to Martha Ginty, whose foot tapped incessantly beneath the table, and snarled, "Keep still, can't you!"

"I'm sorry, miss," said Martha. "I get this way."

"Well, get some other way!"

"It's my son, you see. He went off and he never came back."

"Yes, yes, we know all about it!" Miss Coffin pushed back from the table, at which Bessie pushed back *her* chair and stood in unison.

"Bessie," said Jane, "what *are* you doing?"

"Nuffink, Missus," she said, beaming.

"I don't know what has got into you, but whatever it is, I want it to stop!"

Bessie sat again with a thud, tears springing to her eyes.

"This is a madhouse, that's what this is," said Miss Coffin. "I'm going to bed."

She sniffed contemptuously and left the room. Jane, Bessie, and Martha listened to her footsteps climbing the stairs. The unspoken relief they felt at the woman's departure went round the room; it was as though they could breathe again. Jane moved to sit beside Bessie, touching her shoulder gently.

"I *am* sorry I snapped at you Bessie, but your behavior tonight has been so peculiar."

Bessie hiccoughed and sniffed. "I thought you'd be pleased."

"About what?"

Bessie tilted her head extravagantly in the direction of Martha Ginty and raised her eyebrows.

"I'm afraid I don't understand," said Jane.

Bessie dropped her voice down to a throaty whisper. "About our secret."

"Mrs. Ginty," said Jane, "be so good as to clear the table, will you?"

"Of course, ma'am." Martha rose and began collecting the plates.

Jane turned again to Bessie and lowered her voice. "Yes, Bessie?"

Bessie pulled a folded piece of paper from her bodice. "When Miss Coffin was stirring the pot, I found this in our room. It was hid in one of her boots. I can't read it, but you can, Missus."

Jane hesitated for a moment, then took and unfolded the telegram. As she read, Martha leaned over to remove the meat platter and carving knife. She froze, reading the message over Jane's shoulder.

"Wot's it say?" whispered Bessie.

"She's been lying all this time," said Martha. "Mrs. Field, who *are* these people?"

"Someone is coming to Bow Street, that's clear," said Jane, rereading the slip of paper. "They're setting a trap for someone."

"My Tom's not safe, he's anything but safe!"

"I'm afraid we are none of us safe. Bessie, run quick to the corner and fetch in the first constable you see."

Bessie nodded eagerly.

"Tell him it's for Inspector Field's wife."

"Yes, Missus!" said Bessie, rising.

"What does it mean," said Martha, rereading the telegram, "'use your pins'?"

"*I'll show you*," said Mrs. Andrews, suddenly appearing in the door. She took a long five-pronged hairpin from the right side of her topknot and another from the left. With a toss of her head, her long gray hair cascaded down about her shoulders.

"You lied to me about my boy!" cried Martha. She grabbed the telegram from Jane and shook it at the old woman. "You said this man of yours was a-going to set Tom up in life!"

"And so he will, lunatic, unless you don't behave. In that case you'll never see him again." Jane stared, fascinated: the woman seemed to be putting on the hairpins, like a pair of gloves, one on each hand.

"You *are* Mrs. Andrews, then," said Jane.

"You, Missus Field," the old woman said, "will cut your high-and-mighty ways and leave the running of this establishment to me. Otherwise, my boy will send your husband back in bits."

Martha shook the telegram again. "I didn't raise my Tom to do murder!"

"*My* boy is making history and he's letting your little squib play a role in it, for which you ought to be grateful!" Mrs. Andrews took a step toward the women who all shrunk from her. Jane thought she heard a pounding from above, but perhaps it was merely the blood beating in her own temples.

The old woman drew herself up. "My boy was born special. There was money to be made by it. Was I *not* to make money by it? I *did* make money by it. Fame and glory will follow, and the mighty will tremble before him. If he is difficult from time to time, what of that? He was born different that he might do great things, and history will honor him for it!"

"Me, I'm fetchin' in a constable!" hissed Bessie, backing toward the kitchen stairs.

"Oh no you don't, half-wit!"

Bessie turned and ran, but the old woman leapt after her and swung her about. She thrust at Bessie's throat, but Bessie jerked her apron up to her face and the five prongs of the hairpin went up with it, piercing the apron and sinking deep into Bessie's right cheek instead of her neck. It stuck there, the apron pinned to her cheek, five streaks of blood running down the front.

"*Oi! Oi! Oi! Oi!*" cried Bessie.

Jane came to life. "That'll be quite enough of *that*!" she cried, grabbing the old woman by her long hair and yanking her back. Before Jane knew what was happening Martha Ginty stepped forward and drew the blade of the carving knife swiftly across the woman's throat.

Mrs. Andrews' eyes widened in terror. She struggled to scream, but there was only a spasmodic liquid sound as the blood fountained from her. She fell back against Jane, who just managed to catch her, half falling with her to the floor. The old woman convulsed for a long moment and then was still, her eyes open and staring.

Bessie mewled breathlessly, sinking to the floor, the pin and apron still stuck to her face. Martha knelt beside Jane, staring in confusion at the blade she held. Jane carefully took the knife from her. The three women, covered in blood, slowly became aware of a man standing in the door, Sam Llewellyn fresh off the Dover coach, staring at the carnage in horror and shock.

WITHIN THE HOUR and through the night, No. 2 Bow Street became the scene of intense activity. First, Sam Llewellyn returned to the street to tell the constable he had brought with him that he was free to go; the suspected woman had moved on, no one knew where to. Soon after, Jane employed her nursing skills to clean Mrs. Andrews' body and prepare it for burial. In the dead of the night, Martha Ginty took the old woman's few effects and sunk them in the Thames. Bessie Shoreham scrubbed clean the kitchen. Before dawn, a horse and cart were borrowed, no questions asked, from the widow next door, whose allegiance to Mr. Bucket was fervent.

The following afternoon, Llewellyn pushed through the doors of the Fortune of War, around midday, and approached the bar. Mickie Goodfellow's face fell.

"Oh no you don't," he said. "No, sir. Officer Llewellyn, you are not welcome in my establishment. It took me fully forty-eight hours to be released, and even the magistrate said he didn't know why I'd been arrested!"

"I'll have a pint of your best, Mr. Goodfellow," said Llewellyn with a friendly grin. "No, make it a half, if you please, I have matters to attend to."

The landlord stared at the constable appraisingly, then took a glass from a shelf and pulled the ivory handle marked BEST BITTER. "What's become of Charlie Field, then? Is he dead yet?"

"Gone straight to the top, has Mr. Field, a personal confidant of Her Majesty the Queen."

"Delighted to hear it. I hope he don't neglect to mention *me* to Her Majesty?"

"Not a day goes by, sir."

Llewellyn pushed a coin across the bar, which Goodfellow started to push back before he realized something was attached to it. He frowned and looked closer. It was a bit of string looped through a paper tag that had two words penciled on it: *Will Tailor.*

"I've nothing to do with this," said Goodfellow, any trace of jocularity gone.

"You've still got all your surgeon friends from St. Bart's coming and going, I see," said Llewellyn with a nod to the saloon bar. "I imagine you still provide them with what they want, one way or another."

"Get out."

"What was the name of that magistrate? The one who didn't know why you'd been nicked?"

Goodfellow stared at Llewellyn in silence for a moment. "What do you want?" he said finally.

"Consider it a gift, Mr. Goodfellow. Gratis, as they say."

"What?"

"She's waiting for you out front." Llewellyn put down his half-pint and beckoned Goodfellow to follow. The landlord looked about nervously, then hung his apron on a hook and followed the constable out of the tavern. The cart was stopped directly in front; the horse was tethered to a post and minded by an urchin who ran off when Llewellyn gave him a sixpence. The constable looked about and then lifted one corner of the tarpaulin. Mrs. Andrews' eyes were open, her mouth stretched wide in a parodic rictus and her throat stitched shut with heavy black thread.

"Good God," cried Goodfellow, "cover her up!" He looked up and down the crowded road. "Are you mad?"

"You will take care of her, will you? The Metropolitan won't trouble you or the Fortune of War again."

"Yes, yes! Merciful Jesus, did *he* do this? That's his mother, you know. No! No, I don't want to know! Just wait here, I'll fetch someone directly."

Goodfellow stumbled into his pub. Llewellyn turned up the collar of his coat and rocked back and forth on his heels, in the manner of all waiting policemen the world over.

His mother! he said to himself. *Now I think of it, it makes perfect sense.*

39

COBURG

Charles Field was awakened at dawn in his little room at the Ehrenburg Palace by the sound of high, clear voices singing in the courtyard beneath his window. He rose quietly and looked out. A dozen choirboys, white-robed and ruffed, processed across the inner court toward the chapel, singing a hymn that was somehow familiar to him.

Ein feste Burg ist unser Gott . . .

Sheldon Olderwiser, his voice fuzzy with sleep, sang from the room's other cot.

*A mighty fortress is our God
A bulwark never failin' . . .*

Olderwiser lifted himself on one elbow. "I was a choirboy meself; sang like a bleedin' angel. They say Mr. Martin Luther wrote that one right here, when he was hidin' for his life in that pile o' rocks on the hill—the *Festung*, they call it."

"Is that so?" said Field, watching the double line of boys file into the chapel.

"Mr. Field, you *do* remember that we're all movin' tomorrow? Up to the Prince's old home?"

"I hadn't forgotten. Why?"

"Well, what do you plan to wear, Mr. Field? You seem to be accident-prone and I'm fresh out of shirts and suits that might fit your frame."

"I shall be wearing my own clothes from now on. I shall be myself instead of someone else, and if that's not welcome here, I'll take myself off. I've had my fill of this show."

"Coo," said the young man, stretching himself luxuriously, "*somebody's* touchy."

But Field's everyday attire attracted no particular notice from the Queen as he dutifully followed her about her morning activities. Her Majesty had been told about her grandson's infirmity evidently; the child was brought in at breakfast to greet his grandmama, and his deformed arm was not concealed.

In midafternoon, Albert, Ernest, and Fritz returned to Coburg. Victoria was in flights of bliss to see her husband, and Albert himself seemed in high spirits for a man who had just buried his stepmother.

He can't help it, thought Field. *Having escaped this latest assassin's bullet he feels the danger is over, he feels downright immortal. Well, let's hope he's right, although I never met anyone yet who fit that description.*

TOM AWOKE IN the middle of the night to find Master sitting on a stool beside his pallet. The boy sat up fast, disoriented, his heart racing. Master smiled languidly and glanced at Peter Sims, asleep on his cot.

"Follow me, Tom," he said. "I have instructions for you."

Decimus rose and Tom followed him out into the dark cobble-stoned courtyard. Tom realized that Master was dressed like a stable hand, but it hardly mattered: there was no one awake to see them.

The next day the servants were up before dawn, packing and preparing for the move to Prince Albert's childhood home, Rosenau, a scant few miles from Coburg. A little after noon, three landaus filled with royal family and friends started off, followed by wagons carrying servants, including the new stableboy known to Peter Sims as Thomas. Peter drove the lead coach, which held the Queen, giddy with excitement. Charles Field clung to a brass rail at the back, standing on the little ledge that normally would be used by footmen. Along the way, farmers, dairymaids, peasants, and children paused, dipping heads, curtsying, or touching forelocks before hurrying about their business. As the entourage passed the train tracks where the ambush had been thwarted two nights before and the would-be assassin killed, Albert stared pensively. The crossing keeper, a tall man in a gray uniform with red piping, ducked his head to step out of his hut. He removed his cap and bowed low to Her Majesty.

The ground rose. Eventually they entered a long avenue colonnaded by tall firs. A wooded hill rose at the end of the avenue, and at the top of the hill stood a large white house with black shutters and a steep, step-gabled roof. A single circular tower clung to the left side of the house, accompanied by a very tall pine. The lower reaches of Castle Rosenau were covered by climbing ivy.

Field realized that a conference was taking place within the coach. The landau slowed to a halt, not halfway up the hill. Field jumped from his perch in time to see Albert step down and offer his hand to assist Vicky from the carriage.

"Mr. Field, I am going to show my daughter a secret from my youth, a hidden path to the house that I enjoyed as a boy. Have the goodness to remount and accompany Her Majesty to the *Schloß*."

"Begging leave, sir, to accompany you and the Princess Royal."

"It is not my wish, sir."

"Forgive me, might I have a word apart?"

"This is not the time, Mr. Field."

"But, sir . . ."

"You heard me, did you not?"

"Sir, he's here!" Field lowered his voice. "Our man. Right here, sir."

Reluctantly, Albert approached Field.

"I have been with him, sir. I have spoken with him. It was he who cut me. He is armed and awaiting his chance. I have little doubt he is watching us at this moment." The Prince glanced about nervously. "For your daughter's safety, sir, if not your own, permit me to accompany you, please."

"Very well," said Albert finally. He looked up at his wife, waiting impatiently in the coach. "Carry on, my dear. We shall be along presently."

Peter flicked the reins and the procession resumed its journey up the hill. Albert took his daughter's arm and set off into the woods, trailed at a respectful distance by the inspector. The path Albert led them to was indeed hidden from the road, behind stands of trees, a rise, and a dip. Field speculated that for a boy it would have offered the appeal of secretive adventure and, for the boy's royal elders, might have provided a path for diplomatists or paramours to come and go unseen.

The day was perfect: the weather mild, the sky cloudless, and the air sweet. Albert appeared apprehensive at first but eventually seemed to lose himself in the joys of the moment. He and his daughter walked arm in arm in the dappled light. He was alone with his favorite child on the patch of earth more dear to him than any other. The two of them talked quietly together. Occasionally they laughed.

They had been walking for some time when they became aware of another scent in the air, a sweet, sickly heaviness. Albert and Vicky fell silent. Even the birdsong was suddenly stilled. The sweet odor turned sour. It was a deer, dead on the path before them. Its hide still retained a lustrous tawny glow against the green. The Prince and his daughter gave the carcass a wide berth, leaving the path to circle round it. Field kept an eye on them, even as he approached the fallen animal.

Oh, bloody hell.

The creature lay on its right side. Its left ear was off, not torn by a scavenger but sliced cleanly with the precision of a surgeon with a razor. Field put his hand on the pistol, which was now safely in his breast pocket, and looked about furiously. There was no one there that he could see; there was nothing amiss. He glanced ahead at Albert and Vicky, enjoying a rare moment in which neither of them was anyone but a father and a daughter, sharing the beauties of an autumn day. The inspector scanned the woods again. A light breeze moved in to cleanse the air. It was a sun-dappled paradise again, and the birds again sang its praises. Field took his hand off his gun and hurried on.

40

COBURG
1 October 1860

In the latter reaches of the night a light rain began to fall and continued as the occupants of Rosenau awoke and dressed. By the end of breakfast, though, sun was breaking through the scudding clouds, and the surrounding lawns and woods were glistening. At the insistence of her husband, the Queen endured a morning indoors during which she caught up with her official business. Inspector Field tried to make himself inconspicuous in a library. Vicky and Alexandrine were driven out to shoot and driven back again, smelling of black powder. That was when Sir Horace Dugdale announced he had been obliged to change the afternoon's schedule from the planned tea in Coburg to a royal visit to nearby Castle Kallenberg, the home that Ernest's father had given him and Alexandrine as a present for their ill-begotten marriage.

It was unexpected, but Ernest was happy to lead the tour of Kallenberg. It delighted the Queen. After the hastily prepared lunch,

while the men had drinks and smoked cigars in a room apart, the
women walked out, circling the castle to find a location from which to
do their watercolors, with Inspector Field following. Her Majesty and
her train descended a flight of ornate stone steps to the terrace below,
where their attendants finally placed their easels. The men joined the
ladies not too long after. Sir James Clark planted himself at the edge
of the terrace, his hands clasped behind his back, his chin high and
brow furrowed, as though *he* would be the judge of whether this were
indeed a view suitable for the monarch. He smelled of tobacco and
brandy; Victoria and Vicky were downwind of him and exchanged
amused glances.

"*Ou est Monsieur Kanné?*" said the Queen, dipping her brush into a
paint pot, perhaps reminded of the Frenchman by the aroma of strong
drink and tobacco. "*Nous ne l'avons pas vu depuis des jours.*" No one else
remembered seeing Kanné either, not for days. "One hopes he is not
ill," continued Victoria, frowning in concentration and sighting the
landscape over the tip of her brush.

Prince Albert and his brother, Ernest, walked up and down the
terrace, talking softly; Field watching them closely. A young servant
woman descended the steps, approached the Prince, and gave him a
note.

"Say that I will come directly," he said, scanning the message, "and
let them know in the stables I shall need a carriage." The young woman
curtsied and hurried up the staircase. Turning to his wife and daughter,
Albert said, "My dears, I must leave you to your work. There are people
in Coburg whom I need to see."

The Queen, always serious about her art, nodded and murmured
without looking up from her watercolor, but Vicky put down her brush
and extended her arms. The Prince took his daughter's hands, kissed
each, and then her brow.

"Sir?" said Field, moving to his side.

Suddenly Albert was shouting. "*I am with my family in private conversation, have the goodness to step back!*"

It was as though Field had been slapped.

"Yes, sir," said the inspector, retreating and bowing. "I beg your pardon, sir." He bowed to the Queen, his face aflame. "Ma'am."

Neither the Queen nor the Princess Royal acknowledged his salute; both had experienced Albert's rare but explosive bursts of anger. For the moment neither was royal: they were mere women, keeping their heads down while the man of the house was in a temper. Field turned and climbed the stone staircase. At the top of the steps he crossed the Kallenberg grounds, head down. His intent was to walk back to Rosenau where his trunk was and from there to make his way to the train station in Coburg.

Herr Marx was right, I am the dog beneath the table. Well, no more.

The young servant woman crossed ahead, walking from the stables to the castle. Field hesitated; he could not help himself. "Miss, if you please, do you speak English?"

"I am English, I *should* do," she said tartly.

Field beamed. "Of course you are, my dear, and a credit to your race, I'm sure. If I might ask, my English rose, who was it sent the message you just now give the Prince?"

"Sir Horace Dugdale," she replied, walking on toward the castle, "and none of your gammon, if you please!"

Field walked on irresolutely. He slowed to a stop, listening. He heard voices from below, the Prince's and another's. *Cockney? A boy's voice.* Field changed course and made for the stables where he found Peter Sims, grease-smeared, in a chaos of springs and coils.

"What the devil?" said Field.

"Well might you ask, sir. I can't think how we broke a spring, just from Rosenau to here."

"Who's taking the Prince to Coburg?"

"Thomas. Pass me that spanner, would you, Mr. Field?"

"Who's Thomas?"

"New stableboy. London-born, by the sound of him, but we took him on in Frankfurt, him and his master's horse, the chestnut.

"*What* master? Where is *he*, then?"

Peter shrugged. "Thomas is a sound lad. He asked to go so I sent him."

So now a London-born boy named Thomas, picked up in Frankfurt, is employing his master's horse to carry the Prince off, alone, at the request of Sir Horace Dugdale. Merciful Christ.

"Peter, we've got to go after them."

"I can't very well do that, now, can I, Mr. Field?"

"It's urgent!"

"I serve at the pleasure of Her Majesty the Queen, sir, not you!"

Field felt his scalp tingle. He turned and stepped out of the stable, at a loss. Then he sprinted across the castle grounds, stopping at a stone parapet that bordered the upper terrace. Below, the road was a looping ribbon of switchbacks descending delicately to the plain, threading back and forth between orderly farms, meadows, and copses. It looked like a painting he and his good wife had seen at the National Gallery, thought Field: a man struggled behind an ox-pulled plow; beyond was a brook, and yonder a shepherd and his dog were moving a flock toward town; in the distance a train puffed and hooted.

Directly beneath him, the ornate carriage bearing Prince Albert moved sedately, pulled by a gray and a chestnut and driven by the young top-hatted groom named Thomas, taken on in Frankfurt. As it rounded a switchback, passing out of Field's line of sight, the carriage seemed to be slowing abruptly. Was it stopping? Why should it stop? Field looked directly down and gauged the drop. He stepped up onto the parapet and leapt.

THERESA CHARLOTTE LUISE, Queen Consort of Bavaria, died of cholera after attending a service of thanksgiving in Munich, celebrating the end of a cholera epidemic. This carriage, a small dress barouche, had been hers. It seated two passengers, facing forward. It had a window at the front and on either side. There was a raised back-seat behind the cabin for footmen. It was an elegant little carriage, better suited to formal occasions of state than this simple errand, to deliver one man without pomp a distance of four or five miles, even if the passenger were the Prince Consort of the United Kingdom.

Albert opened the window on his side and leaned out. "Boy? Why are we stopping?"

Tom took no notice, gently reining in Lily and the other horse. The Prince lowered the glass of the front window, just behind Tom's head. "Boy! Driver!"

"I'm sorry, sir," said Tom as he brought the barouche to a stop.

The door on the left-hand side of the carriage opened and Decimus Cobb stepped in, seating himself gingerly next to the Prince with a courteous smile. He was dressed in a gray uniform with red piping. He carried a wooden attaché case.

"Who are you?" said Albert.

"Drive on, Thomas," said Decimus, removing his gray cloth cap. The boy flicked the reins and the barouche jerked into motion again.

Albert's heart raced. "Leave the carriage at once!"

"I feel I need to explain, Your Highness, what is about to transpire, and why. You are going to have an accident, but have no fear: you won't be in a position to feel it. Faster, Thomas, if you please—His Highness is thinking of jumping."

Albert's throat went dry. He struggled to master himself.

"You have no business here," said the Prince.

"I have no business at all," replied Decimus. His eyes moved over Albert's face, scalp, and shoulders, studying them. "Do you think," he said evenly, "I am a monkey?"

"I beg your pardon?"

"There were those who thought they employed me to do *their* bidding in this matter. They deceived themselves. I serve the truth, not them. They are moved by considerations of commerce and power. Not I. I am truth's warrior, and you are truth's enemy. Your true father is the father of lies, and you, if you'll forgive me, are the bastard son of the father of lies."

Albert, never taking his eyes from the intruder, slowly lowered his right hand out the window on his side and made come-hither motions surreptitiously—to whom, God only knew; he did not.

"If you don't wish to lose that appendage straightaway, Highness, I should take it in and keep it in for safekeeping."

Albert quickly did so.

"It only makes sense to stop you. You would spread a disease; I am the surgeon who will excise the disease."

Decimus laid the wooden case across his lap. Albert stared at it. "I don't know what you are talking about," said the Prince.

"Imperial monarch. Empress of India. Defender of the Faith. If a man say a thing, his words travel only a short distance and die. If the monarch say a thing, the word travels round and round the globe like the sun, forever and ever. They got you to remove the demon's name from Her Majesty's list a year ago—we know it was *you* placed Darwin there—but we know that you are still determined to honor the demon, this year or the next or the next."

"I will not. We will not. Darwin will never be knighted, I give you my word."

"Do you think I am a monkey?" Decimus said again.

Tom glanced over his shoulder into the carriage. He saw Master open his kit. The face of the Prince was paper white. Tom turned his eyes back to the road.

Could Tom do it?

You'll only get one chance, you won't get no more.

CHARLES FIELD HURRIED, limping across the fields. He imagined he had entered the painting he had seen from above. He passed the plowman and the ox, he crossed the brook over a small wooden bridge. The hay had been gathered and tied into shocks, which stood about the field like pilgrims in solitary prayer. Somewhere in the distance the train sounded its horn. There was a pain radiating from Field's right ankle that he promised to think about later. He put a hand to the breast pocket where he carried his pistol and realized it was not there.

Fell out when I jumped, didn't it. Well done.

Was he timing it correctly? He had crossed one switchback and should have found her by now.

Ha! There she is!

He put two fingers to his lips and whistled. A half-dozen crows flew up out of the long grass, and the dog stopped in her tracks, confused. She tilted her head quizzically. The inspector beamed and nodded and whistled again. She looked between Field and her master. Field pointed commandingly, whistled again, and the dog sprang into action.

"NO ONE," SAID Decimus, "who has ever dissected a hand, or opened a torso, or examined so much as a *feather*, can believe that creatures change from one thing into another." He was sorting through the instruments in his neatly ordered case, choosing one, examining it critically and then replacing it with a shake of his head. "In the plunder of Egypt, the great Napoleon brought back . . . *what*, your Highness? Do you know?"

Albert whispered, "No."

"Cats. Mummified cats from the pharaohs' tombs, cats two thousand years old. Can you tell me in what way they differed from present-day cats?"

The Prince shook his head.

"In no way!"

Albert opened the door on his side and lunged, but as fast as a snake Decimus had his left wrist in his grip.

"Pull shut the door, Highness."

Decimus produced a brass corkscrew from the box and held it to Albert's left eye; Albert closed the carriage door. Almost playfully, Decimus danced the sharp end of the corkscrew about the Prince's nose, drawing little points of blood. "You are destined to suffocate, but the accident will cause lacerations and contusions, so I have some freedom to enjoy myself here, do you understand me?"

Albert whimpered faintly.

"Do you think, Highness—you, who have never dissected so much as a *cat*—do you think because a man may have a unique feature, that that man has crawled up from something low and vile? Do you think his unique feature is a sign that he is changing into something else? Into something *other than a man*? *Do you?*" Decimus' face was inches from Albert's. *"It is a lie!"*

The carriage suddenly jolted and slowed.

"Thomas?" said Decimus sharply.

"Sheep, sir."

Tom brought the carriage to a complete stop. Decimus peered cautiously out the front window over Tom's shoulder. A line of sheep was indeed crossing the road just ahead, a dog worrying them across, two shepherds moving up and down the line, guiding the flock with shouts and whistles. Decimus sat back in his seat and turned somberly to the Prince.

"We'll take our time," he said, dropping the corkscrew into the box and lifting out a cloth-covered, padded garrote. And then, to Albert's wonder and horror, Decimus began to sing.

TOM'S MIND WAS racing. He had lain awake nights, plotting how he might ride Lily out of his nightmare and into a new life. The plan he hatched was solely for him and the horse; saving the life of a prince had no part in it. Tom scanned the way ahead. Something wasn't right about one of the shepherds—the limping one, he wasn't dressed right—but the shepherd was the least of his concerns. Ahead were open fields and a railroad crossing, on the other side of which dense woods closed in on the road. Tom cautiously leaned forward and edged his way out over the rear of the horse named Lily, to the harness hitch he had doctored days earlier and brought with him, just in case. He worked feverishly, his fingers trembling. He couldn't stop Master; no one could. He could only save himself.

"What's that you're doing, Tom?"

The boy scrambled back up and around, springing a knife from his right sleeve. But it wasn't Master who had spoken. Crouching on the left side of the driver's perch was the wrong shepherd, clinging to the pole that held the ornamental lamp. The man put a large finger to his lips, listening to the singing coming from the coach, his brow furrowed.

Tom recognized him: it was that policeman. The one who thought he could get the better of Master; Tom had encountered him before. He was a fool, that policeman. The dog was racing back and forth before the carriage, moving the sheep off the road. The other shepherd was running away, across a meadow.

"Give us the knife, Tom," said Field quietly. "I need it."

The boy shook his head.

"Are you with *him*, then?"

Tom looked at Field for a moment, then detached the knife in his hand from the metal guide that held it. He passed it handle first to Field.

"When I give a shout, get this rig going again, and fast."

A line of worry crossed Tom's brow. He looked back over his shoulder at Lily.

"Here we go, then," said Field.

Using the lamp pole as a pivot, Field swung round to the side of the carriage, slammed into the door, flung it open, and climbed in.

Decimus turned from the Prince, grabbing in his box as he turned. The corkscrew dug into Field's left thigh, just below the groin, and Field ran Tom's knife across Decimus' face, opening a bright red line. He reached across the Prince to the opposite door, unlatched it, and pushed it open. Albert was gasping for breath, the padded garrote looped round his neck, a lurid red mark on the skin beneath it.

"Oi, Tom!" shouted Field. "Go!"

Decimus turned the corkscrew in Field's thigh with one hand while his other hand found the inspector's throat. At that moment the carriage lurched into crazy motion, swerving to the right, then left, the horses whinnying loudly, tossing the occupants into a jumble. As Decimus' fingers tightened round his throat, Field plunged Tom's knife into the hand that turned the corkscrew. Decimus screamed and Field yanked the screw out of his thigh, along with a chunk of his own leg.

LILY, HER HARNESS released, pulled away from the carriage at a gallop. The gray raced to keep up with her, the carriage jolting along the road with Tom struggling to control it. He watched Lily pulling ahead without him on her and felt something in him die. Then he saw the train approaching the level crossing. Lily might just make it; the barouche would not. From a side lane, a farm wagon pulled up and stopped before the tracks, directly in their path.

DECIMUS WAS ROOTING in his kit; Field was shoving Albert inch by inch out of the barouche. Suddenly Tom was there, clinging to the open carriage door with one hand.

"Pull, boy!" shouted Field.

"*Monkey!*" shouted Tom.

What in God's name . . . ?

"Tom, pull!" cried Field.

"Filth!" screamed Decimus, clutching his bleeding right hand, blood running from his face.

"Show them your tail!" Tom was shouting at the top of his lungs. "Your *tail*, show them! He's got one, you know!"

"Scum!"

"Tom Ginty," shouted Field, "pull this man out of the coach!"

The barouche was jolting wildly. With his free hand, Tom grabbed Albert under his right shoulder and pulled.

Decimus, slick with blood, lurched over Albert's legs, snatched Tom by his collar, and yanked him into the carriage. He threw himself across the tangle of legs, brought his mouth down on the boy's left ear, and ripped. Just as fast, he pulled back, a bit of ear between his teeth and an expression of surprise on his face. Decimus looked down at himself. He shoved his open medical kit aside, but the scalpel was embedded in his abdomen to the hilt. Field got his boot in the man's face and kicked, and all at once Field and the Prince were tumbling out of the speeding carriage, rolling into the ditch below. For an instant Tom looked at Decimus, who was staring at the blade in his gut.

"*I am not the new you,*" said the boy, and then he leapt.

The onrushing train blew its horn. The gray horse swerved abruptly, just short of the wagon at the crossing. The Queen of Bavaria's barouche tipped on its side and slewed onto the tracks where the locomotive burst it asunder.

HISTORY RECORDS THAT Colonel Henry Ponsonby, seeing a runaway horse galloping through the streets of Coburg, came to the remarkably prescient conclusion that Prince Albert had been injured or killed on the road to town. Ponsonby located a doctor and hired a carriage to take them to the scene. They arrived within a half hour of the extraordinary events, greeted by the barking sheepdog.

The Prince insisted that the doctor treat the others first. Field's bleeding thigh was bound up. (*Good job it missed that femoral artery, sir,* said the doctor, *but it wasn't by much!*) Although the young groom, Thomas, had lost half an ear in the mêlée, the damage was not deemed life-threatening. He was shivering, so they wrapped him in a horse blanket and gave him whiskey. Finally the Prince, too, was given whiskey and a blanket. The real shepherd had cautiously returned for his dog and his flock; he was sent off to fetch help.

The fiction began to be written on the spot, authored by Albert with assistance from Colonel Ponsonby. There had been no attempted assassination of the Prince in his own homeland, his brother's duchy, less than five miles from his birthplace, at a time when German unification discussions were at such a delicate pass. Albert's cuts and bruises would be explained by his leaping from an out-of-control carriage. A young groom also had been injured in the accident and would be sent back to London to recover. Inspector Field had not been present, having been dismissed by the Prince and sent away earlier, as witnessed by the Queen and the Princess Royal. Hauptmann Klimt of the German Police *Bund* and his men would be quietly engaged to recover the remains of Decimus Cobb and make them disappear.

Eventually a wagon arrived. The injured were laid in it and driven off to Rosenau. Ponsonby continued on to Kallenburg Castle, where he informed Victoria that her husband had been hurt in a carriage mishap. The Queen, highly distraught, was driven to Rosenau where she found the Prince lying in a darkened room, his injuries bandaged. She wept copiously. Albert, weak and still in shock, found himself, as usual, comforting *her* rather than the other way round. Victoria finally left him to his rest. Her Majesty adored her husband, but she had spent the entire day out of doors and was hungry for her supper.

A few moments after she left, the Prince said, "Mr. Field?"

"Your Highness." The inspector emerged, limping from the shadows at the far end of the room. The dressings on his thigh were covered by his trousers; there were bruises on his face and a bandage across his scalp.

"How is the boy?"

"He is concerned about the horse. If I could assure him that she will be looked after, it might help him sleep, which is what the doctor says he must do."

"Yes, yes, of course. They still have not located the body?"

"Not as far as I know, sir, but they will do. The impact may have hurled it some distance from the tracks."

Albert lay silent for some time.

"Colonel Ponsonby?" he whispered, finally.

"I feel, sir, I may have been premature in my suspicions of the Colonel. I did not like that he seemed to know all about a carriage accident involving Your Highness in advance, as it were. But then, that chestnut mare is a splendid beast. We've all taken notice of her. It's quite possible the colonel simply recognized the runaway horse as one in your service."

"And Sir Horace Dugdale?"

Field shook his head. "Remove him, sir."

"However am I to do that, with the Queen so fond of the man?" Albert sighed. "I have told my people to take pains for your comfort as you travel to London, you and the boy."

"Thank you, sir."

"I deeply regret having spoken to you as I did, Mr. Field."

The inspector nodded.

"I do hope they soon find that man's body," said Albert.

THE INSPECTOR WAS awakened a little before 3 a.m. He was driven by one of Klimt's men to a stretch of railroad tracks about fifty yards from the scene of the day's incident. The scene was lit by lanterns and torches, clustered in the woods.

"There is not much left of him, Mr. Field," said Hauptmann Klimt, "as you can see."

The face was completely obliterated. The torso was more or less intact; the long legs lay decorously together a little farther on, the feet bootless. Bits of gray uniform covered body parts here and there. In the flickering torchlight, the blood and the red piping looked black in color.

Field wrinkled his nose. "What is that smell?"

"Smell?" cried Klimt. "Why, you should know this smell very well, Mr. Bucket! It is the smell of death!"

Klimt's men laughed, then fell silent at a glance from Field. He took a lantern from one of them and moved in a slow circle around the remains, searching the ground.

Too bloody early for him to stink like this, isn't it.

Suddenly he stopped. At his feet lay the half-eaten body of a fox. The sweet-sickly smell was strong. Field looked back doubtfully at the human remains. He approached the torso again and crouched beside it. Reluctantly he lifted a bit of the gray fabric at the base of the spine and studied what lay beneath.

"I'll need to know what the coroner says, Herr Klimt."

"Coroner? There will be no coroner, of course! This matter is now gone forever, Mr. Field! In one hour's time, all this, forever gone!"

IN THE MORNING the Queen was at the bedside of her beloved Prince, fretting over the fact that he might have been snatched from this world the day before. Then, with the morning post, she received another upset. It was a letter from a head butler at the palace, seeking to replace Monsieur Kanné as travel arranger now that he had been dismissed by Sir Horace Dugdale. This was news to Her Majesty. Livid, she summoned Sir Horace to the Prince's suite and summarily relieved him of his position. She may have been fond of Dugdale, but she was fonder still of the Frenchman and was rather firm about making decisions concerning household staff herself. The Prince had propped himself up in bed to witness the courtier's unhappy interview with Her Majesty. At its conclusion Albert caught the man's eye and held it. For the first time, a flush suffused Sir Horace's features. He dropped his eyes, bowed his way out of the room, and was never seen by anyone in the court of Victoria again.

THE WEATHER WAS fine and the Channel calm. Charles Field and Tom Ginty were well wrapped up, sitting side by side on the steamer's deck, gazing at the gentle rise and fall of the gray horizon. The boy had not spoken a word during their first day's journey from Coburg to Frankfurt and on the second day begrudged the inspector only monosyllabic responses to his inquiries. Field hardly cared. He was coming down with fever; by the time they boarded the cross-channel steamer, he was shivering. It was the opinion of the ship's doctor that brisk open air was the best thing for it.

The hum of the engines and rushing splash of the great paddle wheels were irresistibly soporific. The inspector awoke with a jolt to find himself drenched in sweat. He shook out the robe that covered him and then pulled it tighter.

"Tom," he said, over the noise of the steamer, "what was all that about a *tail*, then?"

The boy stared straight ahead. He might not have heard.

"Tom?"

"What was that uniform he was wearin', Mr. Field, and why was he a-wearin' it?"

The gray uniform with red piping had been very much in Field's thoughts. On their first day of travel it had come to him where he'd seen it initially: on the road to Rosenau with the royal party, the attendant at the railroad crossing; a slender man stooping to emerge from his hut by the tracks, bowing and tipping his cap to the Queen. A tall man in gray, outlined by a thin red stripe.

Since then Field had watched Decimus Cobb kill the crossing guard again and again in his mind. Each time, in the dead of night, Decimus laid the body across the tracks in the path of a night train. He might have let more than one train mutilate the body. The corpse was already in place on the day of the attack. If anyone had witnessed Decimus boarding the Prince's coach before the "accident," or leaping to safety after it, it would be the tall man in the gray uniform who would be under suspicion, the man who was now beyond questioning, beyond recognition. The horse would gallop on command, and the dead Prince would be thrown off. The boy would be left on the scene (or, more likely, also killed) while Decimus changed costume yet again and disappeared into the countryside.

It was all very far-fetched. The inspector glanced at Tom and found him still staring at the indistinct, shifting horizon.

"The man's dead and gone, Tom. You needn't worry about him ever again."

Tom shot Field one fierce, accusing glance. Then the boy resumed his examination of the sea and sky divide. The inspector was drenched and shivering again. He rose to return to his cabin but faltered and stood trembling, clinging to the back of the deck chair. Tom stood, took Charles Field by the arm, and led him off below.

PART V

41

LONDON

At the end of his long journey home, Inspector Field was carried from the coach and up the stairs to his bed. His skin was hot to the touch; his thoughts were confused, his speech rambling. Jane, weeping, bathed him from head to toe with cool wet cloths, again and again. Ugly red lines radiated from the wound in his upper thigh. Tom Ginty begged leave to keep vigil in the bedroom. The boy was silent and sober; at St. Thomas' he had seen limbs taken off that were in better condition. Martha and Bessie came and left with broths, which went untasted. Doctors left the room looking grave, speaking to Mrs. Field in urgent whispers, but she always shook her head adamantly.

Sometimes the inspector was able to recognize his wife; a slow smile would spread across his face and he would reach up to touch her cheek. At other times it was hard to say what he was seeing.

"Stop him!" Field cried once. "The bishop is burning the women, can you not stop him?"

Once he laughed. "Come here, girl!" But when Jane rushed to his side, it seemed it was not his wife he was summoning. "That's a girl! That's a good girl!"

And then, bitterly, "I am the dog beneath the table."

Several times he asked for Mr. Bucket, and then, each time, he wept.

On the third day the bedclothes were drenched as never before and in the night the fever broke. By the fifth day he was well enough to ask a question of Llewellyn when Jane was out of the room.

"How did you manage with Mrs. Andrews, Sam?" he whispered.

"She was already gone by the time I arrived, Mr. Field."

"Where to?"

"God only knows, sir. Congratulations, sir."

"What for?"

"Well, you got your man, didn't you."

The inspector lay back against the pillow. He closed his eyes. Llewellyn waited until he heard the long breath of sleep, then quietly left, confident his inspector would keep his leg, that he would live.

DURING HIS LAST days in Coburg, Albert was melancholy. Walking with his wife and daughter, he looked longingly into each valley. He breathed deeply of the pine-scented woods; he smiled wistfully at the tolling of the village bells. His eyes often brimmed with tears, which he would wipe hastily away. Once, though, alone with his brother, looking from Rosenau over the surrounding countryside, he broke down completely and wept, saying he knew he would never see his homeland again.

"Why would you say such a thing?" asked Ernest.

"The hounds of hell pursue me; they may have been chained for a day, but they are not to be turned aside."

Victoria was aware of the change in Albert. On the eve of their departure as he was wishing her a good night, she asked him about it, taking his hand and pressing it. The Prince smiled and squeezed hers in return. "*Meine Liebste*, you and I are quite different. You are full of life. You will give Death a good long chase."

Back in London Albert threw himself into his labors again, working at affairs of state from morning until night but with a haggard, hunted look.

JAKE FIGGIS FOUND new lodgings near his own for Martha and Tom Ginty. At No. 2 Bow Street, the household returned to its former configuration: Charles and Jane Field at the mercy of Bessie Shoreham, their *maid of no work*, as Field called her. The wound in the inspector's leg became reinfected twice, and he was unsteady for a time, employing a hated crutch to get about the house. Worse were the nightmares that plagued him. Again and again he tried to patch together dissected loved ones but would awake in a panic, finding he was missing a vital piece.

Commissioner Mayne gave the inspector leave to recuperate fully before resuming his duties. "Take all the time in the world, Charles! We want you in fighting trim again. You must have done well by the royal party. They seem pleased with you at the palace, although they are rather tight-lipped about what might or might not have happened over there, I must say."

Mayne waited for Field to enlighten him, but the inspector remained silent. The commissioner's smile faded. He drew some papers to him across his desk and picked up a quill. "That will be all."

Field used his crutch to make his way out to the hackney coach that was waiting for him and hurried the short distance home. "Everything all right here, Mrs. Field?" he said the moment she opened the door to him.

"Of course, Mr. Field. You've been gone only an hour." The inspector nodded distractedly and sat down heavily in the ground-floor parlor where he was spending most of his time these days to avoid climbing stairs.

Mr. and Mrs. Field received callers soon after, Sergeant Willette, down from Oxford and, with him, Sam Llewellyn. Willette was delighted to meet the inspector's wife.

"So this is the good woman who took care of old Mrs. Andrews!" he said with admiration. Jane shot an alarmed glance at Llewellyn.

"Yes," she said. "I sent her away with a flea in her ear. She won't trouble us again."

Both Willette and Llewellyn blushed.

"Quite so," said the sergeant, "quite so."

If Inspector Field noticed any awkwardness, he gave no sign of it. He seemed not to be attending. Even when Willette and Llewellyn explained their plan for dealing with the Reverend Carmichael and his crew, now residing in Oxford, Field appeared to be barely interested. He became fully engaged, however, when Jake Figgis came to call a few days later. It seemed that Tom was not the butcher's apprentice he used to be.

"He don't pay attention, Mr. Field. He stares about like he's all the time frightened, and he don't listen. He looks at the meat like it makes him sick. He won't hardly touch a knife, sir! How can he learn the butcher's trade if he won't touch a knife? And his mother, well, she ain't found another position, has she. I paid their first two weeks' rent for them, but I cannot go on doing that. I am that fond of Mrs. Ginty, sir, I would do anything for her and her boy, but I am at my wit's end."

Field nodded thoughtfully. None of this seemed to surprise him. Field called in a favor from a friend in Covent Garden, and within a week Tom was engaged as an assistant at a flower stall. Another friend, a publican, took on Martha Ginty in his kitchen. Field paid their rent for the coming month. At the end of these efforts the inspector seemed pleased, and Jane rejoiced that her husband finally was showing signs of returning to life.

OXFORD

SERGEANT WILLETTE AND Constable Llewellyn watched discreetly from a window of the little Oxford shop, adjacent to what used to be Mrs. Andrews' Guest House. They heard a pump organ playing a dirge. The shopkeeper dusted her shelves and whispered conspiratorially.

"It's an old widow woman they're doing this morning. Mother of four sturdy sons. Mind you, I never asked for no funerals at my gate, Officers. It's lowering of the spirits, if you know what I mean. Still, the Carmichaels order a deal of eggs and loaves from me and I'm not one to turn away custom."

A vibrant male voice could be heard faintly, rising and falling, followed by a ragged choral *Amen*. Not long after, the front doors were opened by a buxom, copper-haired woman in mourning dress. She had a young girl by the hand, also done up in professional mourning. They were followed by a casket borne by members of the dead woman's family and assisted by two tall black-clad young men in top hats draped with crêpe. The casket was lifted onto an open hearse while the two horses, adorned with long black plumes, snorted and shat. More family members emerged. Finally, out came Reverend Carmichael himself, his head thrown bravely back, his long silver locks flowing from beneath his tall silk hat. The cortège moved off at a slow pace. Willette and Llewellyn exited the shop and quietly took their places among the other mourners walking behind the hearse.

Constables halted traffic for the procession as it turned into George Street, the mourners glancing at each other, somewhat surprised at this show of municipal deference toward a working-class funeral. More constables appeared as the hearse began to cross the Hythe Street bridge, on its way to the Botley Road. Still more moved somberly to block the bridge on the far side; police on the near side formed a line there as well, halting the cortège and trapping it on the bridge. Mrs. Carmichael's voice rose in indignation, while the reverend shook his head sadly at a world where such things could happen.

Willette and Llewellyn moved forward toward the bier. At a nod from the former, two local constables climbed aboard the hearse and began to unscrew the casket. There was a murmur from the crowd and a screech from Mrs. Carmichael, who grabbed at the legs of one of the policemen before being restrained by another. The casket lid came off and the constables winced at the odor that emerged. One of them gingerly lifted a bloody, dripping burlap bag from the coffin, and the other held up an empty dress. There was a moment of stunned silence from the mourners and then angry shouts from the family. They surged toward the reverend, surrounding him while Mrs. Carmichael shrieked and kicked.

"She's at the infirmary!" shouted the reverend, warding off the blows. "You can still get her if you're quick!"

Sergeant Willette sent his men in to intercede. In the mêlée, the little girl in black ducked beneath flailing arms and made for the town side of the bridge. Llewellyn pushed his way after her, but by the time he made it to the end of the bridge, she was nowhere to be seen.

Belinda, aka Blinky, had not gone far. She was observing Constable Llewellyn closely from behind a farmer's cart, halted with all the rest of the traffic by the ruckus on the bridge. The handsome officer was looking this way and that in confusion, searching for *her*, she was certain. She remembered him *and* his big comforting partner who had taken her by the hand and promised her food and safety. Their promises had come quickly to ruin and she had been snatched. No, it was better to trust no one. Belinda stayed where she was until the crowd on the bridge broke up and her hated black-clothed master and mistress were taken away in handcuffs. Then she slipped round the cart and doubled back to the railway station.

She was small and quick. She had boarded trains before without a ticket; it really wasn't so difficult. Her mistake lay in forgetting for a moment that she was dressed in the full gear of a funeral mute and much less inconspicuous than she normally was. A porter saw her flash into a closet at the rear of the train. He quietly summoned the conductor.

"Runaway, I expect," whispered the porter.

The conductor merely shrugged and turned a key in the closet door, locking Belinda in. "Let the London police worry about getting her back to her masters."

For Sergeant Willette it was a gratifying day. The Carmichaels, husband and wife, were arraigned on multiple charges, along with their two young men. Sergeant Willette was able to recover the corpse of the widow before she was taken apart by medical students at the Radcliffe Infirmary and to subpoena the surgeon who allegedly had purchased her. Willette divided his time between these proceedings and the Botley Road cemetery, where gravediggers were raising mounds of earth and vacant caskets. It seemed the Carmichaels had been energetic.

Llewellyn was less pleased with his own efforts. To lose the little girl a second time, just when he had been so close to rescuing her, was galling. He crisscrossed the town all afternoon with no result. Finally he gave it up.

42

COBURG

As the last of the leaves fell and a sharp wind swept the countryside round Coburg, rumors traveled from farm to farm: whispers of a phantom who glided like a mist in the night and made off with small animals. A suckling pig, a chicken, a goat. Farmyard dogs were found, silenced with throats slit. A suit of clothes went missing from one homestead, a pair of men's boots from another, and a fish knife from a third. The driver of a night mail coach, sensing a presence in the road ahead, shone his bull's-eye lantern into the darkness and swore he'd seen two spectral eyes staring back, unblinking, before they vanished. When a farm girl disappeared, the stories reached the ears of Hauptmann Klimt.

He traveled alone to the woods where his men so expertly had hidden the burial site of the would-be assassin a month earlier and stood there in the biting cold, pondering his choices. Klimt's stock with Duke Ernest and others in high places had risen because of his recent clandestine labors. To have it suggested he might have buried the wrong man and let the mad assassin go free would not do. No, he decided, these rumors were all a lot of rubbish. The sort of tales old women spin to frighten the young. He would not give them another thought.

HAMBURG

LONDON-BORN MOLLY ENGLISH had immigrated to Hamburg years earlier and worked her way up from the shipyard streets to the higher class of brothel. A tall, striking woman, she still promenaded publicly, but now only in the more fashionable parts of the city. She dressed herself as an affluent British widow of a certain age—old enough to present a dignified bearing but still young enough for a bit of fun. Her attractive face could be made out under the veil she always wore beneath a stylish broad-brimmed hat. The dove-gray fabrics of her garments spoke of wealth; the large black dots scattered here and there across the veil said *naughty*.

When her madam had announced a new customer for her through the speaking tube in her room, she thought the woman had placed an odd emphasis on the word *new*. The knock came; she opened her door.

"Good Lord," she said with a barking laugh, "whatever happened to *you*?" It was Molly's way. She had seen a thing or two in her time and was not squeamish.

The man who stood before her had been tall, she could tell, but now was stooped and skewed. In the wreckage of his face she saw what she imagined to be a livid knife scar from the left side of his mouth to his right ear. The jaw was shifted off-center and the nose flattened. The skin was multihued, from black to yellow to a dirty reddish brown. The eyes were intact, though, and stared at her from a great depth.

In a thick voice he said, "I was hit by a train."

"Well, *I* could have told you *that*, dearie! Never mind, come to Mother and let's see what she can do to make it all better."

He bypassed her and went to the hat stands, which lined one wall of the room, touching the hats, fingering the veils. He opened a wardrobe.

"Come along, come along," said Molly.

He took off his coat and she embraced him. "Tell me if it hurts at all, will you, dear?" She ran her hands down his back and stopped abruptly. "What in God's name is *that*?" said Molly, her eyes suddenly very wide.

His hands leapt to her throat. Molly kneed him in the groin and thrust a fist toward his neck. The struggle was as ugly as most such are, with fingernails and shrieks and snarls. Molly soon knew what the outcome would be. The room swam. The man's eyes grew so large, she thought she was falling into them. She saw her long-dead mother in Dorking, shaking a wet bedsheet as she hung it out to dry. The sharp *snap!* of the sheet was the sound of her own neck breaking; she heard that, too, and then nothing.

WINDSOR

IN DECEMBER OF 1860, the state of South Carolina seceded from the union known as the United States of America. Six more states quickly followed suit, and four more threatened secession. It was all very worrying to Prince Albert. His ardent antislavery convictions were at odds with major commercial interests in the United Kingdom, entities that thrived on cotton and did a great deal of business with the Americans. Although slavery had been abolished throughout the kingdom years earlier, many in Parliament considered it problematic to take sides with the northern states against the nascent Confederate States of America. Wouldn't an *alliance* with the Confederacy be in the better interests of the empire?

One more pot threatening to boil over, thought the Prince wearily, putting down a brief from the Foreign Office. *One more reason for my enemies to wish me out of the way.*

He looked up from his desk to find the Queen regarding him intently.

"You are tired, my dear," she said. "Come and walk with me." The royal couple were at Windsor; there were miles of indoor walking possibilities.

Albert smiled, took off his spectacles, and rubbed his temples. "We humans are capable of such wonders," he said. "Look at what has been achieved in our lifetimes, my dear! Why is it, do you suppose, that we also are so eager to slaughter each other?"

"Come." Victoria offered her hand. He stood and took his wife in his arms.

"If I could," he said, "I would go back in time and return with you to the Crystal Palace on the opening day of the Great Exhibition. I would relive that day happily."

"It was *grand*, Albert."

Arm in arm, then, they made their way to the conservatory. Outside Windsor Castle an icy rain fell, but the air in the hothouse was humid and filled with the smell of earth and fecund growth.

LONDON

INSPECTOR FIELD LEANED on his crutch, watching the boy. It was a cold day in Covent Garden with a spattering of rain; coal-burning braziers glowed beside the flower stalls, and vendors warmed their hands by them. Tom, a cloth cap pulled down over his ears, sat apart on a barrel, staring into space. His master, a Mr. Bowers, nodded grimly at his old friend, the inspector. Field approached the boy.

"What do you think you're a-doing, Tom Ginty?"

Tom sprang to his feet. "Sorry, Mr. Field."

"Save the apologies for your master, boy!"

"Sorry, Mr. Bowers." The flower vendor moved off, leaving Field alone with Tom.

"Mr. Bowers asked me to step round, Tom. He'll not keep you on for my sake—you have to apply yourself, and you won't do that by sitting down on the job."

Tom was silent.

"What's all this I hear about knives, then? Again? You have to handle knives in many of lines of work—you can't shy away from them your whole life!"

"I can handle a knife," said Tom in a leaden voice. His eyes met Field's and he lowered his voice. "He's coming."

"Who is this?"

"Later or sooner he'll come, you know he will. He'll find you. He'll find me."

Field took a deep breath. "Come round to Bow Street at the end of the day, Tom. Mrs. Field is preparing a Twelfth Night feast, she will be expecting you. Besides, someone else there wants to see you."

Tom turned away from the inspector, silent and sullen. Field grabbed his shoulder and spun him back. There was a blade in Tom's hand now, from nowhere; he held it close to Field's face. "I can handle a knife," said the boy again.

In one motion, Field jerked Tom's wrist straight up and kicked him behind his near leg, bringing the boy down to his knees, the knife clattering to the paving stones. Field laid the end of his crutch on the boy's back to keep him where he was and leaned down to speak quietly into his ear. "I can handle a knife as well, Tom. If he comes, we'll see to it, won't we."

Field released him. He picked up the knife and Tom got to his feet. The flower vendor reappeared, looking alarmed, but the inspector shook his head reassuringly. "Police moves, Mr. Bowers," said the inspector. "Boys love 'em. You won't have any further problems with this one, I'm sure of it."

Field returned the knife to Tom and the boy pocketed the weapon. "Next time, Tom, you can try that one on me. Come to supper, now, don't forget."

Field turned up his collar and was on his way. He had mastered his crutch by now and moved through the market at a brisk pace. He found a hackney cab and hauled himself into it.

"No deliveries whilst I was out, my dear?" he said when he reached his home. "No callers, no mail?"

Jane shook her head. "Are you expecting something, Mr. Field?"

"Smells good in here, I must say." He retired to his study, which overlooked a bleak courtyard. The thin rain turned to sleet.

Jane worked all the afternoon, roasting fowl and baking venison pasties, a favorite of her husband's. The plum pudding had been the labor of weeks. Bessie Shoreham assisted by rushing in and out of the kitchen for no particular reason, every now and then dropping exhausted into a chair, blowing strands of hair from her eyes and mopping her brow with a kerchief.

"Lor', Missus," said Bessie, "sometimes I do *not* know why we bother!"

The newest member of the Field household sat on the stairs, staring at the front door and twisting a lock of hair into knots. The inspector emerged from his study and looked up at the girl. He pulled out his watch and pocketed it again.

"All right, Belinda?" She nodded.

At that moment the bell jangled. The girl stood and stared apprehensively. Field opened the door, revealing Tom, cap in hand, the remains of his injured ear exposed: a crusted scab surmounted by the rosy pink flesh of an otherwise healthy young ear.

"Come in, Tom."

The boy stepped across the threshold and stopped, staring up at the girl.

"Hallo, Tom," said Belinda. "You went abroad."

"Blinky."

"Belinda, if you please. *I* went many places, too, you would not believe the places I went. I was snatched, you see, and put in black and made to cry for the dead."

Jane was looking up the stairs, watching from the kitchen door and wiping her hands on her apron. Bessie hovered just behind, peeking over Jane's shoulder.

"I hated my masters, Tom, but I liked what they give me to wear, in a way," continued Belinda, "and it was all new, every stitch of it made to order just for me, and there was even jewelry I wore, too, made for mourning the dead, necklaces and bracelets but all sewn up in black cloth so what was the point of it, I had to wonder. Then I was locked in a cupboard on a train and took by the police and I didn't know what would become of me, but when I told them my name, they said the big policeman was looking for me and they brought me along here to his house where I have my own bed. You needn't marry me, Tom, I think of you more as a brother than a husband, in point of fact; you can rest your mind easy on *that* score."

"Well," said Tom finally, "that's all right, then, Belinda." And for the first time in a great while, Tom smiled.

The bell rang again and Sam Llewellyn arrived, looking wet and cold. Soon after, Jake Figgis and Tom's mother, Mary, presented themselves at the door. Mary still had a distracted air, but Jake put on a brave smile and Tom was very attentive. The inspector ushered his few guests upstairs to the dining room, where supper was ample but quiet, except for Belinda's commentary, which was extensive.

NEAR OSTEND

THE WOMAN IN gray was an invalid; the servants of the great house could tell that much. Master had given them strict instructions: Madame was to be offered every comfort. They never saw the face beneath the veil. Her trunks contained numerous fine ensembles, all in shades of gray, all costly. She seldom spoke; when she did, her voice was deep, somewhat slurred, and her German was British-accented. The girl assigned to be her ladies' maid would prepare Madame's toilette and then clear up afterward; she never saw Madame unclothed. The kitchen staff were ordered to prepare foods that were easily chewed.

Madame walked up and down the corridors of the house using a cane, and when the weather permitted, she paced the terrace in the courtyard. She sent telegrams repeatedly and waited with increasing agitation for replies that did not come.

The months passed. She recovered her strength. The staff took it as a good sign when eventually Madame asked for meat.

43

Early in 1861 Charles Field returned to full-time work with the Metropolitan Police, limping still, but without the crutch. Belinda became a true member of the household at No. 2 Bow Street, Jane Field painstakingly teaching her her letters, and not to steal. The inspector was unable to trace the girl's origins and she herself had no idea what her surname might be, so it was decided that *Belinda Field* would do.

Tom seemed to settle into his situation at the flower market; his master came to be satisfied with his work. He was a frequent guest in the Field home and over time became less withdrawn. Eventually he started talking about the house in Half Moon Street, and once he'd begun, Belinda dared to speak of it as well. Neither spoke of Decimus Cobb and the inspector did not press them, but he learned about the other inhabitants, John Getalong and Hamlet and Mrs. Hamlet. Field decided not to mention Getalong's sad end, but when he told them that Hamlet was dead, Belinda grew thoughtful.

"He was not a nice man," she said, "and he stank, but he was old and stupid and so should be pitied, I imagine."

Tom told Field about the witch he'd met at the guest house in Oxford who came to live in the London house—dressed in black and mean as mean—and she turned out to be their captor's mother. Tom told him about the young woman at the top of the house who was writing a great book.

"Mary Do-Not," added Belinda with a sidelong glance at the boy.

"Her real name was Mary Withers."

"Tom was in love with her."

"Hush!" said Tom.

"She made people perish, that's what everyone said."

"Perish?" said Field. "How did she do that, then?"

"No one knew," said the girl.

"I don't believe it meself," said Tom.

"All them households, Tom! Are you saying all them folk she spoke of dying did *not* get the typhoid and die? She was bad luck, through and through."

Tom didn't answer and Field let it go.

Winter turned to spring, followed by a mild summer. Inspector Field, back in harness, made a couple of notable arrests, including the headmaster he'd been pursuing for the poisoning death of his children's governess. Autumn was glorious but short-lived; winter looked to be arriving prematurely. Slowly the threat of Decimus Cobb receded from Charles Field's mind. Perhaps, after all, the man *had* been cut to bits by the Coburg train.

Through all these months Sir Richard Owen felt a distinct chill emanating from the palace, but his fear of turning a corner one day and meeting Decimus Cobb overshadowed all. Owen's academic work continued to thrive, and his fame grew as the lines were drawn ever more sharply between his camp and the evolutionists. The prime spokesman for the latter, Thomas Huxley, began a series of lecture tours throughout the country, often explaining Mr. Darwin's theories to audiences of working-class men and women who were intrigued by the possibility that everyone might indeed be created equal.

Samuel Wilberforce, bishop of Oxford, felt himself to be haunted unfairly by his possibly infelicitous remarks concerning Huxley's monkey grandparents. He sought to raise himself in public opinion through highly visible charitable works. He was perfectly content, therefore, to interview the modestly dressed young woman sent to him by some choirmaster or other out of his past. He was favorably impressed by her demeanor, her beauty, and her astonishing knowledge of world history. She made him think of an exquisite porcelain doll. He would be happy to lend his name if it might help her to secure employment in an exalted household.

Charles Darwin, confined by illness and fame to Down House, worked tirelessly on his next book, which promised to be even more controversial than the first.

DOWN HOUSE

EMMA DARWIN WAS opening the little parcel when her husband stopped her. "My dear, allow me. I believe this will be yet another finch from a correspondent in Ostend who seems to think I am in need of finches."

She gave the box to her husband with a sympathetic smile. He had been ill again in the night.

"Feeling better?" she said.

"Much."

Moments later, alone in his study off the garden, Darwin carefully unwrapped the brown paper and opened the small box. He was confident it would not contain a finch and he was right. It was a human ear, pressed under a small glass plate. Female, he decided, aged forty years or so. He set the parcel down, pulled the chamber pot from beneath the daybed, and vomited. He opened the garden door and set the pot outside; a winter wind rushed into the room and he closed the door. He moistened a cloth from the ewer at the basin and wiped his face.

A similarly wrapped parcel had come from Ostend a week earlier, also containing a human ear. Gender uncertain but likely female, aged sixteen or seventeen years. Both ears had a characteristic bump in the outermost whorl, a feature that occurred in only about a tenth of the population. At this juncture, it was only a rumor in scientific circles: *Darwin is planning to include humans in his grand theory. One piece of evidence will be the tubercle, the little point in the ear, which he says corresponds to the sharp point of the fox's ear, or the cat's, or the bat's. Or the monkey's.* His anonymous correspondent, therefore, likely was someone in the field of natural philosophy and privy to current scientific scuttlebutt.

Each box held an angry note harping on the same theme, that anomalies were just that and nothing more, and suggesting in graphic terms how Darwin might dissect himself in order to learn from his own mistakes. When he had received the first one, he assumed the severed ear had originated from a legitimately obtained corpse. Now, he had to suspect this was not the case. A madman was killing women. Darwin put a peppermint in his mouth and picked up a quill. The letter went out by the afternoon post to his brother, Erasmus, in London, Darwin's lifelong confidant. *What should one do?* Erasmus promptly sent a note to his friendly acquaintance, Police Commissioner Richard Mayne of the Metropolitan.

As it happened, Mayne was lunching with Samuel Wilberforce when the note was put into his hands. "Good Lord," said Mayne under his breath. He looked up at his companion. "Sorry. It's just that our man, Detective Field, has been claiming for months that there was a violent conspiracy to discredit Darwin, and now . . ."

The bishop put down his fork.

"Yes?" he said. "And now?"

Mayne read the note again. "Well, I had better get him onto it."

"Get whom onto what?"

"This is just between us, you understand," said the commissioner, folding the note and pocketing it. "It seems some anti-evolutionary chap has been sending human body bits to Charles Darwin. I say, old man, are you quite all right?"

The bishop took a sip of wine before answering. "Perfectly, perfectly," he said, but his hand trembled as he set down the glass and he'd gone white as a sheet in an instant.

INSPECTOR FIELD ASKED Sam Llewellyn to accompany him by train to Orpington.

"We'll be traveling on from there by coach to the village of Downe," said Field. "Commissioner Mayne wants us to check on Mr. Charles Darwin and that's where he lives when he's at home, which is almost always as I understand it."

The great man turned out to be far less intimidating than either man might have feared. Darwin had been on the lookout for the policemen, evidently; as soon as they started up the drive, he emerged from the big white house, wearing a greatcoat. He greeted them warmly but steered them away from the front door to a side entrance off the garden and into his study. The day was bitterly cold; Darwin placed his visitors before the fire during the introductions and sent a servant off for a pot of tea. Finally he lowered his voice and said, "Would you like to see them, Mr. Field?"

"I would indeed, sir."

Llewellyn looked at his superior, bewildered. Darwin took two small parcels from a desk drawer and offered one of them to Field.

"The first, sent from Ostend," said Darwin.

Field unfolded the brown paper and opened the little box.

"*Damn me!*" shouted Llewellyn.

"Hush, Sam." A dog somewhere in the house began to bark.

"You said he was dead, Mr. Field!"

"Did I?"

"'Crushed by a train,' you said." Llewellyn ran his fingers through his hair. "You *saw the body*, sir!"

"Others were convinced that the body by the train tracks belonged to our man, and I thought it possible, but with Decimus there was always a niggling doubt."

"Am I to infer," said Darwin, "that you know who this correspondent might be?"

"I believe we may, sir. Might I see the other, please?"

The naturalist put the second parcel in Field's hand. "Again, with an Ostend postmark. This one belonged to a much younger person. Also female, most likely."

"It's got to be him," muttered Llewellyn. "He's on a bloody tear."

"They both feature this little bump here," said Darwin, pointing, "which I call the Woolnerian tip. Others call it a tubercle. You can see from the note that the correspondent seems to think it proves a point, but I'm afraid it does rather the opposite. Who is he, Mr. Field?"

"Man named Cobb."

"Do you think he murdered these women?"

"I am afraid I do, sir."

"Good God. *Why?*"

Field sighed and shook his head. "To look into another man's heart is difficult enough. To read the heart of a monster—if he has one—may not be possible."

Darwin was silent for some moments, staring into the fire. "The heart is a pump," he said finally. "That is all I am qualified to tell you about the heart. And yet I know, in some way not demonstrable, it is something other than, more than, that." He rose and moved to look out the glass panes of the garden door. "I disbelieve in monsters. But I have found ordinary nature to be insupportably cruel, often enough. I left the Church because of it, causing my dear wife great distress. Other men have lost a child and not lost God. I envy them."

The inspector turned to Llewellyn. "Why has he come to life again, Sam? Why does he seem to be aiming at Mr. Darwin now and not Prince Albert?"

"*Prince Albert?*" said Darwin.

The sound of children's voices rose just outside the study door.

"Perhaps, sir, we might continue this outside?" said the inspector.

LONDON

JANE FIELD WAS waiting patiently as Belinda's quill scratched over her lesson. Ink blots appeared here and there on the page like raindrops; Jane winced but said nothing. Downstairs the bell rang. Jane heard Bessie opening the door and some minutes later heard her huffing up the stairs.

"Missus! Someone is askin' after Miss Coffin!"

Jane looked up sharply. "Who is?"

"A boy, but it was the lady in the carriage wot give 'im a sixpence, *she* was the one askin'." I said there ain't no Miss Coffin 'ere, nor was there ever, and when the boy told 'er that, 'e come trottin' back sayin' the lady knows I'm lyin' and has a mind to alert the police!"

"What did you say then?"

"Nothin', I slammed shut the door!"

Belinda ran to the window. "Get away from there, Belinda!" said Jane. "Go and wash yourself, you've put more ink on yourself than on the page, haven't you." The girl turned and clattered down the stairs. Jane went to the window and cautiously looked down into the street.

"The carriage is moving off. What did the lady look like, Bessie?"

"All in gray, with a veil, starin' out the carriage window like she would eat me alive!"

"Did you ever see her before?"

"No, Missus."

"Well, you'll tell Mr. Field all about it when he returns."

"But Mr. Field don't know about Miss Coffin and all wot 'appened!"

Jane hesitated. "I'll think of something."

"Yes, Missus. I don't like to think about 'er—Miss Coffin, I mean."

"Nor do I, Bessie." Jane turned from the window and touched Bessie's cheek sympathetically. Thus, neither woman saw Belinda

cautiously opening the front door below for a peek or the carriage circling back and drawing up to the front of the house.

DOWN HOUSE

THE NATURALIST AND the policemen paced round the
Sandwalk as they talked, their hands thrust deep into coat pockets.
"What's all this about the Prince, Inspector?"

"Did you know, sir, that you were to have been knighted last year,
but your name was struck from the list?"

"I had heard a rumor to that effect."

"The Prince is a great admirer of your work. There are those who
believe if Albert were out of the picture, so to speak, it might help ensure
your name will not appear on this year's Honors List, nor ever again."

"Ah."

"Is it possible, sir," said the inspector as they crunched on over the
gravel, "that a man could have a tail?"

Both Darwin and Llewellyn looked at Field in surprise.

"I'm just curious."

"Yes, it's possible. You had a tail once, and so did I. Every human
embryo displays a vestigial tail for a few weeks, but it disappears before
birth. We don't have the *need* for a tail as we used to do. Mr. Field, I
don't believe you ask this out of idle curiosity."

"It always disappears?"

"Almost always. There are extremely rare instances of humans born
full term with a tail-like appendage, as much as five or six inches long.
Of course, many vestigial organs are not rare at all but quite common,
even universal. Your appendix is one. Wisdom teeth. Gooseflesh. Male
nipples. We seem to be made of bits and pieces of who we used to be."

"Is that so? Mr. Charles Dickens once said much the same to me."

"Indeed?"

"But I believe *he* was talking about the state we're pleased to call
childhood." The inspector's brow furrowed and he stopped in his tracks.
"Very well, let's say it's me, then," he said softly.

"I beg your pardon?" said Darwin, but Llewellyn put a finger to his lips.

"One moment, sir," whispered the constable. "Sorry, sir."

"It's *me* born with a tail," continued Field as he started to walk again. "Different from all others, right from the start. Different in a nasty sort of way. Does anyone *not* wrinkle their nose at me, growing up? Draw back, gasp in horror or mere distaste? My siblings, my mates, if I have any? My own mother? And then, as I grow older, well, I don't like the ladies seeing what I got down there, do I? Not much. But I want the ladies, nevertheless, I got the urge, like anyone else."

Darwin watched, fascinated, as the color rose to Field's face and his breathing changed.

"Makes me angry to feel it, the urge. Just to *think* of it makes me angry, come to that. Enraged actually. Bloody murderous. And then out comes this blighter's damned book and it's saying because of that *thing* at the bottom of my spine, I'm not even a man!" He was shouting now. "That's insult to injury, that is!"

Field stopped again. He clutched his knees and took several deep breaths. "Right," he said with a skewed smile, standing upright again. "That's all well and good, Mr. Bucket, but it don't help us know the man's next move, does it."

"Charles!"

The men turned to see Emma Darwin hurrying toward them, coatless, along the Sandwalk.

"Oh, dear," said Darwin. "I forgot all about our tea. *We're just on our way, darling!*"

She was half-running now, one hand over her mouth.

"Emma, what's wrong?"

She thrust out a small package as she reached them. "What *is* this? The postman just brought it. It's vile. *It's someone's ear!*"

Field quickly took the parcel and Darwin embraced his wife as she began to sob.

"Sam," said the inspector quietly, "the postmark is Dover. He's on his way."

LONDON

Field gave Llewellyn his newly purchased pistol and left him to protect the Darwins, ordering him to join him in London as soon as replacements could take his place. The inspector himself made it to town as a cold, slanting rain began to fall. He went directly to headquarters and briefed Commissioner Mayne, offering him three severed ears as evidence. Descriptions of Decimus Cobb were sent by telegraph to the police in Dover and to the coaching inns from there to London. Plainclothes police were dispatched to Orpington via train and coach, each instructed to look for a tall blond man with striking deep-set eyes. The royal family was at Windsor; Field sent a vaguely worded telegram alerting Colonel Ponsonby, who responded confidentially that the Prince was on the road after paying a visit to his eldest son at Cambridge to chide him for certain unspecified indiscretions.

Just as Field was leaving Mayne's office, a message was put in his hands. A moment later he was running down the stairs and out onto the street. A hackney coach carried him in a freezing drizzle to Bow Street where he found his wife in an agitated state and Bessie chewing her apron.

"I've searched the house from top to bottom," said Jane. "Belinda is gone."

"What? Is that all? Your note said it was urgent!"

"She's been taken, Mr. Field!"

"No, she hasn't, she's run off! Belinda is a street girl, you can't change her ways in a day!"

"Listen to me, Charles. A woman called, asking after Mrs. Andrews—*you* know, that called herself *Coffin*?"

"Yes?"

"When the woman went away, Belinda was missing."

"I don't understand."

"This was on the hall table," said Jane, giving him a note.

What have you done with Mother?

The handwriting was unmistakable: the inspector had just seen three samples of it at Darwin's home.

"It was a woman, you say?"

Jane nodded. Field thought for a moment, then looked keenly into his wife's eyes.

"Mrs. Field, did something happen with Mrs. Andrews that I don't know about?"

"She died."

"Ah. How?"

"Bled."

"How?"

"Throat cut."

"I see." He nodded and took a deep breath. "By whom?"

"Does it matter?"

"My dear . . ."

"Mrs. Ginty did it." Tears coursed down her face. "With my help."

"What did you do with Mrs. Andrews?"

"Mr. Llewellyn gave her to the doctors at St. Bart's."

"Did he now. He neglected to mention it. It was a *woman* who was inquiring, not a man? You're certain of that?"

"A woman with a veil!" said Bessie.

Field stared at the note. It was an angry scrawl.

"Right. I must go. Bolt the door behind me."

"I couldn't tell you," Jane said, weeping. "We killed a woman, *I* did, nothing can ever change that, I knew it would be the end of everything for us, *everything* . . ."

"Mrs. Field." He took her in his arms. "Jane. I begin to feel that whatever happened here in this house may have diverted our man from his intended purposes. Which, in a way, helps me. It does."

Jane clung to him. He gently but firmly disengaged her. "Throw the bolt, Mrs. Field. Admit no one."

THE WHEELS OF the coach rattled over the slick paving stones. Field sat up beside the coachman despite the sleet, straining forward as if willing the carriage to go faster. He leapt down when they reached the market, ordering the driver to wait for him. The inspector ran along the rows of flower stalls, shouting as he ran.

"Where's Tom Ginty? I want Tom Ginty!"

Mr. Bowers appeared in Field's path. "That's just it, Mr. Field—Tom's gone off!"

"Off where, off how?"

"A young girl came and fetched him away."

"Was there a lady?"

"No lady, just the little girl. She was *that* scared, Mr. Field. She said our Tom had to come, or a bad man was goin' to do for you and Mrs. Field. Tom dropped his apron and went, just like that!"

Field turned and ran back to his waiting cab.

"No. 4 Half Moon Street, driver," he said, climbing up to the perch. "Fly!"

THE DAMP CLOTH had come down over Tom's mouth as soon as he climbed up into the lady's carriage. He had struggled against the hand that held it there, staring into the eyes behind the veil, eyes he realized he knew all too well. Belinda, somewhere very close, erupted into screams.

Tom swam down to a great depth.

He came to the surface, coughing. All was dark. When he tried to sit he hit his head. He fell back and struggled to squeeze shut his sphincters. He knew this darkness. He had been here once before.

IT WAS NEAR dark. The sleet had turned to snow. A lamplighter was moving his ladder up the quiet street, pole by pole. To Inspector Field, sitting in the coach outside, the house looked abandoned. The police had sealed the door with wooden boards that already were weathered. No ray of light penetrated the shuttered windows. The steps were thick with sodden leaves covered by a layer of snow; no one had put a foot there. He recalled Belinda saying there was another entrance at the back. Or was Field all wrong? Had Decimus *not* brought the children here?

Then he's on his way to Mr. Darwin with the children, and with God knows what horror in mind.

The inspector put himself in Cobb's place. Decimus, having survived his train wreck, likely would be severely injured, even disfigured. Ladies' apparel and a veil could suit Cobb's purposes when traveling. Decimus had placed his mother in the policeman's own household as a spy. After months of silence he had to know that something was seriously wrong there. But then to discover a former member of his own menagerie living at Bow Street must have come as an unexpected blow to him. So, thought Field, the madman would gather up the remnants of his flock and seek revenge.

Field turned to the coachman. "Can you let me have a jimmy and a light?"

The nails on the boards covering the door came up with raw shrieks, one by one. On his third kick the door shattered messily. He was in.

PETER SIMS HAD accompanied the Prince on his journey to Cambridge and back. Now he helped Albert climb the stairs. The two men were wet to the skin, but Albert was feverish and trembling. Peter called for the Prince's valet, who took in the situation at once and began shouting orders to the other servants. A roaring fire was built in His Highness's bedroom. He was given brandy and put to bed. Minutes later the Queen hurried to his side, only to find him sitting at his desk in his robe, writing furiously.

"*What* are you doing?"

"Palmerston's people will have us at war with the United States of America," said the Prince, still writing. His voice was raspy and tense.

"Stop. Immediately. You were ill even *before* you went on this misbegotten journey. Dr. Clark says you are to *rest*."

"My dear, did you hear me? The Americans—the legitimate ones—have taken one of our ships from the open sea and brought her into Boston Harbor in order to seize two of these rebels from the South." He paused to catch his breath. His face glistened. "The action was imprudent, certainly, but our response must *not* be. This communiqué I wish to amend, if only you will let me, is positively incendiary!"

"Sir James says you must *sleep*. He says you were responding *well* to the regimen he had you on, the gruel and so forth, but *not* if you keep working at this *pace*. He's assigned a *nice* young woman from the kitchens to be in charge of you. You will enjoy talking with her, she is *quite* imaginative."

"This message, Victoria, dispatched as written, with its brash condemnation of the United States government, will draw us into someone else's civil war! *Now, please, leave me in peace!*"

The Queen took a moment to maintain her composure. She went to Albert and put a hand to his forehead. He brushed it away and continued to write.

"I shall *never* forgive Bertie for this," she said. "It is *he* who has made you ill, all along of his *degrading* vices."

"There," said Albert, putting down the quill. "Finished." He started to rise, faltered, and sank down onto the chair again. "Cramps."

Victoria went to the door and told a servant to summon Dr. Clark.

THERE WAS AN odor of gas. Field set down the coachman's lantern, unlit, beside the splintered door, but hung on to the crowbar. He peered into the gloom and listened. Was there a drumming sound? A pounding? Someone somewhere was singing in a high voice. As dim as it was, he could see splashes of wet on the staircase before him. He approached the steps cautiously and crouched to examine them. People had come from the kitchen below and climbed to the upper floors. Looking closely, he saw here and there a scuff of boot blacking on the front edges of the risers. A boot-wearing male had been dragged up the stairs, his heels hitting each step. Field sensed movement directly above him and saw the flash of a large kitchen knife coming down to his neck; his right hand shot up and caught the wrist that held it, all bone, the skin brittle and papery.

"Don't hurt!" squeaked the old woman.

He stood and made out the emaciated features of Mrs. Hamlet. "I thought you was him come back!" she whispered. "He *has* come, you know!"

Field flung her off and began to climb the stairs, speaking to the darkness above. "The children have nothing to do with this, Mr. Cobb." His voice sounded feeble to his ears; it seemed to go nowhere in the close, malodorous air. "Send down the children. When they are safely out of this, you and I can talk."

The singing was coming from above.

Dies irae, dies illa
Solvet saeclum in favilla:
Teste David cum Sibylla!

"You were a Paul's boy, weren't you Decimus," said Field. "You've still got the voice for it, I must say. Send down the children."

The singing broke off.

"The children are only here to fetch you, Mr. Bucket. I've no further use for them."

"Then send them down."

"I'll send them down one piece at a time, Mr. Bucket."

The inspector felt sweat, clammy and chill, on his brow. "No need for talk like that now, is there."

"When I have your tongue out, you won't tell me how to talk."

Field reached the first-floor landing. There were muffled noises coming from behind the door on his right: sporadic pounding, a faint cry, the sounds of a bad dream. Crowbar in hand, he addressed the door.

"Mr. Darwin is most interested in the items you sent him, Mr. Cobb. I've just come from him. He is eager to talk with you about your ideas." Field's mind raced. "This tubercle, or what do you call it—you took him quite by surprise there, I must say. Gave him pause, it did."

"Do you think I'm a child?" The voice came from above him. Field whirled round. In the dim at the top of the next flight stood a figure in women's attire, much disheveled.

"Cobb?"

Decimus pulled off the hat and veil and cast them aside, revealing close-cropped hair and a face creased with scars, the jaw out of alignment with the rest, the nose flattened. Field, wishing fervently he hadn't just given away his pistol, started up the stairs, brandishing the crowbar. Decimus pulled Belinda from behind the folds of his skirt and placed her before him.

"I will see Mr. Darwin, have no fear of that," said Decimus, his voice slurred. "I will demonstrate to him his many errors. I am my own introduction, Mr. Bucket—I have no need of yours."

"Hallo, Belinda. All right, then?"

The girl was shaking.

"Our Tom is here, too, I imagine." The inspector nodded toward the closed door behind him. "In there, perhaps?"

And there it was, muffled, from behind the closed door, Tom's voice crying out, faint but unmistakable.

"Harm them, Decimus, and I will be the one taking *you* apart, I promise you."

A thin brass pincer or forceps of some sort, made for one-handed operation, appeared at Belinda's throat.

"Let's do a trade, shall we?" said Field. "Big bad me for that little thing."

"What did you do to Mother?"

Field stared at the man, whose outward form was now as monstrous as his actions. *No*, he thought, *there ain't no monsters, there's only men. Think!*

"She died, Decimus." He heard a sharp intake of breath from the man. Field took a step up. "You was very fond of her, no doubt—warts and all. Nothing like a mother's cuddle, am I right, Decimus?" He took another step up. "She didn't care that you was born like that, with that *thing* hanging off you, did she? Not her. No, you were her very own little monkey, you were—tail and all!"

"Shut it!"

"I touched that thing once, unintentional, didn't I? Back there in that dark castle room. Disgusting, it was."

"Shut it!"

The inspector climbed another two steps. "No, that mother of yours must have been one in a million if she didn't fling you out onto the streets to be rid of you, or—I don't know—*sell* you to Bartholomew's Fair as a novelty."

Field saw the man above him shudder, his deep eyes staring.

"Got it in one, didn't I, Decimus? She *did* sell you. How many times?"

"She knew how special I was!"

"And that's understating the case, matey."

"I'll nail your lips to the door when I'm done with you! *What did you do to Mother?*"

"Cut her stringy old throat for her, Decimus, and sent her corpse to St. Bart's, like you done so many others."

There was a long silence and then Decimus began to laugh, a high, thin, cascading laugh that went on and on. "Oh, Mother!" he gasped, and then the laugh began again.

Field sprang up the remaining steps and yanked Belinda, tumbling her down the steps to the landing below. He thrust the crowbar at Cobb's face, but the brass forceps closed tight around Field's wrist and flung the jimmy up. It flew from his hand and clattered to the landing below.

"There are twenty-seven bones in the human hand, Mr. Bucket, and I mean to hang each of yours round my neck."

A tentative voice came from the shattered street door below. "Mr. Field, sir?" said Sam Llewellyn. Decimus glanced down the stairs, and Field jerked his own captive wrist over the banister and brought Decimus' forearm down on the rail hard enough to snap it. Decimus cried out, dropping the forceps and Field's wrist was free. He flung himself on the man.

LLEWELLYN STEPPED THROUGH the splintered door and into the house. He saw the lantern on the floor and picked it up. He heard a pitched struggle going on above him, men fighting and a child wailing. He started up the stairs and immediately tripped over a body. He scrambled to his feet. The scrawny crone was sitting on the bottom-most step, staring at him with crazy eyes and tilting her head meaningfully up the stairs. He peered up into the gloom.

"Coming, Mr. Field! Coachman told me you were here. I sent him to fetch more police. They'll be here in minutes, you'll be glad to know."

He took a phosphorous match from a pocket.

"No!" shrieked the old woman.

Llewellyn struck the match against the lantern's side. Instantly the flame ballooned into the lantern and out again, and up Llewellyn's arm with a *whoosh*. He dropped the light, shattering the glass. He beat at the flames on the sleeve of his tunic as a line of fire leapt from the broken lantern up to the wall on the left side of the stairs. It hit the gaslight there with a boom and blossomed into many-hued flames. The fire continued running up the staircase, following the line of the gas pipe, blistering the wallpaper and exploding at each lamp on the way up.

Llewellyn shoved the old woman toward the street door. "Fetch help!" he cried. The constable took the stairs three at a time. He found Belinda shivering in a heap on the first landing and picked her up. "Mr. Field!" he shouted.

Above him, the inspector and Decimus were locked in an embrace, staggering on the stairs like drunken dancers, Decimus clutching a blade to Field's throat and Field struggling to hold it off. Suddenly they both were lit by a brilliant orange light billowing up from the great skirt Decimus wore; it lit his face with a garish glow. The knife clattered down and Field fell back against the rail. And then Decimus' hands were in motion, one struggling to pull off articles of clothing and the other slapping ineffectually at the flames.

Field shouted down to Llewellyn. "Get the girl out, I'll get Tom!"

The inspector half fell down the steps toward the constable who remained transfixed, staring at the sight above. Field picked himself up and rounded the landing, heading to the closed door. "Go on, Sam, *go*!" Llewellyn, clutching Belinda, turned and pounded down to the street door.

Field threw his shoulder against the entrance to Decimus' domain, but it held fast. Flames were spreading up and down the staircase behind him. He kicked twice and put his boot through. He found a latch on the inside and turned it. The door sprang open. There was no time to take in the magnitude of the obscenities mounted throughout the room. He skirted the narrow iron-framed monk's bedstead and made for the casket resting on a catafalque. He tried to lift the cover; it was screwed down.

"Tom!"

Smoke was pouring into the room. Field looked about desperately. He ran back to the landing and searched the floor for the crowbar. Flames were spreading everywhere. *There!* The iron bar was already growing hot.

"Coming, Tom!"

Field levered the crowbar under the casket lid and thrust down, putting all his weight to it. The lid split and the casket slewed off the catafalque, crashing to the floor. He pried off the cover, grabbed for the boy, and Tom's fist hit him just below his right eye.

"It's me, Tom! It's Mr. Field!"

Field hoisted him, still striking out with his fists, up from the coffin and stood him on the floor. The boy's knees buckled and Field caught him. "I've got you, boy!" Tom seemed to focus his eyes on the man before him and suddenly he was sobbing. Field put an arm round his shoulders and led him out of the room. The heat hit them first, and the garish light. A piercing cry drew their eyes to the landing above.

Decimus had flung off his burning clothes. Naked, his body red with the glow of the fire, he turned in circles, swatting at the flames, his tail visible and grotesque.

"Come down, Decimus! Follow me!"

The infinitely deep eyes found the inspector and the boy. He stopped flailing and stood, shuddering. He grasped the rail, took a deep breath and began to sing.

Dies irae, dies illa
Solvet saeclum in favilla . . .

The banister above them gave way, blazing spindles falling about their heads. Field swung Tom clear of the flaming debris. He knelt, drew Tom's arms over his shoulders from behind, then stood and staggered to the stairs. Step by step, with fire on either side, he descended, Tom hanging on his back. A piercing scream came from above. Field looked up in time to see a portion of the staircase above him descend, plummeting straight down like a pillar, carrying a burning human torch atop it into the depths of the building. Field sped, stumbling down the steps.

The night outside was lit by the flames. Constables were keeping back a growing crowd. Snow lay thick on the front steps, glowing from the flames, red and blue and orange, as the inspector emerged from the broken front door, clothes and hair smoking, the boy on his back. A great cheer went up from the crowd.

Inspector Field carried Tom down the steps, walking away toward a snow-covered Green Park. Llewellyn, bearing the girl, followed in his wake. From behind them came, finally, a great roar and a gust of rushing wind.

44

Within days, Inspector Field sent a note to the Prince that contained the series of words they had agreed upon to let Albert know if there were any developments in the case: *We have heard from Bishop Adolf.* He waited impatiently for a reply. At home all was quiet, with Jane Field tending to Tom and Belinda as they recovered from their ordeal. Field's right wrist was bandaged where the brass forceps had cut into the flesh. His eyebrows had been singed off in the blaze; consequently he wore a perpetually startled expression.

Days passed and Field received no answer to his note to the Prince. He felt a need to communicate directly after all they'd been through together. Almost two weeks later, in mid-December, Field decided to pay a visit, without benefit of invitation. The royal couple were at Windsor, where he had never been.

What do I do? he wondered, riding in a coach through the frigid countryside. *Knock at the big front door?*

As it happened, people were coming and going when Field approached the massive, sprawling castle. A man at the entrance had been part of the traveling entourage the year before; he recognized Field and somberly asked him to follow. They walked in a fine drizzle from the lower ward to the upper. Field was deposited within a door there and left to himself. No one seemed to pay him any attention. People moved swiftly and quietly on earnest errands, speaking in hushed tones.

"I beg your pardon," said the inspector to a passing servant. "I'm here to see His Highness, the Prince Consort."

"Follow me, sir," said the man. "The other doctors are keeping themselves close, I'll bring you to them." Before Field could say anything the man turned and walked briskly up a flight of stairs, so the inspector followed after. At the top of the stairs he saw two ladies holding each other and weeping. Further along the corridor they came upon men moving a piano on casters. A butler asked them what they were about and one of them replied, "His Highness asked for it brought near." The butler nodded and they continued.

The servant guiding the inspector stopped at a closed door. "Your name, sir?"

"Field."

The man rapped softly at the door and opened it. Within, a half-dozen grave-looking gentlemen looked up.

"Mr. Field," said the servant. "To see the Prince."

The inspector saw Sir James Clark look up, startled. "*Who* wishes to see him?"

Field walked into the room. "Detective Inspector Field, Sir James, of the Metropolitan Police, you remember me."

"Are you serious? Under no circumstance!"

Colonel Ponsonby crossed the room to speak to Field in low tones. "How do you do, Field. Perhaps you weren't aware, but the Prince is gravely ill."

"Nonsense," said Sir James. "He's rallying." The other physicians in the room looked at each other doubtfully. Sir James raised his voice. "His Highness doesn't need to receive some damned *policeman* just at present."

"On that score," said Ponsonby quietly to Field, "I must agree with our physician friend. The Prince, whatever the prognosis, is ill and not receiving. Sorry, old man."

"I am sorrier than I can say," said Field, "that my lord the Prince is unwell. I just wanted to tell him that the man who tried to do him harm is dead."

Colonel Ponsonby stared at Field. "But he died a year ago, you told me yourself. He was crushed by a train at Coburg."

"As it happens, he survived the wreck and returned to these shores not long ago, intent upon his mischief."

"Good God."

"Fortunately for us all, he perished in a fire before he . . ."

Field trailed off as an elegantly dressed young woman entered the room from an opposite door. With her was a young kitchen maid carrying a bowl. "Thank you, Withers," said Princess Alice, "but he simply will not eat. Let us try again in an hour."

The kitchen maid curtsied. "Yes, miss," she said, and left the room.

"Sir James," said the Princess, "father has asked me to play something, will that be all right? It won't overexcite him?"

"Of course, Your Highness." Sir James bowed and she returned to the sick room. Field caught a momentary glimpse through the door of a knot of somber people—the royal children and their mother—gathered about a bed, and then the door closed.

Sir James turned to Field. "Are you finished?" The inspector nodded and bowed and was about to go when he saw something in the royal physician's eyes, something that he had seen again and again in his long career as a policeman.

Thinks he's got away with something, he does.

"Withers!" cried Field suddenly.

"I beg your pardon?"

"That girl just now, where did she come from? How long has she been here, waiting on the Prince?"

"What are you talking about?" said Sir James.

"Dear God, *he* sent her here, and *you* knew all about it, didn't you! You, Dugdale, Sir Jasper—dear Lord, how many of you *are* there?"

"Steady on, Field," said Ponsonby.

"Whether it's poison she's been giving him, or the miasma, or whatever you doctors bloody well call it, that kitchen maid is killing the Prince!"

"Get this madman out of here!" Sir James shouted. But Field was already leaving, hurrying into the corridor, trying to make out which way the girl called Withers might have gone. From behind him he heard the piano strike up and a female voice singing.

> *A mighty fortress is our God,*
> *A bulwark never failing;*
> *Our helper he amid the flood*
> *Of mortal ills prevailing . . .*

Suddenly the piano and the singing stopped, and so did Charles Field, stock-still. A cry sounded fearfully through the castle; not the voice of a monarch but the wail of a woman who has suffered irretrievable loss.

45

It took some time to sift through the ruins of the house in Half Moon Street. It was grim work. Many of the body parts that the searchers turned up were mounted, labeled, and given fanciful Latin names; others were jumbled together in crates, preserved but unlabeled. All of them were studied by investigators in the coroner's office and at the Metropolitan, who sought to match them with old cases of missing persons. Eventually the thoroughly unmistakable remains of Decimus Cobb were recovered. After the coroner had finished with them, Field ordered them transferred to the Hunterian Museum at the Royal College of Surgeons: a gift from the Metropolitan Police to the famous collection of anatomical aberrations. When Sir Richard Owen demurred, Field sent him a note to let him know that he *would* accept the bones of Decimus Cobb and *would* have them mounted and prominently displayed, for the edification of the public and as a private reminder to Owen of all that Field knew. And so it was done.

From Peter Sims, the inspector learned that a kitchen servant by the name of Mary Withers had indeed left Windsor abruptly, without giving notice; no one knew where she had gone. Field himself was not allowed anywhere near the royal family. The inspector was not entirely surprised to find himself in disgrace with the highest in the land, but it stung nonetheless. It also meant he most likely would have to find new employment.

In the mid-nineteenth century, for the most part, *no one* knew what caused diseases, including typhoid fever. Charles Field did not, certainly, but no more did the leading physicians of the day. In the medical community, bad air—miasma—was considered the likely culprit, a theory that was almost entirely worthless. Prince Albert had not been well for two years prior to his death; he may have been suffering from, and may have died from, a number of other possible diseases. But typhoid's signature rash *had* appeared across the Prince's abdomen. And Inspector Field had made an accusation—*these* things were indisputable.

"I can read the writing on the wall, Sam," he said privately to his young constable, the two of them having a pint at the end of a long day. "I'm for it. I only hope they spare *you*, lad. Here's to Prince Albert."

"To Prince Albert," said Llewellyn. "And Josiah Kilvert."

"To Josiah Kilvert."

Field said nothing to his good wife about his situation. He would find work; he would take care of Jane and the young people who had become the children for which they had always longed.

With Albert's death, the kingdom entered a prolonged period of mourning. For the Queen, the mourning never ended, throughout the many years that were left her. In the Field household, the survivors of blade, flame, and fear shared some of this collective grief. Nevertheless it was Christmastime, and Charles and Jane Field were determined to celebrate the holiday properly. Christmas Eve found the house in Bow Street filled with wonderful aromas, Jane laboring mightily in her kitchen while Bessie Shoreham proclaimed herself *run ragged* between quiet nips taken in the pantry. Up in the dining room, Belinda trimmed the tree from a step stool and rushed to the window every few moments to see if anyone might be arriving.

"God sent us snow," she whispered, although no one was there to hear her. "Just look!" The flakes swirled round the street lamps outside, but within doors the fires blazed and all was warm. The bell jangled and Tom, dressed in a suit chosen by Jane and purchased by Mr. Field, arrived with his mother, who was looking almost her old self again. Jake Figgis arrived soon after, ever solicitous of Mrs. Ginty, and she seemed not unappreciative of his care. Sergeant Willette came down from Oxford with a Miss Draper, young, shy, and apparently happy to be in his company. Sam Llewellyn arrived bearing a bottle-shaped parcel and a bag of oranges.

When the greetings and the coats had been disposed of, Field bundled his guests up into the dining room. The meal was abundant; the wine flowed. During supper the inspector went round the table twice, kissing each of the females, even Bessie, thereby setting a precedent. After the meal, the master and mistress of the house led their guests in toasts, Christmas carols, and much laughter. Tom did not speak often, but Belinda did. The snow gradually muffled the usual noise of the city. It became a nearly silent night in London, and the world, lamplit, seemed almost clean.

AFTERWORD

The Queen lived forty years after Albert's death and wore mourning her entire life. She was the target of several other would-be assassins but survived them all, winning great approbation from her subjects. Victoria, however, withdrew as much as she could from public life. She became a frequent traveler and returned more than once to Coburg. Her late husband's hopes for a progressive Prussia were dashed by the throat cancer that early on took Crown Prince Frederick's life. As for the grandson with the maimed arm whom Victoria had called her *dearest William*, the world, to its sorrow, would come to know him as Kaiser Wilhelm.

Sir Richard Owen was appointed first director of the British Museum of Natural History. His overweening malice eventually caught up with him, however, along with his penchant for claiming discoveries that were not entirely his own. He finally was forced to resign from the Royal Society's Zoological Council because of plagiarism. Nevertheless, his statue stood in the main hall of the Natural History Museum until 2009, when it was replaced by a statue of Charles Darwin. Owen's obituary recounted one of his favorite anecdotes, about a human head he had stolen as a young medical student.

In 1865, despite achieving fame in his own right as a weather prognosticator (and despite his wife's attempts to keep all sharp household objects from him), Captain Robert FitzRoy retrieved a folding blade from its hiding place and cut his own throat with it. He died deeply in debt, but many (including Darwin) contributed to a fund for his widow.

After twenty-four years in the Diocese of Oxford, Samuel Wilberforce was transferred to the Bishopric of Winchester. He died in a fall from his horse near Dorking, Surrey. Thomas Huxley commented that Wilberforce's brain had at last come into contact with reality, and the result had been fatal.

It was in the summer of 1860, not long after the boy named Button had found the bag and the man in the shallows of the Thames, that he made another discovery. A compact wooden chest came squelching from the muck at the river's bottom. It contained a small fortune in coin, which Button managed prudently, having learned from previous errors. His remarkable rise in the world was followed in the press. He was never admitted to society (he remained thoroughly unpresentable throughout his life), but Charles Dickens gave him immortality of a sort and put him (or a distant version of him) in a book.

ACKNOWLEDGMENTS

This story required research. In London Jane Hill helped me greatly with Victorian period detail and language, and Donald Olson directed me to the old operating theater at St. Thomas' Hospital. In Oxford Julian and Alison Munby got me into the room at the Museum of Natural History where the great Huxley-Wilberforce debate took place. At Jesus College, Oxford, I slept on a remarkably uncomfortable student bed, taking research a step too far.

I want to thank early readers for their input and encouragement: Mel and Angela Marvin, Anne Carney, Bill Lawrence, Craig Slaight, Jon Bok, Russell Sharon, Kara Pickman, and Solveig Kjeseth. I am indebted to my indomitable agent, Gail Hochman, and Ira Silverberg who introduced me to Gail and to my editor, Charles F. Adams, a guiding light. For story help, start to finish, I am deeply grateful to my husband, Leo Geter.